**FROM ELEGANT LONDON TO EXOTIC MOROCCO
TEMPTATION LED HER TO THE EDGE
OF DANGER AND DESIRE . . .**

London—Lauren Winthrop had just one year to make Ravissant the world's premier art gallery. International financier Carlos Barzan had offered her a fabulous job—if she kept his involvement secret. Lauren accepted, knowing that in the world of the very, very rich who pursue thrills and money with equal passion, secrets and schemes come with every offer.

Lauren could live with that, as long as she got the success she craved. Until she met collector Ryan Westcott. She had tasted danger before, and in his persuasive kisses she recognized the familiar sensation. There were forces here with deadly intent, sweeping her toward the nightmare she had fled long ago in Marrakesh . . . or toward the sweet darkness of the forbidden pleasures that every woman longs to try.

MIDNIGHT IN MARRAKESH

Also by Meryl Sawyer
BLIND CHANCE

MIDNIGHT IN MARRAKESH

Meryl Sawyer

A DELL BOOK

Published by
Dell Publishing
a division of
Bantam Doubleday Dell Publishing Group, Inc.
666 Fifth Avenue
New York, New York 10103

The author gratefully acknowledges permission to use POEMS OF AKHMATOVA, selected, translated, and introduced by Stanley Kunitz with Max Hayward. Copyright © 1973 by Stanley Kunitz and Max Hayward. "Requiem" first appeared in *The Atlantic*. "Courage" first appeared in AMERICAN POETRY REVIEW.

ISBN: 0-440-20681-2

Printed in the United States of America

Published simultaneously in Canada

April 1991

10 9 8 7 6 5 4 3 2 1

OPM

For Bernie and Frances, and, of course, Jeff

ACKNOWLEDGMENTS

Amnesty International, U.S.A.

Sotheby's, London

Poison Control Center

Counterspy Shop, Beverly Hills

Soviet Life magazine

Angel's Flight—center for runaway children

Veteran's Administration Hospital, Los Angeles

Crisis Center for Sexually Abused Children

I am grateful for the help of many breeders of miniature Vietnamese pot belly pigs, particularly Flying W Farms in Piketon, Ohio. Without the help of these breeders, who unfailingly answered my questions and opened my eyes to the potential of these pets, Pigcasso would never have existed.

A VERY SPECIAL THANK YOU. Two fellow graduates of Santa Fe High School are now involved in the art world. They gave of their time and their expertise to help me with the background information in this story.

Thomas Tavelli, Tavelli Gallery, Aspen, Colorado.

Roberta Brashears, Director, Nedra Matteucci Gallery, Santa Fe, New Mexico.

MIDNIGHT
IN
MARRAKESH

HIGH NOON

We know what trembles on the scales,
and what we must steel ourselves to face.
The bravest hour strikes on our clocks:
may courage not abandon us!

from "Courage" by Anna Akhmatova

1

November 21, 10:00 P.M.: New York City

"I'm not for sale."

"Barzan didn't mean to insult you." Tak's dark brown eyes narrowed a bit more than usual as he studied Lauren Winthrop.

"Then why offer me so much money when he could hire a more qualified person for less?" She ran her hand over her blonde hair, swept back into a French braid, and her silver bracelet caught the light in the semidark room. "It sounds shady."

"It's aboveboard, I assure you. Barzan can afford anything. You're the best and he knows it."

"How could Carlos Barzan possibly know about me?" Lauren didn't believe this story, but she didn't want to insult her best customer by bluntly telling him so. Several years ago, Tak had come into the nightclub, and they'd discovered they had a common interest in contemporary art. She'd accompanied him to galleries and auctions for the last few years, quietly whispering her advice.

Lauren rose from the small table, taking his glass to the black lacquer bar shoehorned into the corner of the private room. He disliked drinking the last few sips of his drinks. Once the ice began to melt, it ruined the taste of the scotch. She counted three ice cubes into the glass, then poured more liquor from the bottle with the gold seal emblazoned with the name Takgama Nakamura.

"Here you are." She handed Tak the fresh drink, bowed, then sat down again.

"Somehow, Barzan discovered you're my secret weapon. Since you began advising me, my art collection has surpassed his. He wants to use your expertise to rescue a London gallery, Ravissant."

"Wait a minute. Wasn't that the gallery involved in the art fraud scandal last year? Don't the Leightons own it?"

"Yes, but Archer Leighton died six months ago. His widow, Vora, has sold half interest in the gallery to Carlos Barzan. Why don't you give him a call?" Tak handed her a business card.

Knowing it was a prestigious gallery that had fallen on hard times didn't ease Lauren's suspicions. *What's the catch?* She deliberately changed the subject. "How's your family?"

"Very well. How is Paul?" Tak asked, as he always did.

"Fine." It was her usual answer, but her brother wasn't well and she feared he never would be again.

"Does he still want to move to Santa Fe?"

Lauren nodded, but they didn't have the money. Living in Manhattan and supporting Paul while he received psychiatric counseling took all she could earn. She was fortunate she earned as much as she did by working at the Sake Sistahs. The nightclub catered to Japanese businessmen who left tips that couldn't be surpassed even by New York's most exclusive night spots.

"Barzan could be your way out." Tak reached inside his jacket for his cigarettes, and Lauren automatically picked up his gold Cartier lighter from the table. After she lit it, Tak took a long draw, then blew the smoke over his shoulder.

"I'll call him," she promised. "But don't you find it strange that Barzan's offering so much money?"

"A million dollars isn't much."

Scion of the family that owned Japan's largest privately held company, Takgama Nakamura was one of the wealthiest men in the world. While his Japanese peers were merely employees of large publicly held companies, Tak wasn't tethered by a corporate bureaucracy and rule by consensus. With a lone-wolf mentality, Takgama Nakamura used his cunning to amass multinational holdings that had given him the edge in the global business marathon the Japanese were obviously winning. A million dollars might not be much to him, but it would take Lauren two lifetimes to earn that much money.

Tak rose to leave and Lauren retrieved the Chivas bottle, making certain to remain discreetly behind him as they entered the bottle-keep area. Like clubs in Tokyo's Ginza district where Japanese businessmen routinely entertained, an American nightclub's status couldn't be measured by posh interiors or beautiful Japanese-speaking hostesses or the requisite lacquer display case—the bottle-keep—lit by a spotlight. Only one thing counted: the names on the liquor bottles' customized labels had to be the right ones. The Japanese doing business in America gladly paid the exorbitant prices—Tokyo prices—just to have the club place a special seal on their bottle with their title and company name.

Other hostess bars catered to middle and upper management, but the Sake Sistahs prided itself on attracting the handful of corporate elite who were the most powerful men in their country. Whenever they were in New York, they visited the Sake Sistahs and retrieved their private stock from the bottle-keep. Lined up closer than passengers on the Tokyo subway, the liquor in the bottle-keep featured Tak's Chivas Regal at center court, telling all who entered that they'd achieved the pinnacle of success like Takgama Nakamura.

While Tak said good night to *Mama-san,* owner of the club, Lauren wiped the fingerprints off Tak's bottle. She placed it in the premier spot, front and center, in the dramatically lit display case.

With a nod to the kimonoed *Mama-san,* her head reverently bowed, Lauren held the door for Tak. The lilting voice accompanying the twangy, three-stringed *shamisen* that came from artfully concealed Bose speakers clashed with the noise of the Manhattan traffic outside. Two paces behind Tak, Lauren followed him to the curb where his limousine waited.

He paused, switching as he always did when leaving the

nightclub from Japanese to flawless English. "Call Barzan, Lauren. He could be the answer to your problems."

She watched the limo's taillights disappear down the street, quickly merging with the midtown traffic. Despite the stiff November breeze, she stood thinking. Tak was shrewd; without asking he knew how bad things were with Paul. Tak could have kept her identity secret, continuing to use her ability to spot talented contemporary artists to expand his already impressive collection. He paid her handsomely for her efforts just as he lavishly tipped her when he visited the Sake Sistahs. As usual, he was right; she owed it to herself, and to Paul, to investigate Barzan's offer.

A neon-yellow taxi deposited a bevy of Japanese businessmen at the curb and Lauren followed them back into the bar. Rapid-fire whispers indicated they had spotted Tak's bottle. Lauren moved around the men, ignoring their stares, smothering her disgust at being nothing more than a modern-day geisha girl who wasn't allowed to greet the patrons outside the shoebox-size, private entertaining rooms. Attuned to the inbred Japanese taste for negative space and their tradition of the serving girl, these rooms became private preserves where the sense of *honne,* true mind, could be spoken.

Mama-san signaled for Lauren to wait. Approaching with slow, precise steps that never ruffled the silk of her ceremonial kimono, she said in a hushed undertone, "Your brother has been taken to the hospital."

Lauren didn't need the portly emergency room nurse to tell her Paul had tried to commit suicide. With the sickening knowledge that this time even Dr. Mortimer West, one of the city's top psychiatrists, hadn't been able to help Paul, she called him anyway.

She tiptoed into the crowded ward and found her brother asleep. Her throat constricted as she stared at his body. Matted with blood, his pale blond hair stuck to his temple; a violet bruise marred the patrician line of his jaw. What happened? The doctor said he'd taken sleeping pills. He must have fallen, too.

Paul's hands lay at his sides. Those same loving hands had

held hers as he'd encouraged her to tell him the truth that day almost two decades ago. With those same hands, he'd tried to take his own life. Twice.

"Paul," she whispered when he unexpectedly looked up at her. His blue eyes, a mirror image of her own, now had the vacant, abstracted look she'd come to fear.

"What happened?" She fought back the hot sting of tears, thinking he'd seemed to be improving lately. The depression about his wife's death had appeared to be lessening. Until now. "Talk to me; there's nothing you can't tell me," she whispered, repeating the phrase he'd said that day in Marrakesh's *medina*. She stared at his hands, thinking of how he'd held her hands then, not letting go until she'd poured her heart out to him. If he hadn't helped her, no telling what might have become of her.

"I don't know what happened." His voice was filled with that desolate quality that had never been there before Marcy's terminal cancer diagnosis. "I took a sleeping pill. Minutes later, I felt dizzy. I guess I fell."

"How many pills did you take?"

"One . . . just one."

One pill wouldn't warrant pumping his stomach or the struggle to save his life. Her fingers curled around his hand. "I've called Dr. West. Talk to him," she said, holding his hand in both hers now. Waiting for him to reply, she twisted the silver bracelet he'd bought for her years ago in Marrakesh.

As she left, Mortimer West met her in the corridor. "He says he only took one pill," Lauren said. "He didn't try to kill himself."

"The ER doc says he had enough Halcion in him to kill ten men."

"Impossible! Paul wouldn't lie to me."

The doctor's frown indicated his doubts.

"There must be something I can do."

The doctor leaned one shoulder against the wall and studied her. "Get him out of town—to Santa Fe. He needs to be someplace where he isn't constantly reminded of his wife."

Lauren nodded, thinking of London and Barzan's job offer.

5:00 A.M.: Marrakesh, Morocco

Ryan Westcott sat up, sliding out of Amal's arms, away from
the warmth of her naked body. He peeled off the condom and
tossed it in the direction of the raffia basket filled with pis-
tachio shells and the wrapper from the Cadbury bar he'd
brought her from London.

"You're leaving?" Only the faintest note of regret tinged
her voice.

Ryan nodded and pulled on the cotton trousers he'd hastily
dropped beside the bed, then turned and smiled over his bare
shoulder at the dark-haired woman. Hell, if she'd been a lady
in London, she would have expected a fancy dinner and a
round of the clubs before he could get laid. Not Amal. Time
was money to her; she never wasted a second on meaningless
chatter.

After slipping his bare feet into *babouches,* Ryan put on a
full-length tunic and belted it. Clad in traditional robes and
slippers, he counted on his dark-brown hair and tan to make
him blend in with the other Moroccan men.

Ryan reached into his pocket for his money clip. He
counted out twice the number of dirhams any Moroccan man
would have paid Amal for her services, most of which defied
the tenets of the Moslem religion, and left the wad on the
leather drum table.

"Beslemeh," she called as he said good-bye and stepped
into the alley.

He stood there a moment, his back pressed to the wall. The
harvest moon backlit the Koutoubia Mosque, its minarets
competing with the vaulted Atlas Mountains for the star-
shrouded sky. The mountains met the desert at Marrakesh,
making the air cool but dry. The fragrance of orange trees,
touched with a hint of cloves and turmeric, accompanied the
heavier aroma of *tajine,* stew left to simmer overnight. No
place Ryan had ever visited smelled quite like the old city, the
medina.

Crossing Jemma el Fna Square, he quickly passed the deserted woven-reed stalls. Most of the human circus—jugglers,
acrobats, fire-eaters, snake charmers, and clever touts—had
gone home. A few unlucky devils slept in the open, covered

only by their burnooses. Out of habit, Ryan checked the darkened doorways for moving shadows as he walked through the skein of narrow streets.

When he returned to his jeep, parked just beyond the crumbling, mud-brick wall encircling the *medina,* the storks nesting in the chinks eyed him suspiciously. He paused before climbing into the ancient Rover to inspect the undercarriage. He found no unusual bulges; he knew he wouldn't. But Ryan kept his guard up, staying alert even though no one knew he was in Marrakesh.

He slammed the junker into gear and left the blue-doored *medina* with its wrought-iron arabesques and keyhole-shaped windows behind, racing down Avenue Mohammed V. The wide boulevard flanked by sidewalk cafes and clusters of orange trees had more of a Mediterranean and less of a Moorish appearance than the *medina.*

On two wheels, he rounded the corner, screeching off the main street, ignoring the *arrêt* sign—there wasn't anyone around at this time of night to stop for, anyway—and turned up Rue de Bab Allen. The bottleneck of cars still parked at the Armstrong villa despite the late hour slowed him down. With the approach of winter in Europe, the wealthy part-time residents of Marrakesh returned. Party time.

He spotted the La Mamounia Hotel's calash in the tiled drive. The Choukrouns, Ryan speculated. Good old Roger and his wife, Regine, often used La Mamounia's horse-drawn carriage. Usually, they had it waiting outside the entrance to the hotel's nightclub they managed along with a far-flung empire of jet-set Regine nightclubs. Ryan figured he'd been in most of them at one time or another. Too noisy. Too many people on the make.

He inched the jeep past the lipstick-red Ferrari everyone in the French quarter knew belonged to Patrick Guerrand-Hermes. Ryan eyed the sleek machine. Must be a hell of a lot of money in scarfs and handbags.

He drove by a classic gull-wing Mercedes. Yves Saint Laurent was in Marrakesh again. No wonder Caroline Armstrong had begun the nonstop entertaining that had made her the social maven of Marrakesh's elite society for years.

Ryan downshifted, slowing the Rover as he looked at the

Grecian-style villa. In his mind's eye, he saw T.J. waltzing on the veranda with the lovely Caroline in his arms. T.J. had never looked happier. Dumb ass. Caroline Armstrong had never loved anyone but herself.

A rapid pulsating at his wrist distracted Ryan. He pressed the stem of his watch twice to indicate he'd received the summons. *Shit! What could have happened?* He jammed down on the accelerator and didn't let up until he arrived at the compound on the outskirts of the city.

The guard recognized him and swung open the heavy, barbed gate as a trio of Rhodesian ridgebacks, their fangs bared, snarled. After a hand signal to the dogs, Ryan jumped from the car and raced inside the villa.

"What's wrong?" he demanded of Adi, the Sikh bodyguard hired by T.J. Griffith three years ago.

"Stirling called," said the tall man whose white turban contrasted sharply with his dark skin and black eyes, meaning Peter Stirling who was Ryan's secret service contact headquartered in London with the MI-5. The Sikh handed Ryan a cryptic note: "He's making his move."

"Barzan," Ryan said, his green eyes gleaming, his heart beating in double time as he slapped Adi on the back.

"What took him so long?" the Sikh asked.

"Who cares? Three years of sitting on our asses bored pissless is over. This time we'll be ready for him."

November 22, 10:00 P.M.: New York City

David Marcus looked across the polished marble coffee table at Lauren Winthrop seated beside Carlos Barzan. Since they'd come back from dinner at Aureole, just blocks away from Barzan's Trump Parc penthouse overlooking Central Park, she'd bided her time, not mentioning the unusual offer. As Barzan's right-hand man, David admired her patience. He didn't see it very often. The scent of money—easy money—was too tempting to most people.

"Did Nakamura explain my offer?" Barzan asked.

As she shook her head, David noted, not for the first time, that she was extraordinarily beautiful, but that she looked several years younger than thirty-four.

"I want you to manage Ravissant Gallery," Barzan said. "Since Archer Leighton died, his wife, Vora, has let it run down."

"It's been slipping for years."

Barzan took a sip of the Louis XIII cognac and pretended to be studying the Rothko on the wall. Despite his sixty-plus years, his hair remained black and his olive skin unlined. Only an intimate like David Marcus could have detected the anger simmering in Barzan's black eyes. Chumming, using money as bait, might not land Lauren Winthrop, so they'd taken precautions. But her brother had survived the megadose of Halcion. Too bad. If he interfered with their plans for Lauren, he wouldn't be so lucky next time.

Barzan grinned, his oft-photographed smile radiating false sincerity. "I want you to step in, protect my investment. You have carte blanche to do whatever is necessary to make Ravissant the world's premier gallery."

"What does Vora Leighton say about all this?"

"She needs money. I've bought half interest in the gallery, that is, one of my holding companies purchased it."

Lauren gazed at the Jackson Pollock on the far wall while both men stared at her. Although they knew she needed the money desperately, David sensed she might not accept the offer. Why not? Was this a ploy to get more money?

Lauren examined the Rothko, one of his most famous works, a single persimmon-colored circle dominating the white canvas. She didn't want to spend the rest of her life working at the Sake Sistahs kowtowing to Asian men, nor did she want Paul to have to remain in New York. Without academic credentials or curatorial experience, she'd have to rely on Tak's generosity to work as an art consultant. Though he gave her substantial consulting fees, she doubted other collectors would trust her.

Barzan was offering Lauren a chance to do what she loved *and* build her reputation. *Why are you hesitating, dummy?* Although he'd died almost twenty-five years ago, her father's words came back to her: "Things that seem too good to be true—are." There was a catch in this deal. What was it?

"I'll pay you a million dollars if you can get Ravissant into the black within a year. Half that if you can't—just for trying."

Barzan's voice was as smooth as the expensive cognac he'd insisted on serving her. "Naturally, I'll include a generous clothing allowance and provide you with a luxury flat."

Still, she hesitated. *Where's the catch?*

"Is there a problem?" David asked.

Lauren avoided looking directly at David Marcus; he made her uncomfortable. His gray hair offset the strangest eyes she'd ever seen. They were the palest shade of blue imaginable—albino blue. "I'd like the job, but I'll need to bring my brother with me. He can keep the books."

"That's out of the question." Barzan walked over to the bar to pour himself another drink and hide his short fuse.

"We don't want to make Vora Leighton uncomfortable." David took over as he always did when Barzan's explosive temper threatened to ignite.

"Then Paul won't work in the gallery. But he must come with me."

"Look," David said, "we're paying you an outrageous sum to bring this gallery up to par. You'll need to be out most nights to become part of the social scene. To rescue Ravissant within a year, you'll want to get to know the movers and shakers."

"Men like T.J. Griffith and his assistant, Ryan Westcott. Have you ever met them?" Barzan asked.

"No, but I've heard of T.J. Griffith. Wasn't he the British collector who was maimed by an IRA car bomb?"

"Yes," David said. "He's still collecting art and remains one of the major forces in determining which contemporary artists become collectible. Since Griffith was disfigured by that bomb, Ryan Westcott has acted as his talent scout."

"Poor Mr. Griffith. He probably lives only for art."

"Don't feel too sorry for him," Barzan interjected, scowling.

The acid edge to Barzan's voice startled Lauren. Evidently, as another major collector of contemporary art, Barzan resented Griffith's head start. Having collected art for thirty years, Griffith's collection was surpassed only by museums. Did Barzan resent Tak as well? Had he offered her so much money to work for him merely to thwart other collectors? There was something strange about the Bolivian man who'd parlayed a family fortune founded on tin into an international empire worth billions.

Barzan sat down beside her, his frown replaced by a concerned expression. "What would all this be worth to you"—he waved his hand indicating the Rothkos, Pollocks, and Mirós lining the walls of the room and overflowing into the entry—"if you lost your brother?"

Mentioning Paul caught her off guard; he'd been in her thoughts all evening. There wasn't anyone meaningful in her life except him. But how did Barzan know about her brother? Evidently, he did his homework. He hadn't become extraordinarily wealthy by carelessly entering business deals. "Nothing. Without Paul, money would mean absolutely nothing."

"Then you know exactly how I feel," he said, the bitterness returning to his voice. "Since my son died"—he rose, walked over to the Rothko, and flung the contents of his glass on the painting—"this is worthless."

Stunned, Lauren watched the amber liquid drip down the orange orb and trail across the white background, puddling on the parquet floor below. All evening she'd watched Barzan, and had decided he was an egocentric billionaire who got his kicks dabbling in art. But a bond existed between Barzan and his dead son that was just as binding as the one she shared with Paul.

When Barzan turned to face her again, his keyboard-white smile replaced his frown. "At this point in my life, I have all the money I could ever spend. What I want . . . what my son, Bobby, wanted was to have a premier gallery."

Lauren tried to remember just what she'd read about Robert Barzan's death just over three years ago. Hadn't he been killed when a diamond deal went awry? "Didn't Robert import diamonds?" she ventured, startled by the odd look in Barzan's eyes.

"Yes." Barzan concentrated on the Rothko. The last traces of the cognac dripped from its frame.

"But that's another story," David said, giving Barzan a cautioning glance. "What do you say?"

Lauren decided Paul could go to Santa Fe now and she would join him in a year. He would be happier there than in

London, especially if she were out socializing all the time. "I'll take the job."

"One more thing. I don't want anyone to know I own part of the gallery. Other than Nakamura, no one does. I don't want people to think I'm manipulating the market."

"The holding company that purchased half interest in the gallery will provide your money," David added. "Your funds will come through them. We want your word no one will ever know Carlos Barzan is involved."

Her eyes narrowed. *This is the catch.* No matter what he says, Barzan intends to manipulate the market. Hiding behind the gallery's name, Barzan could promote artists he collected, creating the impression a prestigious gallery had selected them. She stood up. "Count me out. Good night, gentlemen."

David jumped up and caught her arm, halting her. "Wait a minute. What's wrong? I thought we had a deal."

"I refuse to allow you to use my name to manipulate the market," she said, her voice soft yet uncompromising. "If I'm in charge of the gallery, I'll select the artists."

Barzan flashed his killer smile. It was the best acting David had seen in twenty years of working for the man.

"You'll have free rein with Ravissant," Barzan said. "I'm only asking that my name be kept out of it for personal reasons you wouldn't understand."

There wasn't a catch? Was Tak right? Was Barzan being extravagant because he had more money than he could ever spend? "If—at any time—I even *suspect* you're manipulating the market, I'll leave." When Barzan nodded, she added, "I want half of the million in my Chase account now."

"Agreed," Barzan said.

After David settled the details with Lauren and she left, he found Barzan at the window with the Rémy Martin Baccarat decanter in his hand, staring out at Central Park.

"Shouldn't you have warned her about Ryan Westcott?" David asked. "She needs to know she's in danger. Maybe we should have sent a man."

Barzan didn't bother to turn around. "Never send a man to do a woman's job."

2

February 13: London

"Has your investigator learned anything more?"

"No," Vora said, catching Basil's dark eyes in the beauty salon's mirror. He wound a strand of auburn hair through hers and attached the two with the bonding solution, doubling the length of her hair. "It's a waste of money at this point. Almost a year and nothing."

Basil nodded sympathetically, his head bobbing amid the hanging ferns and multicolored parrots on perches reflected in the three-way mirror. Vora watched while he bonded two more strands, not adding that she'd fired the investigator yesterday. After the art fraud scandal followed by her husband's death and the inevitable taxes, her finances were strained enough without squandering money pursuing apparently groundless suspicions. Archer's death must have been an accident after all. *Close the door behind you; turn out the lights. He's gone.*

"Lauren Winthrop still being difficult?" Elevated a good three inches by high-heeled cowboy boots, the beautician's slight frame seemed overpowered by a lavender paisley shirt. It contrasted sharply with his dark hair, shaved over the ears, with the longer hair on top moussed heavenward.

"I've given up. I could only do so much with her. The dress she's wearing to the opening tonight is straight off the rack at Harrods." Vora smiled as Basil tsked, emphasizing his disgust. "Black velvet, high neck with a pie-frill collar, long sleeves with more pie frills at the cuffs." He shook his head; hopeless, his expression said. "I'm wearing a cocoa-colored Ozbek."

Basil beamed approval at her reflection when he heard the name of the Turkish-born designer once named by Margaret Thatcher as designer of the year. Vora knew how important it was to Basil Blackstoke to have his clients seen at all the exclusive events, wearing the latest fashions. It maintained his standing as London's foremost hairstylist.

"I tried to get her in here, but Lauren refuses to change her hair. She insists on wearing that frumpy bun."

Vora didn't add that Lauren Winthrop's hair was beautiful just the way it was. A stunning, blue-eyed blonde, Lauren had readily allowed Vora to lease and decorate a flat and hire a maid for her. But when it came to modifying her appearance, Lauren politely resisted all attempts to change her image.

Lauren had subtly let Vora know she didn't expect tonight's gala exhibition of Clive Holcombe's acrylics to be a success. *We'll just see.* Convinced Clive was destined to be the next David Hockney, Vora expected him to return Ravissant Gallery to its former status as the premier contemporary art gallery in London.

Basil fluffed her hair, running his fingers through the newly lengthened tresses. "Well, ducky, what do you think?"

Vora peered at the sherry-brown mane with eyes that matched the ringlets. Turning her head, she smiled at the strange feeling it gave her to have hair swishing across her shoulders. "It looks real," she muttered, awestruck at how different she appeared.

"It *is* real hair, dyed to match yours. I defy anyone to show me where I lengthened your hair." Basil wound one long strand around a curling iron. "It'll look even better when I put a bit of curl in it, ducks."

Mesmerized, she stared at the new Vora Leighton. Envious of Lauren's trim figure, Vora had dieted relentlessly, eating only what was green or white—veggies, chicken, fish—until she'd shed fifteen pounds. The eucalyptus wrap in the make-over room up the hall had squeezed her waffle thighs until they were smooth enough to look good in the lacy tap panties she'd bought to wear tonight.

"A new you, ducks, a new you," Basil said after he'd styled her hair, giving her a savage, wanton look.

She nodded and the *Elle*-caliber beauty in the mirror nodded too, dumbfounding Vora. "Clive will die."

Basil, master of the miracle make-over, shrugged dismissively. Women came into Miracles and were plucked, plumped, and pummeled, then made up and coiffed before leaving the high-tech glamour of his salon—changed.

Vora thanked him, deliberately stoking his ego. In an odd sort of way, Basil had become her best friend even though he'd been born under the bells of Marylebone and she'd been raised abroad in a convent school. He'd overcome his Cockney roots as well as his accent by moving to a bed-sitter in Soho and working as a shampoo boy at Vidal Sassoon's first salon. Squirreling away his tips, he'd put himself through a cut-rate beauty school, then gone on to work as a stylist in a fashionable Knightsbridge salon where Vora had discovered him.

Having recently returned to London, she'd had no friends. During her biweekly visits to the salon she and Basil had become close. When he'd opened his own shop and pioneered foil weaving, she'd been his first client. She'd also let him give her an *au natural* perm when he'd been the first in London to use it.

"Have you and Clive set a wedding date yet?" Basil asked.

"It's still too soon." Vora shook her head to get used to the feel of long hair. Her husband had always insisted her hair be chicly short. *Forget it. Archer is dead.*

"I see." Basil pivoted in his lavender cowboy boots with pointed, silver-tipped toes and cooed to one of his prized parrots. His averted eyes told her he knew the score: Clive Holcombe was balking.

"You're the only person who knows Clive and I were . . . seeing each other long before Archer died. It might be better if we waited a bit longer," Vora said, telling half the truth. Clive had stopped insisting they marry immediately after she'd told him about her financial predicament. When Lauren became her partner, things had improved, but she hadn't told Clive that. Her pride demanded he be in love with her—not her money.

Vora kissed Basil on the cheek as she stepped out of the chair. "You're coming tonight?"

"I wouldn't miss it."

On her way out, Vora waved at the receptionist. "Bill me," she said, thankful she was no longer embarrassed by a burgeoning charge account. Taking a partner in the gallery had eased things—temporarily. With Vora's lifestyle, it wouldn't last. Ravissant had to begin making money, starting tonight.

By the time Vora reached her home at Belgrave Square just off Wilton Crescent, she couldn't wait to call Clive. She let the phone ring a dozen times before she decided she'd misdialed. She redialed, but he still didn't answer. Vora thought he must be in the shower and was hanging up when she heard his strangled hello.

"It's me. Were you in the shower?"

"No—aah—yes. I just got out."

"All set for tonight?"

"Tonight? Oh, yes, of course . . . tonight. How does everything look?"

"Great." Vora had supervised the hanging of Clive's acrylics, insisting they be placed exactly as she directed, then left Lauren to oversee the myriad last-minute details while she went to Miracles for a make-over. "Is your dinner jacket pressed?"

"Well . . . I"—he paused—"I bought a Gianni Versace."

"You did?" Vora bit back a reprimand. She couldn't believe he'd spent money he didn't have on a Versace—especially since he'd sulked until she'd bought him a dinner jacket at Gieves & Hawkes. After seven fittings, they'd tailor-made him a jacket. She waited for Clive to explain, but he didn't. Instead, she heard a muffled sound as if he'd put his hand over the receiver. "I'll pick you up at seven thirty."

"No, I'll meet you at the gallery," he said and rang off.

In the basement of Ravissant Gallery where the business offices were located, Lauren found the telephone under a bunch of parsley being used to garnish the hors d'oeuvre platters. Ignoring the frenzied caterers rushing about as they prepared for the eight o'clock opening of the highly touted Clive Holcombe collection, she called her brother in Santa Fe. No answer. She hated being separated like this, wondering if he was all right.

The last time she'd seen Paul had been at Christmas. He'd met her at the airport in Santa Fe and had driven her through the snowy night up Camino de Las Animas.

"What do you think?" He pulled into a narrow drive flanked on either side by a snowcapped adobe wall. Beyond the snow-flakes falling steadily into the tunnel of light created by the headlights, Lauren saw an adobe hacienda with cracked walls.

"Nice." When Paul had been released from the hospital, she'd sent him ahead to Santa Fe while she settled their affairs in New York. Looking at the ramshackle house he'd purchased, she had second thoughts.

"It needs work," Paul admitted, opening a heavy, carved Spanish door. The terra-cotta tile floor blended with the freshly whitewashed walls hung with frayed Navaho rugs. Hand-painted Mexican tiles, many chipped, others missing, formed the hearth of the rounded kiva-style fireplace in the corner. "I've been working on it."

"Don't spend all your time on the house. I want you to shoot some photographs. When I move here, I'm opening a gallery featuring your photography."

"This is why I bought the house," he said as he led her into the artist's studio with a huge skylight. "When you return from London, you'll start painting again."

"How did you know I still wanted to paint?" She choked out the words.

Paul put his arm around her. "Like you, I know talent when I see it. You stopped when we found out Marcy had breast cancer. Don't you think it's time to start again?"

She didn't have the heart to tell him that last week she'd sold the oils she'd painted. They'd been purchased by a discount broker specializing in condo art for decorators, who chose pieces not by the quality of the work, but according to color schemes. Lauren had kept one painting. "Midnight in Marrakesh" that always had had special meaning for her.

Back in the living room, Paul built a fire while she unpacked in her room. Soon the spicy fragrance of the piñon wood filled the house. Lauren came out, her Christmas gift for Paul in her hand. He was sitting on a swaybacked sofa covered by a moth-eaten Navaho rug. With his Reeboks up on a primitive wooden table, he gazed at the shadows the fire threw on the ceiling supported by vigas. The round, fully-exposed beams created linear patterns of dark and light across the crumbling plaster ceiling.

"Here's your Christmas present." She gave him the box.

"I thought we weren't—"

"You said we weren't exchanging. I didn't."

Shaking his head in mock disgust, he ripped the box open. For a moment, he merely stared at the camera. "A Hassel-blad?"

"You've got to have the best, if you're going to be the best."

He reached for her hand and pulled her down on the sofa beside him. "You know, I've never said thank you for taking care of me since Marcy died." He gestured to the house, then tapped the camera with his other hand. "Now this."

"It's no more than you did for me, getting me out of Mar-rakesh." She stopped, not wanting to bring up the past on such a happy occasion. "I'd do anything for you. We have a chance to start a new life, live the way we want. Promise me you won't . . . do anything foolish."

"It was an accident, I swear." Paul ran his fingers through his blond hair. "I took only one pill."

Lauren decided he'd been confused and had a glass of wine and taken several pills by mistake. If the building super hadn't come upstairs with a package and discovered him, Paul would have died.

"It doesn't matter. Luck was with us," she said, looking away, afraid he might see she was lying. She hated deceiving him; they had few secrets. But she'd given her word to Barzan that no one, including her brother, would know about their deal. Paul thought her newfound wealth had come from a real estate investment her late husband had made. "All I have to do is get Ravissant Gallery making money—"

"I should be going to London with you. You're not used to living alone."

"I'll be fine by myself. You can help me most by getting things going here."

The remainder of her time with Paul, until she'd flown to London the first week in January, he'd been upbeat. It was a start. Finally.

Shaking off the memories, reminding herself to concentrate on making Ravissant's opening a success, Lauren went upstairs to street level where Clive Holcombe's acrylics were hung.

The white walls echoed the bleached wood floor; gigantic canvases were spotlighted by a squadron of track lights creating focal points illuminating the art while leaving the surrounding area softly shadowed. She was double-checking the lighting when Vora sailed into the gallery.

"What do you think?" Vora said as she handed the attendant the full-length chinchilla she carried over her arm. She tugged on a long auburn curl.

"I like it, a lot." Lauren smiled her approval, thinking the longer hair was becoming but that Vora should wear less makeup.

"It's a hair extension. I'm going to use it while I let my hair grow out." Vora studied Lauren thoughtfully. "You know, your hair would look fabulous down like this."

"Too much bother," Lauren said, thankful that Vora Leighton had proved to be so easygoing. Her primary concerns in life were satisfied in Knightsbridge where the Sloane Rangers reigned. Like Vora, women in the area shopped incessantly in the trendy boutiques near Sloane Square, earning the name "rangers." Although Lauren wasn't much of a shopper, she and Vora had forged a comfortable relationship. Their goals were the same: To put Ravissant on top. Even if Vora never mentioned it, Lauren suspected their reasons were the same —the need for money.

If Vora thought she was deceiving Lauren, she was mistaken. Any fool could see she loved Clive. He must be terrific between the sheets, Lauren decided, eyeing the canvases. Why else would Vora have exhibited the work of such a mediocre talent? If this showing hadn't been set with advertisements in *Art World* and *Connoisseur,* as well as all the London papers, Lauren would have insisted the opening be canceled.

Vora groaned when a distinguished-looking man with silver-blond hair came in and handed his coat to the attendant. "Finley Tibbetts. He's early. Where *is* Clive?" Vora whispered, then hurried to the door. "Finley, darling, I'm so glad you could make it."

"Nice to see you, Vora. I can't stay long, a'tall."

Two seconds should do it, Lauren thought. By then the *Times* art critic would have written Clive Holcombe off and Ravissant with him. Damage control. It was up to her to defuse the situation and let Tibbetts know subsequent showings at the gallery would be better.

"Hello." She extended her hand. "I'm Lauren Winthrop."

The wide smile he gave her and the approving light in his blue eyes contradicted his reputation as a merciless art critic.

"Lauren's my new partner," Vora said.

"I used to consult for Takgama Nakamura." Bless Tak for giving her permission to use his name. Considering the collection being exhibited, she needed all the credibility she could muster.

"Show me around." With the aura of genuine nobility from a bygone era, he offered Lauren his arm. "Let's see Holcombe's work."

"How about a glass of champagne first?" Delay as long as possible. God willing, he'll have to leave before he gets too close a look.

"I don't understand how Takgama Nakamura built his collection, a'tall"—Finley shook his head and smiled, obviously flirting with her—"in such a short time."

As they sipped champagne, Lauren went into an explanation that included a piece-by-piece description of Tak's collection.

Across the room, Vora watched. Lauren had Finley spellbound. He wasn't even looking at Clive's work. An inveterate ladies' man, Finley would be content slavering over Lauren until he had to leave.

Look on the up side, she'll keep him here at least. Nothing could be more disastrous for a showing than not having the *Times* art critic appear. If Finley Tibbetts left now, most guests wouldn't see him and would assume he hadn't deigned the exhibition worth attending.

Vora greeted guests, seething. Where on earth was Clive? Finally, he appeared without the cashmere topcoat she'd given him, his formal bow tie pointing up at his nose.

"Sorry, I'm late." He smoothed his mussed gray hair.

Vora noted the Versace suit; the high-style Italian dinner jacket accentuated Clive's lanky frame. British tailoring would have made him look better.

"Circulate." She strained to keep her anger from her voice as she straightened his tie. "Finley Tibbetts is over there."

Clive beelined toward the bar where Lauren and Finley were chatting, and Vora realized Clive hadn't noticed her hair.

"Art. I love it. It's so uplifting," gushed a high-pitched female voice. "So inspiring."

Vora turned, groaning inwardly. Mootzie McCallister. Who'd invited her? The platinum blond heiress, enough diamonds on her to have repaid the Third World debt, swanned into the gallery wearing an apple-green lamé dress with a bubble skirt that did nothing to hide her thick waist and wide hips. As far as Vora knew, Mootzie had never been interested in art. Men, yes; art, no.

"Take a look around." Vora managed a tight smile as Mootzie flounced off. Greeting other guests, Vora pondered Mootzie's newfound interest in art. Well, she certainly could afford it.

Born with a silver shoe in her mouth, Mootzie had pots of money. Her father had made a fortune with mini-stores located in underground stations, selling sensible shoes at low prices. The opening of his first store had coincided with the birth of his only child, Matilda, "Mootzie." In celebration he'd named his shops Mootzie's Tootzies. That had been thirty years ago. Now Mootzie had boodles of cash and wore nothing but Maude Frizons on her size ten feet.

Ryan Westcott edged past the mob at Ravissant's entrance. There were too many people packed into the gallery to get a good look at the art from the door, so he angled his wide shoulders sideways and twisted his way across the room. A head taller than most of the men, he had no trouble scanning the Turnbull and Assered crowd that included a sprinkling of lesser-known members of Parliament. In addition to the MPs, a couple of television actors and a few Arabs were sipping champagne.

None of the big players in contemporary art were here— just wannabes. And Finley Tibbetts. The prick. He got off trouncing artists. Worse yet, he was paid to do it.

Tibbetts was smiling at a blonde whose back was to Ryan. Tight bun, tighter ass, great legs. Probably had a face that could haunt a house.

"Ryan," came a sultry voice at his shoulder.

He looked down, forcing a smile. *What the hell was her name? Damned if he remembered.* A long-nailed, lousy lay, she'd left a trail of scratches down his back that had smarted for a week. "How've you been?"

The redhead rattled on and on about her latest shopping excursion to Milan and her new villa in Minorca. Ryan gave her a few seconds, then pointedly looked at his watch. "I've got to be at Crockfords soon," he said, although the gambling there didn't get going until much later.

He eased his way between a fag in lavender cowboy boots and a waiter passing crystal flutes of champagne. "Gin," Ryan ordered, but the waiter shook his head.

Great, leave it to Vora Leighton to serve nothing but wussy juice. He knocked back one glass of champagne, put the empty on the tray, and grabbed another.

The smaller gallery was almost empty as Ryan strolled by a series of works. Drab brown and bile green with intermittent splotches of gray, the paint appeared to have been thrown onto the canvases. Jesus, if art imitated life, then life was a latrine. There wasn't a thing here suitable for T.J. Griffith's collection.

Still, he'd owed it to T.J. to check out Holcombe. When Sotheby's auctioned Jasper Johns's "False Start," which originally sold at just over three thousand dollars and resold for over seventeen million dollars—a record for a living artist— Griffith's collection skyrocketed. There were five of Johns's paintings on display at Griffith's Palace Green residence.

No question about it, art had become the global currency, outstripping gold and diamonds. And increasing in value at a more rapid rate, Ryan thought, recalling the van Gogh of purple irises. What the hell was it called? "Irises." It had sold for almost fifty-four million dollars. That price had been topped last week when another van Gogh, "Portrait of Dr. Gachet," sold for over eighty-two million. Impressionists were netting stratospheric prices. In their wake, modern and contemporary art was increasing in value at astonishing rates.

Ryan polished off the champagne and laughed to himself. Poor old van Gogh. The guy was probably turning over in his grave. During his lifetime, he'd sold only one painting for a few measly francs.

Compared to van Gogh's works, Ryan decided, trotting around to these two-bit exhibitions was bullshit. Then he reminded himself that T.J. had discovered Johns and Hockney and scores of others *before* they'd become big names. Now it was up to Ryan to continue. He had a keen eye; he went on instinct. Like gambling, you won or lost. The higher the stakes went, the more Ryan itched to play.

Vora stood at the entrance to the anteroom adjacent to the main gallery, looking for Clive. He seemed to have disappeared. *Heavens! Who is that?* Standing in the far corner with his back to her, holding an empty champagne flute upside down by its base and swinging it to and fro, stood a dark-haired man in a sport coat. Clearly, he hadn't been invited or he would have worn a dinner jacket. She crossed the room. "Pardon me, but this is a private—" She stopped mid-sentence when Ryan Westcott turned to face her.

He smiled the impudent grin that captivated many females. Not her. Despite his smile, Ryan's compelling green eyes were wary, emotionless. Gypsy eyes. Something about him frightened her.

"Ryan, it's super to see you. When you didn't RSVP, I assumed you were out of the country."

He kept smiling; he knew she was lying. He never responded to invitations, which were really intended for T.J. anyway. If the mood suited Ryan, he showed.

"Got any Boodles?" He wagged the upside-down glass under Vora's nose. He was bored and he still had time to kill before anyone would be gambling at Crockfords. She mumbled something about seeing to it and scuttled off.

Ryan reached down and twisted his gold pinkie ring with

the leopard's head and pinpoint emerald eyes. Over the years, the ring had brought him luck. Once it had failed him. The most important time. He didn't believe in luck—not anymore.

Vora elbowed her way through the crowd to the bar. She was serving Louis Roederer Cristal—the best champagne in the world—and Ryan Westcott insisted on gin. Obviously, he had no taste. Well, what did she expect from a man whose father had been an American and who'd spent his youth in the colonies?

She shoved the empty glass at the bartender. "Get me some Boodles." He looked at her blankly. "Downstairs in the liquor cabinet."

Her eyes swept over the crowd. She had Ryan Westcott waiting, yet Clive was still nowhere in sight. The receptionist caught Vora's eye and held up one finger, the signal that one painting had been sold.

"Who?" Vora mouthed the words, then watched the answer. Mootzie McCallister. Damn! The one person noted for her appalling lack of taste. Vora checked her Piaget; its pavé diamond face told her they had less than an hour left.

Since T.J. Griffith never appeared in public after the car bombing had disfigured him, his assistant, Ryan Westcott, often took paintings on consignment for Griffith to view. If Ryan took home a painting—even if he returned it—the show would be saved. Everyone would assume Griffith was interested in Clive. Where the hell was the waiter with the gin?

She remembered she'd locked the liquor cabinet to keep the caterers from swilling the last of Archer's '37 Armagnac. Mercy! When things went wrong, they really went wrong. Pinpricks of sweat had risen across the back of her neck, and she could feel her curls going limp. She casually wiped the back of her neck with her hand, telling herself to remain calm.

She spotted Lauren, still talking with Finley. Vora edged her way through the group until she reached them. "Lauren, I need you," she said, her voice falsely upbeat.

With Lauren in tow, Vora winnowed her way between guests, and stopped at the entrance to the smaller gallery. "That's Ryan Westcott in the sport jacket," she said, indicating the man with his back toward them. "Entertain him for a while with your Nakamura stories. I'll be right back."

"Damn," Lauren muttered under her breath. Ryan Westcott wasn't supposed to be here tonight. She wasn't prepared for Griffith's assistant yet. She needed a talented artist to capture his interest. More damage control. Maybe she could wave Tak's name and his impressive art collection under Westcott's nose and sidetrack him as she had Finley Tibbetts.

She tried to remember what Vora had told her when they'd discussed the major collectors on the London art scene. Vora hadn't known very much about Ryan except that he was in his early forties and had worked for Griffith for about twenty years. Since the car bomb had exploded, Westcott had moved into Griffith's Palace Green mansion, conducting his business for him. To make Ravissant a first-rate gallery, Lauren needed Ryan Westcott's support.

He stood, his hands on his hips, studying a large acrylic that they'd hidden in here instead of displaying it in the main gallery because even Vora knew it was the weakest of Clive's works. Although Westcott's back was to her, Lauren sensed a certain hostility in the set of his shoulders and the way he had his dark head slightly cocked to one side, his wavy hair brushing the top of his collar.

Her hand extended for a welcoming handshake, her high-voltage hostess smile in place, she advanced. "Hello. I'm Lauren Winthrop."

Westcott swung around to face her, his sweeping glance taking in everything from her smooth blonde head to the silk pumps covering her toes.

"Haven't we met?"

3

The oldest line in the book. Lauren was fighting the urge to tell him this when she noticed the baffled expression on his face. Either he really did think he knew her, or he was a damn good actor. "No. We haven't met."

His incisive eyes assessed her without the spark of lust she usually found in such keen appraisals. "I'm never wrong." Instead of accepting her extended hand, he jammed his fist into his trouser pocket.

Unable to decide how to handle his rudeness, Lauren stood looking at him. With a nose a bit too sharp to be considered handsome, his angular features were tanned, highlighting intense green eyes. His dark-brown hair, worn slightly longer than currently fashionable, glistened like mink.

"What do you think of the exhibit?" she asked to fill the awkward silence.

"It's crap."

Caught off guard by his offensive remark, Lauren struggled to keep smiling. He glared at her, frowning, ignoring her smile. *What a jerk.*

"Here's your gin, Ryan." Vora's voice came from behind Lauren.

Finley Tibbetts, his blue eyes inspecting Lauren's figure, stood beside Vora. While he preached to them about the latest trends in contemporary art, Lauren prayed Ryan Westcott wouldn't voice his opinion of Clive's work to Finley.

"I simply had to have a Holcombe." Mootzie's voice, as she approached, could have been heard on the other side of the Thames.

Earlier, Finley had introduced the heiress to Lauren. Mootzie didn't appear to be the type who collected contemporary art, but years ago Lauren had learned how deceiving appearances could be.

"This is the one I bought." Mootzie gestured to the gigantic canvas on the wall in front of Lauren and Ryan.

"Don't you just love it?" Mootzie directed her question to Finley as a beaming Clive strolled up and joined the group.

Finley thoughtfully sipped his champagne and surveyed the piece. "Interesting. Very interesting."

During Mootzie's gleeful burst of giggles and the polite comments of the group, Ryan bent so close to Lauren's ear that his lips brushed her earlobe. "That's Brit for 'it stinks.' "

"Tell us the meaning of your work," Finley said to Clive, his eyes on Lauren.

The title on the wall plaque read "Descent into Purgatory," but Lauren doubted anyone could read it. She'd told Vora that the plaques were too small and the script too stylized. Next time Lauren would have them made bigger and use block letters.

Clive Holcombe began, "This is Phoenix rising from the ashes of the soul." He indicated a glob of two-inch-thick paint at the lower corner of the piece. He pointed to the irregular mounds of gray and mottled green splattered across the canvas. "These represent man's eternal search for love and fulfillment."

"And I thought all the crap was on the canvas," Ryan again whispered in her ear.

She pretended she hadn't heard him, hoping no one noticed his ridiculing smirk. She had visions of Finley, who was squinting myopically at the piece, smearing Clive and the gallery in one of his infamous reviews.

"I see," Finley said. "It's the transcendental rebirth of the soul. An affirmation of life itself."

Everyone but Ryan and Lauren nodded their agreement.

"This"—Clive pointed to a venom-green smear speckled with gray—"is the culmination: the rebirth of the spirit."

"Then why did he title this piece hell?" Ryan said in a low voice that only she heard.

Desperate to get them away from the painting before anyone else read the title or overheard Ryan, Lauren said, "Is everyone coming to our dinner party?"

Vora had asked a select few to dinner after the exhibition. Parading them through Lauren's home was Vora's well-bred way of letting everyone know Lauren Winthrop had money. To everyone in England she appeared to be a wealthy widow who provided the gallery with an infusion of cash.

"I'd love to come but I didn't think I could make it." Finley smiled at Lauren. "I regretted."

"No problem," she said, wondering if they could fit another chair at the dining table. "We'd love to have you."

"And Mootzie," Clive added.

"Of course," Lauren was forced to say. She smiled brightly, but she had absolutely no idea where they'd seat everyone. Vora had orchestrated a formal dinner with seven courses and place cards. "Run along, everyone. I'll be there as soon as I've closed the gallery."

As the group moved away, Ryan remained behind with Lauren. "Tell me you really like this."

"Well," she hedged, "Finley saw its importance."

"Tibbetts doesn't know his dick from a Dali. Neither does Holcombe."

Lauren winced at his crude but accurate assessment.

"Not only didn't Holcombe remember the title, but the piece is upside down."

"Don't be absurd."

He pointed to the upper left corner of the painting. She squinted, seeing a barely discernible H followed by a faint squiggle that trailed off into the green and brown mire.

"How could I have missed that?"

Vora stood on the curb with the departing guests, waiting for her Jaguar to be brought up as Mootzie's chauffeur-driven Turbo Bentley sped off toward Berkeley Square with Clive aboard. Trust Mootzie to have purchased the worst acrylic in the lot.

Poised as always, Clive had managed to show Finley the true meaning of his work. Too bad he hadn't remembered just which piece he was describing. Luckily, no one else had read the title or Clive would have made a fool of himself—and Ravissant.

Vora drew her chinchilla more closely around her; it was drizzling lightly now. She needed to get to Lauren's flat and let Christian Delteil, the chef from Michelin-starred L'Arlequin, know there would be more guests. Hopefully, the ten-percent overage caterers always prepared would cover it.

"Come on," said a deep voice at her shoulder. "Your fur will be ruined if you wait for your car. I'll drive you over there. I'm parked across the street."

She looked up and met Ryan Westcott's green eyes. "Thanks awfully."

Vora had no idea what to say to Ryan Westcott. Undeniably masculine, Ryan had eyes that gleamed with a permanent expression of defiance many women found irresistible. But she considered him too outspoken, too unpredictable. Uncontrollable.

"I like your hair long like that." He smiled at her, and for the first time she had a taste of what it was other women found so charming. She caught a whiff of his after-shave, Lords from Penhaligon's. Maybe he had a touch of class after all.

"Men like long hair. Like to think of it spread out across a pillow. We don't want short hair we can't get our hands into."

His sexual remark kept Vora from commenting. For years, she'd picked up men like Clive. From the beginning, when she'd met Clive at an exhibition in the Clore Gallery extension of the Tate, she'd been the aggressor. She wasn't sure what Ryan wanted, but she knew she couldn't handle him. She couldn't even handle Clive anymore.

"I read in the *Financial Times* that rents around Berkeley Square now equal the rents in the City," Ryan said. "Is that going to hurt Ravissant? How long a lease do you have?"

"We're fine," she replied tersely, thankful he'd changed the subject. Of course it was a lie, and Ryan Westcott was shrewd enough to know it.

Since Saatchi & Saatchi Advertising had moved their headquarters to Berkeley Square, they'd put the entire neighborhood on a par with the pricey financial district, the City. Moans of alarm had ricocheted up and down the streets adjacent to Berkeley Square. Ravissant, just doors from the square on Bruton Street, was no exception. Its lease would be up in another year, then their landlord, the royal family's Crown Estate, would raise the rent. Ravissant had to be making money by then, or they'd be unable to renew the lease.

"Here we are." Ryan stopped beside his car and fished in his pocket for the keys.

Vora peeped out from under the umbrella and stifled a groan. No wonder Ryan Westcott had found a place to park. While the valets had to hustle cars from blocks away, he'd driven his midnight-black Aston-Martin up onto the sidewalk in front of Barclay's Rolls-Royce dealership.

Ryan paused before inserting the key into the lock. He seemed to be looking at a green light winking at them from the dashboard. He rapped on the window and called, "Get in the back, Iggy."

Inside the dark interior, a small plump brown dog—obviously a mongrel—hopped over the console to the narrow bench seat just inches behind the front seats.

Vora lowered herself into the low-slung sports car while Ryan held the umbrella. She admired the handcrafted Aston-Martin Volante with its dashboard resembling a spaceship, wondering if Ryan's employer, T.J. Griffith, owned it. Since it commanded a price tag surpassing Bentleys and Rolls-Royces, she doubted it was Ryan's.

She felt the dog's moist nose nuzzling her shoulder-length curls and turned to pet the mutt. It snorted. "A pig!"

Ryan opened the driver's door just as the animal leaped into her lap, sniffing and making little snorting sounds. "Here, Iggy." Ryan slid into his seat and signaled to the little pig. "Don't be a pest."

Iggy greeted Ryan with more affectionate snorting as he stroked the pig's ears. "Pigcasso, meet Vora Leighton." The pig snorted once, as if it understood every word. "Don't be afraid. Pigcasso—I call her Iggy—won't hurt you." Ryan flipped on the interior light. "Here, pet her."

Vora gingerly touched the pig's head. In the light she could see Pigcasso wasn't a typical barnyard porcine. Her snout was much shorter than a regular pig's, and instead of having a curly tail, Iggy had a straight tail. The skin beneath her coat wasn't pink; it was brown and her fur was as soft as chinchilla. She was the size of a small dog. "She's still a baby."

"Nope, Iggy's full grown. She's a miniature variety called a Vietnamese pot belly. Bred in China originally. She'll never be any bigger than this."

"Aren't you afraid she'll chew on the upholstery and ruin—" she hesitated, again wondering about the expensive car—"your car?"

"No, Iggy's trained. Uses a litter box. Sleeps with me." He clicked his fingers and pointed to the backseat and Iggy hopped in back.

For an instant Vora pictured one of the gorgeous blondes Ryan was notorious for dating snuggled up to him—and Iggy. People were right; Ryan Westcott was crazy.

"Is there any particular reason she keeps sniffing me?" Vora asked as Iggy leaned forward in the small compartment relentlessly sniffing and wagging her tail like a dog.

"She's checking out your coat. Probably wondering if it's a relative." Ryan turned on the ignition and the engine revved impatiently.

Vora laughed as the Volante, using its famous acceleration, rocketed off the sidewalk leaving the staid Rolls-Royces looking out enviously from the showroom floor. She closed her eyes and prayed while Iggy squealed with delight as Ryan sped through Mayfair's rain-slicked streets to Lauren's. The Volante slammed to a halt, proving its antilock brakes were state-of-the-art, at the Grosvenor Square address she'd somehow managed to give him between Hail Marys.

"Is there room for me at dinner?" he asked, one hand casually stroking Iggy as the pot belly leaned forward from the backseat resting her head on Vora's shoulder.

"Certainly." Vora instantly realized what a coup it would be to have Ryan Westcott at dinner. He seldom appeared in public since Griffith had almost been killed by a car bomb.

"I'll take Iggy over to the American Embassy and let her

foul the sidewalk there, then I'll be back," Ryan said as he walked Vora into the building.

With a sigh of relief, she greeted the ground-floor porter and took the lift to the penthouse.

"Good work," Ryan said to Iggy, who'd reclaimed the passenger seat, then patted the top of her head.

Iggy oinked softly, her doe-brown eyes fixed on Ryan as he turned on the radio, already set on Capital. The Quire Boys' rock music blared out as the sports car streaked down the street then stopped in front of the concrete bunker, the American Embassy. Ryan scanned the area for the Metropolitan police who patrolled the perimeter of the building. Evidently, they were around back; he leaned across Iggy and opened the door. "Go on now. Hurry up. Leave a Holcombe for the Yanks."

As Iggy hightailed it up the gray stone steps, Ryan kept his eye out for the police, thinking of Lauren Winthrop. Created with an artist's touch, her classic features were delicate. Only her lips were fuller, more sensual, less than perfect. Every man's fantasy. Definitely his. He'd bet his life he'd met her before. But where?

Ryan spotted a pair of guards rounding the corner. He opened the door and whistled to Iggy. Snorting rooster tails of vapor into the rain, the pot belly scrambled into the car and Ryan reached for the towel he kept behind his seat. The telephone rang and he tossed the towel over Iggy, then turned down the radio.

"Yes?"

"I had you paged at Crockfords," said Peter Stirling.

"I didn't feel like gambling tonight." Ryan refused to explain any further. He resented British intelligence bird-dogging him all around town. "Anything on Barzan?"

"His operative is in London. Be careful. He may move against Griffith at any time."

Ryan braced the phone between his ear and shoulder, vigorously toweling Iggy with both hands. "What's his name? Got a description?"

"Negative," was the sheepish reply. "That's all we have."

"What a bunch of screw-ups. The Israelis would have pictures, his m.o.—the works. Not the MI-5. Three fucking months we've been waiting, looking over our shoulders. Now all you can tell me is Barzan's man is finally on British soil. What do you expect me to do? Throw a party?"

"Barzan's organization is as impenetrable as yours. We have a mole in place—not in as strategic a spot as we'd like—but better than nothing. You need to be extra careful from now on. Barzan will try to get to Griffith through you. There's no other way."

"Right." He pitched Iggy's towel into the backseat, thinking how much he hated being a decoy. Leave the cloak-and-dagger bullshit to the pros. If he didn't owe it to Griffith, he would have left right after the bombing. Any sane man would have.

"I want you to keep in touch—twice a day. Report *anything* unusual. Let us check it out. The main thing is to behave normally"—Peter hesitated, indicating he had no idea just what was normal for Ryan Westcott—"don't let them know you suspect anything. Has anything unusual happened yet?"

Ryan hesitated, then decided not to take any chances. "Tonight I met a woman. I'm positive I've met her before, but I can't remember where."

"Really?" Stirling paused. Ryan could hear him sucking on his pipe, mulling over this information. "What's her name? Let's see what the computer says."

"Lauren Winthrop." Ryan waited, stroking Iggy's ear, telling himself not to be curious about Lauren. Then why did you invite yourself to dinner? To listen to a cocky little shit like Tibbetts spout off his analysis of art? No. Admit it, buddy, you *are* curious.

"Not much here. Blonde hair, blue eyes." Figures, Stirling's tone implied. "Fluent in Japanese and French. Had an American father who was in the diplomatic corps. He died twenty-two years ago. British mother. She remarried Rupert Armstrong."

"Sonofabitch! That's it. I was sure I knew her." Ryan's triumphant laugh startled Iggy and she nosed under his sport coat to hide. "Lauren's the image of her mother, Caroline Armstrong."

A younger version of the bitch, but the resemblance was unmistakable. With Lauren's hair pulled off her face in a severe bun, he hadn't recognized her. Her mother, Caroline, had worn hers in a classic pageboy.

"What does Caroline Armstrong have to do with this?"

"T.J. was nuts about Caroline Armstrong." Ryan didn't add she'd led him on, admitting only under duress she'd never leave Rupert Armstrong. A listing in Debrett's Peerage along with a multitude of limp-wristed wimps meant more to Caroline than a man like T.J. Griffith who'd made a fortune on his own. The bitch. T.J. had never come even close to loving another woman. "No one knew about their affair except me."

"You're sure?" Stirling's tone indicated his doubts.

"Positive. Caroline would never tell anyone. She was terrified of losing Armstrong."

"Did you or T.J. ever meet Lauren during any of your visits to Marrakesh?"

"No. Caroline Armstrong rarely mentioned her children. I assumed they were problems—into drugs or something. They no longer lived in Marrakesh when T.J. and I met the Armstrongs."

"Interesting," Stirling responded, sucking eagerly on his pipe.

"Anything else on Winthrop?" Ryan wondered why he was asking.

"She studied art at the Sorbonne." He puffed on his pipe a few times. "Let's check deep background."

Ryan waited, wondering if the MI-5 shared its data bank with Interpol or the CIA, but he didn't ask. Even though he'd been cooperating with British intelligence on the Barzan affair, Ryan remained an outsider. They told him as little as possible. That irritated Ryan because he was accustomed to being in charge.

"Not much here. She was born in London, but lived in Japan until her father's death, then they returned here. Caroline remarried. They moved to Marrakesh where Armstrong runs an exporting business. Strange. Lauren wasn't sent to school in England or Switzerland the way most affluent families handle their children. She attended the École Française in Marrakesh until . . . This is odd. She never graduated."

"How the hell did she get into the Sorbonne then?"

"She probably had superior scores on the entrance exams. A

certificate isn't mandatory if you score high enough. At any rate, she married Osgood Winthrop when she was twenty-three and he was seventy-one."

"Must have been loaded."

"Doesn't appear so. They lived modestly in Paris, operating a small gallery specializing in watercolors. He died, leaving her very little. Then she moved to New York; lived with her brother and his wife. After the wife died of cancer, Lauren supported her brother by working in an exclusive bar that catered to Japanese executives."

"Then where'd she get her money?"

"Apparently, before her husband died he'd invested in a real estate deal in Miami. It recently paid off. She used those funds to move here and buy into the gallery."

"I see," Ryan said, staring into the rain-soaked night. Now she was doing what a lot of women did by dabbling in art. It kept them in the right circles, brushing shoulders with the filthy rich. The perfect place to snag a wealthy husband—like mother, like daughter.

By the time Ryan parked his car and went upstairs to Lauren's flat, the party was in full swing. The blush marble foyer with the gilded eighteenth-century Régence chairs set the tone for the rest of the opulent flat. French. Louis the whatever. Figured, she had lived for years in France.

Responding to greetings with curt nods, Ryan nudged his way up to the bar. After he ordered a double Boodles on the rocks, he slowly wandered down the hall past the lavish dining room where a legion of white-aproned maids were scurrying to set up a buffet. On the wall above the table hung a pair of octagonal Spanish vestry mirrors with faceted, Baroque cut-crystal motifs. Lauren certainly knew how to throw her money around. Just like her mother.

Sipping his gin, he sauntered into the library where more maids were setting up chairs beside a prissy peach-hued sofa. Above the carved marble mantel with cutesy cupids blowing kisses to each other hung an oversized beveled mirror.

There wasn't one damn painting in the joint! Strange for a lady with an art gallery. The whole place gave him an uneasy feeling—too much froufrou left over from the reign of a pack of guillotined dilettantes.

Spurred on by curiosity, he strolled down the corridor. A hall of mirrors like Versailles. Through the partially closed door of one of the bedrooms came the unmistakable voice of Mootzie McCallister.

"Hurry, hurry," she moaned.

Through the crack, Ryan caught Mootzie's reflection. Her poison-green skirt was shoved up around her boobs while her panty hose were bunched around her ankles. Above stark-white rhino thighs, a tangle of jet-black curls were partially hidden by Clive Holcombe's hand. Like his art, his taste in women sucked.

Ryan held his nose and whined, "Dinner is served," in his best falsetto voice, counting on breaking up the action. Then he dashed down the hall and into the double-doored suite that must belong to Lauren.

Inside, a crystal lamp revealed acres of swagged blue silk cloaking the windows and canopying a bed that had escaped The Terror. A lone mirror graced the silk moiré walls. The lady loved looking at herself, all right.

An alcove led to a mirrored bath with a sunken tub of pink marble and a heather-colored chaise of silk moiré with a white ermine throw dramatically draped across it. The adjacent dressing area had floor-to-ceiling beveled mirrors accented by miniature spotlights. He walked in and opened a wardrobe door. Arranged by color, most of the clothes still sported their price tags. The only garment that looked as if it had been worn was a violet nightshirt with bold script broadcasting: *Yankees*.

On his way out, Ryan almost missed the silk-smothered French door leading into the rooftop conservatory. He opened the door and went into the dark room. It took him a minute to find the light switch.

Lauren sat on the sofa balancing her dinner plate on her knees as she listened to Finley Tibbett's monologue on the primeval influences in contemporary art. Nearby Mootzie gushed loudly about how handsome Clive looked in his new dinner jacket. Lauren noticed Vora talking to a reporter from

Galleries, but her eyes were on Clive. There was a forced note to Vora's laugh, a definite falseness to her smile.

"I've got to powder my nose," Mootzie announced to the whole room as she rose, clutching her gold Judith Leiber monkey bag.

Who cares? Lauren watched her sashay across the room. Instead of fixing her face, Mootzie should straighten the rhinestone seams on her stockings. They had more curves than a roundabout.

Over the rim of her glass, Lauren's eyes met Ryan Westcott's. She quickly looked away, but not before she noticed the ravishing brunette approaching him. When he left the room, the woman clinging to his arm, Lauren uttered an inaudible sigh of relief. All evening he'd openly watched her, his eyes conveying his dislike. Why? Just her luck to offend one of the few men whose goodwill she needed to promote Ravissant.

Later on her way to the buffet table in the adjacent room to get Finley bittersweet profiteroles and coffee, Ryan intercepted Lauren.

"I think you'd better come see where Mootzie has her tootzies."

4

"Why should I care where Mootzie has her feet?" Lauren replied as smoothly as possible. Ryan's brusque manner and foul mouth made her wish she didn't have to deal with him in order to make Ravissant a successful gallery.

"See the man over by the window?" Ryan grinned as if he knew something she didn't.

"Yes. Who is he?"

"Nigel Dempster. Surely you've heard of him?" She nodded; everyone knew the gossip columnist. "You've been to Annabel's?" Again she nodded. "The scoop that made Dempster's name was the one that smeared Lady Annabel, wife of the owner of the nightclub. Dempster claimed the baby she was expecting had been fathered by an international financier —not by her husband."

"I don't like gossip," Lauren said, wondering what this had to do with Mootzie.

"Neither do I, but the world does. Dempster has a column to fill . . . five days a week." He grinned, but she could tell he didn't think the situation was humorous. "I'm sure he'd love to tell his readers about Mootzie's tootzies. After all, she's made good copy in the past. Now she's in your conservatory."

Lauren stormed down the hall. What was Mootzie doing there? That was her personal retreat. Lauren had allowed

Vora to talk her into leasing this swank apartment only because it had a conservatory. Light filled the glass-domed room even on the dreariest of London days. While Vora and some designer Lauren had never met had decorated the flat, she'd furnished the conservatory herself, setting it up as a studio. So far, she'd only drawn a few charcoal sketches, but she intended to begin painting again.

With Ryan at her heels, Lauren rushed into the small study, one of two ways into the conservatory. Once inside, she halted so quickly that Ryan bumped into her.

Lit up like a West End theater stage, the conservatory could easily be seen by anyone happening into the study or into Lauren's bedroom on the opposite side of the conservatory. Reclining in a wicker chair, buck-naked from the waist down and spread-eagled, Mootzie had her feet braced against Lauren's easel. Kneeling, Clive had his head buried between Mootzie's fleshy, white thighs.

"The artist at work," Ryan whispered. "I tried to stop them earlier—"

"My God!" Lauren turned away from the spectacle. How Clive could do this to Vora after all she'd done for him? "Lock this door. I'll—"

"You bastard! You bloody bastard!" Vora burst through the door from Lauren's bedroom into the conservatory. She flung her drink at the hapless Clive's head. The champagne caught Mootzie smack on the crotch. Her feet slammed to the floor, bringing down the easel on top of them.

Ryan, his hand on Lauren's arm, propelled her into the conservatory just as Mootzie began to shriek "You bitch!" in a voice guaranteed to be heard in Trafalgar Square.

"What are you doing with this slut?" Vora asked Clive, her voice anguished. "Don't you remember? There was a picture of her in *The Sun.* She and some rugby player were arrested for rogging on the steps of the Victoria and Albert. She's a case of AIDS just waiting to happen."

"Bitch!" Mootzie shrieked.

Vora ignored her. "Get out, you bastard." With a mocking smile, she nodded, indicating Mootzie. "She's all yours."

Lauren located Mootzie's shoes and Leiber bag and handed

them to her. "Get her out of here!" she told Clive. "Use the back stairs."

Mootzie huffed out, saying, "You can't keep a man."

"He's not worth it," Lauren said to Vora.

"I know." Vora swallowed a sob, but tears cascaded down her cheeks leaving a trail of mascara.

"Go back to your guests, Lauren," Ryan said. "I'll take care of her."

Hearing voices and not wanting anyone to find Vora like this, Lauren darted into the hall. She ran into Finley Tibbetts and an extremely attractive gentlemen she didn't recall seeing earlier.

"Is something the matter?" Finley asked, and she shook her head. "Nothing a'tall?" Again she shook her head, summoning a half smile. "Good, I want you to meet Ross Benson from the *Daily Express.* He just nipped in for a bit. I want you to tell him all your plans for Ravissant."

By the time the last guests had drained her entire supply of vintage port and the caterers had returned the apartment to some semblance of its original state, Lauren found the conservatory deserted. Vora's chinchilla still hung in the guest closet alongside Mootzie's Fendi, a Russian lynx dyed lime-green with tuffs of garish purple. Ryan and Vora had vanished.

"Will that be all, madame?" asked Selma, the maid Vora had hired for Lauren.

"Yes. Thank you. Good night." She smiled at the older woman, whose gray hair was crimped into a style that hadn't been in fashion since the Second World War.

Suddenly, Lauren felt lonely, lonelier than she had in years. At times like this only one person could make her feel better. She hurried to her room, picked up the telephone, dialed the international code followed by Paul's number. *Please be home. I need you.* No answer. She let it continue to ring. A faint click on the line caught her attention; she'd heard it before. There were two lines coming into the flat; the telephones had lighted monitor buttons, showing which number was in use. Was Selma eavesdropping? Why?

Reluctantly, Lauren hung up. She undressed slowly, carefully putting away her clothes, even though she knew Selma considered it her job. After putting on her Yankees' nightshirt, she unwound her hair and brushed it. Despite a fifteen-round day, Lauren wasn't sleepy. The urge to get far away from the flat—and her troubles—overwhelmed her. Go for a walk; get some fresh air. She grabbed the Russian Bargusin sable Vora had thrust upon her, saying no one would accept her without a "serious" fur. As she went to get her key from her purse, she decided to take her phone card. She'd try Paul again from a phone booth. It might be better to discuss this mess without wondering if Selma was listening.

Lauren tiptoed to the door and into the hall where the hall porter snored noisily. Clearly, he'd just had his busiest night on record.

Lauren took the stairs down to the street where she was delighted to find it had stopped raining. A full moon rode proudly above cumulus clouds. She gathered the fur around her and hurried across the street to Grosvenor Square where a statue of Franklin Delano Roosevelt surveyed the grounds. She rounded the park and stood on the north side of the street, facing the building where General Eisenhower had devised his campaign against the Nazis.

Awed by the memory of the two illustrious men, Lauren slowed her pace. In the greater scheme of things, how important was she? Vora? Barzan? Ryan Westcott?

Discouraged, she turned up Audley, then went onto Lees Place. Ahead of her, two public telephones stood off to the side. Deciding to try Paul again, she went to one and slid her phone card into the slot. She dialed her brother's number.

"Howdy."

Howdy? Surely, she had the wrong number. "Sorry."

"Lauren, is that you?"

"Paul? I've been trying to get you. Where've you been?"

"Repairing a roof."

"Our roof leaks?" she asked, though she might have guessed it did, recalling its appalling condition.

"Not ours, a neighbor's" he responded, an unmistakable smile coming over the satellite connection. "Geeta Helspeth's."

"*The* Geeta Helspeth?" A vision of one of Geeta's glass

sculptures that had catapulted her to worldwide fame sprung
into Lauren's mind. "She's our neighbor?"

"Yup. Drives a temperamental Toyota with a bumper
sticker that says: 'Doo-doo happens.' "

It happens all right.

"Geeta's divorced with two little kids. They beat me at
Nintendo, but now I've got 'em. I bought a book called *Winning at Nintendo.*" He laughed, the first sincere belly laugh
she'd heard from him since before Marcy's cancer diagnosis.
"How are things at Ravissant? Knockin' 'em dead?"

"It's fine." She mustered the courage to ask the question she
wanted to know. "Do you like Geeta . . . a lot?"

Total silence.

"Don't feel guilty," she whispered, tears coming to her
eyes. "Marcy would understand. When she knew the end was
near, she told you to be happy, to get on with your life. Didn't
she?"

"I enjoy Geeta. She's totally different—nothing like Marcy.
I don't know what'll happen."

Relief surged through Lauren. Paul was on the mend. "I'm
glad," she said, a tear tumbling down her cheek. She brushed
it back into her unbound hair.

"You okay, babes?"

"Fine," she lied. Why burden him with her problems?

"Something's wrong. I hear it in your voice."

"Not wrong exactly. I met a man. He could be a big help to
me with Ravissant. But he hated me on sight."

"Ridiculous. There's not a man alive who'd hate you."

"Ryan Westcott's trouble. I can just feel it."

"Don't worry. You'll charm him the way you do all men."
Paul laughed, lighting up the transatlantic connection.

Lauren said good-bye, promising to call next week as usual,
then replaced the receiver. She leaned forward, bracing her
forehead against the call box, thankful Paul was better.

Ryan downshifted, bringing the Aston-Martin to a silent
halt. In the distance he saw a slight figure with blonde hair
streaming down her back standing at the telephone stall.
Lauren. Her maid had said she'd gone for a walk, but she was
making a call. At this time of night? From a public telephone?

He got out of the car, looked quickly around, and walked up the cobblestoned street until he reached her. Although her back was to him, he saw she wasn't making a call. Leaning against the phone, she sobbed a soft, keening cry.

He came up behind her. "What's wrong?"

Lauren spun around and gasped, startled to see him. Tears coursed down her sculpted cheekbones, spilling onto her fur coat. In the moonlight her eyes shone crystal-blue, and her hair hung in loose waves. She looked young, utterly feminine. Not the snooty bitch who'd sashayed up to him at the gallery, already counting him among her conquests. An unexpected twinge of compassion seized him. "Don't cry. It can't be that bad. Tell me the problem."

Tears caught along the serried rows of her eyelashes. He dug out his handkerchief and handed it to her. "What's the matter?" He placed his hand on her shoulder. Her hair, so soft, so fine, shifted under his fingers.

She dabbed at her nose with his hankie and tried to pull away from him. Leaning close, he wiped the last traces of her tears off her cheeks with his thumb. Realizing their lips were just inches apart, he stopped. Diamond-bright, her blue eyes met his. He smoothed the loose curls back from her face, running his fingers slowly through her hair, never taking his eyes from her.

For a second, they froze, lips not quite touching. Then, in one swift motion, he slipped his hand behind her neck, his fingers winding though her long hair and holding her head in place as his lips sealed over hers. Her arms came up around his neck; she stroked him with long, sexy nails.

He kissed her gently, tasting her tears. When he nudged his tongue between her lips, hers was there to greet him. In a series of darting forays, their tongues caressed each other while he ran his hands up and down the back of her coat, feeling as much of her as the damn fur allowed.

She wove her fingers through his thick hair, furrowing it until her nails pressed into his scalp. A low moan came from his throat as he unhooked her coat. Sonofabitch! All she had on was the Yankees nightshirt.

She started to pull away from him, but he backed her against the phone booth. Hot and moist, his lips found the sensitive area beneath her ear and he ran the tip of his tongue across it, inhaling a hint of some exotic perfume.

"What are you doing?"

"Making you stop crying."

His lips found hers again, hungrily kissing her. His tongue darted into her mouth while his hands fanned up and down her slim rib cage, skimming the sides of her breasts.

Their open mouths clung to each other; her breath had an uneven catch to it. Ryan eased one hand over her breast, cupping its fullness, testing its weight while his thumb tested the erect nipple.

She tensed, then twisted in his arms, breaking the kiss. "Don't."

He kissed her anyway, holding her tight with one arm, palming her warm breast with his free hand. Most women said no initially just to go on record as not being easy.

But Lauren wasn't pretending; she remained rigid in his arms. He spanned her chin with strong fingers. "Don't tell me you didn't want me to kiss you."

She turned her head away, her blonde hair falling across her face. "I didn't want you to force me."

Force? The lady didn't know the meaning of the word. Of course, she'd been married to an old man. Probably had to jump start him. Forget it. Like mother, like daughter—conniving ballbusters. The last thing he needed on a trip through hell was a woman.

She hurried away, retreating down Lees Place toward Grosvenor Square.

He caught up with her. "Let me drive you home."

She hesitated, eyeing him warily.

"For crissake, it was only a kiss." He took her arm.

She jerked her arm out of his grasp, but didn't try to walk away.

"What's wrong? Why were you crying?"

"I was crying because I'm so happy."

Happy? Jesus! Would he *ever* understand women? "About what?" he muttered, walking up to his car.

"My brother. He's met a woman."

Tears over her brother's love life?

"Paul's tried to commit suicide—twice. He was desperately in love with his wife. She died. Now I think he's in love again."

Now he's in trouble. It struck Ryan as strange that Caroline Armstrong's daughter would be so loving. Her mother certainly wouldn't have been.

"My sidekick's waiting for us," Ryan said, once they'd reached the car. He paused to check the green monitor light on the dashboard, then looked over his shoulder. Like radar, his restless eyes searched the shadows.

Lauren peered through the window. Iggy pressed her snout against the glass, gazing back. "You have a pot belly! I knew a man in New York who had one. He had to wait months to get it. It cost thousands of dollars." She looked over her shoulder at Ryan. "Hurry up. Let me in."

By the time Ryan let Lauren in and came around to the driver's seat, she had Iggy in her arms and was kissing the top of the pot belly's head.

"What's he sniffing for?" Lauren asked as Iggy nosed open Lauren's coat revealing the Yankees nightshirt.

"She. Her name's Pigcasso. Iggy for short. She has a nose five times more sensitive than a dog's. Her French cousins hunt truffles, so she's checking your truffles."

"Seriously." Lauren smiled, a sincere smile, not the phony grin she'd used when introducing herself. "What's she after?"

Tits by Frank Lloyd Wright. "Nothing. She's just getting to know you." Iggy snuffled, snuggling up against the Y in Yankees, in hog heaven. "Probably likes your perfume."

Lauren hugged Iggy, then kissed her snout.

Ryan inserted the key into the ignition, but didn't turn it when he saw Lauren staring at his hand. She seemed fascinated by his leopard ring. "Married?" he asked, pretending to notice her wide gold wedding band for the first time.

Lauren hesitated, clutching the lucky Iggy to her bosom. "Widowed."

Ryan stared out at the lemony-white light the streetlight cast across the wet cobblestones. Osgood Winthrop had been dead for years, yet she still wore his ring. Why? Love?

He turned on the engine and the sports car barreled down Audley to Grosvenor Square. Lauren was too busy baby-talk-

ing Iggy to notice how fast he went. Love? Hell! Give him a
fast car—and a woman who didn't ask questions.

"Night-night, Iggy," Lauren said after Ryan had double
parked in front of her building and opened the car door for
her.

She didn't say anything more until they were on the lift
bound for the penthouse. "Why did you come back tonight?"

Hell, he'd forgotten all about Vora. "To tell you Vora has
gone to Paris. She needed to get away."

When they reached the top floor, Ryan took her key from
Lauren and unlocked the door. He followed her in even
though she didn't invite him. The absorbed, concerned look
he'd seen earlier when she'd talked about her brother had
again come over Lauren's face.

"Vora will be all right. She's better off without him." He
grinned. "You've got to admit it was funny—Mootzie and
Clive. Dempster would have had a journalistic gem with that
one."

The hilarity of the scene they'd witnessed hit them both at
once. They shared a smile, then a laugh.

"Was she really arrested at the Victoria and Albert?"

"Yes. Mootzie thrives on being outrageous."

"Thank you for helping tonight. I don't know what we
would have done. Ross Benson and Nigel Dempster were
outside the conservatory; if they'd seen Mootzie and
Clive . . ."

He shrugged. "Another scandal would ruin Ravissant. You
need to select artists wisely."

"I would never have exhibited Clive's work, but I had no
choice. Vora had already scheduled it." Lauren gazed
thoughtfully off in the distance, then turned to face him again.
"After the print fraud scandal last year, would you be afraid to
recommend one of Ravissant's artists to Mr. Griffith?"

"No. But if you find a hot artist and reproduce any of his
work as prints, be sure you monitor Ravissant Press carefully.
Get better security. Another problem will ruin Ravissant—
and the artist."

"Like some fake Salvador Dalis I saw in New York. Dali had
released reams of presigned paper. Unscrupulous dealers
printed anything on them, claiming they were Dalis."

"That's why when he died, instead of his originals skyrocketing, they stayed flat, still getting millions, but not as much as might have been expected. If he'd protected his copyrights, his originals would be bringing in astronomical prices. Let his experience be a lesson to you."

"We've improved security. It won't happen again."

"It may not be that simple. Tonight, Vora told me that she suspects her husband's death wasn't an accident. The police were investigating the bogus print operation. She thinks Archer may have been ready to tell the authorities who was behind it and they killed him."

"Do you believe that?" Lauren asked, wondering why Vora had never mentioned this to her.

"Anything's possible. Fraudulent prints bring in a billion dollars a year. High stakes attract criminals who stop at nothing."

"Thank you for warning me. I'll be careful."

"Lauren." He put his hands on her shoulders, then lightly fluffed her hair aside. With his fingers he traced the delicate curve of her cheek where it met her hairline. Her crystal-blue eyes stared up at him. "I was right, you know. I knew you looked familiar. You're Caroline Armstrong's daughter."

She jerked away from him, a bewildered expression on her face. "How do you know my mother?"

"I met her in Marrakesh—a long time ago." He let it go at that.

"I haven't seen my mother in over seventeen years."

"Why not?"

"That's none of your business!"

5

"Clive Holcombe," Lauren said when the houseboy answered the telephone at Mootzie McCallister's Rutland Gate home.

"Mr. Holcombe hasn't arisen," a nasal voice informed her.

"Give him a message. He has until six this evening to pick up his paintings. Otherwise, I'm donating them to the Society to Benefit Distressed Gentlefolk Temporarily Out of Quarters."

She hung up, eyeing the stack of paintings she'd earlier taken off Ravissant's walls and piled against the door. If that creep didn't come for them, she'd let the society for the homeless get what money they could by selling the canvases and frames.

Roaming the empty gallery, her thoughts turned to Ryan Westcott. The image of his gentle hand, the leopard ring winking in the moonlight as he wiped the tears from her cheeks, resurfaced. On an impulse she didn't quite understand, she'd allowed him to kiss her. Obviously, she'd been off balance after she'd talked to Paul. She didn't feel comfortable with a man like Ryan, who probably enjoyed a different sort of woman. Finley Tibbetts was really more her type. Like her dead husband, he had a refined, courteous manner.

Don't worry about seeing Ryan again. Evidently, he thought her callous for not being close to her mother. He'd left immediately when she'd told him what had happened with her mother was none of his business. Bit by bit, the events in Marrakesh had receded until they might never have happened. She wanted it to remain that way. Forever.

Determined not to let the dark vortex of the past eclipse everything she'd struggled to achieve, Lauren picked up a razor. She went to work on the silver mylar letters on Ravissant's window. As she scraped, removing Clive Holcombe's name and exhibition dates from the glass, she didn't see the man standing on the sidewalk until he tapped on the window. She glanced up into David Marcus's albino-blue eyes. While some women might find him attractive, Lauren didn't. He made her uneasy.

The gallery was closed on Mondays, so she'd dressed in work clothes with her hair pulled to the top of her head and cocked to one side in an untidy ponytail. She hadn't bothered with what little makeup she usually wore.

"Hi." David smiled as she let him in, his eyes wandering approvingly over her Jets T-shirt and stone-washed jeans. Great tits, but he liked younger women—twenty years old, tops. "I'm in town for a meeting. I thought I'd see how you're doing. How did the showing go?"

"Super," she said, as he noted the paintings stacked up beside the door. "One collector bought everything."

"Really? Barzan will be pleased. Who is it?"

"Mootzie McCallister. *The* Mootzie McCallister." Lauren's tone intimated David should recognize the name.

"I don't know—"

"Mootzie's destined to be a real force in the art world. She's been written up quite often in the papers here."

"You're off to a good start."

"Griffith's representative, Ryan Westcott, came."

Marcus eased himself down onto the white leather chair beside the reception desk. Maybe Barzan was right, after all. Using Lauren Winthrop as bait to snag Griffith might be better than the other heavy-handed methods they'd considered. The car bombing had been a fiasco. Instead of killing Griffith, it had maimed him, forcing him to employ elaborate security measures that they now had to circumvent.

David smiled again at Lauren, not listening to what she was

saying. He anticipated Barzan's stepping down, leaving the running of the cartel to him. It had been understood that Barzan's son, Robert, would inherit his father's empire. His unexpected death—at Griffith's hands—had changed everything.

For years, David had concealed his dislike of Robert Barzan. Unlike his father, Carlos, Robert went off half-cocked, always trying to upstage David by developing new ways of laundering drug profits. Finally, he'd bitten off more than he could chew when he found himself crosswise with T.J. Griffith.

Robert Barzan had gotten what he deserved when Griffith had shot him. David supposed he should be thanking Griffith, not trying to kill him. But power commanded a high price— one David was willing to pay. Barzan's words replayed, vividly clear. *All you have to do, David, is get rid of Griffith for me. Then I can retire. You'll be in charge.*

At last.

A few days later, Vora returned to the gallery from her stay in Paris. "What did Finley's article say about the exhibition?" she asked, not commenting on Ravissant's bare walls.

"Well." Lauren opted to omit Finley's flattering references to her own talent for spotting first-rate contemporary artists while she'd lived in New York. "He said the collection had 'progressive symbolism which reflected compelling influences.' He cited the 'exuberant use of converging elements.' "

"What does all that mean?"

"Damned if I know." Lauren smiled, but Vora merely looked disgusted. "Hey, he could have leveled us."

"Not you." Vora shook her head, tossing her newly lengthened curls. "You have a great reputation. He could have finished Clive . . . and Ravissant."

"We're in this together—you and I. We'll have Ravissant featured in *Apollo* in no time."

Tears crested in Vora's eyes, spiking her lashes.

"We're friends. Things happen sometimes." At the half smile on Vora's lips, Lauren continued. "I got rid of Clive's paintings. Anyone who repays kindness with crude, inconsiderate behavior isn't going to be in our gallery, is he?"

"No. . . . No, he isn't."

"Now we have empty walls. Where are we going to find another artist?"

"I have no idea. Archer always located the talent."

"Trust yourself. Think. Where would you look?"

"The Royal College. They show students' works. I'd call agents. Look in the galleries along Kings Road, up and down Portobello. Often those galleries don't have exclusives. If I saw an artist I liked, I'd contact him."

Lauren nodded as if Vora's solution was a brilliant idea. The Royal College had been Lauren's first stop, and she'd already covered every gallery in London as well as the agents.

"I might go to Paris," Vora suggested.

"No. Ozzie and I had a gallery there. The dealers are incredibly well informed. If there's a first-rate artist in Paris who hasn't been discovered, he's still in the womb."

Lauren decided it was entirely possible Vora could locate some minor talents through her connections. But Vora didn't know Lauren planned to leave London at the end of the year. It would take a superstar to bring Ravissant to the top within the deadline. Why did Barzan have to be in such a hurry? She needed all the help she could get, Lauren thought, recalling Ryan Westcott's hasty departure from her flat. It would certainly make things easier if he were on her side.

"Did you ever meet T.J. Griffith?" Lauren asked, wondering just what sort of man employed Ryan Westcott. When Vora nodded, she added, "Tell me about him."

"I only met him a few times at exhibitions. He had a reputation as a womanizer and a high-stakes gambler."

"What does he look like?"

"He's in his sixties now, but he's had gray hair since I met him almost twenty years ago—just about the same time he hired Ryan. Griffith's tall. Extremely handsome. Green eyes." Vora shrugged. "I wonder what he looks like now. Some say he's blind, but who knows? No one sees him except Ryan Westcott."

Lauren unwound the last of two dozen tight braids, then arranged the corkscrew curls with a pick before adding black eyeliner around her entire eye and violet mascara to her lashes. Three-inch-long feather earrings the color of New York taxis completed her outfit. She donned enormous Biagiotti sunglasses and quietly slipped out of her building past the snoring hall porter, confident no one would recognize her in the chartreuse tights and thigh-skimming leather skirt.

She hailed a taxi and silently rode to the Bloomsbury Art Festival. *This had better work.* Recalling the "slaves of New York," the network of bohemian artists who dressed outlandishly while they sought recognition as artists, Lauren had decided to go underground. Struggling artists all knew each other. They exhibited in cafes and second-rate shows. On sunny weekends, they hung their work on the fences bordering Green Park and Hyde Park, eking out a few pounds from passing tourists.

It was a long shot, but she hoped by joining the brethren, disguising herself as one of them, she might discover a new artist. If they knew she owned a gallery, she'd be inundated with works to review. She couldn't bear rejecting anyone. She remembered only too well the harsh criticism she'd received when she'd shown her work to Greenwich Village galleries.

When she arrived at the festival, Lauren was surprised to see the huge crowd. There wasn't any question about it: People were hungry for art. No wonder the print market did so well. It was the only fine art the average person could afford. Otherwise they had to settle for this. She looked around at the makeshift stalls with paintings bargain basements would be ashamed to sell.

By the time she'd arrived at the back of the hall where her one painting had been hung, she'd decided it was a terrible idea to ask these amateurs if they knew of an undiscovered artist. No one here knew their rump from a Rembrandt.

"Bad booth," said Thatcher Palumbo, the other artist assigned to her area. His bushy goatee had been tamed by two rubberbands, one at the base of his chin, another several inches lower. "Folks get tired. They never make it back this far."

"Some will," Lauren said cheerfully, but she had to agree. To her the location didn't matter; she had no intention of selling her painting. She'd taken it out of the closet in the conservatory and brought it here only because she had to have something to exhibit. She'd put an outrageous price on it to be certain no one bought it. "There are people who start at the back and go forward."

He grinned. "Which of my works do you like best?"

She gulped, scrutinizing the papier-mâché mounded on the canvas and spiked with fish bones painted Day-Glo orange, green, and purple. "They're all . . . interesting . . . very interesting."

She straightened "Midnight in Marrakesh." Did the young girl in her picture affect people the way Palumbo's works struck her? Long, free-flowing blonde hair shielded her profile, making her face barely visible. Tears coursed down her cheek while disembodied hands—sinister hands—reached out of the darkness for her.

It didn't matter to Lauren if people didn't like her painting. Her talent lay in recognizing great art, not creating it. Right now, she needed to get on with the talent search. "I'm going to look around."

Lauren spent the day roving up and down the aisles. She was able to get a few leads but nothing sounded truly promising. On her way back to give Thatcher moral support, Lauren noticed a young girl with a large display of ceramic earrings. No question about it, an exceptionally talented ceramicist had created them.

"Pardon me," Lauren said to the buxom redhead. Her wiry hair, dragged back into a single braid, emphasized her deep-brown eyes and high-bridged nose. "Did your mother make these?"

"I made them," the girl snapped, eyeing Lauren's earrings with distaste.

"They're beautiful." How old could she be? Seventeen? It was hard to tell with all that makeup. "Do you make anything else?"

"Naw. No money in it."

"There could be," Lauren hedged, wondering why the girl seemed so concerned about money. Didn't her parents support her? "Would you be willing to make me a few things for fifty pounds each?"

"Sure." She beamed. "Like what?"

"Anything except jewelry." Lauren knew there was no

surer way of stifling creativity than telling someone exactly what they should create. "What's your name?"

"Tabatha Foley." She plopped down onto one of the folding chairs in her booth.

"I'm . . . Lucy Wallace," Lauren said, remembering to give the phony name she'd used when registering for the exhibition. She'd chosen it because the name matched the initials on her painting. "Do you live with your parents?"

"No. I live in a flat in Bayswater with six other girls."

Lauren decided not to question her any further about why she wasn't living at home. She remembered the early years when she'd first gone to Paris. Many people had asked prying questions about why she lived with her brother, not her parents.

"You're an art student?"

Tabatha shook her head. "I work in the booth at the Hard Rock Cafe. One day I'm going to have my own shop and sell pricey jewelry like Cornelius on Beauchamp Place."

Lauren had no use for a restaurant whose most popular entree was a T-shirt. She couldn't imagine the talented Tabatha standing in the booth outside the Hard Rock, selling souvenirs to tourists. Nor could she see her limiting herself to jewelry. Tabatha had more potential than that. But Lauren didn't voice her opinion of the girl's aspirations. Perhaps, if Lauren could sell a few of Tabatha's pieces, her goals might change. As creative as Tabatha was, her skill at producing anything but jewelry remained unseen. Lauren still needed that special artist with work that could be exhibited immediately.

"What are you showing?" Tabatha asked, her brown eyes surveying Lauren with curiosity.

"My painting—an oil. I'm in the back with Thatcher Palumbo."

Tabatha snickered. "With Bones? You'll never sell anything back there. The committee always stiffs him, giving him the worst spot. No one goes back that far."

"Maybe someone will buy one of his works today. It's important not to give up," Lauren said, though she'd done just that. When a few galleries had rejected her work, she'd given up trying to find a gallery to exhibit her paintings. "Have you seen anyone you considered particularly talented?"

Tabatha named a few of the artists currently exhibiting at the Royal College. Those she mentioned had already been snapped up by other galleries. "I was thinking of someone"— Lauren waved her hand indicating the group around them— "like us. Someone who hasn't been discovered."

Rolling her eyes heavenward, Tabatha considered a moment. "There is a man. A real queer duck. I met him last summer. He had two of his paintings hanging on the fence at Hyde Park near my stand."

"Did he sell them?"

"Naw. They were too big. He had to bring them in a meat wagon. Everyone loved them, though. He had crowds around him all day."

"What's his name? Do you know where he lives?" She kept her tone casual. This was her hottest lead so far.

"No. I didn't ask. But he shouldn't be hard to find, if he's still working at Smithfield. He brought his paintings in one of their lorries."

"Smithfield?"

"The meat market north of Holborn Viaduct near Saint Paul's. Ask for the Russian. How many of them can there be?"

"A Russian?" Lauren cried. How lucky could she get? Finding an undiscovered Russian would be a major coup.

A swarm of teenagers descended upon the earrings, and Lauren said good-bye to Tabatha after getting her number. As she went to her stall, she mentally crossed her fingers. With Gorbachev's more open policy toward the West, Russian painters not previously seen had come to the art community's attention. In a gutsy move Sotheby's had gone to Moscow and had auctioned Russian art. The now-famous sale had netted capitalist prices for communist art—two to four times projected prices.

Overnight *glasnost* artists were in demand. Russians already living in the West, like Mikhail Chemiakin, watched the value of their works skyrocket. A world-class artist, particularly if he were Russian, would vault Ravissant into the ranks of the leading galleries.

"This is your lucky day," Thatcher informed her, a trace of

bitterness in his deep voice when she returned to their booth. "Someone bought your painting."

"What?" She looked up. "Midnight in Marrakesh" had vanished. She never thought anyone would be interested much less pay such a steep price at a festival where the art sold for a fraction of the price. "How long ago?"

"Two, maybe two and a half hours. Aren't you excited?"

Without answering, she raced off toward the cashier's station where buyers paid for their purchases. "Laur—Lucy Wallace. Booth one sixty-seven. My painting—has it been paid for it yet?"

While the clerk checked the roster, Lauren waited and hoped the buyer was still looking around and she could stop the sale. If he'd left, she'd find him and buy it back. She considered this painting her best work—despite the memories it evoked.

"Here it is. I remember now." The clerk raised one eyebrow. "It's been paid for—all cash."

"Who bought it?"

"I have no idea. We don't keep records on cash sales unless the buyer wants one. Usually they do, but this whole sale was rather odd. What teenage boy has that much cash?"

6

Lauren waited while Finley checked their coats at Sotheby's cloakroom, then they edged their way up the crowded hall to the reception area. People were lined up five deep at the New Bond Street auction house.

"There are the men from the Getty." Lauren's eyes swept over the representatives from Los Angeles's Getty Museum. Other museums lacked the capital to compete in the economic follies that had characterized recent auctions. But the Getty Museum had a three-and-a-half-billion-dollar endowment from the late J. Paul Getty, giving it almost limitless spending power.

"Cheeky Yanks." Finley shrugged dismissively, then smiled at her. "It's too bad Vora couldn't join us. Archer never missed an auction."

"She's still weak." Lauren and Vora had agreed to explain her absence from the auction as a bout with the flu. Vora wasn't ready to face the world yet.

Lauren surveyed the polished group of patrons, thinking Vora would have fit right in. Immaculately coiffed and bedecked in jewels, the women wore the latest in gowns direct from Paris or Milan. The men spoke a dozen different languages, but had one thing in common—tailor-made suits.

Since 1983 when Sotheby's had been taken over by A. Al-

fred Taubman, a wealthy American, their auctions had
changed dramatically. Once the domain of dealers who purchased, marked up, and resold to clients, Sotheby's auctions
now catered to a new breed—the private collector. By creating a friendly environment, Sotheby's wooed new clientele.
At first the management had concentrated on less expensive
art, but as private collectors became more accustomed to
doing their own purchasing, they bought more expensive
items. Today, what had once been the preserve of a cabal of
gray-haired men in pre-World War II dinner jackets belonged
to private collectors from around the world. Many of them
viewed these auctions with the same relish they displayed for
any high-society function they might be invited to attend.
And they dressed accordingly.

As the line moved forward, Lauren wished Ravissant had an
artist who would make these collectors willing to part with
any amount of money. She'd followed up Tabatha's lead and
had checked Smithfield. The Russian was away, delivering
sides of beef to markets along the Scottish border. She'd find
him tomorrow.

"Name?" the receptionist behind the computer monitor
asked when Lauren finally reached the head of the line.

"Lauren Winthrop bidding for Takgama Nakamura."

Instead of punching her name into the computer for the
standard credit verification with international sources, the
receptionist smiled and handed Lauren her paddle and seat
assignment along with a hardbound catalogue. Not only was
Tak wealthy in his own right and therefore a welcome bidder,
but Japanese banks offered open-ended loans—at several
points below the prevailing U.S. prime rate—to citizens purchasing Western art. The impact of the Japanese on the market had constituted a shift in traditional ownership of art from
Europe and America to the Far East.

Waiting for Finley to register at the press station, Lauren
adjusted the belt on her gray knit Alexon suit. Except for the
gold Chanel earrings she wore, Lauren hadn't foolishly spent
Barzan's money on jewelry. In this overcarated crowd, she
stood out as a professional bidder. She scanned those waiting
to check in and recognized Darryl Isley, who'd built Norton
Simon's collection, and Eugene Thaw, who usually bid for

Agnew's of London. Both were noted Impressionist experts, so she doubted they'd be bidding against her since she was interested in the contemporary pieces. She didn't see anyone else that she recognized, but she knew her competition was out there somewhere.

"Nakamura wants the Cocteau, doesn't he?" Finley asked as they walked past the two auxiliary rooms where Sony monitors would display the paintings to less-important buyers. They continued into the main gallery where the most-important bidders were seated and the art to be auctioned hung on the walls.

"You know I can't say."

"There isn't anything else here that suits his collection, not a'tall." Finley led her to the side of the room where a row of black telephones comprised the links between bidders and collectors in other countries. "He wouldn't want the Dali etching until the *catalogue raisonné* is complete. Too risky."

"Mmm." Lauren sat down. Once the list of Dali's authenticated works was complete and the print forgeries identified, the competition would be keen. Now was the time to buy.

"The Cocteau will be an excellent investment. There are only fifty-one around. Most in the Louvre."

Fifty-four, she silently corrected, blessing the deceased Archer Leighton for the fastidious records in Ravissant's computer. "Sevin Wunderman has many of them."

Earlier, she'd searched the crowd, half expecting to see Wunderman, the primary collector of Cocteaus. But the manufacturer of Gucci and Fila watches, who bore a striking resemblance to the now-deceased Cocteau, wasn't here. Perhaps the Californian had sent a representative, one of the men seated beside her at the telephone bank.

Wunderman wasn't the only one who would be interested. Ravissant's records revealed T.J. Griffith's collection was without a finger-painted Cocteau. The father of New Wave cinema and the author of *Les Enfants terribles* had been one of the few artists Griffith had missed.

After Finley left for the adjacent room where the press would view the events via a monitor, Lauren picked up her telephone and verified the connection with Tokyo. Tak's secretary was on the line; she'd put him on when Lauren needed him.

Waiting, she thumbed through the catalogue. Beside each color reproduction was the price of the piece when originally sold, listings of books where the work was mentioned, and places it had been exhibited. And the projected sale price. This collection had been shown in Paris, New York, and Tokyo, returning to Sotheby's home base to be auctioned. After Tak had viewed it and decided to have her bid for him, she'd previewed the collection.

At precisely eight o'clock, Henning Reymont, head auctioneer for Sotheby's for the past three decades, stepped up to the podium, adjusting the lapels of his dinner jacket. As the auctioneer made several announcements, a tall man came up the aisle. Out of the corner of her eye, Lauren saw him take a seat in the front row, not ten feet from her. Someone important. All the seats were reserved, with the front rows assigned to the wealthiest bidders. She looked up from her catalogue at Ryan Westcott's rough-cut profile.

His doubled-breasted dinner jacket made him look larger, more formidable than she'd remembered. Lauren reminded herself to keep her mind on business. She'd earn a substantial fee, if she succeeded in acquiring the pieces Tak wanted. As the auctioneer announced the first painting in English, then in French, Ryan shifted in his seat and their eyes met. Lauren couldn't look away. For a moment, he regarded her with a speculative gaze. Laughter in his eyes, he then smiled and winked.

So that's how he wanted to play it. He planned to battle her for the Cocteau.

When the Dubuffet being auctioned before the Cocteau went onto the easel draped in red velvet, Lauren picked up the phone. Speaking Japanese in a lowered voice, she gave Tak a rundown of those present.

"Who's the main competition?"

"T.J. Griffith's representative, Ryan Westcott, is here."

Lauren envisioned the smile in Tak's inscrutable expression. He loved competition, fed on it. No note of concern etched his voice when she told him the pieces sold so far had gone for double the estimates. Tak was informed enough to realize the boom in Impressionist art and works by old masters had filtered down to the contemporary art arena.

The Cocteau went up on the easel, followed by a flurry of whispers. Lauren resisted bidding for two dozen rounds, repeating the numbers to Tak as she monitored the digital board that displayed the bids in pounds sterling, dollars, francs, marks—and, of course, yen.

Ryan sat, his profile to her, his arms folded across his chest. Like her, he was waiting for the less serious bidders to drop out. And he was on the alert for "bidding off the chandelier." Phony bidders were frequently used to drive up prices—although every auction house would deny it. Since the houses weren't required to post reserve prices, the minimum acceptable to the seller, or announce the names of buyers, it paid to be cautious.

When the bids went above the previous records for Cocteaus, Lauren raised her paddle. "The bid is on the telephone," the auctioneer said.

Instantly, Ryan's paddle went up.

"Two hundred thousand pounds." The auctioneer nodded at Ryan. "The bid is in the front row. Do I have two hundred and twenty-five thousand?"

On the aisle, one of the Getty bidders raised his paddle. Lauren had watched his number eleven go up all evening. They'd already spent a fortune.

"Two hundred and twenty-five thousand. Against you on the aisle. Do I have two hundred and fifty?"

Lauren lifted her paddle as she repeated her bid to Tak.

Before the auctioneer could ask for the mandatory twenty-five-thousand-pound increase, Ryan Westcott raised his paddle.

"Against you in the front row. Do I have three hundred thousand?"

The number eleven paddle went up, bringing an audible gasp from the normally unflappable group. Lauren repeated the bid to Tak.

"Keep bidding," he insisted, though they both knew there was no precedent for such a high bid.

Before she could raise her paddle, Ryan's went up again.

"Four hundred thousand pounds. The bid is in the front

row. Do I have four hundred and twenty-five thousand pounds?"

Lauren wiggled her paddle. A fine coating of perspiration broke out between her breasts; the room felt unusually hot. She glanced up at the glass-barrel ceiling that provided natural light during the day, thinking there was no way to justify bidding any higher.

"Four hundred and twenty-five thousand pounds. The bid is on the telephone."

Again, Ryan's paddle shot up. She couldn't see his face—only the determined line of his jaw. She waited for the Getty representatives to bid.

Reymont looked to where the number eleven bidders sat. "All done?"

"Bid!" Tak demanded when Getty representatives didn't bid.

Reluctantly, she raised her paddle. Before the auctioneer could repeat the bid, Ryan's paddle shot up.

"Five hundred and twenty-five thousand pounds." Henning Reymont dabbed at his brow with his handkerchief. "The bid is against you in the front row."

Lauren bid once more. She quickly said to Tak, "I don't want to overbid."

Ryan topped her bid.

"All done? Five hundred and seventy-five thousand pounds. Five hundred and seventy-five thousand pounds. Five hundred and seventy-five thousand pounds. All done?" The auctioneer's eyes questioned her.

Lauren dropped her paddle in her lap, thankful Tak had taken her advice and stopped.

"All done. Five hundred and seventy-five thousand pounds." He nodded to Ryan. "Your paddle number please."

While the auction continued, Lauren tried to mollify Tak. It took a while to convince him that running up auction bids endangered his reputation as a collector and her professional status. By the time the Dali that Lauren intended to bid on came up, only two other pieces remained on the red damask walls waiting to be auctioned. More than half the bidders had gone; even the Getty representatives had left. She was the sole bidder at the telephone bank.

Ryan sat in the front row, his arm casually looped across the back of the empty chair beside him. He turned and his gaze met hers. She offered him a polite smile even though he'd cost her a hefty commission. Openly amused, he responded with another wink and a broad grin. She kept her smile on hold, not wanting him to see how disappointed she was to lose the Cocteau.

In a frenzy of bids, the auction on the Dali began, but quickly fizzled. Leery investors were worried this etching might be a fake. Lauren wasn't concerned; she'd studied Dali's works when she'd lived in Paris. This etching was genuine, and at this price, a steal. Lauren didn't expect Ryan to bid because Griffith had collected numerous Dalis. She raised her paddle, bidding for the first time.

"The bid is on the telephone."

Ryan lifted his paddle.

Why is he bidding? The last thing Griffith needs is a Dali etching.

"Fifty thousand pounds. The bid is in the front row. Do I have—"

Lauren waved her paddle. It went from Ryan to Lauren. And back again. She wondered if he was bidding merely to aggravate her. With an insolent smile, Ryan looked at her, his green eyes dominated by jet-black irises. Her nerves tightened another notch. In his ill-timed grin, she saw the truth. She told the disgruntled Tak that she wasn't bidding any more.

"Why not? You've authenticated the piece. Once the *raisonné* is complete, it'll double in value."

"You don't know Ryan Westcott. He'll never give up."

He'll never let me win.

Vora hurried down the dark street toward the lighted row of ethnic bars and restaurants. Behind her, a group of drunken men whistled and catcalled. Beyond the West End, London's tourist face was stripped away revealing what every other big city suffered: poverty and crime.

What are you doing here, you fool? You'll be raped or murdered. But she needed that fix, that high only a night of wild, abandoned sex could give her. For the past several years, when she'd been between lovers, she'd taken to drifting about London's seamier neighborhoods, picking up men. One nighters. Nobodies she could leave without a qualm. She'd intended to go to the Indian nightclub she'd frequented before, but the men behind her frightened her. She ducked into a noisy cabaret and glanced around.

No one paid any attention to her except for a man standing at the bar. His black hair, with highlights of gray at the temples, gleamed in the dim light. But he was shorter and stockier than Vora liked. She preferred taller men with lithe frames like Clive.

The gang of men from the street came in behind Vora, jostling her and making crude remarks. She hung the tattered raincoat that she'd bought from her maid on the stand by the door. Vora never wore expensive clothes or jewelry when she came to places like this.

"Hello," she said, stepping up to the bar beside the short man. Close now, she saw he was older than he'd first appeared —late forties. Attractive in a Slavic way, he had thick hair that grew low over his forehead emphasizing his lively brown eyes.

"May purchase you drink?" His words were accented with the harshly blended consonants of a Pole or Czech.

"Scotch, please."

As the foreigner ordered her drink, Vora looked him over, wondering how soon she could get away. This man wasn't her type—not at all. In bare feet, they'd stand nose to nose. But she wanted to get laid. Royally laid. She stole a glance at his well-worn jeans. There was an enticing, fist-sized bulge between his thighs. Very enticing.

He smiled, a cute lopsided grin as he handed her the drink. He said something—she couldn't tell what over the din in the bar. But she decided his accent was Czech. Definitely Czech.

He smiled again, touching her hand, and she noticed his fisherman's knit sweater pushed up to the elbows exposed forearms ridged with muscles. The bulk she'd first attributed to his heavy sweater proved to be strapping shoulders. His body had the well-honed appearance of someone accustomed to hard labor. Obviously he was employed as a stevedore or something.

He smiled—the cutest grin. "I am told this good show."

The lights went out and a blowsy blonde strutted on stage. Vora edged closer to the Czech, inhaling the warm scent of soap. She remembered the other men she'd found in bars like this; at least this one bathed. He turned, his face just inches from hers. She mumbled something, and he moved his head closer to her lips, trying to catch her words above the screeching that was supposed to pass for singing.

She traced the tip of her tongue over the coiled ridge of his ear as she brought her hand up between his thighs. Fabulous, she thought, testing the heavy weight of his balls, the breadth of his cock.

In the darkness, he turned toward her, whispering words she couldn't decipher because of his accent and the noise. One thing she knew for certain—his shaft had grown larger. And harder.

"Do you live nearby?"

"Yes." His expression told her he was shocked. Hadn't a woman ever picked him up before?

She squeezed his cock. "Take me home."

He guided her over to the coat rack. As he helped her put on her coat, she fondled him again. The raw strength in his body with his bulky shoulders and strong arms matched by muscular legs sent a shuddering tremor through her already heated thighs.

"What is name?" he asked when they'd stepped outside. His accent wasn't as thick as she'd first thought. She merely had to listen closely.

"Velma Lesterson." Instead of asking his name, Vora looped her arms around his neck, pressing her thighs against his groin. His dark eyes glittered with disbelief. She kissed him, arrowing her questing tongue deep into his mouth.

"Wait," he said, pulling her to his side with a powerful arm, forcing her to walk up the street.

Whistling "God Save the Queen" he led her for blocks. Obviously, his definition of nearby and hers differed. How would she ever find her way back? He took her down a deserted alley to an abandoned warehouse. Inside, Vora paused. Had she fallen into the hands of a murderer? What was she, nuts? But the man drew her closer, whispering something sweet sounding as he guided her up a flight of stairs to a small room.

He tugged on a frayed cord and an overhead bulb lit the room with twenty-five watts. Twenty watts too many. Vora saw the concave mattress on the floor with its lone pillow and neatly folded blanket—no sheets. The only color in the room came from the Union Jack nailed to the wall.

"Coat, please?"

Vora looked over her shoulder at him as he slid her coat off. Red-faced, he moved away and hung it on a wall rack beside a pair of jeans, two shirts with frayed collars, and a pair of undershorts. Since there wasn't a dresser in the room, she assumed these were his only clothes.

"It's cold in here." No heater was in sight. How did he stand it? Suddenly, she remembered Clive pouting until she'd bought him the cashmere topcoat.

"Want me take you back?"

Her heart lurched. He had nothing. She had everything.

"Of course not. I just want you to keep me warm."

Her words brought an adorable smile to his lips. Kicking off her shoes, she undid the two hooks on the wraparound dress she always wore when she went trolling. It dropped to the floor leaving her stark naked. He tried to take her in his arms, but she went for his belt, unfastening it in one deft motion before undoing the top button of his jeans.

He shucked his sweater while she yanked his pants down. Both naked, they faced each other. Incredible! she thought, examining his burly frame. His thick shaft. Why'd she ever liked them tall and slim? Her hand plunged downward, homing in on his preening cock.

Before she knew what had happened, he had her pinned to the mattress, gasping for breath. She tried to roll over, to get on top, her favorite position. He wouldn't let her, his strong arms held her in place. With a muscular knee, he nudged her thighs apart.

In one powerful stroke he buried his cock to the hilt.

Lauren walked silently beside Finley as they went up New Bond Street. After the auction a reception was being held for the editor from *Apollo*. Despite Finley's placating words, assuring her Ryan had overpaid, she felt she'd failed Tak. Would he ever consult her again?

She didn't believe in luck, not really. But since "Midnight in Marrakesh" had been sold and she'd been unable to track it down, fate seemed to be working against her. She couldn't locate the Russian, and now Ryan Westcott had outbid her. What next?

As they turned up Cork Street, Finley stopped in front of the Bernard Jacobson Gallery and looked at an etching by Lucien Freud. "I don't care for this, a'tall."

Lauren silently disagreed. The numerous elite galleries along Cork were light-years ahead of Ravissant because they had talented artists. Lauren decided she was placing too much faith in the Russian. A one-in-a-million long shot.

"Here we are." Finley stopped at the end of Savile Row and held open a black door with one-inch letters: Albany. "This entrance isn't usually open. Bingham made special arrangements, since so many of us were coming from this direction."

They entered a small garden, then went into the famous apartment house. "How old is the Albany?" asked Lauren.

"Two hundred years. Never say 'the.' That makes it sound like a hotel. The owners don't like it. They refer to it as Albany —the best address in London."

"Oh." She couldn't care less. The British obsession with class distinctions left her cold. So did Albany's location, right on Piccadilly opposite Hatchards. Undoubtedly a prime spot two centuries ago, it was a noisy, traffic-throttled area today.

A hall porter as old as Albany guided them down the marble corridor into a surprisingly small suite lit by an old Waterford chandelier. As Lauren handed the butler her sable, she looked up and saw Ryan Westcott staring at her.

This must be my lucky night. The jerk had cost her a sizable commission and, quite possibly, Tak's respect. She reminded herself that she needed Ryan's goodwill for Ravissant's sake, and forced a smile onto her lips at his familiar wink.

Over savories and vintage port that Finley informed her was a classic '34 from Portugal, the small group's attention focused on Chester Reynolds-Stephens, the editor from *Apollo*. Everyone listened reverently while the ferret-faced expert with a chin that descended down his neck gave what

Lauren considered to be an ill-informed analysis of the ceiling investors should expect in the Impressionist market.

Ryan stood off to the side, his glass of port dangling from his hand in a gesture of bored condescension. She felt his eyes on her, but didn't look up. Instead, she kept her eyes on Reynolds-Stephens, waiting for him to take a breath.

"What do you think of the *glasnost* artists?" she asked when he finally paused to sip his port.

"Some are talented," he said emphatically. "Like Sergei Chepik and Ivan Babij. But the rest are flashes in the pan. I wouldn't advise investing in any of them."

"I would." The group turned to study Ryan, who'd said nothing before this. "They have seventy years of history and repression to tell in their art," Ryan insisted, oblivious to the group's gaping stares. "Best of all they haven't been contaminated by the jackals of the art world from the West. They've painted their lives, their experiences as they've lived them."

In the stunned silence that followed, Lauren's eyes were riveted on Ryan. Exactly! The Russians had the verve, the excitement, the fresh approach the stagnant art world needed.

"Well," Finley hemmed. "I don't know."

"I do," Lauren said. "I would like nothing better than to find a talented Russian artist for Ravissant."

Exhausted, Lauren collapsed on the Frette *duvet*, too tired from the party and the auction to turn down her bed. It was Selma's weekend off, so no one had touched her bed or left the lights on in the foyer. She didn't care. She disliked Selma's officious manner and her snooping. If she didn't need someone to take care of this flat . . . Wait a minute. What about Tabatha Foley? Would the girl be willing to give up her job at the Hard Rock to work as her maid? Definitely—for the right amount of money.

Lauren made up her mind to let Selma go with three months' severance pay to tide her over while she found another job. Then Tabatha could move into the servant's quarters. Good idea. All week Tabatha had been on her mind. She was too young to be on her own. No wonder she'd developed a shell of coldness bordering on hostility. With haunting clarity,

Lauren recalled herself at seventeen. Alone in the world except for Paul.

In the distance, she heard pounding on her front door. At this late hour, it must be Jeeves with an urgent message for her. Had something happened to Paul? Her hair flowing free over her shoulders, she ran down the mirrored hall, across the marble entry, and swung open the door.

"Expecting me?" Ryan Westcott grinned.

"What do you want?" She cinched her robe closed with its belt, looking around for Jeeves, but he was nowhere in sight. Didn't the man ever do his job? No one should be allowed to knock on her door at this hour.

"Let's talk." Ryan walked passed her, heading for the salon.

What unbelievable nerve! He'd deliberately thwarted her at the auction, yet here he was. Seething, she followed him.

"Can't this wait until tomorrow?"

"No." He sat on the loveseat and patted the space beside him.

Remember, Lauren, you need him. She sat in the damask chair opposite him. "Yes?"

"You've found a Soviet artist."

"No." She twisted the silver bracelet she always wore.

"Don't lie. You'll be exhibiting his works next."

"It's a lead," she said, instead of the sharp retort that had first sprung to her lips. *Remember how much easier things will be with him on your side.* "A possibility—that's all. I haven't seen his work yet."

"Count me in."

"I have a partner."

"I can make the Russian a household name. Can Vora?"

Lauren looked away. There was no denying the truth: Vora's comprehension of art was confined to the art of dress. But Ryan, representing the respected T.J. Griffith, could do wonders for Ravissant.

"Didn't you learn your lesson tonight?"

He was actually threatening her. Lauren dredged up another smile, hoping to give him the impression she didn't care, then she reluctantly told him what little she knew.

"Count me in. From now on, I'm your partner. Got it?"

"Why? What do you want?"

"First choice of the Russian's works. I see everything—before any other buyer. I purchase what T.J. wants, then I tout it as the investment opportunity of the decade."

"All right," she conceded.

"When can I meet him . . . partner?"

7

"Eat your breakfast." Ryan consulted his Concord. "The Russian will be back from his deliveries in another half hour."

"I know." Lauren pushed around the sausages on her plate. Mustards Smithfield Brasserie's cuisine didn't interest her. She seemed totally obsessed by the Russian. When Ryan had insisted on becoming her partner, he hadn't realized how important this artist was to her. If she were using the gallery as a means of landing a rich collector for a husband, then why the concern? Why the rush?

He studied her as she took a dainty sip of tea. She still had the vulnerable quality that had captivated him the night he'd found her crying. Despite those tears, he admired her courage. It had taken fortitude to turn her back on Caroline Armstrong. What had happened? Hell, back then, Lauren had been what? Sixteen? Seventeen? The way she'd snapped at him saying her reasons were private told him that she was still sensitive about it. He intended to find out why.

Ryan finished his coffee, recalling how Lauren had challenged the *Apollo* editor with the double-jointed last name. That took guts. Most gallery owners kiss-assed critics. Not Lauren.

Deal from strength, he reminded himself as he watched her. At the auction, he'd shown her that he meant business.

She didn't know the half of it. He admired Lauren's intensity, her commitment. Her sex appeal. But if she screwed with him, he'd take her apart—the way T.J. should have handled Caroline.

When he saw Lauren intended to spend the rest of the time rearranging the food on her plate, he flung a few pound notes onto the table. "Let's go."

They silently walked up Long Lane toward Smithfield. While Covent Garden and Billingsgate, the original produce and fresh fish markets, had relocated beyond central London, the meat trade remained. They'd appeared at Smithfield at dawn, asking for the Russian. He'd already gone out driving the delivery truck.

Ryan took Lauren's arm guiding her around a double-parked delivery truck. Her arm stiffened; his slightest touch put her off. He knew she didn't like him. She was using him. He accepted that. Users were his speciality.

They entered the wholesale market where sides of meat hung from the high ceilings, waiting to be sectioned into chops or roasts. Soon they came to the station where the Russian worked when he wasn't driving the truck.

"Look," Lauren whispered, indicating a stocky man with dark hair. He hoisted a carcass over his shoulder, then tossed it onto the wooden-block table. With a single whack of his cleaver, he split the side of beef in half.

"Irek," Ryan said. "Irek Makarova."

The short man turned around, frowning. "Yes?"

"We'd like to talk to you." Out of the corner of his eye, Ryan watched Lauren. She was staring at the Russian's hands. Blood dripped from large, sinewy fingers. Ryan took her hand in his and gave it a squeeze.

Makarova looked over his shoulder, obviously concerned about wasting time and losing his job.

"We've heard you're an artist," Ryan said, feeling Lauren grip his fingers more tightly as the Russian wiped the blood from his hands using his oversized apron.

"Who are you?" Makarova's voice was guarded.

"I'm Lauren Winthrop, and this is my associate, Ryan Westcott. I have an art gallery."

Makarova's eyes narrowed. He shook his head, backing up.

"You studied with Beliutin?" Ryan took a wild guess before the Russian could walk away.

Makarova stopped. "You know?"

"His students were allowed to exhibit for the first time last year. Did you know that?" Ryan gauged the Russian's cautious nod to mean he was opening up. "Bulgakov, Fillipova, and all the rest."

"Good," Makarova said, but it sounded more like "gut." "The worm—how you say?"

"The worm turns," Lauren said.

Ryan observed Makarova's smile. Another goddamn sucker for a beautiful woman. "Worm turns," the Russian agreed.

"May we see your work?" Ryan asked.

"You no like." He hesitated. "Show galleries. No like."

"When was that?" Ryan felt Lauren squeezing his hand.

"Nine years. When come to England."

As Ryan expected, it was before the Russian vogue hit. The dumbasses in the galleries only pedaled what was popular. "Times change."

"Worms turn," Lauren said with a radiant smile.

That did it. Makarova gave them his address, adding, "Look. Come back if like."

As they left the building, Lauren bounced along beside Ryan, her expressive eyes bright. For once, she didn't try to pull her hand out of his. "What do you think?"

"Don't get your hopes up."

"He studied with Eli Beliutin."

"But his works weren't exhibited in Moscow last year."

"I misunderstood. I assumed they'd shown his early works." Her expression turned grim. "Maybe he isn't any good."

He gave her hand a reassuring squeeze. "Let's see for ourselves."

They were in the car, with Iggy in Lauren's lap, getting her tummy scratched, when Lauren asked, "Isn't it strange Irek didn't give us a key?"

"Where he lives, anything worth stealing has already been stolen."

Ryan raced his Aston-Martin through a neighborhood of dilapidated buildings, some never repaired after the Nazis had bombed London. He turned down a bleak alley; scattering a horde of rats foraging in the gutter, and stopped in front of a building that had stood there since before the First World War.

"How could he live here?" Lauren pointed to the windows broken by street toughs throwing rocks. "It's scary."

"Not many men would take on Makarova." He parked the Aston-Martin on the fractured sidewalk. "Bring Iggy or when we get back, she'll be in somebody's stew pot."

After looking over his shoulder and seeing no one, Ryan locked the car, thankful for the sophisticated alarm system the MI-5 boys had installed. If anyone touched the car, the motion detector would trigger the alarm.

Ryan led Lauren and Iggy up the wooden stairs to the third floor where Makarova had told them he had his studio. An old-fashioned skylight with tiny panes of glass flooded the area with natural light. All along the perimeter of the large room were completed oils. Others were stacked off to the side.

For a moment, neither one of them spoke.

"Oh, my!" Lauren whispered. "He's fantastic."

"Jesus!" Ryan put his arm around Lauren and hugged her. She smiled up at him, either not noticing his arm around her, or being too excited to care. "There's no denying Makarova's talent."

"How would you describe his technique?" Lauren asked.

"Impressionist. A modern Impressionist. Vivid colors like van Gogh combined with softer tones like Monet."

"But Russian. Distinctly Russian. You can see in the shapes of the buildings that this isn't a western artist." She absent-mindedly leaned against him. "How do you suppose he gets those delicate lines?"

Amid the blurred, wavered images often associated with Impressionistic style, fiber-thin lines gave the images form, uniqueness. "Looks like he's used a small brush."

"No. I meant, how does Irek do it? Didn't you notice his hands? Meat hooks."

"Some of the best surgeons are big men with beefy fingers. Why not an artist?"

"You're right. I just couldn't help noticing Irek's hands." She glanced down at Ryan's hand resting on her shoulder.

He'd caught her looking at his hands before and assumed

she was taken with the leopard ring. Most women were. But her comment changed his mind. *What about the hands in the painting, Westcott?*

They walked over to the easel where Makarova's work in progress seemed to be a portrait.

"Odd," Ryan said. "His other works are landscapes or rural village scenes."

"Perhaps he's entering a new phase."

"Maybe." Ryan kept his eyes on Lauren as she studied the unfinished canvas. "Reminds me of a work I recently acquired for T.J."

"Really? What artist?"

"I'm keeping that a secret until T.J. decides if he's keeping it." Ryan was deliberately playing with her by not letting her know he'd bought her painting. He couldn't help himself; he wanted to know more about her. The painting was the key. He'd sensed that from the moment he'd opened the conservatory's closet and had seen it.

"Speaking of showing things, who else knows you have a lead on a Russian? Not Tibbetts?" That sonofabitch would take all the credit for discovering Makarova."

"I didn't tell Finley. I don't think he even suspects."

Ryan interpreted that as a backhanded compliment. He'd figured it out in ten seconds.

"I did mention it to Vora."

"Hell! She'll tell that faggot hairdresser, Basil Blackstoke, and it'll be all over London before tomorrow."

"I only said it was a lead." She again had that pissed-off look she'd had last night when he'd forced this partnership on her. "Are you forgetting Vora owns half of Ravissant?"

"No. But do you want to blow this?"

"You're right. Let's go back and take him to a solicitor this afternoon and have him sign an exclusive contract with Ravissant. Then let's get him some clothes, a decent place to live, a publicist, a—"

"Hold it. Let's get to know Irek. Find out his plans. Look at his art. Irek has a very definite view of life. We can't dress him up and toss him to the barracudas of the art world. He doesn't have any idea what that society is like. It'll make the *gulag* seem like a safe haven."

She nodded as she bent down to pet Iggy.

"He needs friends, not just a contract. Let's invite him for dinner tonight. No bistro with a nose-in-the-air-ambience that'll make Irek uncomfortable. Pizza or ribs or something. We'll find out more about him."

"Vora should come. She has a right to be in on this."

"Just be sure she keeps her mouth shut." Another thought hit him. "Let's all dress casually. Tell Leighton to lay off the jewels. Undoubtedly, Makarova sees himself as one of the proletariat. Rich bitches might make him uncomfortable."

Lauren agreed and turned to study Makarova's work in progress.

"Wear your hair down instead of that bun. You look like a school marm. Makarova probably got into trouble in school."

Her answer was a pissed look. He didn't give a damn. He hated her hair like that. He liked it down, flowing over her shoulders. Sexy as hell. In silence, they walked around the room, taking another look at Makarova's paintings.

"I suppose his early works are in Russia, and there's no hope of getting them out. Russian museums have snapped up paintings they refused to exhibit before *glasnost,* especially the Tretyakov in Moscow."

"No," Ryan said. "This is it."

"How do you know?"

"Even Finley Tibbetts couldn't miss Makarova's talent. If the Russians still had any of his works, they'd have exhibited them along with the rest of Beliutin's Abramtsevo School."

"Irek must have been his prize student. I suppose Beliutin would have shown anything he had of Irek's when the government finally allowed him to exhibit his students' works."

"Damn right, Beliutin would have. But the authorities destroyed Makarova's art—then sent him to prison."

Ryan parked the Aston-Martin in the deserted lot for the Serpentine Restaurant. He got out and buttoned his topcoat against the frost riding the wind ripping in from the North Sea.

Midpoint on Serpentine Bridge Peter Stirling waited. Ryan's contact with MI-5, a bald man in his sixties, stood tossing bits of bread to the ducks swimming in the Serpentine. Stirling had survived in a dangerous business where one mistake was your last. After years in the field, refusing to move up in rank because he preferred covert operations, Stirling's arthritis had forced him to return to London. Thirty years in Her Majesty's service and innumerable citations had earned him the right to a cushy desk job. But he wanted no part of paper pushing; it had taken him a month to learn how to use the newfangled computer system. When they had needed someone with experience—and patience—he'd volunteered for the Barzan case.

Ryan was grateful for Stirling's expertise. He'd personally trained Ryan by polishing skills he'd already developed in Africa looking for diamonds and dealing with scum. Bringing Ryan up to speed on counter-surveillance and high-tech security—waiting for Barzan to strike—they'd forged an alliance. Ryan and Peter respected each other.

"What do you want to see me about?" Ryan asked.

"Lauren Winthrop."

"You're tailing me?" He must be losing it. How in hell had he missed a tail?

Stirling put his finger to his lips and looked around.

"There isn't anyone around. Who'd be stupid enough to come into Hyde Park and freeze his ass off?" Undercover bullshit.

"You're not being followed. Scotland Yard tells us that they're watching the Winthrop woman. It has something to do with the print fraud Ravissant Gallery was involved in. We've asked their man to send us reports on her activities. That's how we know you're seeing her."

Strange, Ryan thought, he hadn't noticed anyone watching her. "Why? You said she was clean."

"The print fraud the Yard's investigating aside, there's something dicey about that Miami real estate deal that brought Lauren Winthrop so much money. The FBI is looking at the Florida records. Since it involves a number of foreign holding companies, the CIA is checking it out, too."

"Shit! I thought this was strictly an MI-5 operation. The CIA always bungles everything. They'll get me killed." Ryan was nervous at not being in control, not running the show. His whole life, he'd not relied on anyone. Now he had no choice.

"Calm down. They don't know anything about you." Turning his back to the wind, Stirling took out his pipe and lit it, then tossed the match into the water. "It might flush Barzan's man out sooner, if you're seen around town more. Force him to show his hand. You'll have to be extremely careful. We'll need the names of everyone you come in contact with—even briefly."

"Start with Irek Makarova."

Stirling jotted the name down in a small notebook. "We'll be following you from now on. Around the clock."

"Be sure to let the Russians and the Israelis know. They throw a shit-fit if a car is parked near their embassies for more than two minutes, let alone overnight."

There wasn't a more secure street in the world than Palace Green where T.J. Griffith's home was located, Ryan thought, although he hated living in that prison. Di and Charles lived to the east, their royal asses under constant guard. Up and down the street were various embassies, all with excellent surveillance. But the Russians and Israelis were rabid about security. They suspected everyone and everything, tenaciously protecting themselves. It had cost a fortune to acquire Greyburne Manor on Palace Green, but living there cut down on security costs.

Nodding, Stirling tapped his pipe on the rail, sending a shower of tobacco down on the ducks. "Be careful, Westcott."

Vora struggled not to look shocked when her maid escorted Lauren into the parlor. She wore black suede slacks that fit like panty hose. They were tucked into knee-high leather boots that were gloss black. A belt with a silver buckle the size and shape of a conch emphasized her narrow waist and rounded breasts beneath a black turtleneck. But it was her hair that surprised Vora the most. Tonight Lauren wore it loose, falling across her shoulders in shimmering waves.

"Your hair looks fantastic!"

"Thanks. I thought I'd try something different tonight." Lauren smiled, looking happier than Vora had ever seen her.

"Where are we meeting them?" Vora asked. When Lauren had called earlier to tell her about the Russian artist, Vora had been surprised that Lauren's lead had proven a winner.

"Pomodoro in Knightsbridge. Irek loves pizza."

Vora hoped this wouldn't take long. She wanted to go back to the cabaret and look for the Czech. Two days. She'd fought it long enough. Tonight, she'd find him again. Nobody—but nobody—did it better.

"Let's go." Vora shrugged into her red fox jacket.

By the time they'd threaded their way up Brompton Place and turned down Beauchamp, they were late. Having a car in London was stupid. Vora silently applauded Lauren's decision not to buy one.

"Ryan and Irek are here," Lauren said as they passed his black Aston-Martin parked on Wilton and went around the block.

Since when had Lauren and Ryan become so friendly? Although she wasn't much older, Vora felt motherly toward Lauren. They'd become quite close these last weeks. Vora didn't want her involved with Ryan. He'd sleep with her, then leave her. Unexpectedly, Clive's face came to her mind's eye. That bastard.

It took another ten minutes to find a spot on narrow Beauchamp Place and walk down the street overhung by Georgian wrought-iron balconies to the restaurant. Although better known for its chic designer boutiques, the short street had several restaurants nestled in between the shops.

"Which way?" Lauren paused at the entrance, looking at the three doors in the alcove.

"This way." Vora hurried down a narrow staircase into a restaurant below the level of the street. *Let's make this quick. A fast hello, then I'm off.*

The darkness caused Vora to blink as her eyes adjusted to the lack of light. There wasn't a single empty table in the tiny cafe. In the corner stood a piano with a man playing it, singing loudly in Italian. Obviously an amateur. The crowd sang along, laughing and quaffing Chianti.

"There they are." Lauren waved.

There was no mistaking Ryan Westcott's tall frame as he stood up in the far corner, signaling to them. Vora tagged along behind Lauren as she gracefully edged her way between the small tables. Conversation stopped mid-sentence when she passed by, unintentionally moving seductively, her tight pants and soft sweater showing her figure to full advantage. But it was her face, with its classic lines enhanced by swishing blonde hair, that captivated the men.

"You're late." Ryan said, his eyes on Lauren, his tone awed.

"My fault," Vora started to say. The words died in her throat. Suddenly, nothing in the noisy room seemed to be in focus.

"Vora Leighton, this is Irek Makarova."

Stifling a gasp of surprise, Vora tried to smile. *Christ! The Czech.*

A raw, primitive rush of shame shot through her. *Don't let this be happening,* her heart whispered. *Not before I have a chance to explain things to him.*

Her gaze met his stunned brown eyes. In that unguarded moment, anguish flared in their depths. Then anger. Or hate.

8

Lauren slipped into the booth beside Ryan. His camel sweater accentuated his tan and intensified the color of his green eyes. As he introduced Vora to Irek, he took the coat Lauren was carrying and hung it next to his worn leather bomber jacket on the hook outside their booth.

"What's with Vora?" Ryan whispered.

Lauren shrugged; she hadn't taken her eyes off Ryan. Right now, Vora and Irek were intently staring at the singer, apparently absorbed in the Italian ditty he was belting out.

"You call what Leighton's wearing casual?" Ryan whispered in her ear, his breath ruffling her hair.

"That's her 'casual' fur."

"Jesus!" Ryan had edged closer to her, their thighs now touching. She ignored him—as she had all day when he'd taken her hand or put his arm around her. He gave her an appealing grin, the first heartfelt smile she'd seen from him, banishing his usual belligerent expression.

"I saw your car. Is Iggy with you?"

"Sure. On our way out, you can pet her."

The singer took a break and Lauren caught Irek's eye and smiled. He responded with a hesitant grin. She noted his sport coat with soaring, swanlike lapels that hadn't been in style for years. They'd dressed down. He'd dressed up.

"What kind of pizza do you like?" she asked Irek.

"Peproni with anchovy—many, many anchovy."

"We've already ordered," Ryan said. "Pepperoni loaded with anchovies—Irek's favorite."

Vora was silent; her face had a drawn look to it. Lauren knew she loathed anchovies. But surely that wasn't the problem.

"I'd like Irek to visit Ravissant tomorrow," Ryan said as he poured Lauren and Vora glasses of Chianti from the carafe already on the table. "He's quit his job so that he'll be able to concentrate on his art."

"Wonderful." Lauren smiled at Irek. His face was flushed; he kept tugging at the frayed neck of his shirt.

Lauren had to kick Vora under the table to get her to add, "We'd love to have you visit the gallery."

What was wrong with her? Despite having the inbred snobbishness common in the British upper classes, Vora usually had an affable manner that put a person at ease. She was too polite, too good-hearted to hurt anyone. *So why is she acting this way?*

"To Irek." Ryan raised his glass for a toast.

Lauren and Vora automatically lifted their glasses, but Irek's remained on the table, clenched in his mammoth fist. Lauren forced herself to look away from his hands. She gazed questioningly up at Ryan whose eyes were on Irek.

"To Anatoly Marchenko," Irek said, his voice choked. "Peace he rest." He kicked back the glass of wine in a single gulp.

"Was he a friend of yours?" Lauren asked. When he nodded, she gave him a sympathetic smile. "I read *To Live Like Everyone* on the plane coming here from New York."

"*Perestroika* late . . . much late for Anatoly."

"Marchenko died in prison, right?" Ryan poured Irek another glass of wine.

"Eight December 1986," Irek said.

Lauren met Vora's questioning eyes; intellectual discussions weren't her long suit. "Marchenko was in and out of prison for thirty years," she said for Vora's benefit. "He wrote: 'Suffering only begins after release from the camps.' Staying for more than three days in a city without an internal residency permit is against the law. Three violations, another trial, then back to jail."

"The law says get a permit, but the military refuses to issue one to former prisoners," Ryan added. "A Soviet Catch 22."

"Is that where you met Anatoly," Lauren asked, "in the *gulag*?" After he slowly nodded, she mustered the courage to ask "Why were you sent there?"

"Put name on painting."

"They sent you to prison for signing your own work?" Vora blurted out.

"Yes." Irek stiffened, angling his body away from Vora as he answered, "Crime to put self before state."

"In the early years after the revolution, the feeling of comradeship ran high. Most artists didn't wish to sign their work." Ryan directed his comments to Vora. "They were content to create in the name of the Soviet Union. But as years passed, more and more artists wanted to sign their works with the name of their artists' group. Later they insisted on using their own names."

"I see," Vora said quietly, her eyes downcast.

Lauren noticed Irek still didn't look at Vora. He kept facing them, his eyes avoiding Vora. Was it her fur? Lauren glanced at the expensive red fox jacket dangling from the coat hook. Or was it her precise diction, each syllable carefully modulated, making her upper-class roots obvious every time she spoke? Ryan had a hint of a British accent acquired, no doubt, by living many years in England. But his use of slang and four-letter words made him seem more American. Lauren knew her own voice bore no British accent. Despite her mother being English, Lauren had been raised abroad and spoke with an intonation that was difficult to typecast.

"You were released, then sent to prison again." Ryan refilled their glasses. "You couldn't get a residency permit, right?"

"Got *propiska*— permit. Sent back for showing"—he took a swallow of wine—"showing paintings with others."

Trying to fight the lump that had risen in her throat on hearing Irek's story, Lauren reached under the table and found Ryan's hand. He gave it a comforting squeeze and she edged closer to him. She'd read about Soviet artists being sent to prison for exhibiting their work, but it had never seemed real. Until now.

"When did you join Eli Beliutin?" Ryan asked.

"Nineteen sixty-one . . . before Manege and Khrushchev."

"Who is Manege?" Vora asked.

Irek took another sip of wine, apparently having no intention of enlightening Vora.

"The Manege Exhibition was held in late 1962," Lauren said, "in Moscow's Central Exhibition Hall. Beliutin organized it as the first avant-garde showing of work since the early twenties. How many artists exhibited, Irek?"

"Sixty. Over two hundred and fifty paintings."

"How many were yours?" Ryan asked.

With a grin, Irek held up three stout fingers.

"Nikita Khrushchev toured the show and immediately closed it, forbidding Beliutin's students from exhibiting anywhere." Lauren smiled at Irek. "The government wanted works that reflected Soviet dogma. Am I correct?"

"Wanted socialist realism in art."

"Beliutin fostered the creative potential of each artist regardless of state theories." Ryan signaled for another carafe of Chianti. "He and his students were banned. They moved from Moscow to Abramtsevo to ride out the storm."

"It was another twenty-five years before they were allowed to exhibit again. But you didn't stay with them in Abramtsevo, did you?" Lauren asked, looking at the Russian.

"Young." Irek smiled sheepishly as the waiter delivered their pizza. "Head hot."

"Hothead?" Lauren asked and Irek nodded. She waited for him to elaborate, but he didn't. He seemed intent on watching the waiter serve each of them pizza.

Lauren eased her hand out of Ryan's, then took a bite of pizza and tried not to grimace. The chef had cornered the anchovy market, smothering the savory pepperoni and cheese that had made Pomodoro's famous. Irek chomped on his slice of pizza, quickly downing it, while Vora, who despised anchovies, commented on how delicious it was. And ate every bite.

"I was a hothead, too," Ryan confessed, "growing up wild in Los Angeles."

Lauren should have guessed that Ryan was from California. He had that West Coast irreverence, a disdain of authority and conventions—an attitude of insubordination.

"Hothead, yes," Irek continued. "Show paintings—putting in train station. All see."

"They sent you to prison again?" Ryan handed Irek the last two slices of pizza.

"No." Irek pointed to his head. "How say?"

"Nut house? Insane asylum?" Ryan asked.

Irek nodded, matter-of-factly munching on his pizza. Again, Lauren found Ryan's hand, clutching it, digging her nails into his palm. An inexplicable look of withdrawal masked Vora's face.

"Pills, shots"—he jumped up in his seat as if hit by a bolt of lightning—"how say?"

"Electric shock." Ryan's voice was barely audible. "Drug therapy—guaranteed to rehabilitate."

Lauren studied Ryan. All traces of his usual hauteur had vanished. Her gaze swung to Vora. Tears crested in her eyes; she quickly looked away.

"Meet Anatoly," Irek said, oblivious to how profoundly he'd touched them. "Have friend. Next get out with Anatoly. Work brick factory. Nights sleep outside top of ovens—keep warm." He took a swig of wine. "No permit. We *bomzhi*— homeless. Catch us and send back."

"How'd you get here?" Lauren asked.

"Exit visa come. Out day next. No call home. No good-bye Anatoly," Irek said, his voice melancholy. "No thing."

The piano player struck up "La Dolce Vita" and the diners sang along. Lauren tried to think of something to say, but couldn't. Vora stared blankly at her wine glass while Ryan sat immobile. They were all shocked by the way Irek retold his story—without bitterness. Finally, Ryan broke the silence by hailing a waiter and ordering coffee.

"Things will be different now. The world will see your art," Lauren told Irek. She could see he didn't expect much. Why should he? So far, life hadn't given him anything.

As they sipped coffee, Ryan chatted with Irek, drawing him

out. The first thing the Russian intended to do, now that he was free during the day, was to take private English lessons instead of going to night school. They discovered he had capitalist aspirations. High on his wish list—should he ever have the money—were a Porsche and a condominium on the Thames. Throughout the discussion, Vora remained silent, watching Irek, who never looked at her.

When the waiter delivered the check, Irek and Ryan both reached for it.

"Mine." Irek covered it with his huge fist.

"No . . ." Ryan hesitated. "All right. Thanks. It was great." He rose and tugged on Lauren's arm for her to come with him. "We'll bring the car around. You two meet us out front."

"Wait—" Lauren started to protest, but Ryan's hand clamped down on her arm. The look in his eye as he helped her into her coat said: Don't argue. As soon as they were out of earshot, Lauren stopped.

"How can you let Irek pay? Did you see what he was wearing? That jacket had to have come out of someone's attic. He can't have any money."

"He's not the kind of person who'll allow himself to become a kept man. The only way I persuaded him to give up his job was by buying one of his paintings. Now he has plenty of money."

"You raided his collection. Is that fair? We're supposed to be partners."

"I bought one painting. What did you want me to do? He wouldn't give up his job without security. What else did he have to sell?" After she reluctantly agreed, he added, "I let Irek buy dinner. Next time, I'll pay and it won't be pizza."

"That's a good idea," she admitted. Prices in London's ritzier restaurants would stun Irek. It would be better to let Ryan handle those bills. "You've done a good job with Irek." She headed up the stairs toward the street. "Why don't you take him to your tailor?"

"Irek has money now. If he wants new clothes, he can buy them. This afternoon he bought what he's wearing tonight. The only time I'm giving him advice is when he asks for it."

"You're right." Lauren stepped out onto the sidewalk; a wet fog obscured her vision. "It's just that my heart goes out to him. He's been through so much. I want everything to be perfect for him."

Ryan put his arm around her, pulling her close. "I know. He's had it worse—much worse—than I expected."

"How can he be so accepting . . . so complacent? Did the drugs, the shocks alter his mind? Is he all there?"

"There's nothing wrong with Irek. He's wise enough to accept what he can't change."

She looked up at Ryan and found the mist had dampened his hair. It clung to the upturned collar of his jacket and waved across his brow, giving him a boyish appearance. What had his youth been like? She didn't dare ask because she feared he'd inquire about hers.

As they rounded the corner, Ryan asked, "What are you thinking?"

"That this has been a special day. I'd fantasized about discovering an artist, but seeing Irek, hearing his story leaves me awed."

Even though it hadn't been what she'd been thinking, it was true. She'd been totally unprepared for Irek's tragic story. Ryan had been far more astute. What would she have done without him? He'd known how to help Irek when she hadn't. Beneath his abrasiveness, Ryan Westcott was a surprisingly sensitive man. A complex man. But his self-assurance bordered on arrogance. Even though she couldn't help admiring his assertiveness, he intimidated her. For years now, she'd studiously avoided domineering men. Men like her stepfather, Rupert Armstrong.

"Irek is special. Tell Leighton to go easy on him. He won't jump in the sack with her and forget it."

"Don't worry. Irek's not Vora's type."

"Irek doesn't know that. He's got the hots for her."

"Be serious. He didn't pay any attention to her all evening. If you ask me, he sized her up as a rich snob."

"When a man's interested in a woman, either he can't take his eyes off her, or he ignores her." He tightened his arm around her waist. "I can't take my eyes off—or keep my hands off."

A tremor of anticipation tiptoed down her spine. He was attracted to her. While that thought thrilled her, it made her apprehensive. The dark undertow of the past warned her to be wary.

They stopped in front of Ryan's Aston-Martin. Water droplets beaded across its buffed surface, making it look as if it had been in a thundershower, not just a heavy fog. Ryan started to step into the street to open the door for her. Out of the vaporous fog appeared a car, its headlights visible only as halos in the mist.

"Careful," Ryan cautioned her, waiting until the car was down the street before he opened the door for her. Lauren climbed in and Iggy leaped from the backseat into her lap, landing awkwardly with her legs splayed. Sniffing.

Iggy squealed twice, high-pitched squawks. Lauren checked to be certain the clumsy pot belly hadn't caught a hoof on the car phone. She hadn't. Iggy bleated twice again. Louder.

"What's wrong with Iggy?" she asked as Ryan slid into his seat.

The pig whined twice more, even louder.

Ryan snapped his fingers three times, silencing Iggy. "Hand over the chocolate, Lauren."

"What chocolate?"

"Iggy can smell chocolate a kilometer away. She has her eye on your purse. You're going to have to give her some." He put his key in the ignition, but didn't turn the engine on. "Not too big a piece. It goes right to her hips and thighs—not to mention her belly."

"I don't have any candy." Lauren opened the worn Bottega Veneta bag she'd purchased secondhand in New York, but hadn't used since coming to London. She'd brought it tonight because it was the only purse casual enough to go with the suede pants she'd had for years. She peered inside. "No chocolate, honest."

Lauren stuck the open bag under Iggy's nose. Wagging her tail she sniffed, inhaling right down to her filed and buffed hoofs, then she squealed twice, disputing Lauren's claim.

Ryan grinned and switched on the interior light. "Iggy's never wrong. Check again."

Lauren unzipped the side pocket and found a bag of M&M's. "I don't believe it! Is this what you smelled?"

Iggy bobbed her head up and down and stuck out her tongue, wiggling it, expecting a treat.

"They're old. I don't remember when I last carried this purse. They might not be good for her."

Ryan took the bag and poured out a handful, then popped them into his mouth. "Stale, but it beats the taste of all those anchovies." He gave Iggy two. "That's it. I mean it. You don't want to be a porker, do you?"

Iggy grunted and stumbled into the back, sucking contentedly on the M&M's.

"Want some?" Ryan offered Lauren the bag.

She put one in her mouth, quickly crunching down on it. It didn't banish the taste of the anchovies, but it helped.

"I can't believe Iggy smelled these."

"Pot bellys have extremely sensitive noses. Can't hide anything from them."

She looked over her shoulder. Iggy gazed hopefully at her. "All gone—honest."

"Lauren." The tone of Ryan's voice had shifted, becoming personal, intimate.

She turned to face him. Green eyes riddled with minute stitches of gold studied her.

"Your hair looks great." He reached over and touched it, then wound the strands through his fingers. "Why don't you wear it this way all the time?"

"I've always worn it up, otherwise men don't take me seriously," she said, avoiding the truth.

"How do you know that, if you've never worn it down?"

Lauren shrugged. It was difficult to deceive Ryan.

"I take you seriously." He leaned toward her, one hand on the wheel, the other on the back of her seat as if resisting the urge to touch her. He kissed her. One quick, unsatisfying kiss.

Heaven help me. Her dawning sexual response must have shown on her face. He grinned. She meant to move away, she really did, but her lips reclaimed hers. He angled his head sideways, his kiss demanding she respond.

She told herself to stop it here, but a shocking heat surged through her as his tongue—agile, insistent—roved between her lips. She became giddily aware of how fast her heart beat. Before she could stop herself, she was running her fingers through his damp, wavy hair. Twining her other arm around his neck, she kissed him lingeringly.

He drew back. "I'm not forcing you, am I?"

"N-n-no," she stammered, mesmerized by his eyes, yet confused by the dangerous, risky passions unfurling inside her, evaporating her will to resist. "I didn't mean that the way it sounded. I didn't know you then. You frightened me."

"Still afraid?" He lowered his head, obviously intending to kiss her again.

"No," she answered honestly, although on some level Ryan Westcott frightened her. Despite his kindness to Irek, Ryan had a disturbing aura about him. His stubbornness at the auction and his insistence on being her partner had forewarned her. A tenacious man, Ryan intended to have his own way.

In one swift motion his arms possessively encircled her, crushing her to him as he sealed his mouth over hers. She thrust her tongue between his lips, eagerly seeking his. Breathless, her pulse throbbed in her ears. She shivered as his hand caressed her bare skin. How had he gotten her sweater out from under her belt without her realizing it? Experience. No question about it, Ryan was an expert with women. He wouldn't try to make love to her here in the confining Aston-Martin. Would he?

She intended to tell him to stop, but the words wouldn't come. Recognizing the urgency in her kiss now, the smoldering heat building between her thighs, she welcomed his touch. He eased the lacy cup of her demi-bra aside and found the nipple beneath. He stroked it with the pad of his thumb. She commanded herself not to sigh, but she did.

"Know something . . . partner?"

She shook her head, not trusting her voice.

"I'm just your type."

Followed by Irek, Vora walked up Pomodoro's stairs toward the street level. After Ryan and Lauren had left, they'd waited to pay while their waiter finished leading the inebriated mob in an off-key rendition of "That's Amore." She'd been tempted to give Irek money, but didn't. She feared it might make things worse.

She'd sat through dinner, her heart slamming against her ribs; a cold sinking feeling leaving her weak. What had she done? She would give anything to turn back the clock. How could she explain?

They stepped outside. A Sherlock Holmes fog, as close to a whiteout as imaginable, greeted them. Judging from where Ryan's car had been parked, it would take a while for them to get back here.

"Irek," she said, touching his arm. Obviously, he'd expected Ryan to be parked at the curb ready to rescue him. "I'd like to explain about the other night. I—"

"You lie!" A glacial glint froze the eyes she'd remembered as warm and loving.

"I didn't tell you my real name because a lady doesn't—shouldn't—isn't supposed to go to places like that. I thought . . ." Her voice trailed off. Compared to places he'd been, the horrors he'd experienced, venturing into a cabaret was nothing.

"You leave—no good-bye." He turned away, looking up the street although the fog made it impossible to see beyond their noses.

Irek hated her now. She didn't blame him. *How would you feel if some man lied about his name, used your body, then left without a word at dawn's first light?*

"Irek, look at me . . . please." When he grudgingly turned around, she said, "Sorry doesn't begin to explain how deeply I regret lying to you, leaving without saying good-bye. Tonight, I was going to go back to tell you the truth." Vora moved closer to Irek. "Do you understand?"

"Yes." His expression told her it was too late. Much too late. "You no like." He thumped his chest. "No good enough."

"You're wrong. I do like you." Compared to the hell he'd lived, what did one lonely woman's opinion matter? Apparently, their night together meant a lot to him. He would be disgusted if she told him the truth about herself. She stood for nothing in life except her own selfish interests. Moral certainty incarnate, Irek Makarova represented mankind's conscience. Man at his best.

"Irek." A note of profound regret rose in her throat, choking her. After a pause, she managed, "I've never met anyone like you. Tonight, when you told us about your life, I knew I'd never be worthy of you. A man like you, with your courage and talent, comes along once in a lifetime. Women like me are everywhere. You deserve better."

Irek eyed her balefully. He fished in the pocket of the trousers he'd obviously purchased at a jumble sale and came up with a fistful of pound notes. He thrust them at her.

"No buy Irek."

She closed her eyes a second, fighting back the hot sting of tears. "I didn't mean to buy you—to make you angry. When I went home, I left you money because I thought you needed it. I wanted to help you, not insult you."

Through the curtain of fog came a car. Irek stepped forward, anxious to escape her, but Vora held his arm. "Never think that I don't care about you, Irek. Or that you're not good enough. You're too good for me."

David Marcus rang the bell on Lauren Winthrop's penthouse door. He knew she wasn't in; he'd phoned the gallery earlier and had learned she had a dinner engagement and was set to join Finley Tibbetts at the Groucho Club after that. It didn't matter. He'd come to see Selma.

Barzan had put David in control of this operation. He was extremely anxious to get this over with and take charge of the cartel. He hadn't worked on any covert operations before, but Barzan trusted him. David realized he was beginning to replace Barzan's dead son, Robert. And David had no intention of letting the old man down.

He buzzed again. Now that Lauren had met Ryan Westcott, they were ready to step up their plan. David had brought Selma more sophisticated bugs to replace the ones she'd originally planted. Fewer would be necessary and they could pick up conversations even through closed doors.

Where is the old bat? He rang three times, barely releasing the button between impatient blasts.

"Give me a bleedin' minute," came a voice from inside. The double door swung open, revealing a teenage girl in a faded flannel nightgown that grazed the tops of her toes. A patched plaid robe hung from her shoulders.

"Who are you?" David assessed the girl in one glance: fly-

away red hair, close-set brown eyes, nose like a ski jump. And
a set of Dolly Parton–sized tits. Fifteen years old—max.

"Tabatha Foley. I'm Miss Winthrop's maid."

"Where's Selma?"

"She got the boot this morning."

Damn! That changed things radically. The bugs were one
thing, but he needed a person on site to move when the time
was right.

"Who are you?"

"David Marcus, an old friend of Miss Winthrop's."

"I don't expect her back until after midnight."

"May I come in? I need to make a phone call."

"I-I guess." Tabatha stepped back, hastily slipping her arms
into the sleeves of her robe and belting it, emphasizing her
small waist and slim hips.

David's prick stirred. Hall of Fame tits usually spelled thick
waists and fat asses. Not Tabatha Foley. Too bad she was stick
ugly. But young. So young.

"The telephone is in there. I'll be back in a minute. I have to
put on my uniform." Tabatha rushed toward the kitchen,
bound for the servant's quarters on the other side.

With an appreciative eye, David watched her tits jiggle as
she went. So young. *Business first.*

He dashed into the library and took apart the telephone
receiver, replacing the older bug with a new one. He covered
the flat, efficiently replacing two bugs with one updated
model, then went into the kitchen. He hid the last one under
the refrigerator. Experts knew the best conversations took
place in the kitchen—not the bedroom. Ice cream loosened
more lips than satin sheets.

"What are you doing?" Tabatha's voice came from behind
him.

He stood up, smiling. "I dropped my pen."

She'd changed into a black uniform that Selma must have
left behind. The oversized skirt hung to her ankles while a
starched, white apron tied with a butterfly bow did little to
conceal the ill-fitting waist. Although the skirt was several
sizes too large, the blouse with its straining buttons was a dam
holding back a floodtide of tits. Silently, David did a double
take. She wasn't wearing a bra.

"Would you like something to eat?" Tabatha's large eyes questioned him, looking even bigger since she'd cinched her hair back with a clip.

"Cheese and crackers would be great."

"I'm not sure what Miss Winthrop has. I just started today," she said, poking around in the refrigerator. "Here's some."

"How old are you?"

She turned, a wedge of Stilton in her hand. "Seventeen."

Liar, he thought, admiring her spunk. She'd looked him right in the eye as she'd said it. "You're awfully young for a job like this."

"I've been on my own for over a year." She opened and closed cabinet doors, apparently looking for crackers. "What kind of biscuits would you like? Carrs? Fortt's?"

"Either." He couldn't keep his eyes off her tits. They shimmied each time she moved. "You came to London to stay with friends?"

"Naw." She located a dinner plate and slapped the cheese on it. "I came alone and got a job."

A runaway, he decided. The hard edge to her voice indicated it hadn't been as easy as she made it sound. She'd lived on the streets and turned a few tricks. No question about it. Great. He liked them young, but not virgins—too much trouble.

"How did you meet Lauren?"

"At an art fair."

"What do you paint?" A germ of an idea came to him.

"I make earrings." She smiled, her eyes bright with pride. "I'm going to open my own shop."

"Come tell me about it," David said, leading her down the hall.

Inside the study, she waited awkwardly, the plate in her hand, the box of crackers under her arm.

"Have a seat." He nodded toward the peach loveseat. "I'll get us a drink."

"I'm not sure I should—"

"Nonsense. Lauren wouldn't mind. Sit down." He opened the liquor cabinet and took out the Louis XIII. David poured two snifters half full. A hundred bucks in most restaurants, he calculated. Who cared? He'd siphoned off millions from the cartel, stashing it in a Swiss account. Now money was nothing —power everything. If Miss Tabatha Foley cooperated, he'd have the power. Soon.

"You know, I admire your courage."

Noting the suspicion in her eyes, he handed her the glass and sat beside her, taking care not to sit too close.

"When I was your age, I left home and went to New York. I didn't have any money. I slept on the streets until I got a job as a busboy." It was a lie. A Jewish prince, he'd grown up in Scarsdale, the only son of a businessman who owned a chain of homes for the aged. "Tell me about the jewelry you make."

"I use Plasticine. It looks like ceramic, but you bake it in the oven instead of firing it in a kiln." She babbled on, describing her work in boring detail.

David prodded her with questions. Winning a young girl's trust was always the first step.

"Do you want to see my earrings?"

"Of course." David followed her out of the room, bringing their cognacs with him. The last thing he wanted to see was half-baked homemade jewelry. He needed her to finish her drink. Nothing spread thighs faster than liquor. So far, she'd downed about half hers, grimacing with every sip. Her back to him, her hips swaying provocatively, he seized the opportunity to pour most of his drink into her glass. Insurance.

Tabatha flicked on the light in the conservatory. "Here's what I painted tonight."

"You *are* talented—better than Paloma Picasso. I knew Lauren had an eye for artists."

"Do you really think so?"

He raised his glass. "To Tabatha Foley, the next Picasso."

He slammed back the cognac in a single gulp—a sacrilege— but he wanted her to finish hers quickly. While she drank hers, David noticed Lauren's sketches. It looked as though she worked beside Tabatha in the conservatory. They would become good friends. Lauren was the motherly type who'd taken care of her brother. Now she had Tabatha under her wing. The idea incubating in his mind grew, fired by his eagerness to see Barzan retire. And his desire to bare Tabatha Foley's tits.

"Tell me again. Where would you like your shop?" His voice

paternal and trustworthy, he casually took her arm, leading her from the room.

"Beauchamp Place."

"I like your style. Right to designer row." His eyes on her blouse, where a button had worked itself open, revealing a tantalizing glimpse of flesh, David hardly listened to her. He understood the important facts. Tabatha wanted to make money—fast. She was greedy and in a hurry. He liked that. Perhaps Selma's replacement would be an unexpected perk.

David guided Tabatha back to the loveseat. This time when he sat down, he moved closer. Her eyes—bright with enthusiasm—had an unfocused look to them now. The cognac was working. "You're saving the money Lauren's paying you?"

"In another two years I should have—"

"You're too talented to wait that long," he said and was blessed with a wide grin. "I'd like to help you."

"Really?" She smiled again, appearing almost pretty.

He took out his Gucci wallet crammed full of pound notes. Slowly, he sifted through the bills, letting her see he carried thousands of dollars. The world's obsession with cocaine spawned money like maggots.

Wide-eyed, Tabatha watched him fold the four fifty-pound notes together making a rectangle. She took her eyes off the money and gave him that greedy smile he'd seen on every continent.

"You know," he said, slipping the cache into the breast pocket of her blouse behind the prissy handkerchief peeking out, "I'm in town several times a month. I'd like to check on your progress."

He eased the folded bills up and down, teasing the nipple beneath the muslin. It jumped to attention. He rubbed the bills back and forth, calculating its size. Jesus! His prick went on full alert.

Tabatha got the message. "Thank you." Smiling, she arched her back, offering him her tits. "Call me whenever you're in town."

"I'm going to help you. But this has to be our little secret. Even Lauren can't know. People would say that I'm too old for you." He whispered these words in her ear, letting the moist tip of his tongue brush her earlobe. "They don't know how mature you are—having lived on your own and all."

"How old are you?"

"Thirty-five," he lied, knocking ten years off his age. "Not so old. Our secret, okay?"

"Our secret," she agreed as she kissed him.

He quickly unbuttoned her blouse. A set of double D's tumbled into his waiting hands. Jesus! What he'd detected beneath her pocket was no illusion. Tight, cherry-sized nipples beckoned. He'd screwed lots of young girls, sampling tits around the world. None topped these. None.

His prick strained against his pants, begging. He buried his face against her warm breasts, sucking one delicious nipple as he kneaded her soft flesh with his other hand.

He barely heard Tabatha's satisfied moans. His thoughts traveled back in time—as they always did when he kissed a sweet young thing's breasts. He closed his eyes remembering . . . remembering the first time. The time he always tried to duplicate. The best time.

It had been after midnight when he heard the tap on his bedroom door. When he answered he found his younger sister, Babs, standing there in a shortie nightgown. Tears were in her eyes.

"Teddy Segal says that I'm all tits and no brain." Babs walked into his room and flopped down on his bed.

"He's a jerk." Personally, David agreed with Segal. Babs' bust measurement exceeded her Binet score. Luckily, he'd gotten his father's brains and Babs had inherited his mother's jugs. "Forget Segal."

"We went all the way. That's why he hates me, isn't it?"

David heard his own quick intake of breath. He'd been away at Princeton the past four years. Since when had his sister started sleeping around? She'd just turned fifteen for crissake! In the two weeks he'd been home, waiting to begin graduate school, he'd gone to the country club daily to play golf with his father. He'd noticed Babs strutting around the pool in a bikini, sporting world-class knockers. Asking for it. A cockteaser.

"You hate me, too." Tears threatened.

David sat down on the bed beside her, reminding himself

not to be too hard on her. She'd grown up in Scarsdale: her mother on the diet; her father on the golf course. She was just a kid. He put his arm around her. "Forget Segal."

She nestled up against his bare chest, and kissed him, her tongue delving deep into his mouth, her hand on his crotch.

"Shouldn't we go into my room?"

David shook his head, then he realized where he was. And who was talking. He wasn't at home in his own bed with his sister. He was in London, years later—with Tabatha Foley.

"Sure." He brought himself out of the fantasy reluctantly.

He inched his hand up Tabatha's leg, nudging the voluminous skirt aside. Her thighs were moist. No panties. He palmed her, rotating the heel of his hand against her soft flesh. She moaned. Like his sister years ago, Tabatha wanted it. Bad.

"How old are you, kid?"

"Seven—"

He squeezed the dense curls, pulling slightly. "The truth."

"Fifteen. But don't tell Lauren. She'd send me home."

Killer tits. And just fifteen. He loved it.

9

When Lauren and Vora reached the Groucho Club on Dean Street, the doorman informed them Finley would be late. While the attendant took their coats, Lauren wondered if Ryan and Irek were having a good time. They'd said good-bye outside Pomodoro's and had gone on to the Mucky Duck pub near Smithfield where Irek, the reigning darts champion, had been challenged.

Lucky for you Aston-Martins are so small. At the thought of how wantonly she'd responded to Ryan, an uncomfortable heat crept up her neck. She'd wanted him to make love to her —no denying it. Why Ryan Westcott? Duty-bound to make love to as many women as possible in this lifetime, he'd had the conceit to say he was her type. Ha! She hadn't made love to a man in over a year. That had to account for her shameful behavior.

Still, she was shocked at herself. She'd been attracted to men—kind, gentle men—like Ozzie and the man she'd dated before Marcy's cancer diagnosis, Grant Fraser. But none of them had left her breathless.

"We might as well have a drink," Vora said as she led Lauren past the brasserie into the bar, "while we wait."

Filled with pleasant chatter, the room had down sofas and comfortable armchairs with modern art hung on the walls, dramatically lit by overhead spots. A pianist played lilting, classical music barely audible above the voices. Vora selected a burgundy high-backed armchair and dropped into it.

Lauren sat opposite her on a loveseat, again asking herself what was bothering Vora. She'd been strangely silent all evening. Was she still moping over Clive? Lauren didn't like to pry, but she needed Vora's help—Irek needed Vora's help—if they were going to successfully market a new talent.

"You know, I wouldn't mind belonging to Groucho's," Lauren said, trying to start a conversation with Vora after they'd given the waiter their order.

"The club is filled and has a long waiting list."

"Too bad. I like it because they encourage women to become members. I despise that all-male-club tradition—especially the old clubs like White's and Carlton. Most of their members are old enough for the great club in heaven, or hell."

Vora nodded her agreement. "You know what I dislike? Club ties. When I'm out and a man trots past sporting his club tie with a perfect Windsor knot, I have to laugh."

Lauren giggled along with Vora, thankful to see her finally loosening up. An image of Ryan Westcott wearing a club tie hit her. Never. "At least Groucho's doesn't insist on men wearing a tie to be admitted."

"The club was named for Groucho Marx. Didn't he say something about not wanting to join any club that would have the likes of him? That kind of attitude doesn't attract members who always wear ties."

As the waiter served them Harveys Bristol Cream, Vora said, "Mark Birley, who founded Anabelles, has a new place, Mark's Club, that just opened. You could probably get in there."

"I don't want a club with dancing and hustling going on nonstop. I like Groucho's because you can have a formal dinner upstairs or something light in the brasserie, then come in here and chat with friends."

Lauren glanced around the bar. If she'd been planning on living in London for more than a year she would definitely have submitted her name to Groucho's membership committee. Unlike other clubs devoted to socializing or obsessed with aristocratic lineage, Groucho's roster included an eclectic mix of interesting people, most of them in the arts.

Looking about, she recognized Ken Follett and an attractive woman. His wife? Probably. Too bad. Nearby sat rock star Eric Clapton in jeans and a baggy sweater. Holding court in the corner was Harold Pinter with his wife, Lady Antonia Fraser. There were many others sitting in small groups that she felt certain were among Britain's intelligentsia.

She turned back to Vora. "What's wrong? You haven't been yourself all evening. Can we stop discussing meaningless topics like Groucho's and talk about what's troubling you?"

"I don't know where to begin." A grim look came over Vora's face. "You wouldn't understand, anyway."

"I'm your friend." Lauren heard the injured tone in her own voice. She'd thought they'd forged a bond by working together, then ousting Clive Holcombe. She'd been wrong.

"You're perfect—beautiful and confident. Everything I'm not."

"Don't be silly. You're extremely attractive." Lauren put her glass down. "I'm not perfect—far from it."

"You know art. All I know is how to dress."

"The reason I've had some success with art is that it has been my whole life. Remember, I studied at the Sorbonne, then married a man with a gallery."

"Archer didn't want me involved with Ravissant. His idea of a partner was a beautifully dressed hostess constantly available to throw gala openings or intimate dinner parties."

Lauren noted the sorrowful look in Vora's eyes. Remembering Archer Leighton's untimely, mysterious death and the problems her own brother had had getting over his wife's death, she asked, "You're having trouble adjusting to Archer's death, aren't you?"

Vora took a slow sip of her drink, then looked directly at Lauren. "In a strange way—yes. He ran around on me constantly. I moved out on Arch once, but found all our friends were his friends. I was desperately lonely. When he asked me to come home, I did." With a wry smile, she paused. "Despite our problems, I miss Archer. He was all the family I ever had."

Lauren considered this revelation, thinking that without Paul she'd be terribly lonely. The hardest thing to bear about his depression had been losing their closeness, their ability to talk about anything. She reached across the small space separating them and touched Vora's hand. "I'm your friend—always remember that. We'll have Ravissant up to par in no time. Arch left great records. You'll use his sources to—"

"Irek won't want me involved. He hates me."

"Look, I know you two didn't hit it off, but—"

"I've slept with him."

It took a few seconds for what Vora had said to register. Lauren couldn't imagine any scenario where Vora Leighton could have met Irek Makarova. She never strayed beyond the West End except for charity functions in Guild Hall and visits to her country home. "How could you possibly know him?"

"Three nights ago, I picked him up in a nightclub near where he lives," Vora said, her tone morose. "Occasionally, I've gone to seedy clubs in questionable neighborhoods and picked up men. Irek was my latest."

Lauren struggled not to look shocked, but it was impossible to conceive of ladylike Vora Leighton doing this. "Why?"

"I like lovers who make me feel superior . . . probably because Arch always let me know what a dunce I was. I discovered how thrilling it is to be with a mysterious, possibly dangerous man."

Mysterious? Dangerous? Lauren swirled the amber liquor in her glass. For years she'd deliberately selected conservative men who reminded her of her father. Had she changed? *Is that why you find Ryan Westcott so attractive?*

"But Irek was different—so different. After he made love to me . . . the first time, he asked, in that cute accent of his, for my opinion on whether Maggie Thatcher would have to go to the country after the poll-tax fiasco. Imagine, sleeping with a man who wants to talk about the PM having to call an election. A political discussion in bed?"

An image of Ryan Westcott flashed through Lauren's mind. Did he talk after he'd made love? She doubted it. He was probably out the door ten seconds later.

Vora smiled. "Irek called the Labor Party a bunch of Bolsheviks in Savile Row suits."

"I'm sure Neil Kinnock wouldn't have appreciated that comment," Lauren said, thinking of the Labor leader. Ryan was right; Irek's mind hadn't been damaged. He'd picked up on the nuances of British politics. England had undergone a bloodless revolution that had put the stamp of socialism on the country. The Thatcher years had reversed much of that trend, but it loomed omnipresent in the shadow government dogging the Prime Minister.

"I'm missing something here. Why does he hate you?"

"At dawn, I woke up in Irek's arms. I panicked and asked myself what I was doing. Never had I stayed the night with any of those men. As I slipped out, I left him all the money I had—about a hundred pounds. I knew he needed it."

"You're right. Ryan and I decided that Irek put all his money into art supplies."

"I don't know what was worse, lying to him about my name or insulting him by leaving the money. Tonight, he all but threw the money in my face. I asked him to forgive me, but he wouldn't. I can't blame him."

"Don't be too hard on yourself. You were trying to be kind, not insulting."

"I'm crazy about him and he hates me. What am I going to do? I don't want to make trouble for you—for Ravissant."

After taking a moment to mull over the situation, Lauren said, "Irek Makarova has dreamed of exhibiting his work. No matter what he feels about you, he won't jeopardize this chance."

"Do you really think—"

"Sssh! Here comes Finley. Remember, not a word about Irek."

Halfway across the room, Finley stopped to greet a brunette with lively blue eyes and her two male companions.

"Elaine Paige, the actress, and Richard Branson," Vora said, "with Big Mac. Finley knows everyone."

"Big Mac? That man owns London's McDonald's franchises?"

Vora laughed. "No. He's Cameron Mackintosh, the producer of a string of hit plays—*Les Misérables* was my favorite. I have tickets for his latest, *Miss Saigon*. Do you want to go with me?"

"Sure, I'd love to," Lauren said, realizing why Richard Branson's name sounded familiar. He was the flamboyant entrepreneur who headed an independent music company. Last week, Fujisankei, Tak's Tokyo-based media conglomerate, had purchased a minority interest in Virgin Music Group. Not content with gobbling up American companies, Tak and his Japanese juggernaut were devouring England.

Lauren hadn't heard from Tak since Sotheby's auction. She intended to invite him to Irek's exhibition. It was important for him to see her Midas touch hadn't deserted her completely.

As Finley moved about the bar, pausing at each table to say hello to friends, Lauren watched. He was extremely well connected. In his own way he could be as much help to Ravissant as Ryan Westcott. Perhaps he'd allow her to use Groucho's club roster to invite the members to the exhibition.

"Sorry I'm late." Finley sat beside Lauren. "I haven't seen fog this thick in years, not a'tall." He signaled to the waiter, who nodded, knowing what Finley drank without asking. "I had a fabulous dinner at the Diplomat. Where did you two dine?"

"At Pomodoro," Vora answered, "with Ryan Westcott."

"Oh?" Finley quirked one pale eyebrow. "Westcott hasn't been around much—until lately."

Lauren wished Vora hadn't mentioned Ryan. Although Finley was too polite to say it, he disliked Ryan Westcott. When they were together, Lauren detected a subtle current of tension between the two men. If Finley knew Ryan was involved, he might not help Irek. "We discussed the possibility of T.J. Griffith allowing Ravissant to exhibit his collection of early Picassos."

"Really?" Finley challenged. "I understood he'd sold them years ago. Vora, don't you remember? Griffith had to raise cash to get Westcott out of prison."

His words sent Lauren's stomach into a free-fall. Her instincts, sharpened since childhood to detect danger, had failed to warn her. Was Ryan Westcott was a dangerous man? Had she let him lull her into believing otherwise?

"I don't know anything about it," Vora said.

"I thought Archer would have told you. About"—he looked at the ceiling—"twelve years ago, Griffith had Archer and

Simon Guthrie from Halford Shead appraise his Picassos. He was selling them to raise cash."

The story had the ring of truth to it, Lauren decided, her uneasiness growing. Halford Shead was Lloyd's foremost brokerage specializing in art. But if the paintings had been sold, why had Ryan chosen them as a cover? He'd suggested that they use the Picasso exhibition to explain his presence at the gallery. That way no one would find out about Irek.

"Did Griffith try to bribe the authorities?" Vora asked. "I thought even an attempt would have landed him in Old Bailey."

"Definitely," Finley agreed, "but it didn't happen here. Westcott was in prison in Zaire."

"Why was he in prison?" Lauren asked, not certain she really wanted to hear the answer.

"Murder. He killed a man—in cold blood. Of course, it was all very hush-hush. I got wind of it from one of *The Times* stringers reporting from Zaire. Then Archer confirmed that he'd appraised the Picassos."

"What were the circumstances?" Lauren asked.

Finley shrugged. "I assume the authorities had irrefutable evidence because the only way Griffith could get Westcott out was with a payoff of several million pounds."

Sickened, Lauren asked herself why she'd become involved with this man. Tonight, Ryan had listened to Irek's story of being in the *gulag* without mentioning that *he'd* been in prison.

"Archer never liked Ryan," Vora said. "He believed Westcott had some sort of hold over Griffith. Except for spending money on art the man was tight. He never bought cars and houses until Ryan came along."

"Even if he didn't have a hold over Griffith then, he must now," Finley added. "Since the bombing, Westcott conducts all Griffith's business. Westcott might be embezzling. Griffith could be too incapacitated to know. It's hard to say because Westcott won't let anyone see Griffith."

"Well, Ryan does gamble constantly at Crockfords, wagering thousands of pounds in an evening. And he drives an awfully expensive car," Vora added. "How much could he be earning legitimately?"

"The car might belong to Griffith and he lets Ryan drive it," Lauren suggested, still tethered to her previous image of Ryan.

"He owns it, not Griffith," Finley said. "Colin Simpson placed an advert with *The Times* to sell his automobile license plate, Art ZZZ. Naturally, I wanted to buy it, but Westcott outbid me. Simpson told me Westcott was the registered owner of the Aston-Martin. He saw it on the records when he sold him the plates."

"I didn't realize people sold their license plates," Lauren said, but her thoughts were still on Ryan and what she'd learned.

"They do," Vora said, "for incredible amounts of money. Archer paid a fortune to get Art 111 for his Jaguar."

While Finley and Vora discussed the rising cost of such plates, Lauren reviewed her options. Getting rid of Ryan wouldn't be easy, but surely there was a way out.

"Lauren, you're not listening, not a'tall."

"Sorry, I was thinking about Mary Cassatt's color prints Ravissant Publishing is doing this month." Lauren deliberately changed the subject. She'd heard enough about Ryan Westcott to last a lifetime.

"Isn't that unusual for Ravissant Publishing?" Finley asked. "Acquiring the rights to an Impressionist when you've specialized in contemporary art?"

Lauren couldn't tell him the truth. Ravissant Gallery was so mired in red ink that she feared she might not rescue it within the year. She planned to surprise Barzan by making money with the publishing subsidiary. "Mary Cassatt has always fascinated me. When she was born, most women stayed home, but she left the United States to pursue her dream."

She added how much she personally identified with Mary Cassatt. Like Lauren, she'd gone to Paris to study art. Cassatt had gone on to become one of the world's most loved Impressionists while success as an artist had eluded Lauren.

"As you know, her color prints have seldom been reproduced, but I acquired the rights through a Frenchman that Ozzie and I knew years ago."

Finley grinned and Lauren smiled, lowering her lashes, a

judicious blend of sincerity and flirtation. It couldn't hurt to have *The Times* give the Cassatt prints a little free publicity.

"The prints should reestablish Ravissant's reputation." Finley's tone indicated his doubts.

"They'll be of the highest quality," Vora said. "No more bogus prints are coming out of Ravissant Publishing. We've increased our security."

"Good." Finley nodded sympathetically at Vora. "I remember how devastated Archer was when those shoddy prints flooded the market." He hesitated a moment. "Has Scotland Yard closed its case on Archer's death?"

At his words Vora looked away, visibly distraught.

"Awfully sorry," Finley said. "I shouldn't have asked."

Lauren opened her mouth to change the subject Vora never discussed—even with her—but her friend spoke first.

"The night before he died, Archer came to me." She paused, looking around, obviously trying to maintain her composure. "He was pale and trembling. He confessed that he'd lied to me when he said that he hadn't known anything about the print fraud the publishing division had been involved in earlier that year. It seems the gallery had been on the skids for several years. Archer had run through his trust fund and was desperate. He'd allowed some men who'd loaned him money to use Ravissant Publishing. He'd thought they were producing mail order catalogues. But they cheaply reproduced a print of an artist we were exhibiting. It was of such poor quality that it was detected before it sold extensively, but it ruined Ravissant's reputation. Now those same men wanted to use Ravissant Publishing to illegally reproduce Dali prints."

"That would have been just about the time that the French border agents intercepted reams of paper presigned by Dali." Finley shook his head. "Poor Salvador. He lost it in his later years. When he let his manager, Pete Moore, go, unscrupulous dealers took advantage of him. I'd guess more than half the Dali prints in circulation are fakes."

"Did Archer identify the men who wanted to use Ravissant Publishing?" Lauren asked.

"No, but he did tell me he'd refused to allow it. Archer feared for his life and warned me to be careful. That night he was killed when his car went off a cliff. I knew—and no one will ever be able to convince me otherwise—he was murdered."

"The police found nothing . . . nothing, a'tall?"

"No. I hired an investigator, but he didn't discover anything either. Nothing. We couldn't even find a record of the loan. It was as if Archer had made up the entire story. But I believe him. I always will."

The words on Ravissant's computer screen were a blur to Vora. She couldn't concentrate with Irek sitting beside her, reading the hard copy of the biography she'd written to go in his catalogue. In halting English, he was making the corrections she was inputting into the computer.

"What is culinary engineer?"

She turned to him. How could a man wearing castoffs be so appealing? "It's a polite way of saying you were a butcher."

His brown eyes narrowed. "Do not be polite. Say butcher. No shame in being butcher."

She made the change. They'd been working on his biography for a week now. Mornings, Irek took English lessons with a private tutor. Then he came to the gallery where Lauren was organizing his work for the exhibition. Vora had been left in charge of the hardbound catalogue. She'd deliberately dragged out the biography section, interviewing Irek, getting the story of his youth, his years in the *gulag*. During their sessions, she'd hoped his attitude toward her would soften. It hadn't. He maintained a stance of cool detachment.

How could she convince him to give her another chance? *It's hopeless. You got what you deserved. Concentrate on making this exhibition the best ever.*

"You're currently living and painting in an abandoned warehouse. Does that sound correct?"

"No. Living in condom at Docklands. See Dog's Island."

"You've moved?" She gazed into his guileless brown eyes. It was difficult to imagine Irek in a condominium on the Thames. Although the Fleet Street papers had abandoned their famous location for new digs on Isle of Dogs, Vora had never been there. The gentrification of London's waterfront had never interested her. Until now.

"Have place at Pelican's Wharf. Much room to paint."

"And heat?" The question slipped out before Vora could think.

Irek vaulted to his feet, his hands on his hips. "Has but no need. England hot, much hot. Siberia cold. Need heat in *gulag*."

She turned back to the computer screen, tears swimming in her eyes. *Would she ever understand him?* They came from two different worlds. In life there were some people who never imagined living without heat. And those who didn't need it.

10

"Exquisite," Lauren said as she examined the vase Tabatha had made. Never having taken more than a rudimentary ceramics class, Tabatha had been reluctant to go to St. Martin's where they had wheels and kilns for her to use. In the two weeks she had been with Lauren, Tabatha had required constant prodding to persuade her to make anything but jewelry. "I'm going to put it on display at Ravissant. When it sells, I'll take a commission. The rest is yours."

"Really?" Tabatha's large eyes grew even larger.

"Yes." Lauren again noted the girl had a hard edge to her. Miserly to a fault, she hoarded her money, buying nothing but art supplies. It reminded Lauren of her early years in Paris. "I've got to run."

"Will you be needing me tonight?"

"No." Lauren preferred to prepare her own meals. "You're taking a class?"

"No." Tabatha looked away. "I have a date."

"Super." Lauren hadn't been aware that Tabatha had any friends, much less a boyfriend. But she was glad she'd met a young man. "Where are you going, the Hippodrome?" The largest club in London attracted teenagers in droves, but it was difficult to imagine Tabatha there. She owned nothing but staid clothes. No counterculture garb or punk hairstyles for her.

"No. We're going to the Odeon . . . I think."

The movies. Well, she wouldn't need a stylish outfit there. Lauren had yet to see her in anything becoming. With her enormous bosom, Tabatha looked off balance, top heavy in everything she wore. "Take my Harrods card. Nip in there and find yourself a new dress. You can pay me later when you're making money."

"I don't need—"

"Get something new, something pretty." Lauren turned to go. "Is he coming by this evening? Am I going to meet him?"

Tabatha looked flustered. "I-I'm meeting him there."

"Have fun," Lauren said as she left. *Stop worrying about her. You aren't her mother.* Still, she couldn't help feeling protective. After all, Tabatha was only seventeen.

As she walked through a fine rain too light to bother with the umbrella swinging from her arm, Lauren went down Carlos Place on her way to Berkeley Square. She slowed her pace, thinking of Ryan Westcott. After Finley had told her about Ryan, she'd intended to tell him that she no longer wanted to be his partner. But the following day Irek had toured Ravissant. From the moment he'd arrived with Ryan, it was obvious that they'd become close friends. Angering Ryan would jeopardize her relationship with Irek.

Face it, you have to put up with Ryan until after the exhibition. She disliked having him around the gallery every day and had done her best to avoid him. If she had to talk to him, she was professional but distant. To date, she'd seen him only a few times. He'd called her flat, but she had Tabatha say she was out. He never left his number.

Crossing Berkeley Square, Lauren spotted Ryan's black Aston-Martin straddling the curb outside Ravissant in the No Parking zone. She fought the urge to skip going to the gallery until he left, but she couldn't. There were piles of bills on her desk and the proofs of the Cassatt color prints to review.

As Lauren passed the Aston-Martin, she peeked in; Iggy wasn't there. A look inside the gallery window revealed Ryan talking with Vora and Irek. Lauren rounded the wrought-iron fence that set off the stairs to the lower level from the sidewalk. A throwback to the years when Mayfair had been a preserve of exclusive townhouses, these sidewalk-level delivery entrances were used today for offices. Quickly descending before the group saw her, she then punched in her security code and entered the subterranean office level.

Inside her small quarters, she saw the message on her desk and called her brother in Santa Fe. "Hi. Is there something wrong?"

"Can't I call you just to see how you're doing?" Paul's voice was upbeat.

"Sure. I've tried to call you. You're never at home."

"Let me give you Geeta's number."

So that's how it is. She smiled as she jotted down the number.

"How's the gallery?"

She told him all about Irek, then invited him to come and bring Geeta for the opening, which they'd set for early May. Surely, Barzan wouldn't care if her brother came for a visit. Paul agreed and said he planned to bring Geeta and her two children. "What ever happened with what's-his-name, the guy who was giving you such a hard time?"

He still is. She decided to let him concentrate on his own life without worrying about her. "It worked out. He's helping me with Irek."

"What'd I tell you, babe? He gazed into your baby-blues and rolled over."

"Hardly. But we are working together."

Paul rang off and she sat there a moment, the receiver in her hand. Strange, she didn't miss Paul as much as she'd expected. Perhaps that was because she was spending so much time with Vora. At first, Lauren had told herself that Vora needed her. The truth was Lauren enjoyed having a friend; she'd never been close with a woman before now.

"Your father's here."

Lauren spun around to find Ryan Westcott, one shoulder braced against the doorjamb, his hands thrust deep in his trouser pockets. A nubby, brown Harris tweed sport coat offset his white dress shirt worn without a tie.

"My father is dead," Lauren replied curtly, ignoring his half smirk. How did he know she was here? Did the man miss anything?

"Consider him resurrected. The old geezer says his name is Grant Fraser. He's waiting upstairs."

"Grant?" A gamut of perplexing emotions shot through her as she pushed past Ryan and took the central staircase up to the gallery level. She paused on the mid-level landing beneath the domed skylight, her hand on the brass banister. She hadn't seen Grant for over a year. What was he doing here now?

They'd dated steadily for over a year and he'd spoken in the vaguest of terms about wanting to marry her. Marcy's death, followed by Paul's tailspin of depression and attempts at suicide, had eroded their relationship. When she was no longer at his beck and call, the wealthy attorney had gradually stopped asking her out. The last time she'd seen Grant, she'd been with Tak, viewing a Hockney exhibit at the Andre Emmerich Gallery on East 57th. A dazzling redhead had accompanied Grant that evening.

Lauren heard Ryan coming up the stairs behind her and hurried up to the gallery level. "Grant." She extended her hand.

He took it, pulled her to him and hugged her. "I've missed you. You look great."

"So do you," she fibbed. Twenty years her senior, Grant Fraser had silver-gray hair that she once thought enhanced his sophisticated appearance. But now, haggard lines etched his face, bracketing his mouth and fanning out from his eyes, muting his urbane features.

"I've missed you terribly." Grant released her, looking sheepish when he saw the shocked expression on her face. "You're upset with me because I didn't say good-bye."

"No. I'm not." She'd been in a hurry to get to Santa Fe to check on Paul. When she'd called to say good-bye and Grant hadn't returned her call, she hadn't phoned a second time. "I'm surprised to see you, that's all. What are you doing in London?"

"I'll be working out of the Lloyd's office here for a while. How about dinner tonight at Rules?"

She started to decline, then changed her mind. The way

she'd flung herself at Ryan the other night showed her how much she missed being with a man. What better man than Grant? She knew him; she could trust him. "Great."

After she and Grant made plans, he left and she returned to her office. She was searching through the file cabinet in her office when she heard someone come in behind her. Ryan. Who else would walk in without knocking? She pretended she hadn't heard him until a soft click signaled the closing of the door. She turned, prepared for a face-off. "What do you want?"

He advanced toward her, his green eyes hostile. A cold knot formed in her stomach.

"You're avoiding me. Why?"

"I'm not," she said, justifiably proud of her calm voice.

He took another step forward. And another. She backed up, unconsciously twisting her silver bracelet. He stepped nearer, closing the distance between them. Two steps back—she bumped into the file cabinet.

"Bullshit!" He placed one hand on either side of her head, bracing himself against the cabinet.

Trapped between his arms and the file, she couldn't move. She glanced first to one side then to the other, apprehensively looking at the snarling leopard ring. Why had she ever thought Ryan's hands were gentle? Panic ripped through her as an onslaught of suppressed memories overwhelmed her.

"Answer me!"

She quelled the spasmodic trembling hidden deep in her chest, reminding herself the past couldn't hurt her. Not anymore.

"I need to work alone as much as possible," she said, telling half the truth. "You handle Irek and I'll be the inside person. You should be coordinating things with Vora. She's in charge of promoting him."

"More bullshit. How about the truth for a change?"

This was a side of Ryan that she hadn't seen. She remembered what Finley had told her. "I-I don't know what you mean," she said, her voice faltering.

"Liar!"

Toe to toe, they stood a hand's span apart, glaring at each other until a ringing silence filled the small room.

She finally found the courage to speak. "Excuse me." She ducked under his arm, trying to get away from him.

He blocked her with his body. "You're not going anywhere until I get the truth."

She looked away, then back, gazing directly into his questioning eyes. "Why didn't you tell me that you'd been in prison for murder?"

He shoved his clenched fists into his trouser pockets. "Who the hell told you?"

"Is it true?"

His gaze shifted to the side. "Yes."

NO! She let out an audible gasp, dismayed at how much she'd hoped that it wasn't true.

"It was him or me," he said, an unmistakable note of regret in his voice. "I had a split second to make the decision that saved my life. It was an accident."

"Why did he try to kill you?"

"I had what he wanted—a thirteen-and-a-half-carat industrial diamond."

A shudder of relief passed through her. There had been extenuating circumstances.

He paused for a deep breath, keeping raw emotion in check. "Money talks—anywhere on earth, but especially in Third World countries. T.J. bribed the right men and I was out . . . seven months later."

The almost imperceptible note of bitterness coloring his final words indicated it hadn't been as easy as it sounded. "Did you ever wonder if T.J. was coming for you? What took so long?"

"Never. T.J. would do anything for me."

Lauren wondered if Vora was right. Did Ryan have a hold on T.J. Griffith? If he didn't, how could he have been so positive T.J. wouldn't desert him? She didn't dare ask.

"Did T.J. sell his Picassos to get you out?"

"No. Why would he when he could borrow against them?"

"Of course," she said, realizing it made sense. An avid collector like Griffith would never sell unless forced to do so. Finley mistakenly assumed the appraisal had been for a sale not just a loan. "Was being in prison in a country like that terrible?"

"Only two things counted: muscle and money," Ryan said, his voice suddenly world-weary. "There's a lot more I could tell you, but your stomach couldn't stand it."

His manner was so disarmingly direct that she had no choice but to believe him. She pondered his revelation for a moment then asked, "What happened to the diamond that almost got you killed?"

"The U.S. government bought the diamond and used it in the Pioneer 2 space probe to Venus. They used it for instrument-viewing ports. Only diamonds are transparent to infrared light, yet able to withstand the intense heat and pressure of Venus's atmosphere." He gave her a wry smile. "Industrial diamonds aren't exactly the glamorous end of the business, but necessary. Despite all mankind's technology, diamonds are still the hardest substance on earth."

Lauren had no idea what to say. His story was too wild not to be true.

Ryan put his hand under her chin and tipped her face back, forcing her to look him in the eye. "Is there anything else you'd like to know? If there is, ask. Don't go sniveling around pissed off."

Lauren didn't respond. She'd never met a man who'd killed anyone—no matter the reason. She didn't know what to say.

"My turn?" His cocksure grin forewarned her. "Can the old fart still get it up?"

It took a second for her to realize Ryan meant Grant. "He's not that old."

He placed his hands on either side of her head again. "Compared to me, he is."

She didn't hazard a glance at his hands, instead she looked him straight in the eye. "I had a right to ask those questions. Your background affects our professional relationship. Our personal lives should remain just that—personal."

"That's bullshit. Be honest. You're dying to get me in the sack. Admit it."

"You creep!" She slammed both hands against his chest, trying to push him away. He didn't budge. She angled her body sideways, attempting to escape. "Move. I don't have anything to say to you."

"Stop lying to yourself. The other night you were hot to trot. If I'd taken you home—"

"All right. You caught me at a weak moment—that's all. It doesn't mean—"

"Shut up."

With savage intensity, his mouth swooped down. Her thoughts fractured as his lips slanted across hers and his arms clamped around her. She jammed her fist into his chest. Once. Twice. He continued kissing her, breaching her taut lips with an insistent thrust of his tongue. She struggled to shore up her weakening defenses. Her pulse skittered alarmingly, sending currents of desire through her as his tongue flowed around hers. His sexual magnetism stimulated her with a sense of urgent anticipation she'd never before experienced. Each time she was with him, the pull intensified.

Be honest, you want him. Why not? You've played it safe for years. You're ready for a real man now. Aren't you?

She kissed him back, pressing her body against him. The elusive scent of after-shave wafted up between moist kisses, triggering within her the memory of those kisses in his car. She'd wanted him then; she wanted him even more now.

His arms relaxed their tight grip and his hands slowly roved down her back to cup her bottom. Heat coursed through her, heightening her desire. He brought her up on her toes; her softness jammed against a rigid erection. With a quick intake of breath, she cradled it between her thighs, easing herself up and down. Not here. She couldn't possibly, could she?

Unexpectedly, Ryan pulled back, breaking the kiss. He looked at his watch as if it had bitten him.

"I've got to go. It's important."

Words eluded her. She watched him fiddle with the stem of his watch as he headed for the door.

"I'll pick you up at eight."

A wave of embarrassment surged through her. She'd thrown herself at him and he had something more important. *What kind of fool are you?*

"I have a date," Lauren said in the calmest voice she could manage.

"Break it." He bounded up the stairs without another word.

* * *

Of all the dumbass luck. He'd had Lauren right where he wanted her. What the hell had happened to make Adi send an emergency signal?

As soon as the watch had vibrated, Ryan had pulled twice on the stem of his Concord, signaling Adi that he'd received the summons. Now he had to find a public phone. There were two numbers he'd been warned to keep secret at all costs: Stirling's MI-5 number and the number of the Palace Green estate. Phoning from the gallery would give someone a number to trace. No one was ever to suspect the MI-5 was in on this.

"Irek," he called when he reached the gallery level.

"Here." The gruff Russian voice came from the antechamber.

"Something's come up. Can you get home on your own?" At Irek's nod, Ryan continued, "I'll pick you up tonight. Lauren's coming with us." He hesitated a moment, looking at Vora. "We're going to a concert tonight. Come with us?"

Vora glanced at Irek, almost as if she needed his approval. "Come." Irek didn't sound as if he meant it.

Had Vora been such a highfalutin' bitch that she'd discouraged Irek entirely? Ryan didn't have time to worry about it. He dashed out of the gallery and across the street past Moyses Stevens' flower shop to the Coach & Horses. The half-timbered Elizabethan pub looked out of place among the brick townhouses that had been converted into chic shops and offices.

Inside, he dialed the secret Palace Green number. Adi answered on the first ring. "Call Stirling."

Ryan punched the number and Peter Stirling's voice immediately came over the line. "Where are you?"

Ryan told him and Stirling gave him the name of a pub nearby where he'd meet him. More cloak-and-dagger crap, Ryan thought as he left the Coach & Horses. Stirling always insisted on meeting out in the open where he could spot anyone trying to eavesdrop, or in crowded places where their conversation would be garbled even to the most sophisticated listening devices.

Ryan drove to the Duke of Albemarle Pub and managed to sandwich his car into a nearly nonexistent space. He entered the pub and looked about, squinting his eyes to adjust to the darkness. Stirling hadn't arrived. He made his way up to the bar and wedged himself in beside two men discussing the Players Cup, then ordered a pint of Goose Eye bitter.

Sipping the beer, he examined the tavern with its silken oak and horse brasses. Once a hangout for footmen working in Mayfair, carrying messages between elegant townhouses, today the pub hosted wealthy businessmen whose offices were nearby.

With a smile, Ryan recalled the story of Winston Churchill receiving a congratulatory telegram after England had finally won a battle. The message had come from a drunken mob assembled at the pub. They'd flippantly signed it: Duke of Albemarle. Of course, there was no such duke. The title had been retired. Wishing to respond, Winnie's staff had spent hours sifting through peerage records, mystified at not finding the duke.

What a bunch of jerk-offs! They should have been concentrating on Hitler, not answering telegrams. It was a miracle they'd won the war. Not really, Ryan conceded. T.J. had been in the RAF. And Airey Neave, Margaret Thatcher's advisor, had also been a war hero. Both men had been victims of car bombs. A lifetime's work and dreams—wiped out. Ryan bet Margaret Thatcher still missed Neave. He'd helped shape her political views just as surely as Griffith had changed Ryan's life.

"Pint of Guinness." Stirling slipped in beside him.

They pretended not to know each other, passing a few pleasantries until Stirling had his stout. "How is the pig?"

It pissed him off that Stirling kept calling Iggy "the pig." When Ryan had insisted on buying Iggy, Stirling had stared at him as if he only claimed earth as his permanent residence. "Iggy's fine."

"The Rottweilers?"

"Adi puts them through their paces every day. What's wrong? You got me out of an important meeting."

"David Marcus, Barzan's top man, is in London . . . again."

"He couldn't be the man Barzan sent to get T.J. You said the operative is already living here."

"That's our information. Barzan's man is living in London and has a year to get T.J." Stirling took another swig of beer. "I'm concerned because it's Marcus's third trip here in the last six weeks."

"Aren't you tailing him?"

"Lower your voice." Stirling looked around with a false smile. "We can't follow all Barzan's men. He wouldn't send his top man in to do the job. Marcus's passport records show numerous trips to the Caymans and other offshore banking countries as well as Switzerland, not London. We want to know why he's suddenly coming here."

"Don't you have any idea? Shit!"

"We're working on it. We put a tail on Marcus the last time he came though—the night you were at Pomodoro with the Russian. Our man lost him in the fog, but Marcus went into a building on Grosvenor Square. We're not sure just which one. Marcus didn't turn up at the St. James Club until early the next morning."

"He got laid by some woman who lived on the square. Big deal."

"That's the same block where Lauren Winthrop lives."

"So? There are dozens of apartment buildings there."

"Caroline Armstrong's daughter—the image of her mother —shows up in a gallery where she's bound to come to Griffith's attention, sooner or later. Then Barzan's top man starts coming to London and goes to visit someone on the same block where Lauren Winthrop lives." Stirling paused as the bartender passed by. "Too many coincidences."

"Last night, you said her real estate deal came up clean."

"It did, but those international transactions are impossible to trace. David Marcus makes sure of it. That's how David Marcus has laundered untold millions for Barzan and gotten away with it. Proving anything is difficult . . ."

"Lauren's not involved," Ryan said, recalling her panic when he'd cornered her in her office and forced her to tell him what was bothering her. Women who frightened that easily weren't destined to be Mata Haris.

"It's time that we put her to the test. Have her meet T.J., but don't let her prepare in advance. I'm betting she uses her ace in the hole—being Caroline Armstrong's daughter—to try to cozy up to T.J. and get invited back to Palace Green. The next time we'll give her plenty of notice that she'll be seeing T.J. and let her show her hand. She'll come prepared to kill him."

"You know, this tops all the half-assed ideas I've ever heard. She's not part of this. I'd stake my life on it."

Stirling reached in his pocket and brought out his pipe, then began patting his pockets, searching for his matches. He studied Ryan with concerned eyes. "You're not getting involved with her, are you?"

"No," Ryan lied. For the first time in years, he'd been looking forward, not back. He had no intention of living constantly looking over his shoulder. Why the hell didn't Barzan make his move so Ryan could get on with his life?

"Good. If she tries to kill T.J., you might have to . . ." Stirling found his matches and lit one with his thumbnail. He looked Ryan squarely in the eye. "I don't want you hesitating, understand?"

11

"It's not like Lauren to make a date and not keep it," Vora said to Irek. They waited in the theater lobby for Ryan to place advance orders for intermission drinks.

Irek checked his new Mickey Mouse wristwatch—the concert was set to begin in three minutes. She knew Irek thought Lauren had done it on purpose the way she'd left him without a word that night. Why had Lauren gone out when she was expecting Ryan?

"We're set," Ryan said. "Two gins, one vodka."

Vora walked beside Irek, wondering how she'd last through the evening. Livid that Lauren had stood him up, Ryan hadn't said much on the drive over. As time passed, he'd became more withdrawn—not less. Through it all, Irek kept looking at her as if it were her fault.

The usher showed them their seats, and the two men sat with Vora in the middle. She glanced at the playbill, then asked Irek, "Did you know Boris Grebenschikov when you lived in Russia?"

He shook his head. "Russia is a big place. Grebenschikov lived in Moscow. I lived in Kiev . . . and *gulag*."

His English was improving rapidly, Vora noticed. His pronunciation was clear, but his syntax still needed work. "He plays the guitar?"

"Writes and sings also."

"In Russian?" This promised to be a *long* concert.

"Made record in English in America. Call *Radio Silence*."

"Oh." Vora scanned the program. The singer had been booted out of college for appearing at a rock concert and hadn't been officially recognized until recently. "All his recording in Russian was done underground."

"Cannot sing certain songs or sing in way government not like. Grebenschikov lucky he not go to *gulag*. Very lucky."

Vora stole a glance at Ryan as the house lights dimmed and the curtain rose. Arms folded across his chest, he stared dead ahead, as if he'd been transported to another planet.

A commanding figure walked onstage with a guitar in a hand that sparkled with a ring on every finger. Clad in tight leather pants, Boris Grebenschikov had a black shirt unbuttoned to midchest to reveal a succession of gold chains festooned with rock crystal and zodiac medallions. His dark blond hair was caught back in a ponytail and he sported a gold hoop in one ear. Grebenschikov's square jaw and masculine profile gave him a breathtaking virility.

She looked to her right and caught Irek smiling at her.

"Russian men," he said, lifting his eyebrows.

Singing in fluent English, the guitarist strummed songs with a soft-rock beat, delivering his insightful themes. He dedicated his final song before the intermission to his favorite British singers, The Cocteau Twins.

"Who are they?" Vora asked as the house lights came up for intermission.

"Avant-garde musicians," Ryan said, rising. "Too bad Grebenschikov has to go home after this tour."

"He still lives in the Soviet Union, looking like that?" Boris appeared be so thoroughly Westernized that Vora would have sworn he'd come over from Camden Lock, the area that had replaced King's Road for London's trendsetting youth—not Russia.

"Yes. Many dress like Boris . . . now."

"At least now they can sing and compose what they want," Vora said as they moved up the aisle to claim their drinks. For the first time in her life, she appreciated the term "artistic freedom." Before it had always seemed to be an excuse ballet dancers used to escape to the West and set up Swiss bank accounts.

"Can you two manage if I leave?" Ryan asked.

They nodded and he left. An uneasy feeling overcame Vora. Now was her chance. But what should she do? When she'd discussed the situation with Basil, he'd insisted most women weren't good listeners—they loved to hear themselves talk. The hairdresser had advised her to get Irek to talk to her.

About what? Ballet! Wasn't it in all Russians' blood like their music by great composers like Tschaikovsky? Like all those Russian authors with long, complicated names who wrote even longer, more complicated novels?

"The Bolshoi will be in Covent Garden in May with Mukhamedov performing in *La Bayadère*," Vora said, but Irek merely looked at her as if she were berserk. Wasn't he interested in seeing the world's finest male dancer? Tickets for the Russian's performance were already sold out, or being hawked for ten times their face value.

"Do not like ballet." He claimed their drinks from the counter and handed Vora hers. "Butterflies in tut-tuts."

When the bell rang signaling the end of the intermission, they went back to their seats. Vora sat through the remainder of the program, hardly hearing the music. Maybe what they'd experienced that night at his place hadn't been magical, after all. Perhaps the afterglow of uninhibited sex had blinded her, making her think they'd been communicating. Now she seemed unable to relate to him on any level at all.

When the curtain went down, Irek jumped to his feet yelling, *"Bravo! Bravo!"*

"Shall we go backstage and talk with him?" Vora asked.

"Nyet." Irek grabbed her arm—the first time he'd touched her since that night—and led her up the aisle. "Grebenschikov come to West, but must go back." He pointed to himself. "In *gulag* much time. Have bad name. *Glasnost* today. Tomorrow . . . who know?"

"You're right," she replied, slipping her hand into the crook of his arm. "The Berlin wall has fallen, but Eastern Europe is still a work in progress. The perils of *perestroika*. Who knows what tomorrow will bring? Look what happened in China."

As the taxi they finally found chugged up Piccadilly bound

for Vora's, she wondered how to handle the situation. Normally, her escort would take her to his club after the theater, or if they went to her place, he'd expect her to invite him in for a drink. But would Irek think she was making a pass at him if she asked him in? She didn't want to do anything to make things worse.

The taxi arrived at her home and Vora gave it a go. "Would you like to see my Sorollas?" She'd overheard him telling Lauren that Sorolla was his favorite Impressionist.

"You have Joaquín Sorolla in house?"

"Yes. Come see." He'd be astonished to find she had twenty-three of the Spanish painter's oils.

A cast-iron fence capped by gold-leafed spears surrounded 11 Belgrave Square, enclosing a manicured yard and an English oak planted during Cromwell's reign. While the fifty-foot frontage was unusual, even in opulent Belgravia, the house itself, with its triangular portico supported by Doric columns, bespoke wealth attained the old-fashioned way—inherited over generations.

Irek paid the driver, then took her arm, guiding her up the steps past the stone planters brimming with lavender tulips. As usual, the butler had left all the lights on inside the mansion, even though she wasn't home. Filtered light from crystal chandeliers shone through the Palladian windows, revealing a grand salon swathed in charvet silk and filled with priceless French antiques. When they came up to the double doors, Vora clanged the brass knocker.

"No key?"

She shook her head; she never carried a key. One of the staff was always at home. A moment later, Chiswick opened the door, his eyes on Irek and the dated suit he'd dredged up for the concert.

"Madame?" he said, staring at Irek with ill-concealed contempt.

She stepped forward. "Chiswick, take Mr. Makarova's"— she stopped herself before saying "coat"; she doubted he owned one—"umbrella. Have Millicent bring us coffee in the—" She halted. Which room would be best? "In the study. And have her bring a torte as well."

Holding his breath, Chiswick took Irek's battered umbrella

and dropped it into the umbrella stand by the door. Then he removed her Burberry with the same flourish he affected when handling her chinchilla. He pivoted and minced off to the kitchen.

Turning in a slow circle, Irek surveyed everything in the oval foyer from the marble floor hand-laid in a black-and-white diamond pattern to a Rubens painting hung above a bombé chest that had been a personal possession of Louis XIV, the Sun King.

"Fock!"

It took her a second to realize what he'd said. He was spending absolutely too much time with Ryan Westcott. She grabbed Irek's arm, leading him up the polished mahogany staircase to the second-floor hall where the Sorollas were hung. They strolled silently down the corridor viewing the parade of oils dramatically lit by special spotlights.

"This like museum," Irek said, pausing in front of a scene of children at the beach, one of Sorolla's best-loved subjects.

Suddenly, Vora felt ashamed at having so many fine paintings. She walked by them every day without even looking.

"Sorolla my favright Impressionist."

"Mine, too," she answered honestly. Never Archer's favorite artist, Sorolla had been placed upstairs while other Impressionists, collected by Archer's father, were on display downstairs.

After Irek had viewed the collection twice, pausing in front of each painting and stepping back to get the overall effect, they went into the study. The room had always been Archer's hideaway, but after his death, the mammoth house had seemed so lonely that she'd taken over the cozy room. The study had reminded her of him—too much so. Habits of a lifetime.

One day she'd wandered into Davies on Great Newport Street and had fallen in love with the traditional English style David Davies used. She'd retained him to redecorate the study in heavily upholstered sofas and acres of English chintz. Davies had banished Archer's ghost, but his ancestors remained immortalized in an armada of silver frames clustered on a table. He'd revered his family as much as he had art. If she and Archer had been able to have children, their marriage would have been happier.

Irek walked into the study and went over to the table with the photographs. "Your family?"

"No. Those are my late husband's relatives."

"Late? He come home soon?"

"Late—a polite way of saying dead."

"Like culinary engineer?"

His tone told her he was teasing her and she shouldn't take him seriously. Relieved, she smiled at him.

Millicent delivered a silver tray with a sterling urn of coffee and a chocolate torte topped by six inches of white chocolate curls. Irek's mouth gaped.

"Death by Chocolate Torte," Vora explained, waving Millicent out the door. She wanted to serve Irek herself.

"Eat and die?"

She opened her mouth to explain, then realized he was joking. Progress—at last.

Keeping up a light banter about the gallery and his exhibition, Vora served him coffee and a double portion of the torte.

Between mouthfuls, Irek pointed his fork to the group of photographs. "Where is your people?"

"I'm an only child. My parents are dead."

"No photographs?"

"A few." Of course, Archer wouldn't have wanted them mixed in with his relatives. While he'd been alive, she'd never even broached the subject. She had no idea why she hadn't told Davies to replace the pictures with her own family photographs. Archer shouldn't be able to rule her life from the Leighton crypt.

Irek studied her curiously. "You do not like your family?"

"I hardly remember them."

She explained how her parents had been killed in a plane crash on Malta. There had been no one to take her in except an uncle, a senile bachelor.

"Senile?"

"It means old and forgetful. Uncle Nigel's memory was poor for most things except his garden. There he could remember the watering and fertilizing schedule as well as the botanical names of each plant." She took a deep breath, seeing in her mind's eye Uncle Nigel religiously tending each cherished cutting, ignoring the small child tagging along beside him, anxiously waiting for him to say something. Anything.

"What is wrong?" Irek asked, obviously seeing the distress the painful memories evoked.

"When I was eight, a neighbor gave me a tangerine-colored kitten. Tangie became my only friend. You see, we lived on a vast estate out in the country. I had no playmates, so I would dress the kitten in my doll's clothes and push her around Blyforthe Hall in a pram. One day, I was strolling Tangie through the garden in the pram when I tripped and fell into his tulips, crushing dozens. Uncle Nigel threw the kitten down the well." She ignored the catch in her voice. Even after all these years, she could still hear Tangie's terrified yowls. Then silence.

"He ordered the servants to lock me in my room. I had to stay there until he found a convent school in Italy where I could board. I lived there year round except for holidays. Whenever I came home, he locked me up—treating me as if I were a small child even when I was older."

Irek gave her hand a comforting squeeze, then asked, "Uncle . . . late?"

"Yes. He was seventy-seven when I was four and came to him. He died of a heart attack while pouring beer into saucers in his flower beds."

"Waste of beer!"

"He always did that. He'd heard on a Beeb radio program about gardening that beer attracted snails. They crawled into the saucers and drowned—happy."

"I not listen to BBC radio." Irek pinched his nose closed, saying, "Too much gardening talk by men with I-better-than-you voices."

Vora giggled. He had a point. Would the Beeb—radio or television—survive the onslaught of programs geared to the changing times and the waves of immigrants who didn't share the same cultural background?

"Tell me about your family," she asked. During their sessions on his biography for the catalogue, he had disclosed no more than the barest details. As far as Irek knew, his parents, two brothers, and a sister were alive and living in Kiev.

"I grow up in apartment—same size this." He indicated the small study. "One room for sleep. Kitchen with table, but all could not eat at same time. Father and sons eat. Mother and sister last." He shrugged. "We were rich. Had machine that wash in bathroom. Let its water go into tub, then we have bath. No one else in building has machine. My mother happy, happy."

"How did you get the washing machine?"

"My father in party. Have good job."

"Have you heard from them since you left?" she asked. *Glasnost* had opened many doors. The first to swing wide was uncensored mail. Surely Irek's family had written.

He looked at the sterling ranks of Archer's ancient ancestors. "I write much times. No answer." His gaze swung back to her; sorrow tinged his eyes. "They angry still. I make much trouble. Police tell Father make Irek behave. He try. I run away—end up in prison. When I get out, Father say no come home. Irek not his son anymore."

Vora wanted to reach out—to cradle him in her arms. The years in prison enduring torture hadn't hurt him as much as his family's continued rejection. On this level, at least, she understood Irek. Years of never knowing the comfort of a family's love swept over her. She'd married Archer Leighton because she'd desperately wanted her own family.

"No worry. Things is wonderful now."

He rose to leave. She wanted to say something to make him stay, but she couldn't think of anything, so she followed him downstairs and had Chiswick ring for a taxi. It pulled up immediately, enticed by a fare in Belgravia. Wait until the driver heard the Wapping address. Although the waterfront was being revitalized, it was surrounded by a neighborhood best avoided after dark.

"Dushinka," Irek said. "I sorry Uncle Nigel bad to you."

She clung to his arm. How on earth could he feel sorry for her? How?

"Good night, *dushinka.*" He brushed her cheek with his lips.

Vora returned to the lonely house and picked up her Filofax. She found the number and dialed Carleton Amestoy's home. When the houseboy put Arch's old friend on the line, she said, "Carleton, this is Vora Leighton."

There was an audible pause and she consulted her Piaget. After midnight. Good manners allowed no calls at this hour short of an emergency.

"Yes?" he asked, considerable alarm in his voice.

"I'm wondering," she said, knowing he'd imported sable from Russia for years, "if you could tell me what '*dushinka* ' means."

"What?"

"*Dushinka . . . dushinka.* What does it mean?"

"It's hard to come up with a literal translation. Russian, in some ways, is a lot like French. There are infinite variations of every word. English, you know, is an imprecise language."

"Give me the closest English translation."

"It means darling."

"You're sure you don't want any dessert?"

"I ate every bite of the woodcock. I don't have room for anything more," Lauren said, smiling across the table at Grant Fraser.

The nostalgic atmosphere at London's oldest restaurant had made her temporarily forget her waistline. Considerate Grant had known she would love dining at Rules where H.G. Wells, Thackeray, Galsworthy, and a host of other notables had eaten. The paneled walls displayed hundreds of caricatures and ancient programs from the Queen's Theatre. The romance of the Edwardian atmosphere enthralled Lauren. She could almost see Edward VII and Lillie Langtry at their favorite table by the latticed window. Forbidden love. A heartbreaker for Lillie.

Forbidden. Ryan Westcott's brash smile flashed through her mind. The way she'd thrown herself at him showed her that her hormones were out of whack. Her happiness evaporated. He'd be furious that she'd stood him up. What did he expect? She didn't break dates on demand.

"Lauren." Grant covered her hand with his, stopping her from fiddling with her spoon. "I have something for you."

He handed her a maroon-velvet box so small that only one piece of jewelry could fit inside it. Her blue eyes questioning him, she slowly opened it. A nine-carat diamond, so perfect it refracted blue-white light, glittered in the box with the initials H W for Harry Winston embossed in gold inside the lid.

"I'd like you to be my wife."

Once she'd thought she wanted to marry Grant. She was no longer certain what would make her happy.

"I know I should have asked you long ago but . . . Well . . . I wasn't sure I wanted to be tied down."

"Marriage is a commitment two people who love each other make." She snapped the lid shut on the ice-cold diamond. "Neither person should feel tied down."

"I know that . . . now." He took her hand again, gently squeezing it. "I want to spend the rest of my life with you. I love you."

She stared at him, disbelieving. Why, in the year they'd dated, had he never once said those words?

"Just after Christmas, I had a massive coronary. I had to have a triple bypass. Lying in that hospital bed, I thought about my life. You're warm, loving—the best thing that ever happened to me. I just didn't know it. I need you now."

What about me? What do I need? Grant needed her; he didn't love her. Not the way she wanted to be loved, anyway. She'd already spent ten years nursing an elderly man. She hadn't minded because she'd needed Ozzie as much as he'd needed her. He'd been the reincarnation of her father, a man who made her feel safe. A man who helped her banish the horrors of her past. But her life was different now. What she wanted was a man to be there for her should she need him.

She handed Grant back the velvet box. "I like you very much, but I don't love you. I can't marry you."

The happy glow on his face faded. "There's someone else, isn't there? That Westcott fellow?"

She hesitated, wondering what would make Grant say such a thing. The two men had barely exchanged hellos when she'd introduced them that afternoon in the gallery.

"I'm not in love with Ryan," she answered truthfully. In lust better describes it, she thought, remembering her heated responses to his kisses. "I'm sorting things out right now. My focus has to be on Ravissant, not my personal life."

"Promise me you'll think it over." Grant pocketed the box.

"I'm not taking no for an answer. I'll be working here. Let's see each other as often as possible. I'll bet the old spark is still there."

On the drive home, Lauren tried not to encourage Grant. She needed to back off from men entirely until her life had more direction. When she moved to Santa Fe, that would be the time to consider a permanent relationship. As they turned the corner in front of the American Embassy, Lauren thought she spotted Ryan's Aston-Martin. He wasn't still waiting for her, was he? Well, he didn't scare her. He would merely rant and rave, pulling the quintessential macho routine because she'd had the audacity to stand him up.

"Good night," Lauren told Grant as he walked her to the ground-floor lift.

"No nightcap?" His beguiling smile implied he expected much more than Le Paradis or Louis XIII cognac.

"Another time; I'm tired. Thanks for a lovely evening." She stepped into the lift and pulled the antique grillwork door shut.

"I'll phone you tomorrow," Grant called after her.

She stepped off the lift at her floor, then paused to check the time. Midnight. Had Ryan waited all this time? She shook Jeeves, the porter, who was slumped in the chair beside the lift, emitting a foghorn snore. He was awake only for elevenses and his afternoon cuppa.

"How long has Mr. Westcott been here?"

"Who?" The old man stared up at her with rheumy blue eyes.

"Never mind." The man was worthless. She went over and opened her door a cautious crack. The only light in the foyer was the overhead spot that bathed the George III chinoiserie mirror in subtle light. The salon and study were dark. Apparently, she'd been wrong. It hadn't been his Aston-Martin.

She hung her sable in the hall closet, then went down the long, unlit corridor to her bedroom. Tabatha hadn't turned on the bedside lamp as Lauren had instructed. She hurried across the plush carpet and clicked on the light. Lauren unzipped her black cashmere sheath and walked into her dressing room. After kicking off her high heels, she shimmied out of her dress and tossed it into the dry-cleaning hamper.

She was about to take off her slip when something in the dark bathroom beyond the dressing area caught her eye. Certain her imagination was playing a prank on her, she flicked on the bathroom light. Lying on the chaise, a half-empty glass in one hand, was Ryan Westcott.

"You're not going to stop now, are you? Take it all off."

"What are you doing here?"

"Watching a strip show and having a drink." He gestured to her bidet. He'd filled it with ice and was chilling a bottle of Boodles in it.

She grabbed the terry robe that always hung on the back of the door. "Leave—now."

He swilled his gin and grinned, then wadded the ermine throw into a pillow and put it under his feet.

Lauren considered dialing 999, the emergency number, but thought the better of it. With her luck, the incident would end up in Nigel Dempster's column. Or Ross Benson's.

"Why are you in here?" she asked in her calmest voice.

"Your joint's so full of prissy French crap, I thought I'd settle back and wait where the crap really belongs."

She had no idea how to respond to such an outrageous statement.

He vaulted to his feet and slammed the bathroom door shut. She jumped aside as he turned on the shower full force. Too stunned to stop him, she watched him turn on the tub, both sinks, then he flushed the toilet.

"What are you doing?" she shouted as a hot cloud of vapor engulfed the room.

Ryan advanced on her and grabbed her by her shoulders. He whispered in her ear so softly that she could barely make out his words above the noise of the running water. "Griffith has your painting. He wants to see you."

"Really?" she asked, unable to conceal her thrilled surprise. T.J. Griffith, the renowned collector, had her painting. "But how—"

"Don't say another word; just put on your clothes and come with me."

12

In a howling wind, the Aston-Martin raced up Kensington Road and veered right. Slowing only slightly as he drove up Palace Green, Ryan waved to the guard in the kiosk.

Long known as "Millionaire's Row," the private tree-lined street with its mansions, many converted to embassies and ambassador's residences, was owned by the Crown Estates. The small enclave of leaseholds basked in their proximity to Kensington Gardens and Holland Park. The kingpin of the imposing estates was nearby Kensington Palace. Home to the Prince and Princes of Wales, Princess Margaret, and Prince and Princess Michael of Kent, each family living in their own quarters.

Along with the prestige of a neighborhood bordering the royal residence, the street boasted embassies belonging to two of the world's most powerful—and security-minded—nations. Guarding opposite ends of Palace Green were the Soviet and Israeli embassies. The area graciously accepted a perquisite it had come to regard as its right: patrols by the Diplomatic Police. Numerous private protection forces augmented their efforts. At this late hour, the mansions' windows were dark, but ultra-bright security lights lit their perimeters and surveillance cameras relentlessly checked the grounds.

The wind whipped through the trees arching over the

street, battering their limbs, threatening to break them. A
hunter's moon, shining brightly earlier, had been eclipsed by
curdled clouds bloated with rain and high winds, harbingers
of a storm blowing in off the North Sea.

Lauren pulled her sable closer, thinking about Ryan's explanation of how he knew she'd painted "Midnight in Marrakesh." He claimed to have seen it when he checked the
conservatory closet, looking for a jacket for Vora. When he'd
spotted it again at the fair, he'd paid a teenage boy to buy it for
him so no one would suspect T.J. Griffith was interested in the
artist.

Please let Griffith like it and keep it for his collection. In the
past few weeks, she'd done a few sketches. Since coming to
London something in her mind had been freed. She created
easily without the tortured struggle that had characterized
her earlier works. The result had been charcoal portraits. If
Griffith thought she had promise, she'd chuck her plans to
open a gallery in Santa Fe. Instead, she would seriously pursue
a career as an artist.

The car halted in front of a tall wrought-iron gate, the single
opening in a ten-foot-high wall that resembled stone ramparts
of medieval times—except it was capped with electric prongs.
Cameras mounted in the gargoyle-topped pillars flanking the
gate surveyed the occupants of the car.

"Face the camera," Ryan ordered.

She turned and looked at the winking red light. The camera
spent a full minute on her face, then tilted to one side, inspecting the interior of the car. The gate swung open and a coven
of Rottweilers, their collars spiked with barbed steel, stalked
the car into the courtyard.

"Not too friendly, are they?"

"All thirteen are trained to kill first and bark later."

Without warning, a bolt of lightning flooded the courtyard
with a violet-white glare, backlighting leafless trees standing a
deathwatch over Greyburne Manor, revealing an ivy-
shrouded stone fortress three stories high. Then a volley of
thunder rocked the car. Lauren gripped Ryan's arm with her
gloved hand as she watched the dogs whipped into a frenzy by
nature's unusual display of temper. Fangs bared, they snarled
viciously, hovering around the Aston-Martin, their muscular

bodies tense beneath gleaming black coats, their eyes glowing with hatred.

The car inched forward, coming to a stop before a double-wide garage door partially hidden by an archway of clipped yew. A camera mounted on a motorized pole greeted them, inspecting the car's exterior and its undercarriage.

The garage door opened and exposed a room as brightly lit as a midsummer day. At the far end stood a dark-skinned man in a white turban and sweeping white robes that billowed about his long legs. A wide scarlet sash held a lethal-looking dirk in a scabbard studded with nailhead points of gold. He held Iggy in his arms, her front legs flailing.

"Who's he?"

"T.J.'s bodyguard." Ryan waved to Iggy. "Adi is a Sikh, the best in the business—trained from childhood to fight. Loyal."

"Tell that to Indira Gandhi," Lauren said, recalling how the Prime Minister's prized Sikh bodyguards had turned on her.

"That was a special case. They're the preferred bodyguards. Ask anyone whose life is in danger." Ryan opened his door and got out, nodding to the Sikh.

The guard put Iggy down and opened Lauren's door for her. She stepped out, smiling up into the most merciless eyes she'd ever seen. A shadow of alarm touched her; she looked away. Iggy sniffed, inspecting her sable as if it were a long-lost cousin. Lauren bent to pick her up.

"Don't touch!" The Sikh's voice bounced off the walls.

Lauren jerked back, looking for Ryan. He must have gone inside the building; he wasn't anywhere in sight. Behind her, the garage door clanged shut, sealing them off from the vicious attack dogs. And the outside world.

Iggy squealed three long, heart-rending cries. She stood on her back legs, pawing the air, begging Lauren to pick her up.

"She's used to me carrying her."

The Sikh nodded curtly and Lauren lifted Iggy into her arms. The pot belly nuzzled her ear sniffing her perfume.

"Stand here," the Sikh commanded.

"Another camera?" Really, this was overkill. But she walked over to the spot he'd indicated.

"Stand still."

Obediently, Lauren waited while the camera zoomed in on

her eye. Just what kind of a man was T.J. Griffith to insist upon all this security? Did he really think the IRA would try to kill him again? Why had they in the first place? They didn't have vendettas against individuals, unless like Mountbatten or Ian Gow, the person was closely allied with the government. The whole thing didn't make any sense.

The door parted, soundlessly gliding open, and Lauren stepped forward. She found herself alone, Iggy in her arms, in a dark hall lit by a single wall sconce that shot light toward the ceiling, leaving the rest of the area in deep shadows. Clutching Iggy, Lauren let her eyes grow accustomed to the lack of light.

Uneasiness crept over her. Where was Ryan? She squeezed Iggy tighter as she passed through an unusual archway and walked down the empty corridor. Her stiletto heels made sharp clicks on the bare marble, throwing the sound upward to the vaulted ceiling. She came to a vestibule that must be the entrance hall. Another strange-looking arch framed the front door. The room was empty except for the walls honeycombed with priceless paintings haphazardly hung from the ceiling to the wainscoting.

"Ryan?" The word echoed, unnaturally amplified by the emptiness, the stone walls, and marble floor. A person could scream forever and the sound would never go beyond these walls.

A bolt of specter-white lightning seared across the room; a clap of thunder, almost directly overhead, was muffled by the thick walls. Iggy shrieked and burrowed under Lauren's open coat, seeking refuge against her bosom.

"Ryan," she yelled, her eye on the door as she fought the urge to flee, remembering the dogs.

Out of nowhere, the Sikh appeared. "Mr. Griffith will see you now."

She followed him down a long hall lined with paintings until they stopped in front of a fortress-style door. The Sikh took Iggy from her, then helped her out of her coat. He silently opened the door and motioned her forward.

Inside the pitch-black room was a single light as bright as sun on the Sahara. The spot focused on a trestle table where an easel displayed "Midnight in Marrakesh." The light was so intense she couldn't look into it. She shielded her eyes with her hand. Back against the door, she waited for her eyes to adjust.

Beyond the spotlight, Lauren detected the outline of a man sitting in a chair. Positioned behind the blinding light, he was cloaked in shadows, making it impossible to tell much about him except that he had an unusually large frame.

"Sit down." The voice sounded distorted, as if it were coming from a mechanical device like the voice boxes victims of throat cancer used.

Squinting against the intense light, Lauren walked to the empty chair at the table and sat down beside her painting, opposite the man. She reminded herself that T.J. Griffith had been mutilated by the bomb. He didn't want anyone to see him, hence the concealing use of light directed away from him. Still, she couldn't help being apprehensive. This whole encounter was simply too bizarre.

"Tell me about your painting," the voice croaked. "Why do you call it 'Midnight in Marrakesh'?"

"I used to live there."

"That's not why. Tell me the real reason."

It wasn't the real reason but Griffith had no way of knowing that. Anxiety gnawing at her, she twisted her silver bracelet, praying he liked her work.

"I asked you a question."

"I answered." She hated the tentative sound of her own voice. Her jitters increased as she looked into the hazy backwash of the light. Griffith wore a khaki bush jacket and some sort of hood, or perhaps a ski mask. The kind terrorists wore.

"The child in your painting. Is that you?"

"No," she lied. "It isn't anyone in particular. She's a product of my imagination, that's all."

Griffith shifted in his seat. She doubted she'd fooled him. She'd never been a good liar.

"And the hands," the garbled voice demanded, "why are they reaching for the girl? What does that signify?"

Lauren switched on her hostess smile; she desperately wanted him to like her work. If he did, she'd know she had talent, not just ambition. "The hands represent the forces of evil in the world, reaching out to tempt the girl."

His shadow moved; he cocked his head to one side. She couldn't tell if he was studying her or something in his lap. "Why did you leave Marrakesh . . . and your mother?"

Every fiber in her body tensed. Her mother. Why would Griffith even think to mention her mother?

"To study at the Sorbonne." That was only part of the reason, but it was true enough so that her voice no longer had a false ring to it.

"Why are you in London?"

"To make Ravissant into a premier gallery again. I'm sure Ryan's told you that we've found an exceptionally talented artist."

An unnatural silence filled the room, like the deceptive quiet after a crack of thunder. Waiting for him to respond, she looked beyond Griffith and saw a floor-to-ceiling window swagged with heavy portiers. They were probably velvet, but with the light in her eyes, she couldn't make out the fabric or the color. The table beneath her clenched hands trembled as another round of thunder shook the stone walls.

"Why are you lying?" His voice sounded almost normal.

Panic raised the hackles across the back of her neck. Her worst enemy had caught up with her. The past.

"You think because you're beautiful you can lie and get away with it, don't you?"

"No—"

"The only thing you've said that has been true is you're here to rescue Ravissant. The rest—nothing but lies."

"No."

"I have a voice modulator tracking your responses. It's more reliable than a lie detector."

Perspiring beneath the glare of the hot light, her pulse thudded erratically. She hated lying. But she had no intention of telling anyone—certainly not a stranger—the truth.

"Why are you lying?" His voice was diabolically insistent.

He had his nerve, questioning her like this, dredging up the past. It was none of his business. "I don't wish to discuss the meaning of my painting," Lauren said as nicely as possible. Griffith's approval meant more to her than she'd admitted before now. "Interpretations of an artist's work are dependent on the viewer. Each piece should be judged on its own

merit. It should evoke an emotional response in the be-
holder."

"Bullshit! You're lying. I want to know why."

The anger smoldering inside her flared. "The meaning of
my painting is personal. It's not any of your business. Either
you like it, or you don't. If you don't wish to keep it"—she rose
—"I'm prepared to give you your money back. Good-bye."

He responded with a ragged chortle that she took to be a
laugh. She was too furious to speak. This whole meeting was a
game to him. And Ryan Westcott was probably in on it. They
were only playing with her. No one had ever seen any artistic
merit in "Midnight in Marrakesh." No one ever would.

Just as she reached for her painting, thunder hit the room,
shaking it like an earthquake's aftershock. The lights flick-
ered, then dimmed to an amber brown. She stared at the window, realizing that she had yet to see any lightning pre-
ceding the volleys of thunder. Either the window wasn't real,
or it was sealed like a prison. The film of perspiration on her
skin became an icy sheath.

The room plunged into total darkness. Trembling, she told
herself not to be afraid. It was only a power failure. Suddenly,
Griffith was beside her; she could feel the heat of his body. His
hand, covered by thin surgical gloves, brushed her cheek. Past
and present merged. Fighting the urge to scream, she
wheeled away from his hands.

"We have a backup generator," he said, his voice strangely
soft as he moved closer. "It'll be on in a minute."

She had the insane notion that he was going to take her into
his arms. And kiss her. She turned, sprinted for the door,
banged into it, fumbled until she found the knob, yanked on
it, telling herself not to panic. Locked.

"It can only be opened from the outside."

"Let me out this instant. I want to go home. You have no
right to keep me in here."

"You'll leave . . . when I say so."

As she pounded on the door, trying to get Ryan's attention
—surely he wouldn't desert her—her hand touched the wall.
Padded. She was trapped in a soundproof chamber without a
window. Griffith was deranged; she was convinced of it. Kicking the door as hard as she could and screaming for Ryan to let

her out, she realized no one knew she was there. Ryan had hustled her out of her apartment. She hadn't even left a note for Tabatha.

The lights flashed on; she turned, ready to confront Griffith. He'd vanished along with the painting. With her back braced against the door, she waited, panting. Suddenly, the door opened and she stumbled backward.

"You okay?" Ryan caught her, then pulled her around to face him.

Still breathing hard, she hugged him for a long moment before her anger returned full force. "Where is Griffith? He has my painting. I want it back. I demand you take me home —now."

"Easy, easy." He held her in his strong arms, running a soothing hand up and down her back. "Did he frighten you, partner?"

"No . . . a little. Get me out of this tomb." Pivoting, she jerked out of his arms. "What kind of a room is this? A torture chamber?"

Ryan chuckled, a dry cynical laugh. "What an imagination."

He flicked on the overhead lights, revealing a barren room except for the table with two chairs and a cot standing off to one side. What she'd thought was a window was actually an avant-garde-art wall sculpture.

"Why are the walls padded?" she asked, feeling foolish.

"Sometimes T.J. can't sleep. He comes in here. He hung that piece of crap over the only window so he can have total dark when he needs it. The padding keeps out the noise." He pointed to the walnut-paneled wall. "There's a hidden door over there."

She felt silly now, but was determined not to show it. "I want my painting back . . . then take me home."

"No way. T.J. wants that painting."

"He does?" She couldn't believe it. "He has a strange way of showing it."

"Did he get a little heavy-handed with you?" At her nod, he continued, "He didn't mean to. It's just that you remind him of Caroline Armstrong."

"He knew my mother? How?"

"He met her in Marrakesh several years after you'd left. It's a long story. Come up to my suite and I'll tell you about it. Besides, I have something up there for you."

Reluctantly, she let him squire her up the stairs. "Griffith didn't buy my painting just because of my mother, did he?"

Ryan shook his head, but she wasn't sure she believed him. An accomplished flirt, Mother had always had men swarming around her, anxious to curry her favor. She'd even managed to wed Rupert Armstrong, a man whose status as a peer should have elevated him above a marriage to an impoverished widow with no social connections.

"I thought you were going to explain," she said as they ascended the final flight of stairs to the third floor.

"When we're in my rooms," Ryan said, his voice low as he looked over his shoulder. The Sikh stood at the bottom of the stairs, his brows tilted inward in a puzzled frown.

On the third floor was a set of double doors. Ryan stood directly in front of a fish-eye peephole like the one downstairs.

"What's that?" she demanded.

"An ocular scanner. It makes a computer image of your iris. Adi scanned your iris as you entered. Now no one can ever pretend to be you and get into Greyburne Manor."

She'd heard of biometric scanners where a finger or palm was placed on a receptor to gain admittance to a high-security area, but this defied her imagination. Was Griffith really in enough danger to warrant this?

Inside the walnut-paneled room, lined floor to ceiling with crowded bookshelves, was a sofa upholstered in masculine tones of maroon and British racing green. It faced a fireplace where an oak log burned, its low flames throwing scrims of shadow and light across the floor. Facing the sofa was a suede chair in a deep shade of cranberry with dozens of issues of *Scientific American* heaped on it. Across the arm was the leather bomber jacket Ryan had worn the night they'd had pizza with Irek.

He whistled and Iggy came shambling out of an adjacent room, crossing the Persian rug covering the plank floor. She tripped on the rug, then clumsily plopped down on her haunches in front of Lauren. She lifted the pot belly into her arms and Iggy inhaled deeply.

"She loves my perfume. Bluebells by Penhaligon's. Next time, I'll bring her a bottle of her own."

"T.J. invited you back?" A gleam of surprise fired Ryan's green eyes.

"No. I mean next time I see you I'll give you a bottle of Bluebells. You won't get me back here on a bet." She sat on the sofa, putting Iggy down beside her.

"Don't be too hard on T.J. The last few years haven't been easy."

"I know, but he acts strange and dresses—"

"There's nothing left of T.J. Most of his face and neck are gone. Luckily, he still has vision in one eye. Both forearms are artificial."

Instantly regretting her callousness, she swallowed hard, unnerved by what she'd learned. Griffith had suffered the tortures of hell, and she'd let the dark abyss of her past make her overreact. "Does he use some sort of a lie detector that measures changes in a person's voice?"

"Yes. T.J. has every security device currently available. He believes someone's trying to kill him."

"Who? The IRA? Why?" she asked, her mind on Griffith. She'd lied and he knew it, yet he still wanted to keep her painting. He thought she had talent!

"Not the IRA, though the papers claimed they were responsible for the bomb that almost cost T.J. his life. A case of mistaken identity, most likely. Since then, we've been living under constant guard. T.J. won't admit the truth—he's already dead."

"What do you mean?" Her words were a stricken whisper.

"He's lived his entire life as a gambler." Ryan picked up the worn bomber jacket and tossed it to Lauren. "This was T.J.'s. Sixty-seven missions with the RAF. Shot down three times. Look at the lining."

Lauren opened the jacket, inhaling traces of Ryan's aftershave that clung to the leather collar. Inside was a crude, hand-drawn map of France and the English Channel.

"He counted on surviving by finding his own way home. He never expected anyone to come to his rescue. It was the same thing when we kicked around Africa chasing diamonds. T.J. thrived on tackling projects where the odds were against him.

Now he won't even go out into the courtyard. He might as well be dead."

"I-I see." Her voice wavered as she realized how pathetic Griffith's life had become. She put the jacket down by the snoozing Iggy who'd stretched out, taking up half the sofa.

"Don't discuss seeing T.J. tonight with anyone. He doesn't want the world to know how bad off he is. You're the only person who has seen him besides Adi and me."

"I won't tell anyone." Poor man, alone and suffering. He'd chosen her above all the artists he could have called to Palace Green, and she'd let him down by lying to him.

Ryan studied her intently for a long moment, then walked over to a pecky cypress hutch, apparently considering the subject closed. "Would you like a drink?"

Lauren almost declined, then reconsidered. Despite the warm fire, the scene with Griffith had left her chilled.

"Harveys, if you have it."

Ryan handed her the drink and sat close beside her, one arm negligently draped over the back of the sofa. As she looked into his brooding eyes, a warning shot through her. She knew what his gaze signaled: the universal male look of lust. Usually, she retreated when faced with it. Not tonight. All along, something inside her had been responding to this man despite her reservations.

She suppressed her feelings, remembering why she'd come up to his room. "What about my mother and T.J.?"

"They met fifteen years ago this coming July. T.J. and I were in Marrakesh concluding a deal with Rupert Armstrong. That's when T.J. fell in love with your mother."

Same old story. "She hooked him, then tossed him aside, angling for another catch."

"Not at all. They carried on an affair for over a year, meeting daily at a secret spot in the *medina.* She claimed she was going to leave Armstrong."

"Mother loved Rupert's money, his title. She never would have risked it all by cheating on him."

"You never saw T.J. in action, honey. He could have had any woman, but he loved your mother. And she loved him—in her own way." Ryan studied her thoughtfully, all traces of sexual interest had vanished. "But you're right. She had no intention of leaving Armstrong. T.J. never got over her."

"It was better that way. My mother never would have stuck by him, living in this prison."

"My mother would have."

The unmistakable caress in his voice astounded her. He'd never used that tone with her. But with his next words the timbre of his voice again changed, becoming disturbingly bitter.

"My father was a lazy drunk who beat my mother every chance he got and she still made excuses for him."

Embarrassed at the emotion in his voice, Lauren realized she'd witnessed a momentary crack in his tough shell. Not knowing what to say, she deliberately changed the subject. "How did you come to work for T.J.?"

"I came to London after my tour of duty in Vietnam"—Ryan hesitated a fraction of a second—"to meet a relative. I went to work for T.J. I've been with him ever since. We have a lot in common. Mainly, we like to gamble." He took a sip of his drink. "Not just on cards, but on other things—like art. That's how T.J. got started collecting. As you can see by the way he displays his paintings, he doesn't do it for the love of art. He does it as a gamble—to see who'll be a winner."

"He's done amazingly well at something most collectors devote a lifetime to studying." She looked at Ryan and asked, "Is that what you two are doing, gambling on me?"

"It's not a gamble. You have talent. You just don't know it." He leaned forward and gently kissed her. "Sorry I ran out on you this afternoon. But you paid me back by not showing tonight."

Lauren had wondered if he was going to mention it. In spite of his calm statement, she sensed he was angry. "I said I had other plans. I don't break dates."

"I'm glad you didn't sleep with him."

"How do you—" His kiss extinguished her reply.

Leave now before it's too late, common sense said. *Don't be crazy,* her heart clamored, *you want this.*

She wound her arms around his neck; instinctively her body melded against his. There was a dreamlike intimate quality to their kiss now. He unbuttoned the blouse she'd hastily put on before leaving her place, inching it down until it exposed the tops of her shoulders. Then he slid her bra straps off, leaving her shoulders bare.

He stopped and gazed at her with a suggestive smile that made her heart somersault. "Almost perfect." He quickly removed her hairpins, unraveling her high-fashion chignon, tossing the clips onto the rug. "Perfect."

He wove his fingers through her hair, close to her scalp, then clinched the loose strands in his strong fists. He pulled her face close to his, never loosening his hold on her hair, stopping just short of kissing her. For a moment, a surge of panic gripped her as she felt his hands in her hair. But the tender look in his deep-green eyes told her she had nothing to fear.

For a long moment, he gazed at her. She had the unsettling thought he was memorizing her face because it was the last time he would see her. Well, he was famous for his numerous, brief affairs. *That's all right. You couldn't handle him for more than a night, anyway. He's not your type.*

He continued to hold her, staring at her, his green eyes reflecting wavering spokes of gold from the fire.

"Ryan," she said to break the spell. "Downstairs, you said you had something for me. What is it?"

He smiled, the lopsided grin she'd come to expect before one of his off-color remarks. After releasing her hair and spreading it across her bare shoulders, he took her hand and kissed the center of her palm. Another cocky smile. "I have something for you, all right."

He guided her hand down to the V of his thighs, forcing her fingers closed over his erection.

13

"Ryan." Lauren twisted her lips away from his. She looked around the dark bedroom where he'd taken her.

"Mmmmmm?" He nuzzled her neck.

She hesitated to put her suspicion into words. After all, she'd overreacted earlier; maybe this was just her imagination, too. She tried to concentrate on being in bed with Ryan, enjoying his expert lovemaking, but she couldn't. The uneasiness wouldn't go away.

"Please"—she reached for his hand as he outlined the tip of her breasts with his fingers—"listen to me."

He stopped kissing her, but his hand kept roving, caressing her. "I'm listening . . . partner."

She lifted her head off the pillow, bringing herself up on her elbows. "I know this sounds silly but . . ." She looked around his bedroom, lit only by the light of the dying embers in the fireplace in the adjacent sitting room.

"What's the matter?"

"Is there any chance—any chance at all—that someone is watching us?"

A muscle flinched in his jaw; he was trying not to laugh. "T.J. is not watching us. I promise."

Crushing her to him, his mouth pressed against hers as his tongue eased between her parted lips. She wanted to kiss him, to feel that heady passion that had overwhelmed her in the other room as he'd slowly undressed her, caressing her with such mastery that she'd begged him to move into his bedroom. But she couldn't concentrate now. This wasn't her imagination. Someone was watching.

Ryan stopped kissing her and spread her hair across the pillow. "T.J. really spooked you, didn't he?"

"Yes, I guess he did. I can't shake the feeling someone's watching. It must be all the security gadgets around here. Any hidden cameras?" She tried to make it sound like a joke, but it didn't.

Ryan raised himself up on one elbow and peered around the room. Then he eased himself back down on the pillow and whispered in her ear. "It wasn't your imagination. Turn your head to the right."

He quickly switched on the bedside lamp. She saw Iggy hiding in the armchair next to the bed. She peeped over the upholstered arm; only her cocked ears and doe-brown eyes were visible. Iggy spotted them looking at her and nose-dived under the slacks Ryan had slung onto the chair when they'd gotten into bed.

"Beats anything she's ever seen." He turned off the light. "Can we get back to business?"

He kissed her slowly, his tongue gently parrying with hers, easing in and out, mimicking the churning rhythm of his hips against hers. All her doubts fled, eased by the passion radiating through her body.

The magnitude of Ryan's desire stunned him. Earlier, he'd teased her, seducing her slowly, deliberately arousing her, intending to make this special for her. But by the time he'd undressed her and had her in bed, he discovered waiting was impossible. When she'd stopped him, thinking someone was watching, he'd suffered a moment of uncertainty.

Now he was in control again. The ardor in her kisses and the way she offered herself to him reassured him. He eased his hand downward, across her slim hips to her legs twined with his. His fingers slipped between her soft thighs, cupping her. The dewy heat plunged him into a sensual tailspin.

He poised above her, then joined her body to his with one masterful thrust. She shuddered, digging her nails into his shoulders. Hurtled beyond the point of no return, he tangled his hands through her hair, his lips on hers. His body insistently stroked back and forth.

He wanted to slow down, to make this right for her, but he was beyond stopping. He thrust harder . . . deeper. Until he came in one powerful, white-hot explosion of pleasure.

He collapsed, exhausted, beside her on the pillow. *What the hell happened?* He hadn't gone off like that since he was thirteen. Some lover.

Lauren lay staring at the ceiling. No man had ever made love to her with such tenderness and passion. Everything he'd done, every place he'd touched her left her breathless, wanting more. By the time her breathing returned to normal, she realized Ryan hadn't moved or said a word. Had she done something wrong? Maybe she wasn't good enough, experienced enough. She waited, listening. The storm had passed, stalked by distant thunder, leaving behind a somnolent dripping from the eaves.

Lauren turned on her side, facing the armchair. The fire had died, making the room dark, but she could sense Iggy's presence. Lauren wanted to run and hide, but couldn't. The place was a prison; she wasn't going home until Ryan drove her. To hide her embarrassment, she snapped her fingers once, summoning Iggy.

With a squeal, Iggy was airborne, sailing across the small space. She belly flopped into Lauren's tummy. As the pot belly stumbled to her feet, her back hoof caught in the sheet and she fell, snout first, against Lauren's breasts. After Lauren freed her, Iggy pawed the mattress impatiently.

"I don't have any chocolate, I swear."

"You're on Iggy's pillow."

Without a word, Lauren surrendered the pillow. Iggy took it in her mouth and dragged it to the foot of the bed. She stomped on it a few times, flattening it, then collapsed on it, sighing.

"Here, you can share mine."

Too embarrassed to look at him, Lauren scooted onto his pillow. Should she suggest going home, or wait for him to make the first move?

"I'm better than that," he said quietly.

It took her a second to realize what he meant. He had to be joking, taunting her with his offbeat sense of humor. Or perhaps he wanted praise. That was it. The man's ego could consume London. She wasn't about to give him the satisfaction of telling him no one had ever made her feel so . . . so aroused.

He rolled onto his side and touched a wisp of her hair as it lay damp along her cheek. There was just enough light for her to see his eyes. He was serious. Completely serious. He didn't think she'd enjoyed it and he blamed himself. What did he usually do to top that performance? True, her experience was limited—she'd never indulged in casual sex—but still . . .

"It's your own fault, you know."

"What?" she gasped as his lips crowned one nipple.

He didn't bother to answer for a few seconds. Instead, he whorled his tongue around, sending a sensuous message. When he lifted his head, he whispered, "You were a tease. Admit it. From the first time I kissed you until this afternoon in the office, you've teased me. Any wonder I came so soon?"

"I didn't mean to, really, I didn't."

He wasn't listening. She watched the top of his head as he devoted his full attention to her breasts. She ran her fingers through his tousled hair. Then she moved beneath him, spreading her legs, a silent invitation.

"Stop. Don't rush it. This one's for you."

"It was wonderful the first time, honest."

He stopped, rolled onto his side, and regarded her solemnly. "Let's get one thing straight. I expect you to be honest. You didn't have an orgasm. Don't pretend you did."

She didn't deny it. Of course, she hadn't had an orgasm. She seldom had. Until Ryan, sex had been a part of the bargain she'd mentally made with first Ozzie and then Grant. In exchange for their company—hopefully their love—she'd allowed them to make love to her. She'd never really enjoyed it. Until tonight.

"Don't pretend I've satisfied you, when I haven't." He kissed her lightly. "Tell me what you like."

She had no idea how to respond. What did she like? Everything he did.

He slid his hand down her belly to the exposed mound of

downy hair, then caressed her with expert fingers. "Don't be a prude, Lauren. You know you like this. Say it."

"I like it." She moved her hips upward, showing him how much.

Ryan paused, reveling in her uninhibited response to him. The moistness of her aroused body and her undulating hips thrilled him. She wanted him. Every time he kissed her, she made that clear. So, she was inexperienced and couldn't talk about it. What the hell? Most women talked it to death.

In a mind-reeling kiss, Ryan's tongue eased back and forth imitating the motion of his hand. Erotic lightning arced through her, careening her pulse out of control. A shocking heat invaded her body, commanding her to languidly move her hips. Soon, a series of spasms trembled through her.

"Better?"

She smiled and snuggled up against him. Totally exhausted now, she wanted to fall asleep in his arms. "Yes."

His voice was low—a promise and a threat. "I'm not finished with you yet . . . partner."

"Hello?" Carlos Barzan's deep baritone came over the line to David as he sat in his London hotel room.

"I'm all set here."

"Westcott has taken the bait?"

"Absolutely," David assured him. "He just took Winthrop to meet T.J. Griffith. He tried to camouflage his voice by turning on the water. It didn't work. Those new bugs are the best. We caught every word." David couldn't help smiling. It had been his idea to buy the state-of-the-art technology from the CIA operatives seeking to make a few bucks on the side. "Right now, Lauren Winthrop is face to face with T.J. Griffith."

He didn't add that in ten minutes Tabatha Foley was due in his suite. Barzan didn't have to know everything. David had performed for his employer beyond anyone's expectations. Years ago, Barzan had sought a man competent in the emerging computer technology field. David had made certain Barzan never regretted his decision to hire him. Using computers and banks overseas, David had hidden the source of Barzan's assets, cleverly laundering funds in a series of financial gymnastics until Uncle Sam had no idea Carlos Barzan's empire was based on cocaine, not a multitude of international investments. While he was at it, David had siphoned off millions for himself, stashing the funds in a Swiss bank account.

"Do you have Griffith's phone number yet?"

"No," David reluctantly admitted, "but I will soon."

"Good. Call me when you're ready to strike. I want to be there. I have to do it in person, understand?"

"Yeah, yeah," David said. How many times did the old coot have to tell him? Barzan insisted upon killing Griffith himself. Carlos Barzan had an unrivaled passion for revenge. Over the years, Barzan had personally killed anyone who'd crossed him. But his obsession with Griffith exceeded Barzan's previous schemes.

"Be certain you're not followed when you're in London."

"Griffith isn't into counter-surveillance. He's fronting a rearguard effort. At best. He's protecting himself. That's all."

David heard Tabatha knocking on his door. At last. "Don't worry. I've got this under control."

"Anything else happening?"

"Winthrop's Cassatt prints are selling like crazy, and she's found some hotshot artist to exhibit. Ravissant will probably be out of the red before the end of the year."

Barzan rewarded him with a burst of sincere laughter—the first David had heard since Griffith killed Robert Barzan. "Just what we need—more money."

"The print scam is ready to go again. I would have flooded the market with phony Cassatts but I didn't find out about them in time. They're sure to run a series of prints after the exhibition. We'll bootleg those."

Barzan grunted his satisfaction. "Keep me posted. Remember, I'm ready to retire—if you get Griffith."

David hung up. Retire? It couldn't happen soon enough. With the United States government putting increased pressure on the Medellin cartel, Barzan's smaller, Bolivian-based operation had experienced an unexpected bonanza. Business they hadn't dreamed would come their way several years ago was now falling into their laps. Soon it would take an army of financial wizards and a phalanx of computers to launder the money.

David relished the challenge. While the Colombian drug

lords set up fiefdoms, living lavishly, taunting their government, he intended to follow Barzan's example. He would live in New York, conceal his source of income, and cultivate his reputation as a wealthy philanthropist. Then he could do exactly as he pleased. Behind closed doors.

Another loud knock interrupted his thoughts. David had spent his last night in London with Tabatha two weeks ago. He'd had a hard-on, waiting to get back to her ever since. A quick study, she'd instinctively known how to please him. As an added bonus, it had been shamefully easy to convince her to spy on Lauren Winthrop. Money parted thighs, loosened lips. Eased consciences.

He opened the door, and found Tabatha wearing a blonde wig.

"Hi," she said as casually as if she'd left him two minutes ago, not two weeks ago. She tossed her coat aside, revealing a youthful dress. Suggestive, but not revealing.

He walked over to the bed and lay down, his head propped up by a pillow. "Come here," he said, an order, not an invitation.

Fluffing her long blonde curls with her hand, she slowly walked up to him, seemingly innocent. His sister all over again, pretending while being the aggressor. Becoming increasingly assertive. Demanding.

"How have you been?" he asked, his prick ramrod straight, belying the gentle tone in his voice.

"Fine."

"How is the jewelry business?" he asked and she smiled. "Is Lauren painting?"

"Every night."

Fabulous. Everything was right on target.

She stood beside the bed; yanked off the cheap blonde wig he'd insisted she wear when visiting him. He needed to be careful. He didn't want Barzan to find out about his penchant for young girls. Barzan insisted everyone in his organization maintain complete respectability.

Tabatha slowly undid one button on her dress after another. It slowly opened, revealing more and more braless skin.

She hiked her skirt, exposing a wealth of dark pubic hair,

and straddled him, dangling her world-class knockers in his face. "Suck me."

Uncomfortably hard now, David did as he was told.

When Lauren realized the heartbeat throbbing beneath her head wasn't her own, she came fully awake but lay listening to Ryan's heart beating. Hypnotic. Seductive. She slowly opened her eyes. The hazy gray light of emerging dawn revealed her tumbled waves of hair spread across his chest and threaded between clumps of dark-brown hair that trailed down, disappearing beneath the sheet covering his hips. She stared at the masculine bulge, covered but hardly concealed, and blushed, remembering.

She hadn't really . . . had she? *Admit it. You enjoyed every minute.* She stared at his hand and the gold leopard ring grinned at her. Who would have believed Ryan Westcott would have such gentle hands? She felt her cheeks heat as she remembered all the places he'd put those hands. She hadn't been able to get enough.

Easing herself from his grip, Lauren slid out of bed. She smiled at Iggy who still slept on the pillow curled up very much like a cat. Somehow she'd managed to snooze through an entire night of sexual highjinks.

A glance at the window disclosed carbon-colored clouds sulking on the horizon. She tiptoed across the room, following a trail of discarded clothes, gathering her things as she went. By the time she'd covered the sitting room, she discovered her bra was missing. A lacy creation from Janet Reger's pricey lingerie shop, the peach demi-bra matched her panties. She hated to lose it. Hadn't Ryan tossed it on the floor by the sofa? She would have sworn he had.

She went into the bathroom, quietly closing the door behind her, and turned on the shower. Inside the stall, she found an oatmeal-colored bar of soap that smelled faintly like horse leather. As the water ran over her, the shocking realization of what she'd done hit her.

Why Ryan Westcott—of all the men on earth? He wasn't the kind of man she needed. What made a great night didn't make a good marriage. And that's what she wanted—a happy marriage. And children. Wedding bells with Ryan Westcott?

Definitely not. Even if he were a domesticated male—which he obviously wasn't—he wouldn't make a good father. Unless she fancied kids with four-letter-word vocabularies.

She washed herself, thinking about sexual addiction. *Cosmo* had been full of it back home. She'd laughed, believing it was nothing more than a gimmick to sell magazines. Now she wasn't so sure. It had happened to Vora. If she didn't get rid of Ryan Westcott, it could happen to her.

End it right now. Tell Ryan you won't see him again. She fortified herself by remembering the big-boobed, blonde bimbos Ryan was famous for loving—then leaving. Don't join their ranks.

Toweling off, she heard the telephone ring and Ryan's sleepy hello. A stab of primitive longing swept through her. What was wrong with her? *He's not your type. Remember that.*

She rifled through the bathroom drawers, astounded to find the man didn't own a blow-dryer or a brush, just a comb with several missing teeth. She was toweling her hair dry when Ryan burst into the bathroom without knocking.

Swaggering in naked, he said, "Round four."

He was actually counting, like a gunslinger notching his holster.

"Just kidding, partner." He sauntered over to the toilet and lifted the lid.

Mortified, Lauren turned her back and scrambled into her clothes, blushing and struggling to ignore the sounds coming from the opposite side of the bathroom. The man she intended to marry wouldn't violate her privacy. When she'd been married to Ozzie, they'd had separate bedrooms. Grant Fraser never let her see him naked, maybe because he had a paunch, but it didn't matter. Ryan Westcott was a crude man. Definitely not her type.

"I have to leave town for a while," Ryan said as he washed his hands. He caught her eye in the mirror. "What's the matter? Don't be upset. I'll be back soon."

Did his body have to be so perfect? His masculine frame ridged with muscle and long, powerful legs kindled an instinctive response, a yearning ache, that she was powerless to prevent.

He beamed at her—the warmest, most engaging smile she'd ever seen him give. Except when he'd mentioned his mother. His smile almost triggered an answering smile, but she banked it with a firm reminder. Every woman was entitled to one reckless night. One.

She ran his miserable comb through her hair, affecting a carefree voice. "It was fun, but it's over."

His response was an insolent grin.

"I'm serious. Last night was a mistake. Let's keep our relationship professional." She started for the door, but he caught her arm and spun her around to face him.

"You're so full of shit your eyes are turning brown. You wanted it as much as I did. We can't pretend it didn't happen."

"Let's behave like adults. I'm not seeing you again except professionally."

"I don't have time for this crap. I've got a major problem with T.J.'s company. I have to leave for the continent this morning. Be honest. Why don't you want to see me again?"

Because I'll fall in love with you. "Because you're too crude. I can't carry on a decent conversation with you. All you do is swear."

"That's a bunch of shit and you know it. What's the real reason?"

She gazed at his gentle hands, resting on his hips as he stared her down. "You remind me too much of Rupert Armstrong."

$\mathcal{M}$IDNIGHT

When you really want love,
you will find it waiting for you.
Oscar Wilde

14

The sun hadn't yet climbed over the Atlas Mountains, dominated by snow-clad Djebel Toubkal, when the alarm sounded. Ryan awakened slowly, still exhausted by three days of traveling incognito from London to Marrakesh. The ten-hour drive awaiting him demanded he start now. After dressing in traditional robes, he grabbed a wool burnoose and hurried down to the Rover. He checked the fuel and double-checked the petrol cans lashed to the side. The road to Ouarzazate was no place to become stranded.

He signaled to the guard to open the gate in the ten-foot-high wall surrounding the compound. The Rhodesian ridgebacks, under a stay command, watched the Rover choke to a start then rumble down the street beyond their territory. Rooster tails of red dust streamed out from the tires as the car sped down the road.

Dry, translucent air enhanced dawn's first light, a pale pink that brushed the rooftops then, deepening into mauve, spotlit the cupola of the Koutoubia Mosque. An orchestra tuning up for the morning sun, birds burst in song from bamboo thickets and waterfalls of bougainvillaea, welcoming the new day. In minutes, it would officially be dawn and the *muezzin* would begin his singsong chant calling Allah's faithful to morning prayers.

As the legions of date palms swayed in the breeze, their fronds whispering, Ryan left the groves behind, racing south on P31 across the *bled*, the rich red alluvial soil of the plain surrounding Marrakesh on all sides. The road edged its way upward along the skirt of hills that soon became the Atlas Mountains. He negotiated an unending series of switchback turns that would carry him to the summit.

As he drove, he struggled to keep his mind on the road's lethal curves. He couldn't. Lauren Winthrop's face kept blinding his vision. Her behavior when she'd met T.J.—almost panicking—assured even the skeptical Peter Stirling that she wasn't in cahoots with Barzan. Still, the way she'd treated Ryan proved she was a bitch. Just like her mother.

Had he fallen for Lauren just as T.J. had for Caroline Armstrong? No, buddy, this isn't the same. Not at all. Caroline had strung T.J. along, promising to leave her husband. She would have kept on seeing T.J. forever if he hadn't forced her to choose. Lauren had been satisfied with one night in the sack before she'd tossed him aside. And she hadn't bothered to let him down easily. No. She had to tell him that he reminded her of Rupert Armstrong.

Jesus! She'd punched his hot button with that one. Armstrong had to be the biggest prick he'd ever met. He even topped Buck Westcott. Not only was Rupert a mean sonofabitch, he was worse than a common criminal. But few people knew the whole truth. To most he was a wealthy exporter with a flair for gracious living and a wife whose beauty was legendary. *The* Caroline Armstrong.

What the hell made Lauren think he was one bit like Armstrong? He didn't get it. Probably never would. After Lauren had cold-cocked him with her statement, he'd stormed out and told Adi to take her home.

To hell with her. She was nothing special in bed—that was for sure. Inexperienced as hell. Definitely not his type. Then why couldn't he forget her? Was this how it had been for T.J.?

Ryan stared at the crimson sphere edging its way up from the Sahara desert, flooding the new day with heat and light. But he didn't see the serpentine road or the Moroccan sun. Instead he pictured himself on that early morning—years ago—as he'd come home to Los Angeles from Vietnam.

* * *

Ryan walked down the jet-way into a mob of anti-war protesters brandishing placards: GET OUT OF VIETNAM. STOP THE BOMBING. NO MORE NAPALM.

"Killers! Murderers!" chanted the mob.

Several of the GIs walked together, closing ranks against the outside world. Not Ryan. He strode out ahead of them, his eyes eagerly scanning the crowd for his mother. Hadn't she gotten his telegram? Didn't she know how much he'd missed her?

As he pushed his way through the jeering mob, a girl wearing hip-hugger bell-bottoms and garlands of love beads stepped in front of him. Her board-straight hair hung in dirty hanks to her waist.

"Killer!" She spit on him, landing a glob on his cheek.

He raised his hand, set to slap her across the terminal, but stopped himself, wiping his face with back of his hand instead. *Don't be a fool. That's exactly what they want you to do.* Jesus! What had the world come to?

Did the dumbasses think the soldiers had any control over what was happening in Vietnam? Uncle Sam drafted—you went. No choice in the matter. Unless, of course, you were a rich kid with a student deferment. Then you could stay home and protest while someone else went through hell for you. What had happened to the Home of the Brave? A pack of dickless wonders had handed it—and their balls—over to a bunch of women who'd burned their bras.

Ignoring the taunts, his eyes skimmed across the terminal, searching for a short woman with curly brown hair and loving eyes. *Come on, Ma, where are you?*

Ryan made his way to the baggage-claim area and waited for his Army issue duffel, trying to ignore the happy soldiers with their girlfriends draped around their necks and their beaming parents at their sides. He claimed his bag and caught a bus that let him off within sight of the ocean.

After hoisting the duffel over his shoulder, he walked through Venice's streets. Named for some fancy place in Italy, the beachside suburb where he'd lived his entire life sounded glamorous. What a crock. The only time water filled the canals was after a rain, which happened two, maybe three times a

year. The rest of the time, people used the canals as giant
garbage cans.

He passed row after row of clapboard bungalows with yards
the size of his duffel bag and cars parked on the weed-choked
lawns. When he came to Sycamore Street, he didn't look
down it to check out Sherry Brinkley's house. The bitch.
When he'd been home on leave, he'd gone to see his former
girlfriend. She'd stammered and blushed, tossing her blonde
hair from side to side, apologizing for not answering any of his
letters. Didn't he know she was in college now? She'd been
too busy.

Then she'd told him she was in love with an SAE. Ryan had
pretended not to see the knowing smile on her mother's face
as she stood in the kitchen listening. What the hell was an
SAE? He racked his brains, reviewing the initials he knew all
too well. DMZ, VC, NLF, GI. The worst—MIA. The best—R
and R. No SAE.

Turned out to be a college fraternity—draft dodgers. He'd
asked her if the SAE cared that she'd lost her virginity to a GI.
Sherry's mother had come screaming out of the kitchen,
wielding a spatula. He'd left with her yelling at him saying he
was no good and wouldn't amount to anything.

As Ryan rounded the corner and came onto his block, he
wondered if that was true. Didn't a Silver Star count for anything? Not anymore. Once he'd thought he was hot shit. That
had been in high school when he'd been the star on the football team with every chick in school including Miss SAE crawling all over him. Then Stanford had offered him an athletic
scholarship, and he'd been on top of the world.

He hadn't counted on 'Nam. When his draft notice had
come the summer before he was going to college, he'd expected to talk his way out of it. The rich kids in Beverly Hills
and Brentwood always did. No luck. His draft board, number
101, covered the ritzy West Los Angeles area where highfalutin' lawyers had already gotten too many rich brats defer-
ments. The hard asses had a quota to fill. The next thing he
knew he was in boot camp.

You're okay, buddy, he told himself. You made it out of
'Nam, didn't you? You've got some money saved. You could

still go to college. But after the protesters in the airport and memories of Miss SAE, he wasn't sure what he wanted to do.

Ahead he could see the yellow stucco house where he lived; he picked up his pace. The paint was peeling. What else was new? Buck Westcott spent the time he wasn't working on the assembly line at McDonnell Douglas drinking at Joe Mama's Tavern and jaw-jacking with his buddies. Not only was his father a lazy cuss, but he was a mean drunk.

Buck would tie one on and slap his wife around. He'd sent her to the hospital once. For as long as Ryan could remember Buck had come after him with his fists when he was drunk and with a vicious tongue when he was sober. The summer Ryan had turned fourteen, he'd put a stop to the beatings. He'd always been big for his age, but then he'd started to fill out. Every day Ryan had worked out with the team, getting ready for football season. When Buck slapped his mother—for not guessing when he would come home from Joe Mama's and not having his dinner ready—Ryan had gone after him. He'd landed a half-dozen choice punches before Buck had kicked the shit out of him. But he'd gotten the message: Ryan had grown up and soon the day would come when he wouldn't be able to lick him. Buck never hit either one of them again. But he'd found other ways of tormenting them.

The minute Ryan had taken a job after school to earn money for college, Buck had stopped giving Mary household money, saying it was Ryan's turn. Household expenses had taken all he made, leaving little to buy their clothes. Whenever Ryan took a girl out it meant he and his mother ate macaroni and cheese for a week. And Ryan was continually embarrassed because Buck never let him use the car.

Ryan bounded up the steps of his house and jerked open the screen door. It creaked shut behind him—same as always. But inside everything was different. Ma had rearranged the furniture and bought new curtains. He took a second look. Yards and yards of hot-pink dotted Swiss covered the windows. Definitely not his mother's usual style. The picture of Ryan in his cap and gown holding a Scholastic Excellence certificate was missing from the top of the television.

His sixth sense kicked in, warning him as it had on numerous missions, saving his butt more than once. Earning him a

Silver Star. He moved silently, as if through jungle loaded
with VC, across the tiny living room into the kitchen where he
heard a radio blaring "You're So Vain." Edging his head
around the doorjamb, he saw a middle-aged woman in hot
pants with her legs up on his mother's kitchen table painting
her toenails shocking pink.

"Who the hell are you?"

She shrieked, jerking her feet to the floor and dropping the
bottle of Cutex, sending it skidding across the yellowed lino-
leum leaving a trail of hot pink. Standing now, she stared at
him, her hand over her mouth, which was painted the same
shade of pink.

Not one of Ma's friends. None of them would wear bright
pink short-shorts that revealed flabby thunder thighs, or a
halter top harnessing humungous breasts that sagged to her
waist. Her flamingo-blonde hair had been ratted into a bee-
hive and preserved for eternity by Spray Net.

"Where's my mother?"

"Well, sugar, you must be Ryan." She flitted a set of mas-
cara-embalmed eyelashes at him.

"Who are you?"

"Lulu. I can see Buck didn't tell you."

His throat tightened with the metallic taste of fear—like
knowing the VC had you in their sights. "Tell me what?"

She pulled out a dinette chair, saying, "Sit down, sugar."

He grabbed the broad by her skinny throat. "Tell me!"

"L-let g-go first," she croaked, tears filling her eyes.

He released her. She was scared spitless—too damn bad.

"Your mother is dead."

"Liar! I just had a letter from her—" How long had it been?

"Look, sugar. I'm sorry." She clawed at a tear with a vibrant
pink nail, deftly removing the droplet without disturbing her
pancake makeup.

Ryan collapsed into the chair. No force on earth could have
kept Ma from coming to meet him. "When? How?"

Lulu pulled out a chair and looked at him, genuine sympa-
thy in her eyes. "Seven weeks this Saturday." She reached out
and touched his hand with hers, running her phony nails
across his knuckles. "A blood vessel busted in her brain. She
went quick. She never knew what hit her."

A hollow, lifeless feeling sapped his body of its energy. Thank God, he thought. Thank God, he'd told his mother he loved her. All through the years she'd repeatedly told him she loved him. But he'd never said it, thinking if she really loved him she'd leave that sonofabitch, his father. When she'd said good-bye, sending Ryan back to 'Nam after his leave, he'd finally told her how much he loved her. He said it not because she deserved to hear it—had always deserved to hear it—but because he thought *he* might die. Not her.

"Where? Where did it happen?"

"She went in her sleep, sugar. One of the neighbors found her in the morning."

"Not Buck? Where was he? Joe Mama's?"

Lulu's lower lip curled outward in a neon-pink pout.

He slammed his fist on the table. "Where was he?"

"With me. At my apartment. Bucky filed for divorce."

"Liar! My mother would have written—" No. Ma wouldn't have. She would never have wanted Ryan worrying about her when his life was at stake.

"We moved in here after she passed on to her great reward. After all, Bucky owns the house."

Bucky? Ryan stared at the woman, the opposite of his mother. Mary Bailey Westcott had been a proper English lady who'd worn hats and gloves. Even drank tea. The kind of woman that would make any man proud. Not good old "Bucky." After making her life miserable for years, forcing her to slave over a sewing machine, mending other people's clothes while he hung out at Joe Mama's, good old "Bucky" had left her.

Had she been able to make ends meet during those last months? It must have been difficult. She'd never made much doing alterations. Ma had wanted to open her own shop, but Buck wouldn't hear of it. No wife of his was working outside the home.

"Where's she buried?"

"At Heaven's Gate . . . somewhere." Lulu smiled, revealing a dentist's nightmare. "I gave her things to charity except that old hatbox with her letters in it. 'Course your things are still in your room. Bucky didn't want to throw them out until he talked to you."

Ryan stood up.

"Where ya goin', sugar? Set a spell. Have a Coors."

He shook his head. "I'm going to the cemetery."

It took hours—you were lost in LA without wheels—to get to Heaven's Gate and find his mother's grave among the inexpensive plots facing the freeway and its ever-present hum of traffic. He looked at the grass with the faint rectangular line marking the spot where the turf had been lifted to lower the coffin into the ground. Cheap sonofabitch. Buck had only paid for a plain marker. Ma was probably buried in a cardboard box.

She deserved better.

Ryan trudged down the hill and went into the mortuary's office. He ordered a marble tombstone with an epitaph chiseled in Old English script: Forever in my heart.

Then he took a bouquet of wildflowers, her favorites, to the gravesite and placed them on the ground. He sat down beside her. "I made it, Ma. I'm still alive. You'd be proud of me."

As he ran his fingers through the grass, it occurred to him that she'd already been dead when he'd led the charge up Hill 666—The Devil's Hill. He'd fought like a sonofabitch, rescuing seven buddies and a green lieutenant trapped by the VC, earning a Silver Star. While he'd been struggling to keep his men alive without being killed himself, there hadn't been one person on this earth who cared if he lived or died. Not one.

With his fingers, he dug a hole in the grass, carefully lifting a small square like a lid. He buried the Silver Star in the soil and replaced the grass on top.

He stayed until the sun set over Santa Monica Bay and the guard came to tell him he was locking the gates in ten minutes. Weary from the long flight, Ryan returned home to get his things. No way was he spending the night under the same roof with the hot-pink whore. No way.

The house was dark and empty after he'd finally found a westbound bus and returned to Venice. Ryan changed into his worn Converse tennies and Levis, then rifled through his belongings, deciding what to keep. On the top shelf of his closet Lulu Hot Pants had put his mother's old Harrods hatbox. It contained a green hat that looked like something uprooted from a cabbage patch. He'd never seen his mother wear the crazy thing. But it had always been in the top of her closet in the hatbox where she saved the yearly Christmas letter sent by her best friend in London.

He picked it up, playing with the forties-style veil, wondering why his mother kept the hat. Treasured it. But never wore it. Then he felt something stiff under the lining. He peeled back the felt and discovered a picture. Immediately, he recognized his mother as one of the two women in the black-and-white photo. Happier than he'd ever seen her, she was smiling at a strikingly handsome man in an RAF bomber jacket.

Ryan's eyes were riveted by the second man, standing beside his mother, but with his arm around another woman. A dead ringer for himself! His Uncle Garth. Ma always said he was the image of her brother who'd been killed when the Nazis had shot his plane down over the English Channel. Why hadn't she shown Ryan this picture?

He'd stared at his uncle for a minute before he realized why she'd kept the photo hidden. Buck would have gone nuts, seeing her with another man. Her adoration was obvious as she looked at the tall man, her face radiantly happy. So, Ma once loved someone else. Good for her. Why had she married Buck? He'd been stationed in England after the war and had met his mother. The man she'd loved must have died in the war.

A drunken laugh followed by a fit of giggles heralded Buck Westcott's return. Ryan went into the living room.

"Lulu told me you'd come back."

Buck Westcott hadn't changed a bit: short, bald, with a belly that slopped over his belt buckle. Just Lulu Hot Pants's type.

"You're a cheap sonofabitch, you know. I bought Ma—"

"Don't start on me, boy." His words were slurred. "I paid for the funeral. I didn't have ta do nothin'."

"Why, you—" Ryan bolted across the small room.

"No," screamed Lulu. "Don't hurt him."

"Don't you touch me, boy. You owe me."

"Owe you? That's a joke."

Buck looked at Lulu, then at Ryan, then at Lulu again.

"Tell him, Bucky, tell him. Get rid of him. He scares the daylights out of me."

"Tell me what?" Ryan stepped forward.

"Stop," wailed Lulu, "or I'm callin' the police."

"Get away from me." Sweat had broken out across Buck's forehead; he swiped at it with the back of his pudgy forearm. "I took pity on you, boy. I gave you a name."

"What's that supposed to mean?"

"I promised Mary I wouldn't tell you. But she's gone and I ain't putting up with your shit no more. You're not my son. Your mother was knocked up when I married her. She promised to have my son. What'd I get, boy? Nothin' but you."

Ryan stood paralyzed just as he'd been the first time he'd looked down the barrel of his M-16 and realized if he pulled the trigger a man would die. It made sense. Buck had always hated him, never attending any of his games, never taking any pride in Ryan's superior grades. He'd pretended he hadn't cared, telling himself that his mother loved him. But it had hurt—as much as Buck Westcott's fists—when the other boys had asked where his father was and he'd made excuses.

Finally Ryan was able to ask, "Who is my father?"

"She refused to tell me."

15

A light drizzle was falling in London when Ryan arrived from Los Angeles. He hailed a taxi and gave the driver the east London address. Tillie Clary had written Ma each Christmas for twenty years from the same address. But with his luck she'd have moved this year.

The taxi came to a halt in front of a crumbling brick building. The windows on the lower floor had been boarded shut, but the pack of kids stampeding up and down the steps indicated the place was still occupied.

"Any of you know which apartment is Tillie Clary's?" Ryan asked after he'd paid the driver.

"This way." A young boy led him into the unlit building.

Cabbage. Jesus, in England they actually ate the stuff. He tried not to breathe too deeply as he walked up a flight of stairs to meet the widow who'd been his mother's closest friend. Surely, she could tell him about his father.

Upstairs, the kid stopped in front of a door at the far end of the corridor. "This is it." He stuck out his hand, palm up.

Ryan fished in his pocket and brought out a dollar bill.

"Don't you have any real money?"

He gave the boy five pence.

"Gee, thanks. Thanks a lot."

"Yes?" came the muffled response to Ryan's knock.

"It's Ryan Westcott, Mary Bailey's son."

"Mary's boy?"

The door swung open revealing a stout woman with chestnut-brown eyes and hair several shades darker. She wore a faded print dress and clodhoppers with nylons rolled down around her ankles like miniature inner tubes. She couldn't be more than forty-five, but she looked sixty.

Tillie Clary took one look at him, her eyes wide with astonishment. "No. It can't be."

Ryan reached into his jacket pocket and brought out the picture. As he started to hand it to her, he saw she was crying, silent sobs vibrating her stout frame.

"M-my stars," she sobbed. "I can't believe it. I just can't believe it." She drew a threadbare hankie from between her breasts and dabbed at her nose. "You look just like him."

"I know. My mother told me that I look just like her brother." He guided Tillie over to a sofa with a crocheted cover on it that didn't quite hide the patches beneath. He eased her down, sitting beside her, hoping the contraption could support them both.

Tillie smiled at him with the same loving smile he'd seen so often on his mother's face. "You're even better looking than Garth was. And he was something. You look just like your uncle—except for the eyes." She wadded her handkerchief into a moist ball. "Did your mother tell you Garth and I planned to be married?"

"Ma told me."

"How is your mother?"

He took her hand. "Ma died almost two months ago. A blood vessel in her brain broke. She died instantly."

"No. So young." Tears again welled up, seeping out of the corners of her eyes and trickling down the sides of her nose.

He showed her the picture, hoping to distract her. He hated it when women cried; he never knew what to say. "Here's a picture of my mother and Uncle Garth."

She gazed at it a moment, tears still bordering her eyes. "My stars, look at me. Doesn't that beat all?"

Ryan did a silent double take. It definitely beat all. He would never have recognized Tillie Clary. She'd been blonde then and slim.

"Wasn't your mother pretty? Look at that hat. I remember going with her to buy it. She tried on every hat at Harrods—she didn't care what they cost—to get the right one to please . . ."

He waited, alerted by the look on Tillie's face. "Who'd she want to please?"

Tillie pointed to the man in the RAF bomber jacket. "Your father, Throckmorton Jaymes Griffith." She looked at Ryan, obviously surprised by the expression on his face. "My stars, didn't your mother tell you?"

"She never told me who my real father was. That's why I'm here. I want to find my family, my grandparents . . . my cousins."

"There isn't any family that I know of. T.J.—that's what everyone called your father—was raised in an orphanage." She smiled wistfully. "Garth and T.J. were in the RAF together. That's how Mary met him. They were heroes, not just to us but to the entire country."

A bittersweet current warmed Ryan's heart. That's where he'd gotten his courage—from his father and his uncle, not from that sonofabitch Buck Westcott. If only he could have known them, they would have understood what he'd been through in Vietnam.

"Every time Garth and T.J. went on a mission, Mary and I prayed that it wouldn't be the last time we saw them. One day our prayers weren't answered."

"They were both killed on the same mission?"

"Garth died. Your father was shot down I don't know how many times, but he always made it back. T.J. was too feisty to let the Nazis get him. He's still alive and living like royalty right here in London."

"He didn't want to marry my mother?" The idea astonished Ryan. His mother was pretty, a lady. What more could a man want?

"No. He flat refused. Mary had no choice but to marry Buck Westcott. Or get rid of you."

"If she had to do it all over again, she probably would have had an abortion. Buck made her life hell."

"Don't say that." Tillie brought herself to her feet. "She sent me a letter just last Christmas. It was all about you and

what a joy you'd been." She rummaged through a drawer. "It
was strange, though. After all these years, this was the first
time she'd ever mentioned T.J." Tillie handed Ryan a letter.

He slowly read the pages filled with how proud she was of
her son and how brave he was to be fighting for his country.
She expressed her fear that he might be killed. The last para-
graph was devoted to Tillie, who'd evidently written to his
mother after her husband's death, saying even though he'd
been a good man, she had never stopped loving Garth.

> I know what you mean, Tillie dear. You and Garth would
> have been happy together had God not taken him. And I
> can understand how, after all these years with another man,
> you still long for Garth. I confess I've never stopped loving
> T.J. At times, when I'm alone, I cry for what might have
> been had he wanted my love. I've forgiven him. I love him
> still. I always will. He gave me the greatest joy of my life, my
> son. God love him for that.

Ryan found Griffith's place in Hampstead Heath. The bastard wasn't home.

"Whom shall I say called?" The man who answered the door
looked at Ryan as if he'd opened a body-bag in 'Nam and had
taken a whiff.

"A long-lost relative."

"I wasn't aware that Master Griffith had any"—he looked at
Ryan's worn jeans and shabby windbreaker—"relatives. You
may wish to call again tomorrow. Master Griffith will be playing at Crockford's until late."

Once celebrated for its grasslands where bawdy fairs and
cattle markets were held, Mayfair now sported the most glamorous casinos in the world. Within the walls of these palatial
establishments—the Aspinall, the Ritz, the Clermont, and
Crockfords—high rollers gambled, wagering more per person
in these clubs than anywhere else in the world.

The centerpiece of these casinos royale, Crockfords, was
the legacy of William Crockford. Born the son of a fishmonger,
he'd developed modern-day gambling early in the nineteenth
century. So popular were his numerous clubs that Crockford

separated many of the aristocracy from a substantial portion of their inheritances and retired a fabulously wealthy man. Over the next hundred years, gaming clubs came and went until after the Second World War when the most exclusive establishments settled into one square mile of the Mayfair district.

Morton Fields had been the doorman at Crockfords since he'd returned from the war. No other club had a better doorman, and he knew it. Morton stood watch, greeting members with the respect their wealth demanded. Most who entered the Georgian door with its classic fanlight were regular members. A privileged few were not.

According to British law, first-time gamblers had to fill out a formal application and wait forty-eight hours for their membership to be approved. This supposedly prevented impulse gambling by visitors who might later regret their actions. While other less prestigious establishments found themselves processing applications constantly, Morton seldom saw more than a few new applicants a month. The exorbitant membership fee and the astronomical table stakes kept undesirables at bay. Those few punters who did apply generally accompanied members. If not, they had been recommended by casinos in Monte Carlo or the Bahamas.

As Morton stood under the portico supported by Doric columns painted gloss white, he didn't dream the hulking youth swaggering up Curzon Street was headed for his club. Morton adjusted his top hat and smoothed a nonexistent wrinkle from his frock coat. A frisson of alarm shot through him when the young hooligan stopped and looked at the club's gold-plated plaque mounted on the pillar.

There hadn't been any trouble at Crockfords during Morton's tenure except for two Italians—what did you expect—who got into a punch-up over a misplaced bet. He took three steps back, clasped his white-gloved hands behind his back, and hoped the misfit would disappear.

Ryan studied the joint. Didn't look like a casino. But who was he to say? His knowledge of England came from his mother's tales of the war and classics he'd read in school, like *A Christmas Carol* and *Tom Jones*. So far, London was greener, wetter, and older than he'd ever imagined. But the same hippies they had at home clogged the streets here, wearing long, straight hair and playing Beatles' songs on their transistor radios. London also had more than its share of old men dressed in clothes from Dickens novels, like the man at Griffith's and the guy guarding this club's door, looking down his beak at him.

Ryan bounded up the steps, two at a time, and stopped beside the doorman. "I'm looking for T.J. Griffith."

"It's club policy not to disturb any of the members," Morton said, but the youth shoved past him. "Now see here. You can't go in there."

Inside it was so quiet Ryan thought he'd stepped into a mortuary. But when he entered the main room, throngs of men were crowded around roulette wheels and gaming tables. Dressed for a wedding, most gamblers wore tuxedos. A few Arabs, dressed in long white robes, hovered around one table.

Ryan's eyes skipped around the room past the hunt scenes hung on the walls, up to the two golden American eagles perched above one window, over the sexy bodies of the female dealers, across the nameless faces—mostly male—until he found the one man fitting the description Tillie had given him from a recent photo she'd seen in *The Times*.

Beyond the softly lit main room an archway led to a smaller room. There he saw a tall man with silver-gray hair. Ryan walked past the curious gamblers casting dubious looks at his Levi's. In the smaller room where Griffith was playing, the stacks of chips on the roulette table were much larger. High rollers. Griffith's luck had just run out.

Ryan paused in the arched doorway, staring at the man with his back toward him. The set of his shoulders and the way his head was cocked to one side as he watched the wheel and the ivory ball hop from black to red to black to red suggested confidence.

"Griffith!" Ryan's voice cracked through the silent room like a round from an M-16.

Griffith turned. "Garth? It can't be!"

Ryan charged across the short distance and came face to face with his father. The eyes staring at him from the handsome face were the same ones Ryan had seen in the mirror his entire life. He slammed a fist into Griffith's stomach, then caught his chin in a brutal upper cut. Griffith sagged against the table for a second, giving Ryan time to land still another punch. The punishing blow rammed his nose and blood splattered across the felt table.

Griffith hammered Ryan with two surprisingly strong punches. But Ryan's skills had been honed by the necessity to survive, and the blows did little but make him angrier. Ryan knocked Griffith to the ground, then straddled him, delighting in the fear he saw in Griffith's eyes. He grabbed the bastard's throat, squeezing.

"Who are you?" Griffith asked between gasps for air. Twin streams of blood gushed from his nose, flowing down his chin onto Ryan's hands.

He didn't have anything to say to the prick, so he just kept choking, intending to stop just short of killing him. But Griffith didn't know that. A whap on his back jolted Ryan; he looked over his shoulder.

A bobby stood, brandishing a billy club. "Awfully sorry. Couldn't we take this unpleasantness outside?"

Since the bobby was reinforced by a dozen officers, Ryan didn't argue. He clutched Griffith's throat and gave it one last choke. Ryan stood up while the doorman scurried to give Griffith a handkerchief to stop the bleeding. As Griffith pressed the linen square to his nose, a gold pinkie ring with a leopard's head glistened on his broad finger.

"Fuck you." Ryan flipped him off with a raised middle finger and sauntered out of the casino, ignoring the shocked stares. As he passed a cute blonde dealer he hadn't noticed earlier, he winked at her.

Under the watchful eyes of the bobbies, Ryan cooled his heels on the porch until Griffith appeared, his nose no longer bleeding.

"Sir," said the bobby who'd stopped the fight, "you'll need to come with us to press charges."

Griffith gazed at Ryan. "That won't be necessary if he agrees not to touch me."

A squadron of domed hats emblazoned with silver shields swung toward Ryan. Curious eyes studied him.

Ryan had no intention of killing Griffith. He'd had enough

of killing in 'Nam. Hitting Griffith had vented his anger. Now a hollow ache reminded Ryan that this trip had been nothing more than a wild-goose chase. On the flight over, he'd dreamed about finding his family and having them welcome him with loving arms. Fairy tales.

"I won't hit him again."

The bobbies trooped down the stairs and piled into the white squad cars with horizontal blue stripes. Ryan followed them down the steps.

"Wait." Griffith trailed behind him at a safe distance. "You're Mary Bailey's son, aren't you?"

Ryan didn't answer.

"Why are you angry with me? I was your Uncle Garth's best friend. And Mary—" Griffith paused. "—Where is Mary?"

"She's dead—an aneurysm in her brain."

Griffith's handsome forehead corrugated into a frown; his eyes were no longer lively but sad. "That's terrible. I'm sorry." Griffith touched his arm. Their gazes locked; matched pairs of green eyes stared at each other. "You're my son, aren't you?"

Ryan turned away, having nothing more to say to Griffith. But he followed Ryan, easily keeping pace with his angry strides. As they walked, Ryan realized that he'd inherited more than Griffith's green eyes. They were both several inches over six feet with long legs and powerful frames. But that's where the resemblance ended. T.J. Griffith was strikingly handsome while Ryan was a dead-ringer for his uncle—thank God.

"Mary never told me that she had the baby." When Ryan didn't respond, Griffith said, "Listen, son—"

Ryan stopped dead in his tracks. "Don't you dare call me son. I'm Mary's son, not yours." He shoved back his jacket sleeve and showed Griffith his forearm. A patch of taut brown skin stood out. "Four years old. Not old enough to know toasters can burn. Buck found me playing with the toaster. Where were you when he made sure I learned toasters can burn? Where were you when Buck locked me in the toolshed for two days because I'd torn my pants sliding into home plate? When I needed someone to help me stop Buck from slapping Ma?" He started walking again. "I'll tell you where you were.

Over here, gambling with a bunch of candy asses. I'm not your son. I never will be."

Griffith stopped beside a sleek red Ferrari. "You've made your point. Now listen to me."

Ryan paused, his eyes on the car. Every man's dream. Definitely his. "You've got one second. Spit it out."

"Do you have any brothers or sisters?" When Ryan shook his head, Griffith continued, "Then, like it or not, I'm all the family you have."

"I don't give a damn."

"What would your mother have said? Would she want you to come all this way and not at least talk to me?"

Ryan decided talking to him couldn't hurt. This would be the only time he would ever see the bastard.

Griffith tossed him a set of keys. "You drive."

Momentarily speechless, Ryan stared at keys with the prancing horse logo on them. A Ferrari. Griffith owned that bitchin' red Ferrari. Ryan climbed into the low-slung sports car and gripped the wheel as if he drove Ferraris every day. Nothing could have been further from the truth. In high school he'd occasionally driven friends' cars, all old clunkers. In 'Nam, he'd driven the company jeep whenever he'd gotten the chance.

"Where are we going?" Ryan asked after he'd turned on the ignition and the Ferrari purred to life.

"Where are you staying?"

"Nowhere. My things are in a locker at Heathrow."

"My place then. Go right on Audley."

By the time Ryan had crossed Oxford Street, he'd fallen in love with the Ferrari. When he made some real money, he'd reward himself with a great car. He reminded himself not to let the sports car distract him. He turned toward Griffith and found him studying him. "I thought you wanted to talk?"

"Don't you think you should tell me your name?"

"Ryan Bailey Westcott."

"Ryan?" he said as if wondering if the name fit him. "You must have recently discovered that I'm your father."

"Yeah. When Ma died, Buck told me."

"I never knew you existed. If I'd only known—"

"What would you have done?" Ryan kept both hands on the

wheel, not trusting himself to keep from hitting Griffith. "You refused to marry her."

"To be honest, I never loved your mother, but I would have married her if I'd known she'd had my child."

"If you didn't love her, why did you knock her up?"

"It was an accident."

"Bullshit! You would have used a safe. Even when I was in 'Nam and spent time with whores, I made certain to use a rubber. I can sleep at night without worrying that my kid is going to bed hungry or crying."

"You were in Vietnam?" He gestured, indicating Ryan should go right. "Were you decorated?"

"Yes, but stop trying to change the subject. Were you too dumb to use a safe or too lazy?"

"I always use one. They're not completely reliable."

Ryan punched the accelerator and the Ferrari rocketed up the deserted street. He was an accident. A stupid accident that had ruined Mary Bailey's life. He came to a roundabout and whipped around it three times. It didn't let off any steam.

"Turn here," Griffith said quietly. "Then it's a quick left and a right."

Still traveling faster than he'd ever driven in his life, Ryan guided the Ferrari through the white-knuckle turns. He loved driving fast—on the edge. In 'Nam he was famous for it. The guys always insisted he take the green recruits for a spin in the company jeep. Anyone who chickened out got the shit details.

"Left here." Griffith's voice was level.

Ryan veered left. Jesus! The Ferrari was smooth. Any other car would be on two wheels. He ventured a peek at Griffith, expecting him to be scared pissless. The man was smiling. Ryan floored it. Griffith started to laugh. Ryan took his foot off the accelerator; the car slowed. "What's so damn funny?"

The question only made Griffith laugh harder. Ryan pulled the car to the side of the street, slammed on the brakes, bringing the Ferrari to a whiplash stop.

"Why are you laughing?"

Griffith raised both hands in mock surrender. "You have Garth's face but even if you didn't have my green eyes, I'd know you were my son. Garth would never have had the nerve to waltz into Crockfords and beat the tar out of anyone.

And he never drove over five miles an hour. There isn't a policeman in London who has to ask my name when he writes up my speeding ticket."

"Uncle Garth was brave—a hero."

"I'm not saying anything negative about Garth. I still miss him. But Garth didn't have raw courage. He had the quiet type of valor that comes out in a crisis—in a war."

"What about the time Uncle Garth climbed that high pole with the statue of what's-his-name on top of it?"

"Nelson's column. Who told you about that?"

"Ma. She said Uncle Garth climbed it and hung a big sign from Nelson's hat that said, 'Fuck Hitler.' "

"I scaled the column. Garth waited at the bottom."

"Yeah?" Ryan said, disconcerted. "What about the time Uncle Garth took on four Nazi planes in a dogfight?"

"*I* had no choice. They were going after one of our crippled planes. They wouldn't have made it unless I distracted the Nazis. It took guts, not just on my part, but on the entire crew's—particularly the tail gunner. We were damn lucky we lived."

There was no doubting the sincerity in Griffith's words. Had all the wild tales Ma told with undisguised love in her voice been her way of telling him about his father without Buck knowing? Would she ever have told Ryan the truth?

"Are we going to sit here all night?"

Without saying another word, Ryan followed Griffith's directions and raced to his home in Hampstead Heath. As Ryan got out he gave the Ferrari's leather wheel a good-bye squeeze.

"Come in a minute. I have some pictures of your uncle and your grandparents."

Ryan hesitated. Unexpectedly a vision of the Westcott clan came to him. Slovenly. Stupid. He'd always been ashamed of them. What had his real family been like? This is what he'd come to England to find out.

As Ryan entered the house, his eyes swept across the lavish furnishings. He'd watched plenty of television in his formative years, his ideas of how the rich lived came from *The Beverly Hillbillies*. What he saw here—the mellow paneling, the priceless antiques—had to be what his mother called "class." But he wondered if all classy, rich people hung their paintings from ceiling to floor.

Inside a small room lined with shelves haphazardly crammed with books, Griffith brought out a worn photo album. Ryan slowly looked through the first dozen pages, which were all pictures of Uncle Garth and Griffith and their planes: lounging on their wings, clowning in the cockpits, standing on the tails, hanging from the propellers. Any fool could see they were best buddies and they loved to fly.

"Here"—Griffith pointed to an older couple on the next page—"are Louise and Tom Bailey, your mother's parents."

Ryan took a closer look. He had his grandfather's square jaw and sharp nose. "They died in the Blitz?"

Griffith nodded, visibly saddened. "I took these pictures"— he turned to the next page—"at a family party they threw for me. Several days later the Nazis scored a direct hit on their building. Luckily, Mary and Garth weren't home."

Ryan examined each black-and-white snapshot. His mother arm in arm with Tillie, wearing the cabbage-patch hat. His mother and Uncle Garth mugging for the camera. His mother displaying a pie she'd obviously made for the occasion. His mother wearing Griffith's bomber jacket.

"What's this?" he asked, indicating a picture of his mother holding the jacket's lining to the camera.

"That's the map I'd drawn on the lining. I never knew when I'd be shot down or where. I wanted to be able to find my way back on my own."

The hair across the back of Ryan's neck prickled. In 'Nam, he'd never gone out on a mission without taking his own copy of the latest recon map.

Shaking his head, Griffith smiled. "It worked, too. That's why we were celebrating. I'd been shot down and had been missing for two weeks. I was hiding in a French fishing village and waiting to find a boat going across the Channel. It was difficult since the only French I knew was a phrase your mother had taught me. *Vrai amour ne se change.*" Griffith chuckled. "You don't get far saying true love never changes."

The sonofabitch took her love for granted. She was probably just one of a parade of women through Griffith's life. He was too damn handsome with his perfect features and compelling green eyes. Griffith needed a warning label tattooed on his forehead.

"Cognac?" Griffith asked as he moved over to a fancy TV tray with a decanter on it and several itty-bitty glasses.

Ryan nodded nonchalantly as if he drank cognac everyday. Griffith handed him a glass less than half full. Cheap bastard. Ryan kicked it back in one gulp. It hit the bottom of his stomach, igniting like napalm, flaring all the way up his throat. He coughed twice, then watched Griffith cradle his glass in both hands for a minute before he sipped it.

"When I met Garth, we immediately connected. Do you know what I mean?"

Ryan nodded. He'd felt that with Brad Samuels. The second lieutenant had taken over his unit when Ryan was halfway through his first tour. They'd immediately became insepara-ble. Until Hill 666. Of the men Ryan had rescued, Brad had been the only one too severely injured to walk. Ryan had carried him out on his back, crawling most of the way. When he'd finally reached the medic, Brad was dead.

"The Baileys included me in all the family gatherings. For the first time in my life, I was happy. I know it sounds crazy because we were in the middle of a war. But then I had everything I wanted—things I don't have today. A family. A best friend. A sense of belonging, of really being needed. And flying, knowing I might die, gave me a thrill I haven't experi-enced since."

"What about my mother?"

"She knew exactly what kind of a man I was. Through the entire war, I dated one woman after another. I liked Mary as a friend. I never encouraged her, not just because she was Garth's sister and he wouldn't have wanted her hurt, but because Mary"—he looked away—"wasn't my type."

"She was loyal and devoted. The best mother in the world." The words came out from between clenched teeth. "Exactly the kind of woman I'm going to marry."

"I felt responsible for Mary, so I spent as much time as I could with her after Garth and her parents died. She didn't have any other relatives. But I never touched her—until sev-eral years after the war. I was at loose ends then. I had nothing to do. All of England was digging out, rebuilding, so I worked

as a chippie—a carpenter. I had an idea for a new business and
I needed to save as much money as possible to start it. Mary
knew all this; I saw her several times a month to make sure she
was all right. Garth had asked me to look after Tillie and his
sister. I owed it to him."

"You've done a great job with Tillie, too. She's living in a
slum."

"I had no idea. After Mary went to America, I never saw
Tillie again. She was furious I didn't marry your mother. I'll
see if Tillie will let me help her now."

"Too late. I've already taken care of it. She wants to move to
Stow-on-the-Wold. I gave her the money; she'll pay me back
when she can."

Griffith's eyes narrowed as he assessed Ryan thoughtfully.
"About your mother, I don't know how it happened exactly,
but one night I made love to her. Like most women, she
equated sex with love. I apologized for doing it, but she cried
and clung to me, saying she'd always loved me. I stopped
seeing her."

"Come on. One time and she got pregnant? I don't believe
it."

"The rubber broke. When she came to me and told me she
was going to have a baby, I couldn't believe my bad luck. I
gave her money to get rid of . . ." He sucked in his breath
and closed his eyes for a moment. "I assumed she had. The
next thing I knew she'd married Westcott, an American army
private stationed here. I'm sorry their marriage didn't work
out. And I'm sorry Westcott was so hard on you."

"I could handle it." He hadn't meant to cry-baby to Griffith.

"Listen to me for a minute. Don't say anything until I'm
finished. I have a job you might be interested in. It's dangerous so it pays well—a twenty-five thousand pounds a year."

Ryan struggled not to look shocked. He could never make
that much money at home without an education. But did he
want to work for the man who'd deserted his mother?

"You would be based here. But the job entails traveling to
Africa frequently. I need someone with guts and a quick
mind. I don't want you to answer right now. Think it over."

Mumbling a terse good night, Ryan stood up. He was halfway to the front door when Griffith called to him. He turned just in time to catch the keys to the Ferrari.

"Take the car; you won't find a taxi at this time of night."

"How do you know you'll ever see the Ferrari again?"

A slow smile revealed white teeth below a nose that had swollen but hadn't marred Griffith's handsome face. "I'm not worried. You're Mary's son."

16

"Your vase sold," Lauren said as she came into the kitchen where Tabatha was bent over the oven, removing a cookie sheet brimming with fresh-baked earrings.

"Really? So quickly?" She grinned, the first sincere smile Lauren had seen from the girl.

Lauren put the money on the counter. "I had inquiries the moment I put it on display. Do you have a second one?"

"No. I-I never thought . . ." Tabatha grabbed the money.

"I know talent when I see it. Don't limit yourself to jewelry." Lauren walked toward the swinging doors leading out of the kitchen. "Don't make dinner for me tonight. After work, Vora and I are going to see *Miss Saigon*."

She rode the lift to the ground floor where she stood and stared out at the curtain of rain that obscured her view of the square. Two toots from a maroon Jaguar announced Vora's arrival. With her umbrella shielding her, Lauren dashed for the car.

"All set for Finley and the other critics?" Vora asked.

"I guess, but I'm not looking forward to it. I'll try my best to charm them. I want Irek to get good reviews."

Vora drove toward Ravissant saying, "I'm worried about the two of us promoting Irek. England is a very chauvinistic society. We may have a queen and a PM who are women, but look at the level below. What do you see? Unlike the United States, few women are in high places in business or industry."

"It's no different there, not really. I doubt if a woman—no matter how qualified—could be elected president. I'd like to think she could, but I doubt it."

"The point is that in America there are now enough women in executive positions that men don't resent them," Vora said as she maneuvered the car through a deep puddle at Brook and Davies.

"I wouldn't say that. They've been forced to accept us."

"British men haven't accepted women; maybe they never will. Don't forget that good-old-boy tradition started right here in the men's clubs."

"What are you trying to tell me?"

"I'm worried about the critics. I want Irek to be a success. I think the critics would take us more seriously if one of us were a man."

"Have faith in yourself. We're going to do just fine."

Vora pulled into the car park and they got out and popped open their umbrellas.

"Please don't worry. I can handle Finley."

"Awfully sorry, but I can't help worrying about Irek. You know how much I care for him."

They rounded the corner, walking quickly through the downpour. Ahead Lauren saw Ryan's Aston-Martin. Instead of straddling the curb as usual, it was up on the sidewalk in front of the gallery. Of all the nerve! How was it his car was never booted with an immovable tire clamp for illegal parking?

In spite of herself, Lauren's pulse quickened, thinking she'd have to face him for the first time since she'd slept with him. Three long days ago and three even longer, lonelier nights. Despite his outrageous comments—"I have something for you"—and his counting rounds, she missed him. *He's not your type,* the right side of her brain kept insisting. *Yes, he is,* the left side responded.

Why was she being so indecisive? She'd done what she had to do. Now forget him. She doubted if she'd have to worry about her rebellious hormones after she'd told Ryan that he reminded her of Rupert. Ryan had maimed her with a glare, leaving without another word.

Why had Rupert's name slipped out? He was nothing like Ryan. Nothing. Few saw behind Rupert's suave facade. Brash to the point of being crude, Ryan said exactly what was on his mind. They were nothing alike—except they both were accustomed to getting what they wanted, although in different ways. That must be it. Her subconscious had culled out the one similar trait the men shared. Warning her.

"Irek is using Ryan's car," Vora said, obviously upset.

"What's the matter?" Lauren asked, thankful she didn't have to contend with Ryan yet.

"I mentioned the menu for the opening to Irek, and he wants to discuss it with us."

They entered Ravissant and tucked their drippy umbrellas into the brass stand beside Irek's frayed one.

"Hello," Irek said as he came toward them. "Raining dogs and cats."

As usual, he wore a sweater that had seen better days over a shirt with a collar that was no longer in style. He sported a new watch, replacing the Superman watch he'd worn the last time Lauren had seen him. This one's tangerine band clashed with the poison-green face and violet hands.

"I understand you want to discuss the food we'll be serving at your exhibition. It'll just be hors d'oeuvres. The buffet after the showing will be at Basil Blackstoke's new penthouse. Naturally, what he serves will be up to—"

"Irek doesn't want caviar at the opening," Vora said.

"Slimy, smelly, salty." Irek screwed up his nose.

"Let me assure you that we aren't serving salmon roe. We're not even serving golden osetra. In your honor, the caterer has ordered Royal Beluga flown in fresh from the Caspian Sea."

"No caviar."

"But it's typically Russian," Lauren said before she caught Vora's warning look.

Irek shook his head, digging his heels in. "*Nachalstvo* are only Russians who eat caviar."

"Party bosses," Vora interpreted for Lauren's benefit.

"Only *nachalstvo* afford caviar. Ask the peoples who waits hours in line for one fatty chop if they have ever has caviar."

"Things are different here," Lauren argued. "We don't stand in line. We buy whatever we can afford. Our guests will expect the best. That's why we're serving Royal Beluga iced in silver dishes and Cristal champagne."

"Champagne is wuss."

"Wuss?" Lauren asked and Irek flapped his arms like a bird preparing to leave the nest. She looked to Vora for an explanation.

"Irek means real men don't drink champagne."

"Of course they do." Then she thought of Ryan. He hated champagne and had transmitted his dislike to Irek. Great. He could fly off to God-only-knows-where and still manage to make trouble for her. "We're having a full bar as well. No one has to drink champagne unless they wish to." She smiled, considering the subject closed.

"No champagne. No caviar. Cheese and English vodka," Irek insisted. "Burrough's."

Vora put her hand on Irek's arm. "Burrough's is good but maybe not England's best. Tanqueray is now making a first-cabin vodka called Tanqueray Silver. Let's serve it."

"Burrough's is good," Irek persisted. "Not *sivukha*—not gut rot."

"Tanqueray Silver will go better with Stilton, English Cheddar, and Single Gloucester." Vora smiled at him, her tone accommodating. "And Dorset blue."

Flabbergasted, Lauren stared at her friend. Vora didn't seriously propose to serve cheese and vodka and nothing else. Half their guests would drink the Cristal and the rest would expect first-rate liquor, most likely twenty-five-year-old Glenfiddich. And caviar.

"I am a British subject born from Russia," Irek said proudly. "At my show I want best English vodka and best English cheeses, no thing else." He winked at Vora. "*Deke zabeb* eat much, much before meal—ruin dinner. No need for such waste."

"*Deke zabeb?*" Lauren asked.

"Crazy Westerners," Vora said.

"Telephone, Mrs. Winthrop," the receptionist called. "It's from America."

It must be Paul. She turned, thinking of how much better her brother seemed each time she spoke with him. His recovery meant everything to her. She stopped, then walked back to where Irek and Vora were standing. "You know, in the greater scheme of things what counts isn't what we're serving, but the art we're exhibiting. Call the caterers, Vora. Tell them to create something special with cheese."

"Paul," she said after she'd finally picked up the telephone.

"No. David Marcus. I've just read your report on Ravissant's progress. Very impressive. Your gamble with the Cassatts worked out well. What I don't see is a contract with Irek Makarova. I assume you neglected to send it for my approval."

"We don't have a signed contract, just a verbal agreement." Since when did she need his approval?

"You can't seriously mean you intend to exclusively market Makarova and publish his prints without putting the agreement in writing? What if you sink all this money into promoting him—you've already spent thousands on the exhibition—and he walks?"

"Well, I . . . ." How could she explain to someone like Marcus that Irek was a man of integrity and principles? They'd discussed a contract, but Irek had been adamant. Didn't need, couldn't understand, only made solicitors richer.

"Get it in writing. That's how business is done. When you have it signed, FAX it to me."

Reluctantly, Lauren agreed and hung up.

"Super news, super." Vora beamed at Lauren when she hung up. "I just called Tanqueray. They're donating the vodka. They want to promote their product to the most affluent market in the world."

Lauren nodded her approval, not just of the unexpected windfall, but of Vora's initiative. She was really doing her job nicely and with more confidence as each day passed. Turning to Irek, Lauren said, "Could you run me over to La Tante Claire? It's not too far. You'll be back in time for your appointment with Dr. Digsby."

When Lauren and Vora had expressed concern over the time Irek had spent in prison, worrying that the media might not understand that he'd been a political prisoner, Ryan had suggested a visit to Dr. Denton Digsby. The doctor advised people on how to take advantage of media attention.

"Irek," Lauren said when they were in the car zipping past Berkeley Square. "I think that we should have a contract—for your protection."

"Do not worry for me. I am not afraid. You are my friends."

"But Irek." She tried to keep her tone smooth, sensing his stubbornness. "Anything could go wrong."

"I am not worried. Ryan says contracts are no good. Fine print is bad news."

Ryan again. Although from different worlds, they thought alike, viewing life with a no-nonsense—or should she say, no-bullshit—attitude. Lauren gave up; she had no reason to press for a contract. She'd just have to put off Marcus until it was too late for him to stop the opening.

Irek slowed the car for the usual snarl at Hyde Park corner, worsened by the heavy rain. "Why did you not come go with Ryan when we see Boris Grebenschikov?"

Not Ryan again. "I told him I had other plans."

"More important then Ryan?" Disbelief colored every word.

"No," she replied carefully. "But I had already promised another gentleman I'd have dinner with him. It wouldn't have been fair to break our date, would it?"

Unconvinced, Irek shrugged and nursed the Aston-Martin up the street. "It mean much much to Ryan. He has not asked a lady for a date in three years."

"Three years? No. He has a reputation for being a playboy and dating lots of different women. You must have misunderstood."

"He tell me that after the bombing he was a different man. Knows what is important. Like me after *gulag.*"

Lauren stared at the wipers slap-slapping back and forth but only clearing the rain for a split second. Could what Irek said possibly be true? What did she know about Ryan, anyway? Only what Vora and Finley had told her. To Lauren, he seemed every inch the macho playboy. Was his brusque manner camouflage?

His hands. The tenderness in Ryan's touch surprised her.

He seemed to know, to anticipate whatever her body needed. If only—if only he was a different sort of man. Gentlemanly, polite to match his magical hands. But he wasn't and if she didn't stop thinking about him, she'd go nuts. She should be thinking of Grant, who called every day, or Finley, who'd asked her to spend a weekend with him at his country house. Think of anything but Ryan Westcott.

Irek brought the car to a stop outside the restaurant. The doorman rushed forth with an umbrella the size of a pup tent and opened her door.

Before she could get out, Irek caught her arm. "Do not be bad to my friend. He like you much . . . much. *Liubov'* even."

"Liubov'?"

"How you say?" He put his hand over his heart and thumped twice. "What we feel deep, deep inside for those we like much."

"Love?"

"Yes. That is the right word."

Lauren said good-bye and stumbled out of the car into a wind-driven rain. As she ran into La Tante Claire and stopped to shed her rain gear, she mentally reviewed the time she'd spent with Ryan. He had a cavalier attitude that indicated she was nothing special. Had she missed something? No. Other than being determined to make certain she had an orgasm— which merely validated his sexual prowess—he'd never given her any sign he cared one whit about her. Irek was mistaken.

What if he wasn't?

"There you are." Finley came up and offered her his arm.

She smiled, reminding herself how important these critics were. Stop thinking about Ryan Westcott.

Finley guided her across the crowded La Tante Claire where diners either made reservations weeks in advance, or didn't bother to ring for a table. Since he ate there every day, Finley always had the best table.

"Lauren, you remember Chester Reynolds-Stephens from *Apollo.*"

Her hostess smile in place, she extended her hand to the critic she'd met after Sotheby's auction. "Wonderful to see you again."

"My pleasure," he responded, shaking her hand with a hand as smooth as a powder puff and every bit as soft.

"This," Finley said as a short man with a pixie face and diminutive frame stood with his hand reaching for hers, "is my oldest friend, Rutherford Ames."

"Hello." Lauren shook his hand. She noted the delicate flaring of his nostrils and the rapid way he blinked as he looked at her. Although he was smiling, Rutherford Ames had taken an instant dislike to her.

Shaken by that thought, she kept her smile on hold and sat down. She allowed Finley to order for her. Grilled plover. Simply La Tante Claire's best. Couldn't be topped, not a'tall.

Lauren sipped a glass of Malvern Water with a double twist of lime and listened politely as they discussed the upcoming exhibition at the Tate.

"Will you all be able to attend Irek Makarova's exhibition?"

"Wouldn't miss it," Rutherford assured her and the other two men voiced their agreement between bites.

"Has anyone had a chance to read his press kit?"

"You're using a new advertising firm?" Finley asked.

"Yes," Lauren said, encouraged by his smile. "Vora has been in charge of the promotional end."

Rutherford quirked one elfish eyebrow, but said nothing. Lauren didn't elaborate. The entire design and advertising concept had been Vora's. She'd done it in-house to avoid anyone finding out about Irek until the last possible moment.

"May I suggest," Chester said in his usual waffling manner, "that next time you promote a new artist you send out press kits that look less . . . less slick."

"I agree," Rutherford jumped in. "The Russian's kit reminded me of that American chap, Jeff Koons.

If Lauren hadn't just taken a bite of plover, she would have blurted out one of Ryan's four-letter words. Comparing Irek to Koons. Ridiculous. A former publicist for New York's Museum of Modern Art, Koons had spent several years on Wall Street before deciding to become an artist. While most artists used highly discreet methods of publicizing themselves, Koons's campaigns—which successfully vaulted him to worldwide attention and stratospheric prices for his works—were media events.

What Vora had done for Irek was nothing like that. Her professional press kits were navy with dove-gray lettering. Hardly slick. The hardbound catalogue echoed the same color theme. And the advertisements planned for the major papers and the art magazines featured a shot of one of Irek's landscapes. Unlike Koons, Irek didn't pose beside his works like a male model. "We've sought to bring an exciting new talent to collectors' attention without resorting to shameless grandstanding."

"Critics have to be careful," Finley said. "There are so many Russians nipping about these days."

"When Sotheby's auctioned the avant-garde Russians, scholars claimed two of Popova's oils were forgeries," Chester said. "But Sotheby's disputed the authorities and auctioned them anyway."

"Rather a nasty business. Not a'tall what Sotheby's would have done in the old days."

Lauren ate her plover to forestall a sharp retort, but she got the message. When Taubman sought to purchase Sotheby's, he'd had to go before Britain's Monopolies and Mergers Commission. He'd left the impression he would keep Sotheby's as it had been since the mid-eighteenth century. But once he owned it, Taubman diverted much of Sotheby's prime business to the New York branch. The Brits hadn't taken it well, harboring ill feelings for Sotheby's. Maybe she was being paranoid, but she couldn't help wondering if they resented her not only because she was a woman, but an American as well like Taubman. She wanted to protest that her mother was British and that she held a British passport, but her pride wouldn't let her.

"Bad show," Chester said. "Prices for contemporary art are rather out of hand. Willem de Kooning's 'Interchange' just sold for . . ."

"Twenty-one million," Lauren said. "A new record for a living artist."

"And now we're faced with the Saatchi affair," Finley said.

He'd said this in such a hushed undertone Lauren would have assumed he was referring to a torrid love affair, not the business problems of London advertising mogul, Charles Saatchi. In the early 1980s Saatchi had acquired works of numerous contemporary artists. Because the market hadn't yet exploded, the artists allowed Saatchi to stockpile their work, believing he intended to have his collection tour museums the way Armand Hammer's collection had. Unfortunately, a financial pinch Saatchi had experienced prompted him to sell certain artists' work.

New dealers jumped at the chance to buy blocks of works by artists such as Eric Fischl and Anselm Kiefer whose prices were past the million-dollar mark. When these dealers put the paintings they'd recently acquired from Saatchi on the market along with the artist's more recent works, this saturated the demand. There simply weren't that many buyers of million-dollar-plus paintings. Many of the artists found themselves unable to sell their current work. Saatchi made money. The dealers made money. But the artists found their careers stalled.

Lauren supposed it would level out—eventually when the glut was absorbed. She nodded to Finley and his friends, a guarded smile on her lips. Vora was right. For a variety of reasons, they'd already made up their minds not to like Irek's paintings.

While they ordered Tirami Su and discussed the relative merits of other restaurants serving the marscapone and ladyfinger dessert, Lauren tried to reassure herself by thinking Ryan had already taken two paintings for Griffith's collection. Still, niggling doubts badgered her. How often had she seen unfavorable reviews whither a talented artist's hopes? In the critics' eyes animated works became frivolous. Serious subjects pretentious. Vivid colors garish.

"Dash it all," Rutherford said. "I've got to run."

After he left, Lauren turned to Finley. "I need to return to the gallery soon. Thanks for the lunch. I'd like you to be my guest tonight. I have superb tickets for *Miss Saigon*."

Media consultant Dr. Denton Digsby's one o'clock appointment, Irek Makarova, was late. Digsby waited in the alcove behind a two-way mirror overlooking the receptionist's desk. The first time he saw new clients, Digsby liked to observe them without their knowing it. How they treated his receptionist told him as much about that person as an extensive interview did.

As a young boy, Digsby had wandered into the parlor where his mother was watching Rev. Malcolm Oggstone on television. He'd concluded his weekly telecast, as he always did, by asking the brethren to send a pound and he'd say a prayer for them. Amazingly, his mother did just that, ignoring her son in his thrice-handed-down shoes and the empty larder.

Digsby had immediately seen the opportunity to better himself through religion. From then on, he never let his eyes veer from his goal of a television ministry in which he could pray for pay. Consumed by the idea of ruling the theological airwaves, Digsby enrolled in a religious correspondence course.

Praise the Lord. He was awarded a title: Doctor of Divinity. But Digsby was too bright to believe a piece of paper would be his entree into the world of television. He saved money for two years and then enrolled in a television course. Finally, his turn in class came and he stepped in front of the camera, primed to practice the first of many profitable sermons. Before Digsby finished his opening sentence, the audience of students erupted in laughter. When he watched the replay, he realized why. His close-set eyes ringed by dark circles above a priggish nose gave him a raccoonlike expression. He did not look like anyone's apostle. And he never would.

As disappointing as that year, 1958, was to Digsby, the following year provided divine inspiration. The British general election was covered by television for the first time. The BBC carried the Nixon-Kennedy debates. Mesmerized, Digsby stared at the television, thinking of the power of the camera.

The one true God.

He offered his services—free of charge because he had no experience—to Wilber McCallister, owner of the Mootzie's Tootzies shops in underground stations. Wilber had taken to the telly, touting his latest venture, Sox Trot. Located in barnacle-sized spaces, also in underground stations, the stores sold nylons and men's socks at underground prices.

Red-faced and wattle-necked, McCallister appeared on television trussed up in a frock coat and white shirt. His affected Etonian accent fooled no one. The backlash was tremendous. No one wanted to buy anything from the shoe-faced sock salesman.

Digsby spent hours with McCallister, practicing in one of the BBC's many studios that a friend arranged for him to use. He dressed McCallister in simple, work clothes—like those his customers might wear—and told him to drop the bogus accent. "Always target your audience" became Digsby's axiom. McCallister wasn't selling his cheezy shoes and socks to the royal family, so why pretend he was?

When the revamped commercials hit the telly, sales skyrocketed. Digsby's career took off along with the shoes and socks. He advised politicians who'd been shell-shocked by the election coverage as well as wily MPs who'd watched Kennedy and discovered a new word—charisma.

As the years passed, the one true God was blessed with an ever increasing flock as media events, photo opportunities, and thirty-second bites replaced traditional journalism. Digsby increased the scope of his media-consulting business, adding speechwriters, wardrobe planners, makeup consultants, and poll takers to measure results.

Today, Digsby watched the door to the reception area as it opened and in walked a pretty brunette. A burly man lagged behind, his ragtag umbrella dripping as he eyed the Chagall hung above the receptionist's desk.

"I'm Vora Leighton and this is Irek Makarova. We have a one o'clock appointment with Dr. Digsby."

"Today?" The receptionist feigned confusion.

"Yes. I'm sorry we're late. The rain . . ."

The receptionist leafed through the appointment book as if she had no idea who they were. Vora looked over her shoulder and smiled apologetically at the Russian. So that's how it was, Digsby thought with amusement. The receptionist left the room, pretending to be checking on the mixup.

"Now, don't forget to call me the minute you finish that portrait we've been waiting on," Vora said, obviously trying to take the disgruntled Irek's mind off the confusion over the appointment.

His scowl softened as he looked at her. "I will call the minute I finish. I am almost done."

"Good. We need to include it in the catalogue and arrange

display space." She smiled another heartfelt smile, then looked worriedly at the door to the inner office.

The receptionist returned, muttering apologies. A temp had handled the appointment; you couldn't get decent staff these days. "Go right into Dr. Digsby's office, Mr. Makarova. He'll join you straight away." She turned to the brunette. "Mrs. Winthrop rang earlier. She needs to speak to you immediately."

Digsby remained behind the two-way mirror and watched Vora use the telephone.

"Lauren? Is something the matter?" Vora's voice had moved up an octave. She listened silently for a moment. "I don't mind. If it'll help Irek, I'm all for it. Go ahead; take Finley. I've already seen the play once. . . . I just spoke to Irek about it. He promised to let me know as soon as he's finished the painting."

Digsby waited until Vora had been escorted into his private office for the preliminary interview. He entered, noting the overbright smile on Vora Leighton's face and the suspicious look the Russian didn't attempt to conceal. Digsby didn't offer his hand as he introduced himself. He avoided touching anyone—couldn't be too careful these days—except his wife, who'd worked as his receptionist since the day he'd opened his first office.

"Tell me, Mr. Makarova, what will you do with all the money you'll make from this exhibition?"

"Buy a Porsche," he replied without hesitation.

Digsby understood completely. There were certain material rewards a man needed. "What do you think will be your biggest problem, assuming you're tremendously successful?"

Irek pulled a watch from the pocket of his well-worn jacket and handed it to Digsby. On the oversized face was a cheap rendition of Marc Chagall's "Joseph the Shepherd," the same oil Digsby had purchased for his reception room.

"Commercialism is any artist's enemy. Much much more for son of Russia. Not used to Capitalist Olympics. Goes to—" He pointed to his head.

"I believe the Lord will show me the way to help you, Mr. Makarova. But you *must* do exactly as I say."

The Russian's brows pinched over his nose in a wary frown.

"He'll do whatever you say," interjected Vora.

Irek cast a sidelong glance at her. She encouraged him with another high-voltage smile. "Ryan thinks it's a good idea."

"I will do as you say," Irek told Digsby.

"Good. Now what are you doing about your accent?"

"I go to teacher every day. Practice at night: The city sheriff shoots silver six-shooters. Say over and over—fast as I can."

That topped the rain in Spain bit Digsby usually heard. "Stop taking lessons. Practice by talking to as many different people as possible. Part of the reason your English isn't good is because you worked at a job where you had no chance to communicate." He ignored Vora's questioning gaze. "Watch as many news broadcasts as possible. Then find a mirror and practice looking into it repeating what you've just heard."

"Pretend I am on television?"

"Yes. Because you will be soon. Always remember to look directly into the camera. Looking away gives the impression you have something to hide or you're lying." He rose and gestured for Irek to come with him. "Now you're going into my studio and let my crew drill you. We'll stay here."

When the Russian left, Digsby asked, "Mrs. Leighton, are you in love with Irek?"

She looked away. "Yes," she finally admitted.

"Then let me give you a bit of free advice. Get rid of the phony hair. Keep your hair no longer than chin length with natural curl to give it bounce. Perm it if you must, but keep it soft, springy." He squinted through the glasses he wore, not to enhance his vision, but to hide the dark circles racooning his eyes. "What are you hiding under all that makeup?"

"Freckles. Lots of them."

"Perfect! Don't try to hide them. Just wear a peach blush and tint your eyelashes. Nothing else. Understand? Also dress down, not up. This will be your salvation."

"You mean Irek will . . . like me better?"

"The good Lord willing."

"May I go check on him now?" she asked.

"No. He has to face the pit bulls alone." At her grimace, he clarified. "That's what I call my crew—pit bulls. They're going to jostle him, jam cameras and microphones in his face, and ask the rudest, most personal questions imaginable. They'll put the fear of God into any man."

Vora laughed, a mellow sound that Digger recognized as being cultivated in the most exclusive of schools, probably abroad. "You can't frighten Irek. He's been in prison."

"He's never faced the British press."

"Fock off!" reverberated through the well-appointed office as Irek exploded through the door.

Vora jumped to her feet. "What happened?"

Irek waved a clenched fist in Digsby's face. He stood his ground. The Lord was with him.

"They call my mother *bepchek*. Say she spread legs for any man in Politburo. Lies. Lies."

"Sit down, Mr. Makarova," Digsby said. "Let me explain to you how the Lord works."

17

Ryan stood beside the Rover on the Tizi N' Tichka Pass above Marrakesh and looked west, shielding his eyes from the descending sun with his gloved hand. Far below, the red sandstone of the plain encompassing Marrakesh had blurred to a soft blush. Flanking the road, an unending series of hairpin turns, were forests of thuya and ilex, their crowns concealed by thickets of pink oleanders. *Ksours*, fortified Berber villages, were perched on promontories, clinging to their mountain hideaways well beyond the grasp of the modern world. At the summit, the bosky terrain gave way to a moonscape of yellow-amber boulders and pinnacles that had erupted from beneath the earth's surface centuries ago.

Sheer drops and dangerous escarpments marked the apex of the drive through the pass. Built by the French during their tenure in Morocco, the road had enabled them to extend their control of the country to the remote southern region. The route through the Atlas Mountains, nature's bastion against the Sahara to the east, had been ruled by the fiercely independent Berbers since before biblical times.

When the French withdrew, the mountain route lost some of its importance. Still a lifeline to the Draa Valley and the Algerian border, the road was seldom traveled except for Berbers on their horses and the trucks bringing manganese down from the pure vein the French had struck while paving the road. This remote route led to Ouarzazate, the last outpost of civilization before the unforgiving sands of the Sahara.

Ryan gathered his burnoose around him, seeking the cloak's protection from the summit's chill, and climbed into the Rover. Without a backward glance at the lush west face of the Atlas Mountains, he headed east down the barren ridges and ravines scoured by centuries of wind-driven sand.

He checked his Concord; it was mid-afternoon in London. What was Lauren doing? A man was in deep trouble when he couldn't get a woman out of his mind. Sleeping with her had triggered something deep inside him. Something he'd never even suspected had been there. She was provocative, mysterious, elusive. Or maybe just plain confused.

Above all she was a liar. She hadn't told the truth about the meaning of "Midnight in Marrakesh." Said it was personal, private. Hell, she had a point. She didn't owe anyone an explanation. She was entitled to her secrets—no matter how much Ryan wanted to know them. Perhaps that was why he was so intrigued by her. Most women were easy to figure out. Not Lauren.

On two wheels, the Rover rounded a sharp turn. Ryan slammed on the brakes to avoid hitting a mounted patrol of Berbers crossing the road. Their white robes trailing over their horses' rumps, the riders saluted Ryan with long-barreled rifles held horizontally in one hand and raised above their heads. Ryan responded with a smile and a straight arm pointing skyward brandishing his Walther.

Bound for Telouet, just off the summit, these Berbers belonged to the fiercest clan in the region, the Glaoui. Ryan remembered the first time he'd seen them. That day, almost fifteen years ago, he and T.J. had been traveling, not east, but west on their way from Algeria to Marrakesh. Around a dogleg turn, a band of Berbers had blocked the road, their rifles trained on them.

"Shit!" T.J. jammed on the brakes, and the Rover fishtailed to a halt. He grabbed the Walther PPKS that years of kicking around Africa had taught them to leave on the dash. Ryan silently said his first prayer.

Aiming the automatic at the leader, T.J. vaulted from the car, swearing in sharp, guttural Arabic. The chieftain grinned at T.J., revealing blackened stubs of teeth, and palmed his rifle, turning it parallel to the ground. Then he thrust it skyward, waving it above his head in a weather-hewn hand. Laughing, his men followed suit, hoisting their rifles to the azure sky. Ryan heaved a sigh, blowing upward and ruffling his unkempt hair.

The Berbers led them off the main road down a trail washed out by spring rains and left to bake in the unrelenting African sun. At their village, Telouet, they were served mint tea and a feast of roast goat, *mechoui,* so tough Ryan's jaw ached for two days.

Later, on the way into Marrakesh, T.J. explained that a show of power always commanded respect. Then he launched into his usual diatribe on the decay of the West in the face of the pistol-packing Communists. His generation had fought—and won—the Battle of Britain; Ryan's generation was faced with the Battle of Bullshit. Ryan nodded, but he wasn't listening.

Since he'd come to work for T.J., he'd spent hours talking to him. Although he didn't like to admit it, Ryan found they agreed on most things. Blondes, good gin, gambling. And fast cars. Ryan had bought himself a secondhand Aston-Martin Virage like one James Bond drove in *Doctor No.* He'd taken his mother to see that movie—she adored Sean Connery—and Ryan had promised her one day he'd have a car like Bond's. She hadn't laughed; she'd always encouraged his dreams.

Ryan liked living in England. Not only was he by rights British, he felt little allegiance to a country who'd turned its back on the men it had sent into Vietnam. He learned to eat bubble and squeak—leftovers fried with potatoes—as well as drink warm beer while hanging out in pubs playing darts and shooting the breeze. He found the British interest in politics, with the average man in the street informed about the day's vote in Parliament, an improvement over the attitude of many Americans who didn't give a damn.

But he didn't share the Brits' obsession with the antics of the royal hangers-on. Unlike *The Times,* with its ironic, educated tone that Ryan liked, dozens of sleazy tabloids trumpeted the lowdown on the upper crust. God Save the Queen from her

relatives. Still, Ryan couldn't pass a news rack without opening one of those papers to the third page, which featured a
topless cutie.

Changed tremendously from the green kid who'd taken T.J.
apart in Crockfords, Ryan now headed Griffith's diamond operation. During the Second World War, T.J. had foreseen the
world's dependency on oil. Desperate grabs for the precious
resource had influenced both Japanese and German military
goals. T.J. had realized drilling equipment would bring pre-
mium prices during the post-war boom. He'd saved his money
and started a drill-bit company that manufactured diamond-
studded drills for oil-producing countries.

Griffith didn't need gem-quality, D-flawless, one-carat diamonds to slice through icy tundra or pure bedrock. Bort, low-
grade diamonds available only in crushed form, would do the
trick. But he did need a continuous supply. He could have
dealt with conventional sources, purchasing industrial diamonds in bulk through the market centered in London. He
didn't.

When he'd founded Griffith International, T.J. had been on
a shoestring budget and needed to obtain bort below the
carefully controlled market price. He'd gone to the source
and purchased slag diamonds in Africa from "artisan miners,"
men who smuggled diamonds out of the mines and sold them
below market value. By the time Ryan had come to London,
T.J. was fantastically wealthy. Still, he insisted on circumventing the established market and finding diamonds from his
own sources.

At first, Ryan thought Griffith was cheap, but it didn't take
him long to realize T.J. couldn't resist the challenge. The
markets fluctuated constantly as the tightly controlled diamond cooperative shut down suppliers doing business outside
the carefully monitored system. It didn't matter. Another
source always replaced a lost one.

Ryan didn't mind sifting through Kimberlite, mica rock
where diamonds were formed, and checking the bort, but he
had his own private dream. It didn't include spending a lifetime in the bush, studying chemistry textbooks by an oil lamp
at night while being eaten by mosquitoes as big as helicopters.
T.J. paid him well to negotiate with the suppliers and live in

African backwaters. One day, Ryan would have enough saved to start his own business. Pursue his own dream.

"Now that's civilization." T.J. pointed to the city looming ahead of them, rising from the red plain like one of the Seven Cities of Gold.

The last rays of the sun were settling across Marrakesh, glazing the miles of ochre walls with amber light as the *muezzin* chanted his sunset call to Allah. It was Ryan's first visit to the Berber stronghold of bygone days. He'd expected another dusty oasis, not a glowing gem shaded by thousands of date palms filled with colorful birds trilling a good-bye to the sun.

Everywhere there were gardens bursting with flowers creating a limitless palette of color against the canvas of terra-cotta walls and buildings. Vibrant blue-violet jacarandas lined boulevards reminiscent of France, while high walls typical of Arab cities were softened by bougainvillaea or six-foot-high hedges of daisies. The blending of cultures, dominated by the Berber ramparts surrounding the *medina*, gave the city an exotic allure.

"Is Marrakesh on an underground spring?" Ryan asked. The plains they'd driven across were too dry to support the lush vegetation he saw everywhere.

"One of the Pashas had the water from the Atlas Mountains diverted to Marrakesh. He built the *khetteras*, underground channels lined with stones. They still supply the city with water."

They halted at an *arrêt* sign behind a bus full of veiled women and men in turbans. Perched on top of the ancient vehicle were bales of straw, tethered goats, and bicycles. Leaving a wake of red dust and diesel exhaust, the contraption chugged along a wall sectioned off at regular intervals by jutting towers and arched entrances decorated with reliefs of geometric symbols. They followed the bus along the perimeter until T.J. found a spot wide enough to pass.

"Largest *medina* in the country," T.J. said as he downshifted.

Ryan nodded. "Do you know where we're going or should I be looking for a particular street?"

"I know. More or less." He pointed to another arched opening that led into the *medina*. "Each *bab*—gate—has a name.

That's Bab Ahmar. We're looking for Bab Larissa. The Armstrongs don't live too far from that gate."

They easily found the Armstrong villa near Jardin du Hartsi. In Nairobi the previous month, Rupert Armstrong had invited them to stay at his home in Marrakesh while they concluded a business deal.

"Cocktails in an hour," said the servant who escorted them to their rooms. He was dressed in a white uniform with a scarlet sash and matching tarboosh. The tassel swished back and forth across the hat as he walked.

Following him down a marble corridor, Ryan eyed the Greek villa with its pretentious air of opulence. The servant led Ryan to a room overlooking a reflecting pool cloistered by garnet-colored impatiens. After a bath, the first hot water he'd had since London, Ryan joined T.J. on the terrace.

"Quite a place," T.J. said as they strolled through the topiary garden past a brace of peacocks preening by the marble fountain.

"Is this supposed to be a party or something?" Ryan asked. There were a dozen guests dressed formally. He felt out of place in his lightweight sport coat worn without a tie. T.J., of course, could wear a sport coat he'd slept in for a month and still look like an advertisement for high-priced scotch.

"Just a dinner party. Nothing special."

It never failed to amaze Ryan how unaffected T.J. was by wealth. He'd made it on his own; he was confident. Few material things impressed him. Fewer people.

They ordered Boodles on the rocks, as they always did, then sipped their gin, savoring civilization. Crossing the terrace and greeting guests, Rupert Armstrong made his way up to them.

Flame-red hair, immaculately barbered, made his pale complexion seem even more washed out. His brown eyes dominated his face beneath eyebrows so light they couldn't be seen until you were close to him. As Armstrong made small talk with T.J., Ryan silently watched. He didn't like Rupert Armstrong, although he really couldn't say why. Just a feeling. He wished T.J. hadn't agreed to export Armstrong's phosphorus to Japan for him.

Who needed the aggravation? They didn't know shit about

exporting fertilizer. And they already had plenty to do with Griffith International as well as the multitude of investments T.J. had made over the years. On top of everything, T.J. relentlessly pursued the art market, and that took time. But T.J. insisted he needed to try something new. Plain and simple—he was bored.

"Let me introduce you around," Armstrong said, leading T.J. toward a cluster of guests babbling away in French.

Ryan knew Armstrong didn't mean him; he considered Ryan a flunkie. But he tagged along anyway. Few people noticed his eyes were dead-ringers for T.J.'s. Probably because T.J. was a strikingly handsome man. But he wasn't just another pretty face. He had an aura of masculinity about him that men admired while the female population was left weak-kneed.

Ryan didn't mind having only average looks. He got his share of the action. And he didn't care that no one dreamed he was T.J.'s son. Not only didn't they look alike, but Ryan had appeared on the scene as an adult with his own separate identity. He had insisted T.J. keep their relationship a secret. He was Mary Bailey's son. End of discussion.

"Your Highness, may I present Mr. T.J. Griffith?" Armstrong paused as T.J. kissed the woman's extended hand, politely murmuring a greeting. "And his assistant, Mr. Ryan Westcott. Gentlemen, this is Her Royal Highness, Princess Sophia of Bulgaria."

Bulgaria? Another throneless freeloader. Europe was crawling with them. Tack a title on a name and presto, invitations galore. No need for honest work. Just mooch your life away.

"Your holiness." Instead of kissing it, Ryan pumped her hand, secretly delighted at the laughter in T.J.'s eyes.

Armstrong mumbled a few platitudes to the dumpy dowager and they moved on to be introduced to a succession of no-accounts possessed of little more than their titles. The only one who seemed the least bit interesting was a three-hundred-pound black man decked out in a pure-white military uniform decorated with gold braid and epaulets. The King of Tonga. Luckily, Ryan remembered his geography and knew Tonga was out in the South Pacific and really did have a king, or he would have said something crude.

"Notice," Ryan whispered to T.J., "the only person here not taken with himself is the only one who has a throne—other than the one in the loo—to call his own."

"This party looks like a real snoozer, all right. As soon as dinner is over, we'll go over to La Mamounia Hotel and do a little gambling."

"Over there," said Armstrong, materializing before them again, "is the Sultan of Brunei's nephew. Let me introduce you."

Ryan guzzled his gin and headed back to the bar for a refill. When he had it in his hand, he turned and saw T.J. signaling for him to join them. Great. Just what he needed—a Bedouin pretender.

"This is His Royal Highness," Rupert began as Ryan came up to them, then proceeded with a litany of Arabic titles three sentences long.

Ryan mentally dubbed the Arab the Baba Yaga after a fairy tale his mother used to read him. He was about to write him off as another royal pain-in-the-ass when he noted the eleven-carat-diamond pinkie ring on one hand and the flawless star-ruby sapphire on the other. This guy had money—black gold.

"Your Potentate," Ryan said and the Baba Yaga smiled, a broad, sincere grin, as he shook his hand. Had to be the real thing.

Ryan was about to see if the Baba Yaga needed a lifetime supply of drill bits when the music being played by a combo hidden behind a cascade of iridescent bougainvillaea halted mid-song. All eyes focused on the landing above the sweeping staircase that led from the second floor to the courtyard.

A shapely woman in a toga-style dress of ice blue stood motionless, moonbeams playing over her blond hair. Sculpted with flawless symmetry, every line, every plane of her face was perfection. From a diamond necklace, as fluid as wine, dangled an aquamarine pendant that echoed the color of her eyes. The diamond bezel surrounding the stone nestled between her breasts provocatively refracting the light in the courtyard.

Sonofabitch! Things were looking up. She floated down the stairs, one step at a time, basking in the attention. Halfway down, she paused and the light from the torchiers illuminated her beautiful face.

Damn it. She was old enough to be his mother. Close anyway. He looked at T.J., who had his glass of gin pressed to his lips but wasn't drinking.

"Amore mio . . . amore mio," twittered a high-pitched female voice from behind them. *"Bella notte. Bella. Bella."*

Ryan turned as a woman beelined for Rupert, then hugged him, smacking him noisily on both cheeks with full, painted lips which matched Rupert's red hair. Dressed in a crimson silk gown shot with silver that shimmered with each undulating swish of her hips, the attractive brunette had a neckline that dipped to her navel revealing Atlas-size tits.

"Silicone," Ryan remarked to T.J. "I prefer original equipment."

T.J. grunted his agreement, but he wasn't looking at the twin peaks. His eyes were on the woman who was still poised on the staircase. Her sleek blonde hair, worn in a classic pageboy, cast a shadow across her face. But it didn't hide the lethal look in her polar-blue eyes as she stared at the Italian bimbo.

"That must be Caroline Armstrong." T.J. didn't take his eyes off her.

A servant handed the woman a glass of champagne. She remained where she was, holding the glass like a scepter, until Rupert disentangled himself and came over to her. Ryan couldn't tell what she whispered, but any fool could see she was pissed. Didn't like being upstaged.

Rupert made the rounds with Caroline regally holding his arm. When he introduced her to T.J., she asked him if he knew several of her friends who belonged to Boodles. T.J. lied and said he didn't. She dropped a few other names of exclusive clubs with the same result. T.J. didn't give a damn about the nuances of dress, manners, and clubs that keyed men into London's social strata. Though he had many friends in those clubs, the only club he'd joined was Crockfords. She nudged Rupert and they moved on to the Bulgarian freeloader. Caroline fawned over the dour dowager.

The dinner bell rang, a series of melodic notes, and the guests went into dinner with pomp suitable to Buckingham

Palace. Ryan found himself seated next to the Baba Yaga, who only spoke Arabic, and opposite T.J. and the Italian number, whose name was Lola Ciatti. They were at Caroline's end of the table, though a French couple sat between them and their hostess. Ryan spoke passable French from taking it in high school and spending a fair amount of time in Algeria. But he pretended he didn't when he was introduced to the distant relatives of Baron de Rothschild, who appeared intent on spending the night bashing Chateaux Margaux and Haut Brion.

Ryan sipped his wine and settled in to watch Lola paw T.J. When they'd been introduced, Ryan had decided she wasn't his type. Both he and T.J. preferred long-legged blondes. Lola had an overblown figure that promised to run to fat after one more plate of ravioli. Still, he winked at the Baba Yaga and peeked at her cleavage just once. Okay, twice. Three times. What the hell? He was damn horny after months in the African bush.

"Yves Saint Laurent moved here last week," Caroline told the de Rothschilds' kin.

Who cared? Ryan looked at Caroline and decided she never sincerely smiled at anything—except her own reflection.

Lola kept snuggling up to T.J.'s arm, giving him frequent closeups of her breasts. She didn't speak much English and little French, but she managed to chatter nonstop to T.J.

Between polite conversation with the Baba Yaga in Arabic —he didn't need any drill bits—Ryan listened to Caroline.

"Tomorrow we must visit the Comtesse de Breteuil at her Villa Taylor. She'll show you the tower where Churchill had President Roosevelt carried to see the sunset on the mountains."

"Quand es-ce que ca s'est passé?"

"In 1942, I believe, after their conference in Fez," Caroline answered.

Forty-three, Ryan silently corrected. Had to have been after the Casablanca conference. He continued to listen to Caroline, dropping names like confetti. She reminded him of the dimwits who'd come to his mother to have their clothes altered. Impressed with themselves, they'd lorded their money over his mother by name dropping. Shallow bitches—just like Caroline Armstrong.

Disgusted, Ryan turned his attention to Lola and T.J., who were carrying on a flirtation. She kept making suggestive remarks that became bawdy jokes after she'd had more wine. Ryan got the message; she wanted to hop in the sack with T.J.

The Baba Yaga was dozing off when the servants presented the third course. Lola told them it was pasta blackened by combining squid ink with the semolina.

"*Puta nesca*—whore's hair." Lola giggled suggestively.

Ryan made it a point to never eat anything black, so he put down his fork and listened to Caroline toasting the frigging frogs with *"Santé."* He leaned across the table and raised his glass to Lola and said in a low voice,

> *"Acqua fresca,*
> *Vino puro,*
> *Fica stretta,*
> *Catzo duro."*

Lola howled, laughing so loudly that Ryan's ears rang and T.J. turned red. The Baba Yaga jerked to attention, his gaze on Lola's breasts. Then he rolled his eyes heavenward and muttered something to Allah.

"Pray tell, what is so funny?" Caroline asked T.J.

"Just a toast," T.J. said smoothly without bothering to look at Caroline.

"Repeat it for us."

Speaking in Italian, T.J. rapid-fired the toast, keeping his eyes fixed on his glass.

"Could you say it in English?" Caroline asked, clearly miffed.

Ryan stifled a laugh.

"Doesn't translate," T.J. said, "not literally."

"Do your best."

This time, Ryan chuckled, and T.J. kicked him under the table.

"Fresh water," T.J. began, "pure wine, straight roosters, and nice kitties."

Ryan stifled a laugh at Caroline's confused frown. T.J. had

the water and wine bit correct, but he'd altered hard cocks and tight pussies.

"Kitties?" Lola asked. "Kitties?"

"Pussy," T.J. whispered.

"Pooo—sie?" Lola said in a voice so loud that the King of Tonga, seated at the opposite end of the table, turned toward them. "Pooo-sie?"

The Baba Yaga smiled, flashing a king's ransom in gold. This was one word he knew. He stared at Lola's boobs and listened as she loudly regaled them with a tale of the time her "pooo-sie" got loose in the Paris Ritz. She chased it into the Ritz Club, but she couldn't find it because of all the dancers. When she'd discovered him, he'd already helped himself to an exotic fish from the aquarium.

Ryan noted Caroline hadn't taken her eyes off T.J. She knew she'd been had and didn't like it one bit. Too damn bad. Heart-stopping looks couldn't disguise a ballbuster. She was the type of woman who'd turn a man to stone with a single word or frosty look. He preferred women with smiling eyes and ready laughter. He didn't find bitches like Caroline Armstrong a challenge. T.J. did. To him the whole world was a challenge, a gamble.

T.J. laughed heartily at Lola's story and asked if she had her pussy with her. Sure thing—Ryan would have bet his life on it. She was staying at La Mamounia, and she'd be glad to show T.J. her "pooo—sie." Ryan, who'd been whispering translations to the Baba Yaga, added this as well. The Baba Yaga invited himself along to check out the famous feline.

Caroline was glaring at the four of them now, but Lola was too tipsy to notice, and Ryan didn't give a damn. The Baba Yaga was too obsessed with Lola's breasts to care. T.J. didn't look her way. Out of the corner of his eye, Ryan watched Caroline. She wasn't used to a handsome man making fun of her.

"I detest felines," Caroline said, her eyes zeroed in on T.J. "My daughter had a kitten once, but I got rid of it. I found the odor of the kitty loo offensive."

"Pooo-sie looo?"

The whole table roared except for Caroline. She rose with a martyred smile and swept from the room like a queen leaving her uncouth subjects behind. Lola pooo-sied again, undermining the royal exit. Ryan grinned. What a tight-ass.

After dinner everyone except Caroline went over to La Mamounia to gamble. T.J. and Ryan gambled together while the Baba Yaga tried his luck upstairs with Lola.

The next night they wanted to get out of dinner, but Rupert wouldn't hear of it. This time when they went into dinner, T.J. had been seated next to Caroline. When dinner was over, T.J. was too tired to come with them to La Mamounia.

On his way to bed, his pockets full of winnings, Ryan stopped by T.J.'s room. Just as he went to knock, he heard Caroline's voice. Jesus! Leave it to T.J. He could score with any woman. Even Mrs. Tight-Ass.

18

"I'm flying back to London tomorrow," Ryan told T.J. It had been six weeks since they'd arrived in Marrakesh to work out the phosphorus deal with Rupert Armstrong. Ryan was bored pissless.

"I still have a few more things to attend to here."

Ryan knew exactly why T.J. was lingering. They'd tied down all the loose ends in their export deal with Armstrong. Staying so long required them to move into suites in La Mamounia and keep in touch with London from there. The only thing keeping T.J. in Marrakesh was Caroline Armstrong.

He'd never mentioned her name. Not once. But Ryan knew. Each afternoon, T.J. would make his excuses and slip away into the *medina* and meet Caroline. Nights, T.J. spent on the social circuit—where he could see her—while Ryan gambled at La Mamounia.

For the next six months, Ryan hopscotched between London and Marrakesh. T.J. was too preoccupied to come home to handle his affairs, so he gave Ryan carte blanche. During that time, Ryan ran T.J.'s business. He should have been happy with so much power, but he wasn't. He finally admitted to himself that he missed kicking around with T.J. What did he see in Caroline Armstrong?

One night T.J. unexpectedly appeared at Crockfords and dragged Ryan away from a winning streak at the wheel.

"We're moving permanently to Marrakesh," T.J. informed him as they walked past Morton.

Ryan generously tipped the doorman. "Move if you like, but I'm not going. I'll find another job."

"Let's go over to your place and talk about it."

Ryan reluctantly agreed, although he couldn't imagine what T.J. could say to change his mind. He'd lost respect for him over this affair. Caroline Armstrong had to be the reason T.J. wanted to move. What did she have that his mother hadn't?

When they arrived at Ryan's maisonette in Mayfair, he poured them a round of Hennessy Extra and sat down, waiting to hear what T.J. had to say.

"I love Caroline very, very much. I know she seems cold, but she isn't. She's had a hard life."

T.J. paused to take a sip, and Ryan thought of his mother. Caroline Armstrong didn't know shit about a hard life.

"She came from a very poor family. She married an American who was here with the embassy. He was transferred to Tokyo. She adored him, but he was killed. She had to marry Armstrong because she had no way to support her two children."

"Now you're going to marry her."

T.J. nodded. Ryan was surprised. He hardly knew the woman, but word around Marrakesh was the flames of social climbing fired Caroline's every move. Hobnobbing with the jet set, she fancied herself to be a princess. She'd better be prepared to give all that up. T.J. wasn't about to sit around all day sipping vintage wine and kiss-assing peers of the realm.

"Come with me. I've purchased a villa. We can—"

"No."

T.J. clasped his snifter and stared at the amber liquid. When he lifted his eyes, they were troubled. "Let's keep the London office open with you in charge. I'll handle what I can from Marrakesh. You come down whenever . . . whenever you feel there's something you need to see me about personally."

They left it at that. For the next four months, Ryan rarely spoke with T.J. and he didn't go to Marrakesh. When they spoke, T.J. didn't sound happy but Ryan never questioned him.

Something came up unexpectedly and Ryan had to fly to Marrakesh to get T.J.'s signature. He pulled into Griffith's high-walled compound on the outskirts of the city at noon. T.J. answered the door himself.

Ryan walked in. "What's the matter? You look terrible."

"It's getting to me," he confessed. "The only time I see Caroline is when she can sneak away."

"Thought she was leaving Armstrong."

"She is, but she doesn't want to hurt him. He's been very good to her and the children. She's waiting for the right time to tell him."

That was months ago, buddy. Ryan handed him the document and watched T.J. as he signed it. He'd aged in the last few months. His hair was even grayer, and his eyes had lost their luster.

"Let's go to lunch down on the boulevard. We'll sit around at one of the sidewalk cafes and watch the girls."

Ryan almost declined, but the eager look on T.J.'s face changed his mind.

Shaded by fragrant orange trees, they sat at a sidewalk cafe on Avenue Mohammed V sipping a local *vieux pape* and watching the black-robed Moslem women swathed in veils walk by amid women dressed in Western clothes. Too soon, it was time for T.J. to meet Caroline.

"Wait here," T.J. said. "I won't be gone long."

"Aren't you meeting her at your place?"

T.J. shook his head. "Caroline doesn't want to chance being seen—until she's told Rupert. She disguises herself by dressing like a native. We meet in the *mellah* at our secret spot."

In the *mellah*? Clever. The Jewish quarter was decrepit, even by the standards of the *medina.* The last place anyone would take a lady. It was depressing as hell. How could T.J. go there every day?

Located within the *medina,* the *mellah* was an area created simply because the Moslems needed a section to segregate the Jews. Although the Koran guaranteed freedom of religion, the reality was quite different. Through the centuries, Jews had suffered sharp restrictions. They could bear no arms, were required to wear distinct clothes and pay a special tax. Naturally, they weren't allowed to participate in the government. Often, they were massacred or dragged through the streets behind camels.

The Moorish influence, followed by the Europeans, elevated many Jews who were self-taught. Better educated than the Moroccan Moslems, the Jews quickly became traders and then bankers. Their lot improved when the French colonized Morocco, and Jews held government positions. Over the years, they used their banking and commercial interests to establish connections in Europe that allowed the Moroccan Jews to become fabulously wealthy. But with the French withdrawal and the creation of Israel, most fled, terrified by the prospect of a Moslem state.

As it turned out, the Jews had little to worry about. Mohammed V and his successor, King Hassan, both valued their expertise and encouraged the Jews to stay. Those remaining in Morocco had suffered far less than Jews living in other Arab countries. Morocco was the closest to the West—the farthest from the Middle East and its rising tide of Moslem fundamentalism and anti-Israeli militancy. But to this day, the fear remained. Wealthy Jews, living in various parts of the city, carried French passports. Just in case.

Today, the *mellah* was home only to the poorest, least educated Jews. The few times Ryan had become lost in the *medina* and found himself in the Jewish quarter, he'd been overwhelmed by the squalor. No chance anyone would look for Caroline there.

Over the next six months, Ryan frequently visited Marrakesh. He kept telling himself that T.J. needed him. One day while he was hanging around the villa, Ryan checked the records of the phosphorus they were exporting for Armstrong, which T.J. had been handling on his own from Marrakesh. Something wasn't right. After kicking around Africa, dealing with shysters circumventing the legitimate diamond market, he'd developed a sixth sense about withheld information.

Ryan had been watching the phosphorus market in the *Financial Times.* The Japanese kept overpaying Armstrong.

He shouldn't complain. They were making a killing. Still, his suspicions nagged at him, and he decided to investigate.

While T.J. was off on his usual afternoon tryst in the *mellah,* Ryan went down to the *fondouk* to check the phosphorus shipment. The warehouse was located on the east side of the *medina* not far from the dye vats where unspun wool was dipped in pits dug into the ground and lined with copper. It was dark inside the mud-brick building, but the light coming through the cracks in the roof guided him. He checked several crates. Phosphorus.

Then he noticed the Xs which appeared on some containers, but not others. He pried one open and touched its contents. Dried blood accumulated around his finger, revealing the mammoth elephant tusk beneath. He imagined the poor beast lying in the brutal African sun, wounded but not yet dead—the elephants' hides were too tough to ensure an instant kill—as the poachers chainsawed their tusks off. Enraged, he opened another Xed box, and still another. More ivory. He'd bet it came from the Masai Mara game preserve in Kenya. After all, they'd met Armstrong in Nairobi doing "business."

Most African countries had poaching laws, but they were too poor to strictly enforce them. Undoubtedly, Armstrong wanted to take advantage of the market. He didn't want his name tainted—should anything go wrong—so he'd contracted with T.J. to transport the contraband.

Japan. It figured. The Japanese had an insatiable appetite for ivory. And they paid top price for it.

Ryan spent the rest of the afternoon relabeling the boxes. Instead of reading Griffith International, they now were marked as merchandise from Armstrong Unlimited. Without waiting to tell T.J. what he was doing, he flew back to London. He used the computer to alter his records. When the banks opened the following day, Ryan persuaded a few cuties at Barclays to help him out. Satisfied no trail led back to Griffith International and every finger pointed to Armstrong, Ryan went to see Dr. Denton Digsby.

One night at Crockfords, an inebriated MP had confided in Ryan that he owed his election to a preacher turned media maestro. Apparently, the wizard could transform a coffee klatch into a media event. When Ryan reached Digsby's office in a stately building known to house the royal gynecologist among a legion of other overpaid private physicians, he had his doubts. This uncertainty increased when he'd called the cross-eyed stick of a receptionist hot lips, and Digsby bounded into the reception area like a lion from his lair. The doctor of divinity had gotten real pissy, but calmed down when Ryan explained that he was not seeking media attention for himself. Then he went on to give Digsby the ugly facts.

"Heavens," Digsby said. "The Lord won't like this. He didn't have Noah save his creatures, loading them two by two on the ark, to have them slaughtered."

Ryan left the preacher's office, not knowing if he should call for the straitjacket corps or not. He kept the faith, praying Digsby would come through, but hedged his bets and contacted Interpol.

Before he could call T.J. and tell him what he'd done, T.J. appeared in the London office.

"I'm moving back."

"Why?" Ryan blurted out before he could remind himself that it wasn't any of his business.

"I gave Caroline an ultimatum," he answered, his tone desolate. "Me or Armstrong." He walked over to the frost-whorled window painted opaque silver by freezing sleet and stared out. "She said she loved me more than anything on earth. But I couldn't give her the social position she needed."

Ma would have followed you to the end of the earth.

Ryan let T.J. brood until that evening when they were having dinner at Crockfords. Then he told him about the contraband ivory. T.J. was still too shell-shocked by Caroline's decision to say more than "I like the way you handled it."

"Don't you understand what I'm saying?" Ryan asked, trying to break through to the T.J. that he knew. He loved animals and would never condone poaching. "Not only was Armstrong poaching full-grown elephants, he was killing babies as well. Two of those crates contained tusks not more than six inches long. How much do you suppose they're worth?"

"That small? Less than a pound sterling, about two dollars. Only the larger tusks are valuable."

"Right. He clubbed baby elephants, leaving them to suffer a

slow death beside their butchered mothers—for less than a pound."

T.J. shook his head; Ryan knew what he was thinking. Caroline had chosen a man like Rupert Armstrong over him. Ryan questioned the depth of T.J.'s character. Although Caroline was a beautiful woman, she was a very shallow person unworthy of T.J.'s love. T.J. must see this. It had been obvious to Ryan from the start.

Like a frag grenade exploding, the truth hit Ryan. After years of winning, conquering numerous women, T.J. had lost. Caroline's attraction wasn't her beauty. The challenge she presented fascinated T.J. Was T.J. capable of real love, the kind that lasted a lifetime? The way his mother loved T.J. until the day she died? The way Ryan wanted a woman to love him?

T.J. interrupted Ryan's thoughts with "I hope the press screws Armstrong—royally screws him."

It did. The pussyfooting preacher came through with press and television coverage of the Interpol confiscation of the Armstrong Unlimited crates in Japan. It hit the news at just the right time—nothing else was happening. The Cold War was at a standstill, Parliament didn't have anything interesting on the docket, and none of the Windsors had been caught in clandestine clenches. The press harped on the poaching for weeks. Armstrong weaseled. Hadn't known, some mixup, wasn't his fault.

Digsby got some gruesome pictures to the tabloids, which then went after Armstrong like a pack of pit bulls. The attack extended not just to Rupert, who hadn't resided in the UK for years, but to his relatives who did. Ryan had to admit it was a great ploy. The only thing that beat peer pressure was a guilt trip from your family. Garrick Armstrong, Rupert's father, took out full-page advertisements in *The Times*, denouncing his son. An entire branch of the Armstrong family discovered a long-lost relative and double-jointed their name, becoming the Armstrong-Smythes.

The best thing to come out of the exposé was that the BBC sent a film crew to Africa and filmed a documentary, which played around the world, keeping the plight of the elephants at the forefront of the news.

Ryan expected a monumental bill for the media blitz of the

decade. When none came, he called Digsby's office. Hot lips put the fruitcake doctor on the line.

"The good Lord never charges to protect those who cannot protect themselves."

"Amen," Ryan rang off.

After a time, T.J. seemed to become himself again. He never mentioned the Armstrongs, but Ryan noticed he made no move to sell the villa in Marrakesh. He figured T.J. still held out the hope that Caroline would change her mind.

To divert T.J.'s attention—and give him the challenge he craved—Ryan got them involved in the hunt for the industrial diamonds with NASA specifications to be used in America's space program. Why the hell not? He and T.J. were out there anyway. Might as well keep their eyes out for diamonds with NASA specs.

It wasn't as easy as they'd expected. The competition, particularly from the Israelis, was fierce. Everyone wanted in on the action. Finally, they located a thirteen-carat diamond in Zaire that fit the specs. All they had to do now was get it to America.

Late one night in Zaire just outside the lean-to that passed for a terminal at the Kisangani Airport, an armed black man jumped out from behind a parked truck, demanding the diamond.

In an explosion of movement, Ryan tackled him. "Run," he managed to yell to T.J. before he knocked the attacker to the ground. Ryan pinned the man, who was too overweight to be much of a threat, and took his gun from him. Now what to do with him? The last thing they needed was for him to blab to the police that they were transporting diamonds. T.J. had the diamond in a briefke. For generations, diamond brokers had used a simple square of paper folded five ways to transport loose stones. T.J. had it hidden in his film canister because they didn't have an export permit.

Ryan decided he'd have to hold the man until T.J.'s plane left. That way if the subject of the diamond came up, it would be his word against Ryan's. He waved the gun, motioning for the man to stand. As he came to his feet, he lunged for Ryan with a Tomcat in his hand. The deadly knife was aimed at his heart. Ryan fired one round and the man slumped to the ground. A geyser of blood gushed from the point-blank shot in the chest and oozed into the thirsty African sand.

Instantly, police dressed in khaki-colored uniforms with the Bermuda shorts of the tropics descended upon Ryan. He looked at the terminal and saw T.J. coming back for him. Ryan motioned for him to leave. There wasn't any problem here; this was a clear case of self-defense.

But there was a major problem. The Tomcat had somehow disappeared and Ryan was at a loss to explain why he'd shot an unarmed man. That's when he discovered he'd watched entirely too much television in his youth. No one had read him his rights. He wasn't allowed to call his lawyer, the embassy, or anyone. Due process—bullshit.

They took him into a concrete prison whose windows were six-inch barred slits just below the ceiling. The ripe equatorial smell of damp earth and garbage melded with sweat and feces. Down a corridor, deep in the bowels of the jail, the guards stopped before a cell that was twelve feet square. With their flashlights, they panned across the small space, awakening nine natives. Several appeared to be too ill to stand. The others had savage eyes with the predatory look he recalled in the eyes of the Viet Cong. Inured to violence—and death—they valued nothing. Human life was meaningless, because their own held no memory of a happy yesterday or the promise of a brighter tomorrow. Death meant nothing to them. Their own or his.

A rush of primal fear curdled his blood as the guards unlocked the door and shoved him into the stuffy cell, then left him in total darkness. Within seconds the other prisoners were all over him, trying to take his clothes from him, checking his pockets for food, grabbing his balls. Ryan lashed out with both fists and a couple of karate kicks. In the tomblike darkness, some blows connected, others missed. Footsteps retreated a few feet and a volley of Swahili followed. Ryan kept his back to the door; 'Nam had taught him to protect his ass. He waited for them to attack again. They didn't. But he knew it would only be a matter of time.

The hazy gray light of early dawn gradually filled the cell. Still plastered to the door, Ryan waited. The men began to stir and he realized they were too far inside the prison to get any real light. Peering around the cell, Ryan tried to determine who the cell leader was. Every rat pack had one. He decided the leader must be the tall black with teeth askew, several protruding like fangs. The man swaggered over to the putrid hole in the floor that served as a latrine and pulled out his dick.

Ryan pounced, grabbing the guy's balls in one hand and giving them a violent twist. With the other hand he grasped the man's Adam's apple. Using the full weight of his body and the element of surprise, Ryan shoved him up against the wall. He banged the man's head repeatedly against the concrete wall while twisting his balls.

"Nobody touches me, you cocksucker. Nobody. Understand?"

Of course, he didn't. Probably he didn't comprehend more than a handful of words in English. But the terror in his eyes said he got the message. Ryan released him and walked over to the choicest spot in the cell, the corner. He could sit there and be protected on two sides. He kicked the two men occupying the small space aside. "Get the fuck out of my place."

They scuttled away and Ryan sandwiched himself into the corner. Every eye in the cell was on him, their eyeballs gleaming unnaturally white in their dark faces. They thought he was crazy. Let 'em. The best defense is a good offense.

At first, Ryan wasn't terribly worried. He and T.J. had worked out a plan to cover just this sort of thing. Whoever was on the outside would get a little "dash" to the right people. Bribes went a long way everywhere in Africa. The people were too poor not to be swayed by easy money. But when days became weeks, he grew increasingly apprehensive. He imagined T.J. had been killed or else he would have heard from him.

Finally, an attaché from the American Embassy appeared to inform Ryan that he'd been charged with murder. When the trial would be held, he couldn't say. Weeks, months, who knew. Sorry. You know how it is around here.

Ryan didn't realize T.J. had done anything until the guards started giving him extra food. They even managed to pass him a small bar of soap. It didn't do much good. The single shower was no more than a leaky faucet trickling out brown water pumped directly from the river. Few men ventured into the shower; it was an invitation to be raped. He wasn't concerned. He'd pulled enough stunts to be a certified loony tune even in this group. But he didn't shower because he knew most rivers in Africa were contaminated with bilharziasis or roundworm larvae. Both deadly.

Days became weeks, then months as he sat with his back to the wall, allowing himself only the briefest of catnaps. Weakened, he had to be on guard constantly. 'Nam had only been a dress rehearsal.

Time no longer had meaning, merging as it did into an endless stream of dark nights and bleak gray days. He would have lost hope as well had it not been for his increased rations. T.J. was out there somewhere. What the hell was taking so long?

One day the guards appeared and opened the cell door, calling his name. All nine men charged. The guards beat them back and Ryan shoved through the melee into the corridor. After being in the hole for so many months, he had to keep a hand over his eyes as the guards led him into the captain's office.

Through the spaces between his fingers, he saw T.J. His usually animated face froze. There may have been tears in his green eyes.

"Ryan?"

"Who the hell are you expecting?" He hadn't said more than a dozen words in the last two months; his voice was hoarse.

T.J. handed him his sunglasses and Ryan put them on, but he still had to squint to see.

The captain shook T.J.'s hand and smiled, revealing a picket fence of ivory in his dark face. "The charges have been dropped. Mr. Westcott is free to go."

T.J. guided him out to a waiting jeep that took them directly to the airport. Ryan didn't say a word as they drove to the field. Inside the single-engine plane flown by a bush pilot typical of Africa, Ryan waited, holding his breath for the take-off. *Let's get to hell out of here.*

The engine coughed to life and the plane skipped down the buckled tarmac until it gained enough speed to soar into the welcoming blue sky. Ryan sagged back in his seat. "Where are we going?"

"Nairobi," T.J. answered as he handed him a cold Tusker from the small Styrofoam cooler near the bulkhead. "I want you to see a doctor."

Ryan sipped the beer. He couldn't imagine what he looked like—or smelled like. He was still in the same clothes he'd worn the night of the shooting. Blood stained the front and concentric rings of dried sweat circled the material beneath his armpits. He'd lost weight; he'd long since traded his belt to a guard for a piece of rope that could be tied tight enough to hold up his pants.

According to the doctor in Nairobi, other than his weight loss Ryan had only one small intestinal problem. The worms he'd acquired from eating tainted food would be taken care of by a bottle of pills.

When they reached their hotel where T.J. had booked a huge suite, Ryan deadheaded for the shower. Forty minutes later he emerged and found T.J. had put a toilet kit on the counter and a suitcase full of clothes still bearing their Harrods tags on his bed. Ryan shaved, first having to clip the shaggy beard he'd had no choice but to grow. When he finished, the face staring at him from the steamy mirror wasn't his own.

You look like a piece of dogshit after a rainstorm.

Naked, he collapsed on top of the bed and fell into a dreamless sleep. Ryan was vaguely aware of T.J. coming in several times. Once he covered Ryan with a sheet. Another time he put his finger on the pulse point at Ryan's neck.

When he finally woke, it was dark. Across the chair beside his bed were several new pairs of slacks—in a smaller size. He dressed and went into the sitting room where he found T.J. sipping Boodles and reading the *Times.* He jumped to his feet when he saw Ryan.

"Feel better?"

Ryan nodded. "I slept longer than I meant to."

T.J. picked up the telephone. "I'll bet you're starved. Let's get room service right away. What would you like?"

Shepherd's pie the way Ma used to make it with sour cream in the mashed-potato topping. "Whatever."

T.J. ordered while Ryan poured himself a gin. A double. Then he slumped down on the sofa. T.J. came over and took a seat beside him.

"Ready to talk? There are some things I need to say to you. I've been doing a lot of thinking."

"So have I." He'd survived, partly because he'd let his mind drift beyond the confines of the cell. He'd mentally planned the rest of his life.

"Sorry it took so long to get you out. Don't think you weren't on my mind every minute of every day. Arranging something like this took longer than we ever thought."

"It's not your fault. We never anticipated I would be held for murder."

T.J. picked up his gin and took a long drink. "While you were in prison, I took a close look at myself and I don't like what I see. I almost got you killed because I'm an overgrown boy too immature to act responsibly. There's no reason for us to be chasing around after diamonds. We can afford to buy them on the open market. But I've done it for years. Why? For the thrill of it."

"This last time was a little *too* thrilling."

"You're right. I almost got you killed because I've been trying to recapture the excitement I had flying for the RAF. I had no right to involve you, to risk your life."

"I'm a big boy. I knew what I was getting into."

"From now on, we're going to live and enjoy ourselves. No more cheap thrills. We'll expand Griffith International into new, safe areas."

"I've got an idea," Ryan said. "Promise not to laugh." T.J. nodded and he continued, "I want to make diamonds from methane gas."

T.J. looked at him blankly for a second, then he roared, laughing until tears ran down his face.

Pissed, Ryan got up to answer the knock on the door. A waiter wheeled in a cart laden with food. T.J. came over to tip him.

"Sorry I laughed. But there's only one other person on earth who'd think of turning shit into diamonds." He pointed to himself.

Ryan couldn't help chuckling.

T.J. slapped him on the back and bear-hugged him, holding him tight. "It's great to have you back."

Ryan didn't know what to say. This was the first time any man had shown him the least bit of affection. T.J. had always treated him in a breezy, casual way as if they were friends. Ryan clutched T.J., then dropped his arms.

"I want you to have this." T.J. took off his gold leopard ring and slipped it on Ryan's pinkie. A perfect fit.

"I don't want—"

"Listen to me. This ring was left with me when my mother abandoned me at the Bolingford Orphanage. It's a man's ring, obviously. My father's?" T.J. shrugged, his eyes melancholy. "I haven't a clue. But as I grew up, I looked closely at every man and woman I saw, looking for some resemblance. At night, I'd lie on my cot and dream that I'd been left behind because of some terrible mistake, and that my parents would discover where I was and rescue me."

Ryan nodded, thanking the Lord for his mother.

"When I left Bolingford, I tried to trace the ring. All I found out is that it's one of a kind and had been made in India. Had my father been with the military there? Is that where I got my courage? I never found out. But when I flew for the RAF, I wore the ring. Before each mission, I rotated it seven times. It always brought me luck."

Ryan managed an encouraging smile, but he wasn't superstitious. People made their own luck.

"When you were in prison, I thought my luck had run out. But it held. Now I want you to have it, just as you'll eventually inherit everything I have."

"Hold it, I—"

"You're my son. You can't deny your birthright. Besides, my solicitors have already revamped my holdings. We're partners now. But you're going to earn your share."

Ryan stared down at the ring with the mysterious past. During the lonely months in prison, he'd realized how special T.J. was and how proud he was to be his son. If only T.J. had loved his mother.

"Your mother was a wonderful woman," T.J. said, almost as if he'd sensed Ryan's single reservation about admitting he was his son. "She did the right thing by not getting rid of you.

My life would have been empty without you. You're the best friend I lost and a son—all in one."

"Ma loved you to the day she died. She would have done anything for you."

"You have no idea how many times in the last few months I've reminded myself of that. You see, I had a great deal of difficulty finding the right person to get you released. I spread a lot of money around. Nothing happened. I might as well have stood in Trafalgar Square and tossed it to the pigeons."

"They gave me more food because of your money."

"For all the good it did." T.J. shook his head. "I could see I wasn't going to get you out until I made contact with just the right person. Otherwise, they'd keep taking my money and putting me off. So I went to Caroline. I knew Rupert had done business for years in Zaire."

"Yeah, in Haute Zaire poaching gorillas, sending their noses to Hong Kong to be ground up for aphrodisiacs and selling their hands for ashtrays."

"I was desperate. I knew he had contacts at the highest levels of government. I begged Caroline to get me a name, but she refused. She was afraid that Rupert might find out. Then I reminded her of all the times she'd said she loved me. I told her if she really meant it, she'd help me. She could find a clever way to ask Rupert without his knowing it was to help us."

"She wouldn't do it?" Figured, selfish bitch.

"No. I got the name through the BBC boys who'd done the exposé on poaching." As he looked at Ryan, his voice wavered. "I never loved Caroline, not the way your mother loved me. I don't know why." He paused, shrugging apologetically. "Maybe it was because I was raised in an orphanage. No one loved me. I didn't learn to love anyone." His eyes shifted away from Ryan's questioning gaze. "But I love you, son. If I'd lost you, I . . ."

The heat rose to Ryan's cheeks as T.J. faced him. He wanted to tell his father he loved him—had always loved him even though he hadn't known he existed—but the memory of his mother and her lifetime of suffering stopped him.

19

Vora stood nude in her dressing room in front of a three-way mirror, and ran her nails through her amber curls. Did she look better with her hair cut to mid-chin and left to curl naturally as Dr. Digsby had suggested? Basil said no, advocating keeping her artificially lengthened hair until her own grew out, but Vora trusted Dr. Digsby. Only a kind man could employ that ugly crosspatch of a receptionist. Vora had immediately taken his advice. Since Lauren had asked Vora for her tickets to *Miss Saigon,* she'd had nothing better to do after the session with Dr. Digsby than to go to Miracles and have her hair restyled.

She did a slow pirouette in front of the mirror, checking her pared-down hips. Amazing. With Clive out of her life, she'd continued to lose weight. It had to be her nonstop running around for Ravissant. For Irek.

She shrugged into her silk dressing gown and went into her bedroom, thinking of the Russian. Lauren had told her the luncheon with the critics hadn't gone well. Without ever having seen his work, they were lying in wait for him. She wasn't surprised; she'd expected it.

Lauren's bold plan shocked Vora. She would know in a few more hours if Lauren's scheme to outwit the critics was on track. She had promised to call as soon as she came home from the theater.

Vora pulled out a box of Cadbury's Biarritz chocolates from her stash in the Louis Quinze secretary and plopped down on her bed. She flashed the remote control at the telly, and it immediately sprang to life. She scanned the channels. Nothing. She missed Emma Freud's *Pillow Talk*. The great-granddaughter of the psychoanalyst had had the inspiration to do a chat show in bed with her guests. Clad in jammies, they let their guard down, revealing more about themselves than they ever would have under normal circumstances. Vora clicked off the telly when conservative MP Terry Dicks's face came on the screen.

She took Jilly Cooper's latest novel off the nightstand and opened it, tossing the sterling silver bookmark aside, and tried to remember where she'd left off. The telephone rang. Normally, she let Chiswick screen her calls, but tonight she suspected it might be Lauren calling from the loo at intermission with a progress report.

"Hello," she said, ignoring the click from the line in the butler's pantry.

"Vora?"

She recognized Irek's voice. What was wrong? Why was he calling? He didn't have his own telephone. Didn't want, didn't need, only interrupted his painting. "Are you all right?"

"Yes. I am finished."

Finished? Was he backing out on them now? Was he that upset over Dr. Digsby? After the doctor had explained the power of the media and Irek had spent two hours with his "pit bulls" learning how to handle himself with the media, she thought that they had things under control.

"With the painting. With the painting."

He'd finished the portrait. Finally. She'd never seen it, but Lauren had spoken so highly of his most recent work—the one he'd agonized through an artist's block trying to finish. She'd been holding a special page in the catalogue for it, and Lauren had reserved a place of honor for it in the gallery. "Good. Thanks awfully for calling to tell me. I can hardly wait to see it."

"I will be there in five or four minutes. Am at Bellington's place."

"Bellington? Where does he live?" His friend probably lived near the Thames-side complex where Irek had moved. Other than Ryan, Irek had no friends on the West End.

"Hyde Park corner. Be there soon."

Vora scrambled to her knees clutching the receiver, listening to the dial tone. Bellington. He meant Wellington. Of course, the Apsley House. England's grateful gift to Arthur Wellesley, Duke of Wellington, was now a museum. Driving Ryan's car, Irek was at Hyde Park corner. Less than five minutes away.

She dashed into her dressing room and automatically grabbed her bottle of specially blended foundation. She shook it, then stopped. Let the freckles show. Hesitating, she took a second look at herself before reaching for her sable brush and dusting her cheekbones with soft-peach blush.

After pulling on leather pants she'd bought for the country and had never worn, Vora slipped on a camel-colored cashmere sweater. Her reflection didn't look right. Too formal. She sprinted down the hall into Archer's old room and rifled through his closet, thankful that in all this time she hadn't had the heart to give his things away. She found his worn tweed hacking jacket. He'd been tall, but narrow shouldered. After rolling up the sleeves, she put it on. Perfect.

The bell rang downstairs. "I'll get it," she yelled to Chiswick as she reached the landing.

She raced across the cold marble and came to a stop with her hand on the brass knob. As she opened the door, she realized she had bare feet.

"Vora?" A frown furrowed Irek's forehead.

He hates my hair. I should have listened to Basil. "Come in."

As he stepped into the entry, she noticed his new clothes—off the rack, certainly—but brand new. A nubby cranberry sweater increased the breadth of his shoulders, and gray flannel slacks made his legs look longer. He raked his hand through his hair, a slow smile lighting his face, and she noticed yet another watch. This one was a diver's watch with a luminous dial.

"You cut your hair." His smile widened and he nodded his approval. "Beautiful. Much beautiful."

She fluffed her hair with one hand, joy bubbling inside her. "I'm glad you like it." *You don't think my freckles are ugly, do you?*

He kept smiling—that tender smile she loved—and looking her up and down. Her toes curled against the cold marble.

"Did you bring the painting with you?"

"Too big. You come with me and see it."

Surprised delight rippled through her. He'd made a special trip to get her. She'd be the first one to see his latest, his best work. "Let me run up and put on some shoes. I'll be right back."

Upstairs, she surveyed the rows of shoes her maid neatly shelved for her, and selected a pair of brown Bally loafers. Halfway down the stairs, she heard men's voices. As she rounded the landing, her hand on the freshly polished newel post, she saw Irek speaking with two men. She raced to the bottom.

"Vora, they are from Scotland Yard and Imperpole," Irek said.

"Interpol," corrected a pudgy man with receding gray hair. "I'm Brian Dunfee, Interpol. And this is Alan Coombs from New Scotland Yard."

"Gentlemen." Vora shook their hands. Had Irek done something wrong?

"We'd like to speak with you privately, Mrs. Leighton."

Vora breathed a silent sigh of relief. "About Archer?" She reached for Irek's hand, her fingers trembling. His warm hand closed over hers with a reassuring squeeze. "This is Irek Makarova. He and I are close . . . close friends. I'd like him to stay with me."

"Read rights." Irek's voice was gruff.

"Mr. Makarova," Dunfee said, "you've watched too many telly programs from America. There is no need to Mirandize anyone here. Besides, Mrs. Leighton isn't under investigation. We merely want to speak with her."

Irek didn't look convinced; he moved closer to Vora.

"Let's go in the parlor." She led them into the adjacent room, taking Irek to a brocade loveseat opposite two wing-back chairs, and sat down. He moved close to her, sitting with his shoulder touching hers, his hand covering hers.

"Mrs. Leighton," Alan Coombs said, his voice somber. "We believe your husband was murdered."

"Who did it?"

"We're hoping you can help us," Coombs replied as he flipped open a notebook he had across his lap.

"I told you all I knew when I came to you last year."

"The Yard didn't conduct a complete investigation," Coombs said, "because the death occurred in the jurisdiction of the Scarborough Police Department. All I have here is the preliminary report from the officer who interviewed you then. I'm with Special Investigations. We're cooperating on this case with Interpol."

"Why?" Vora edged closer to Irek.

"Well, ma'am," Dunfee said. "We suspect your husband was murdered by a gang of highly organized and sophisticated thugs dealing in fraudulent prints. It's an international syndicate. That's where Interpol comes in."

"What took you so long to decide Archer had been murdered? It's been more than a year."

"The Beverly Hills Police contacted Interpol when they were investigating the fraudulent prints being marketed by a gallery in Beverly Hills. Are you familiar with the case?" Dunfee asked.

"Yes. It's been in all the trade publications. They were accused of selling bogus prints by Dali and Chagall as well as fake oils."

"We're after the source of those prints. We suspect there's a syndicate using printing facilities in a variety of countries. They don't care that the quality is appalling—often nothing more than cheap photocopies."

"That's exactly what Archer said when he caught them using Ravissant Publishing. The prints were terrible. That was odd because we do nothing but prints of the first water."

"Exactly," Dunfee said. "Quality means nothing because they're using these prints to conceal their profits from the drug trade. Through a series of shell companies it's easy to show buying prints and reselling them at a profit. On the books, it appears to be a legitimate business."

"Would not a gallery owner know bad print from good?" Irek asked.

"I'm afraid too many gallery owners see the print market as a way to make easy money. With the runaway prices of originals, prints are the only type of art most people can afford. There are some unscrupulous gallery owners who buy obviously fake prints at prices far below market value. Then they foist them off on an unsuspecting public."

"The syndicate printing them," Coombs added, "makes no money off the prints, but they don't care. All they want to do is to camouflage money that really comes from dealing in drugs."

"Certificate of Authenticity," Irek said. "Do not buyers ask for?"

"Easily forged, I'm afraid." Dunfee shrugged.

"It can destroy an artist's reputation," Vora said, apprehension seizing her as she thought of Irek's fledgling career. If anything happened to his prints, it could ruin his career before it got off the ground.

"We're trying our best to put a stop to it," Dunfee added. "You can help us by recalling exactly what happened when your husband died."

Vora recounted her conversation with Archer on the evening prior to his death. "It was the last time I saw him."

Coombs made notes on a ruled yellow pad. "Other than his warning the previous evening, did anything else about his death make you suspicious?"

"Arch's Jaguar was less than two months old—too soon for the brakes to fail so it went off a cliff. But more important, what was he doing all the way up in Scarborough on a lonely road? He'd planned to meet Finley Tibbets at Boodle's after dinner. He never even called to cancel. That wasn't like Archer."

"But he did try to call you about teatime?"

"Yes. He called home from York where he was appraising some paintings for a client. I didn't take the call, but later Chiswick told me that Archer had said it was urgent."

Coombs consulted his notes. "You were at Miracles?"

"Yes. Chiswick told Archer, but he didn't call there."

"You were still there at teatime after going in at eleven? Isn't that a long time for a cut and blow-dry?" Dunfee asked.

"Here's a list of services Mrs. Leighton received." Coombs handed Dunfee a lavender sheet of paper with Miracles' logo.

Dunfee lofted his eyebrows. "Pore vacuuming, volcanic-ash-mud pack, almond and aloe facial, lash tint, brow contouring, manicure, pedicure, full body wax, steam bath, massage, eucalyptus treatment for cellulite, one-hour session in the immersion tank, root tint, avocado conditioning for damaged hair, style and blow-dry, consultation with makeup artist, full makeup session."

"Surprised you not still there," Irek said, a laugh in his voice as he squeezed her hand.

Vora felt utterly stupid. What would Irek say if he knew she spent an entire day each month at Miracles? "Afterward, Basil, the owner, took me for a drink at the Goat in Boots on Fulham, then to dinner at Bibendum. The police called shortly after I came home. I chartered a jet helicopter to Scarborough that night. When I saw the crash site, I knew he'd been murdered."

"How?" Irek asked.

"The dirt road went off the main route into Scarborough. Arch would *never* have taken the Jag down an unpaved road."

"Fog," Irek suggested.

"No, but it did rain late that night. It was impossible to tell if there were any other tire tracks on the road."

"Other than these men who'd loaned your husband money, can you think of anyone who would want to see him dead—for any reason?" Coombs looked at her, his pen poised.

"He'd recently broken up with Elizabeth Hartley, his mistress of long standing," Vora said after hesitating and wondering if she wanted to remember the unhappy hours Liz Hartley had caused her. "But I doubt if she would have had the cheek to kill him."

"She didn't. We checked her alibi. She was gorilla trekking in Zaire, deep in the bush on her hands and knees, hoping to spot a silverback." Coombs tapped the eraser tip of the pencil against the pad and appeared to be very uncomfortable with the personal turn in the conversation. "She was very angry, though. It seems your husband had promised her that he was leaving you. When she called him on it, he walked."

Vora didn't trust her voice. So, Arch had refused to leave her for Liz. She'd needlessly worried and tried to make Archer jealous with meaningless affairs.

"Just how was he killed?" Vora asked. *Please say he went quickly.*

"He'd ingested a dose of brucine. It acts almost instantly. Someone was up on that cliff with him. They gave him a lethal dose of the poison then pushed his car off the cliff into the surf sixty feet below."

Tears stung Vora's eyes and her throat seemed to close up. Poor Arch. Irek put his arm around her, hugging her tightly. The room was quiet for a few minutes. Only the rhythmic tick-tick of the portico mystery clock, one of Cartier's finest art-deco pieces and Arch's favorite, could be heard.

"Why push car into ocean?" Irek asked.

"To cover up his murder and make it look like an accident."

"I insisted they double-check the cause of death," Vora said. "Why didn't the coroner realize Arch had been poisoned?"

"Brucine is almost impossible to detect with just a routine autopsy," Coombs said. "Only the most sophisticated laboratories can discover its presence. You kicked up a bit of a tiff with the coroner. He took tissue samples, but found nothing. Luckily, he saved them. The laboratory at Fort Halstead in Kent uncovered the traces of brucine."

"Please," Vora said, her voice thick. "Find his killer."

"We've given this case top priority," Coombs assured her.

Assuming they'd finished, Vora started to rise.

"Just a minute," Dunfee said. "Just how much do you know about Lauren Winthrop?"

Lauren sat beside Finley in Groucho's bar and sipped something called a velvet. Champagne and stout. She didn't see its attraction, but she kept drinking it anyway to hide her nerves. She'd been waiting all evening for the opportunity to ask Finley for Groucho's membership roster. During lunch, she'd decided to hedge her bets. Irek would be a major talent—she was convinced of it—but it might take longer than she anticipated if the critics scuttled him the first time out. She had faith that other artists—writers, pianists, actors, even rock stars—would recognize talent. If collectors like Jeffrey Archer, who'd been purchasing art for years, bought Irek's work, the critics could go to hell.

"Finley, I don't know what I would do without you," Lauren began with a coy smile. "You've been such a tremendous help with this exhibition."

"I don't mind, not a'tall." He gave her a sly look she took to mean he would like a few favors in return.

"I was wondering . . . no, I don't suppose it would be possible. Never mind. Forget I said anything."

He took her hand in his. For a second she didn't see his long, thin fingers capped by immaculately clipped and buffed nails. Instead, she saw strong, thick fingers and the back of a hand peppered with hair like fire. The haunting image vanished as quickly as it had appeared.

"You can ask me anything, Lauren. You know that."

Still she hesitated, playing the moment for all it was worth. Finley Tibbetts was a man who thrived on being needed, on knowing it all. "After the exhibition, Basil Blackstoke is having a special reception at his Palace Green penthouse."

"Three A, Palace Green, David Goldstone's development. I have a number of friends in the complex. The only apartment building on 'Millionaire's Row.' "

"Basil is terribly excited about his penthouse. He had Nina Campbell do the interior. What he would like, what I would like is a real bash, not just another post-exhibition party. I'd like to invite some actors, some ballerinas, some writers—you know, people with talent. Like yourself."

"Good idea. How can I help?"

"Well, if you gave me the names of anyone you thought interesting, I would send them an invitation to the party."

"I'll have my secretary make up a list."

"Wouldn't it be a good idea to include the members of this club?" She smiled encouragingly, her fingers mentally crossed. "Could you get me a roster?"

"I don't know. It isn't really cricket, not a'tall."

She lowered her lashes and expelled a disappointed sigh.

"Well, I suppose I could do it—just this once. I wouldn't

want anyone to know I gave it to you. You'll have to be mum on that."

"This is so sweet of you." She brought her glass to her lips, so he wouldn't see her triumphant smile.

"I'll expect a favor in exchange, of course. I'll need to have an exclusive interview with Irek Makarova before the exhibition."

"You sad for Archer?" Irek asked after the investigators had left and he was driving Vora to his place to see the painting.

"Yes. He didn't deserve to be murdered."

"Do you . . . love him still?"

"I loved him but I wasn't in love with him."

"*Deke zabeb*—crazy Westerners. What do you mean?"

"I liked him, but I didn't want to be with him every minute." *Not the way I do you.* "He was a tremendous influence in my life. I wasn't as happy as I could have been, but I wasn't lonely the way I'd been as a child." She paused, wondering if she should be totally candid now that Irek seemed to be forgiving her. "For the last two years, I was involved with another man."

Irek studied her, his dark eyes serious. "Love two men?"

"No. I didn't love Clive either. I was just lonely, confused." How could she possibly explain? She couldn't imagine what she'd seen in Clive Holcombe.

They drove in silence until the Tower Bridge and the sparkling lights of the Thames loomed before them.

"You angry at Lauren?"

"No," Vora said, eager to change the subject. "I'm certain she's not involved in this. You heard what I told the inspectors. Lauren didn't invest in Ravissant until almost six months after Archer's death. Then she didn't come to England for another two months. She couldn't possibly be involved."

"You are right. I know peoples. Lauren is a good woman. So why they 'look into it'?"

"They have to investigate every possibility. That's their job." Irek had an inbred distrust of the authorities. She couldn't blame him after all he'd been through. Perhaps this investigation would restore his faith in justice. And hers.

"Here is my home." Irek drove the Aston-Martin into an underground car park.

They took an elevator up four flights to an open-air walkway. Even from here she could see the Thames and smell the briny tang of the river. Inside his penthouse, Irek threw on the lights and looked at her expectantly. There was no getting around it. Red. Every shade imaginable, many not compatible. How could a man with his artist's eye for color decorate like this? She mustered a weak smile; he looked so awfully proud.

"Other than Ryan, you are the first here."

The first? She *was* special. What did the color matter? "I wish I'd brought you a housewarming gift."

"House warm?" Irek scowled. "I turned on heat for you."

She rushed up to him. "A housewarming gift is a present brought to a friend's new home. Next time I come I'll bring you a present." She reached for the hand that had held hers through the ordeal with the inspectors and gave it a loving squeeze. "It's nice and warm in here."

"You like?" He nodded to the penthouse.

She never took her eyes off him. "I love."

"*Deke zabeb.* You love everything. Love is most overused word in your language."

"Your language, too. You're British now and don't forget it."

"Never forget. I am proud. Here is justice. Police will find your husband's killer."

Vora wanted them to find the killer, not just to give Arch the justice he deserved, but to help Irek. She couldn't help being apprehensive. What if the forgers struck again? She didn't want to think about it, so she asked, "Where is your studio?"

Irek led her upstairs to a spacious loft overlooking the Thames. He flicked on the overhead lights. "The paint is not yet dry. I finished as the sun go down."

At this distance, all she saw was a large canvas rippled with muted colors outlining the naked back of a woman who was looking over her shoulder. As Vora moved closer, she gazed at the auburn-haired woman with the loving smile on her face. The indistinct lines of Irek's quasi-Impressionist style would hide the subject's identity from most people. Not Vora. Those freckles were too familiar.

How had he known? Then she remembered the night she'd slept with him. She'd trotted down the hall—her teeth chattering and goosebumps covering every inch of her—to the bathroom. She'd washed her hands and splashed ice-cold water—there wasn't any hot—on her face.

She ventured a glance at him. Their eyes met and a jolt of astonishment rushed through her. He was looking to her for approval.

"You like?"

"I love." She waited, not knowing what to say, stunned that he liked her enough to paint a portrait of her.

"I watch you with Dr. Digsby. I understand you care much, much what happens to me. You mean your words when you say you like me. When I know this, I finish much, much quick."

She wanted to tell him that she loved him. Had been waiting for him a lifetime, but the word love sounded too shallow. "Do you have a title for it?"

" 'Velma Liubov'. "

He seemed pensive, not disturbed or angry as he looked at her, waiting for her to say something. Why Velma? was all she could think. "What does lee-buv mean?" she mumbled.

He spanned her cheek with his wide hand, then smoothed back the free-flowing curls grazing her cheek. "Love. First night, I know I love you. Love Velma. Real love—*liubov*'— not like the word *deke zabeb* use all the time."

"Don't love me, Irek. Don't. You deserve someone better— more talented. Soon the world will be at your feet. You'll have—"

"Don't want the world. I want you. I am happy when I am with you. This afternoon, your *deke* Dr. Digsby was funny. We laugh together after. No?"

"Yes." Her thoughts filtered back to that night she'd slept with him; she should have known she'd loved him. No one had ever made her respond like that, nor had she ever enjoyed talking with a man more. Then his English had been halting, more difficult to understand, but the wit, the incisive intelligence had been there. "You know I love you—*liubov'*. I'd do anything for you. Anything."

His mammoth hands held her face; he looked directly into her eyes. "One night me and Anatoly were in Kiev. We try and stay warm, so we sit backs to furnace that burn trash during day. We talked all night and decide what will make us happy."

"What?"

"To write and paint what we wants, not what state tell us. In Russia, police tells us 'live like everyone.' They mean do not make trouble. Here, I have freedom. Now I want to live like everyone in West. To have a home and friends. The woman I love. Really live like everyone."

He pulled her against him. Her soft curves molded to the strong contours of his body as his lips met hers. She quivered at the sweet tenderness of his lips as they brushed hers and then drew back. A second later they returned, lingering longer this time. Holding her passion in check, Vora savored the moment, remembering what he'd said.

Liubov'. She'd never known the meaning of the word.

20

A *sirocco*— the fiercest of African sandstorms—pummeled the Rover, blasting the already pitted windshield with sand. On the horizon Ryan saw Ouarzazate backlit by the rising sun, its handful of palm trees bent submissively to the punishing wind off the Sahara. Unlike Marrakesh with its exotic allure or Casablanca with its aura of mystery, Ouarzazate was a town with few pretensions. Built by the French in the 1920s in their quest to subdue the southern region, it was newer than most cities in Morocco. Its concrete buildings constructed by the government stuck out like gray tombstones among the traditional mud-brick structures.

As might have been expected, the French withdrawal hadn't brought the demise of the man-made city in an area where the desert oasis had always determined the location of the population centers. Ouarzazate thrived because it was the most logical place to garrison some of the soldiers who continued to fight the twelve-year battle with the Polisario faction of the Sahrawis.

The disillusionment that followed in the wake of independence in many African nations, spawning rebel movements, was even more acute in Morocco, which had annexed the territory to the south. Claiming the area they'd occupied since biblical times, Polisario rebels fought Morocco for the Western

Sahara. The Polisario had appealed to Morocco's longtime rival, Algeria, for aid and received the military supplies necessary to wage a nettlesome but largely ineffective civil war. To protect his territory, King Hassan ordered his troops to use bulldozers to erect a fourteen-thousand-mile-long wall of sand. Equipped with movable radar detectors, it had kept the Sahrawis tribes out of all but the smallest portion of the Western Sahara—their native land.

Two years ago, Algeria, faced with crushing economic problems, had withdrawn their financial support of the rebels. Most Westerners expected the Polisario to fold. They didn't. Colonial empires had been dismantled in Africa and nationalist states replaced them. But no one had bothered to consult the nomads who had wandered for centuries untethered by borders. The Polisario remained rigid in their demands for a separate state, so King Hassan was forced to keep troops along the southern border, guarding a sea of sand dunes. Although most of the Sahrawis were camped southwest of Ouarzazate in the area around Tindouf, an Algerian border town, a royal garrison was based in Ouarzazate. Just in case.

Ryan steered around the town, headed for the two immense *Kasbahs* on the outskirts of the city. Inside the forty-foot-high walls, fortified by massive ramparts, was the original village built a mile from the site the French later chose for Ouarzazate. He drove through an archway into the second *Kasbah.* Despite the sandstorm's near whiteout conditions, chickens squabbled in the streets while innumerable children played beside them. He parked the Rover near a typical mud-brick building, its cracks sealed by an adhesive mixture of straw and camel dung, and walked inside.

"Where is Avi?" he asked in Arabic.

The boy sweeping the concrete floor with a palm-frond broom pointed to the next room that housed the laboratory. Inside, the Israeli whom Ryan had met years ago in Botswana sat at a wooden desk making notes in a ledger. He looked up and a welcoming smile crossed his broad face. "Look."

Ryan stepped up to the desk and saw strips of film.

Avi rocked back in his chair, balancing his bulk on the two back legs. "It passes all the stress tests."

"Sonofabitch!! Is this why you sent for me?"

"Why else did you think I called you to the back of the beyond?"

"You said something about moving out. I thought you meant the Polisario was infiltrating the area."

"No chance. The U.N. is in Tindouf, trying to establish who is entitled to vote. When they figure it out—if they figure it out in this lifetime—they're going to have an election to see whether the Western Sahara wants to remain part of Morocco or not."

Ryan nodded, but he'd barely heard Avi. "You've perfected the formula? The equipment?"

Avi nodded with another hearty smile. "Five fucking years. But we did it."

"You did it."

"Producing diamonds from methane gas was your idea. I just had the chemistry background to do it. Without your money—"

"Don't forget T.J. It was his idea to locate out here." Ryan again looked at the handful of film. "We'll have to file for patents quickly, though, before the cartel gets wind of it."

Ryan imagined the shock at the diamond cartel's marketing headquarters in London. There, prices on diamonds from rough bort used industrially to the finest gemstones were set and so rigidly controlled that anyone who dared to cross them was swiftly eliminated.

Several years ago Zaire had had the audacity to leave the cartel. As the second-largest producer of diamonds, they might have been expected to do well on their own. Although the cartel would deny it, everyone knew that they had forced Zaire back into the fold. They'd flooded the market with the same type of low-quality diamonds that Zaire was trying to sell. Economic havoc followed in the African nation whose sole resource was diamonds. The shaky government nearly toppled, saving itself only by again relinquishing the marketing of their diamonds to the cartel.

Now Ryan had the capacity to make diamond film to strengthen the drilling equipment Griffith International produced, eliminating the need for bort. He'd never have to pay the cartel's set prices again. This would blow their asses right out of the water. About time.

The diamond film passed the stress tests, proving it was as tough as the natural stone. It could be directly applied not only to the drilling equipment they already made, but to semiconductors, surgical tools, and a wide variety of other instruments in the burgeoning computer-technology field. Griffith International would take a quantum leap forward with this invention—the greatest advance in materials since plastic.

Now registering the patent was crucial. To keep their work secret—and protect their lives—they hadn't filled out a single patent application. For years General Electric and Japan's Asahi Group had been attempting to develop a technique of producing industrial-diamond material. Eighty Japanese companies and a score of American firms were working on producing synthetic diamonds as well.

"In two weeks, I'll have the prototype machine ready to move," Avi said.

"We'll have to get everything out of here without anyone suspecting what we're doing." Ryan would have to explain to Stirling what was happening. So far, he'd evaded the MI-5's questions. They hadn't pressed because Stirling understood that Ryan had a business to run. As long as he cooperated with them—as best a civilian could—they were happy. But they'd be pissed to find out he'd left the country with Barzan's man gunning for T.J.

Ryan had been exceedingly cautious. Other than Avi, no one else knew about the laboratory in Ouarzazate. The same results could never have been accomplished in London. The paper-pushers would have had a go at every phase of the testing. It would have been impossible to keep the cartel from discovering what they were developing.

"We can't be too careful," Ryan said. "Remember Robert Barzan."

Lauren walked into the conservatory and found a blank canvas on her easel. Primed and fitted with stretcher bars, it was ready to use.

"Tabatha," she said to the girl studiously bent over a pair of earrings. "Have you taken up painting?"

Her eyes were downcast. "No," she said shyly. "It's for you."

"Really?" For a girl so chary with her money, this was extremely extravagant. Lauren was touched.

"I wanted to thank you," she said, head still bent, "for taking me in. For helping the likes of me."

"You didn't have to thank me like this." Lauren walked up to her worktable. "You earn your way cooking and cleaning."

"I still wanted to thank you. You should be painting, not just sketching. You're always harping on me to be more creative."

Tabatha had a point, Lauren conceded. "Thank you. Thank you very much. I'll start painting tonight."

She waited a moment, but Tabatha didn't look up. Lauren didn't understand her. When they'd toured the Portobello Ceramics Show, they'd seen dozens of artists with far less talent than Tabatha. Most were selling their pieces and making good money. But Tabatha didn't seem to be particularly interested in attempting anything other than earrings and matching necklaces. *You've encouraged her; you can't tell her how to live her life.*

Tabatha walked across the room and retrieved another cookie sheet of earrings. "How is the exhibition coming?"

"Great." Since Tabatha seldom talked, Lauren seized the opportunity to get to know her better by giving her a short rundown of their plans.

"You're serving vodka and cheese?"

"It's what Irek wants. The caterers pitched a fit and refused to go along with the new plan, so Vora gave them the boot. She's hired someone new—a woman, Sally Clark. I've sent you to her shop on Kensington Church Street for cheese."

"I remember," Tabatha said, though she didn't sound particularly interested.

"Do you think you could have another vase ready by the time Irek's exhibition opens? It would be the perfect time to show it."

"With Mr. Makarova's paintings?" Her tone was incredulous.

"Irek won't mind. I'd suggest a ceramic wall hanging but frankly, we're tight on wall space. I can easily put the vase on a small table where everyone will see it."

"Yes," Tabatha mumbled. "I guess I could."

"Super. You'll need a new dress for the opening. Use my Harrods charge again."

"I can't. I-I haven't paid you yet for my other dress."

"Don't worry about it. We'll work something out."

Lauren walked over to the canvas Tabatha had given her. Why was it already primed—overprimed actually? Tabatha must have purchased it at a cut-rate shop that catered to amateurs. Like most professional artists, Lauren primed her own canvas. She preferred a light coat nowhere near as thick as this. But she didn't say anything. Why hurt Tabatha's feelings when she'd so obviously done something special for her?

"Do you think your boyfriend—what's his name—will be able to come to the exhibition?"

"David. No. He won't be in town." Tabatha scurried from the room, cookie sheet in hand.

Lauren had squeezed an assortment of colors onto her palette and had blended a dozen or so others and was making her own shades when the doorbell rang.

Lauren went to the door and found Vora, a delighted smile on her face. Her hair had been cut and styled into a corona of loose curls that were more becoming than the longer hairstyle she'd been wearing. "Come in. Where were you all day? I wanted to tell you what happened with Finley last night."

Vora walked in, wearing expensive leather pants and a butter-soft cashmere sweater topped by a hacking jacket that had spent one weekend too many grouse hunting. For a woman obsessed with the fit and the line of everything she wore, this was an odd outfit.

"I was with Irek. He's finished the portrait. It's beautiful," she said, tears cresting in her eyes. "He's forgiven me. I'm moving in with him."

An unexpected twinge of jealousy pricked at Lauren. *What's wrong with you?* "I'm so happy for you." She hugged Vora. "You're not rushing things, are you?"

"No," Vora said emphatically. "It'll take a lot of compromising on both our parts. He'll have to turn on the heat, and I'll have to learn how to live with red." Vora giggled. "And someone will have to learn how to cook."

"You *can't* cook?"

"Uncle Nigel had two cooks, and at school all our meals

were prepared for us. When I married Arch, he had a full staff including a French chef. I never learned. Until now, Irek never had more than a hot plate. All he can make is borscht."

"I suppose you'll work it out."

"Of course we will. I love him. No man is perfect. But Irek's perfect for me."

Lauren smiled at the undisguised love in her words. An image of Ryan Westcott jumped into her thoughts. No man is perfect. Was she being unrealistic in her expectations?

"Finley gave me the Groucho's list," Lauren said, determined to take her mind off Ryan, "but he insisted on doing an interview with Irek before the opening. I know we'd decided no interviews until that night, but—"

"Irek will be fine. Dr. Digsby's crew worked with him at length. They have several more sessions scheduled."

"You know I'm not worried about how Irek appears to the media. This Digsby thing was Ryan's idea. What upsets me is giving Finley the chance to pan Irek before the opening. But I circumvented that by making Finley promise not to run the interview until after the exhibition."

Vora frowned; her eyes became less animated. She told Lauren about the visit from Scotland Yard and Interpol. "I'm awfully concerned about them, investigating you."

"Don't worry. I have nothing to hide."

That was true, Lauren reassured herself as she saw Vora to the door. She had a legitimate business deal with Carlos Barzan. She wished she could tell Vora about it, but she couldn't. She'd given her word. Still, she couldn't help wondering if Barzan knew about the gallery's outstanding debt. She'd thought about this weeks ago when Vora had first told her about the mysterious investors who'd loaned Ravissant money and yet had disappeared, never claiming their due.

There was something about this that didn't seem right. So far, Barzan had lived up to his agreement. He hadn't attempted to manipulate the market as she'd originally feared. She'd sent him an invitation to the exhibition, but he'd declined, saying he'd send David Marcus in his place. He appeared to be acting with the utmost propriety, yet her niggling doubts remained. If the authorities questioned her, she'd have to tell them about her deal with Barzan. She'd have no choice but to tell the truth.

After Vora left, Lauren went into the empty conservatory and stopped before her easel. A vision sprang to life on the canvas, clear and sharp in her mind's eye. She picked up a brush and dabbed it in the brown paint, adding black and gold until she had just the right color.

The first strokes came with difficulty; she was unaccustomed to the slick, overprimed surface. Once she'd gotten the feel of the smooth canvas, the picture came easily, more quickly than anything she'd ever painted.

As the dome of sky visible from the conservatory turned pearl gray with the light of yet another overcast London day, she'd finished most of the painting. Only a few details remained unfinished.

"Wonderful," Tabatha said, startling Lauren. "My gift inspired you, didn't it?"

Hermès briefcase in one hand, David Marcus walked into his Manhattan office and saw his sister, Babs, waiting for him. Ignoring her, he crossed the ultramodern reception area with its gray Berber carpet and collection of Koons paintings. His secretary, Julia Hartley, smiled. Her blonde hair brushed the tops of her shoulders—professional but sexy. Her blue eyes revealed nothing more than a businesslike relationship. He collected his messages.

Babs looked up from *Town and Country*. "David, I need to talk to you."

He shut his office door on her, leaving her in the waiting room. Babs was the last person he wanted to see. She disgusted him. Three kids and her body had become a bloated marshmallow with pendulous tits. She nagged nonstop, browbeating her accountant husband. And anyone else who would listen.

He answered his messages diligently. Keeping the overseas banks behind him had been one of the secrets of his success. With the government getting more aggressive by the day, he needed to keep abreast of any investigations or possible leaks. Finally, he decided Babs had stewed long enough. Making her wait never got rid of her. It only made her whine, louder and longer.

He picked up the receiver on his desk. Julia's throaty voice came over the line. He could picture her shaved crotch, warm and soft. At thirty, she was much too old for him, but he used her when he was between young girls. "Send in Mrs. Horowitz."

Babs burst in saying, "You kept me waiting forever."

"What do you want? I'm busy."

She deposited her bulk in the armchair opposite his desk. What had he ever seen in her? Even the Chanel suit she wore couldn't disguise her lumpy body. Hours at spent at Georgette Klinger having facials didn't hide the spray of crow's-feet around her eyes or the hard lines creasing her forehead. "Mother is worse."

David grunted. He doubted it. Whenever Babs prepared to hit him up for more money, she said their mother, who was living in the Jewish Home for the Aged in Scarsdale, was worse. She was always the same. Senile, but alive.

"Dr. Gross wants to do more tests."

"So what's stopping him? He knows where to send the bills."

"He thinks it might help if you came to see her."

"What for? She doesn't know who any of us are. When was the last time she recognized you?" He silently cursed his father for dying on the golf course of a massive coronary and leaving him to deal with his mother and sister. "What is it you really want, Barbara?"

She sniffed, feigning tears.

He took out his checkbook and reached for his solid gold Dupont. "How much?"

"Tiffany needs braces, and Josh's fee for camp is due. You know Brian doesn't make a decent living."

Brian Horowitz made plenty—enough to support a dozen wives in most countries. Barely enough for one in Scarsdale. Especially his sister. Poor sucker.

"How much, Babs? How much?" Did she think he was made of money? Fortunately, he channeled enough of the cartel's funds to his own account to cover Babs's endless expenses.

"Twenty-five thousand dollars." She rattled on, itemizing repairs to her home and things her children needed.

David wrote out the check, but he wasn't fooled. She would use the money to pay off her bill at Barney's or Martha's or some other equally expensive shop. For one summer of sex—always initiated by Babs—he'd spend the rest of his life paying. Not that she ever directly mentioned those nights. But the guilt was always there.

Babs grabbed the check and stuffed it into the quilted Chanel bag that matched her red suit. She huffed out, leaving a wake of noxious but undoubtedly expensive perfume.

David buzzed Julia. "Take a letter."

She walked in and quietly closed the door behind her, bending slightly to give him a provocative view of her long shapely legs and nicely rounded derriere as she locked the door. Too bad she wasn't younger. With her British accent, Julia Hartley was all class. He'd been shocked the first time she'd come on to him. Now he took her services for granted. Efficiency itself, she handled the office or a blowjob with equal skill.

"Come here, doll." His cock was already aching. Hot. He'd spent most of the night dreaming about Tabatha Foley.

Julia took her time crossing the room, her hair swishing across her shoulders. He spun his chair to the side facing her as she came up to him. Her eyes dropped to his crotch where his parted legs revealed a world-class hard-on. She looked at him; their gazes locked.

She slowly sank to her knees, positioning herself between his legs. Her hand cupped him, stroking him through the material, running sexy fingernails along the perimeter, then down to the root. He leaned back in his chair, throwing his head to the side.

"Julia will take care of you straightaway," she crooned in a sexy British accent that reminded him of Tabatha.

Inch by inch, she slowly unzipped his pants and eased out his distended penis. She ran her tongue up the seam and down, then blew across it. He held his breath, his eyes closed as he thought of Tabatha.

He came in a matter of seconds—same as always. Julia was quick, but not innovative like Tabatha. Just as she reached for the moist towelettes he kept in the top drawer, his personal line rang. It was probably Carlos calling from his penthouse for the daily report. He'd get an update and go on to a high-profile board meeting for some museum or other charity. He was the master of keeping up a front.

"Hello," he said, still leaning back in his chair.

"David?" Tabatha's sultry voice took him by surprise. She had his private number, but had been instructed not to call unless she had something important to report.

"Yes?" He jerked upright in his seat.

"Yesterday I picked up the canvas from your man."

"Good work, angel." The sound of her voice combined with Julia's cleansing strokes brought a hot ache to his groin.

"Lauren began painting on it last night."

"Wonderful."

Julia had a puzzled expression on her face. He was getting hard again. He motioned for her to stay.

"She's almost finished a portrait of Ryan Westcott."

Hot damn. "This means something special for you, angel," he said, between clenched teeth. His cock was rigid again. The sound of her voice topped by her news had done the impossible. "I'll be in London on Friday. I'll give it to you then."

"Friday? Oh, all right. I guess I can see you." She didn't sound the least bit interested. But then she never did. That was part of her appeal. "I'm going to make you"—her voice suddenly became assertive—"give me exactly what I want."

He could hardly wait.

David hung up and found Julia looking at him with curiosity. He knew what she wanted. Happy to oblige, he unbuckled his trousers. Then he eased her skirt up her slim hips and hooked his thumbs under the waistband of her panty hose. Peeling them down, he watched for the tantalizing mound of shaven flesh.

He glanced up and caught her staring at the sharp letter opener lying across his personal mail. For a moment, he had the crazy feeling she was planning to grab it and bury it in his heart.

Instead, she smiled and parted her legs.

21

Peter Stirling strolled through the Snowden Aviary and studied the faces of passing zoo visitors, searching for Ryan Westcott. Nothing. It was a chilly spring day outside, yet it was humid and warm inside. Despite the lush tropical vegetation and the twitters of exotic birds in the huge open space, Peter had never liked this building. It looked like a television antenna that had been caught in a hurricane. He was too old for modern architecture. Too old for wild cards like Ryan Westcott.

"I say, old chap, have you a match?"

Stirling whirled around, instantly recognizing Ryan's teasing voice. Westcott didn't ask what Peter wanted. When Ryan had arrived home last night, he'd called. Peter hadn't bothered chastising him over the telephone.

"Where have you been?" Stirling asked in a voice so low it could barely be heard above the birds' incessant chirping.

Ryan gave a one-shouldered shrug. "Away on business."

"You're supposed to let us know where you are—at all times. What if Barzan had made his move?"

"Adi had his instructions. He wouldn't let anyone in, and he would have called you if anything happened. What do you expect me to do? Sit on my ass waiting while my business goes to hell? We've been waiting years and nothing has happened."

"Barzan is taking his time, encouraging us to let our guard down. You're playing right into his hands." Peter heard the irritation in his own voice. He wanted to retire on top with this case—the most extensive undercover operation since the war. But the chances of trapping Carlos Barzan rested on one man—Ryan Westcott. If Ryan were a MI-5 agent, Peter wouldn't be concerned, but Westcott was a civilian who had a lone-wolf mentality that meant he never truly leveled with them. "You've perfected your diamond process, haven't you?"

Only the briefest glimmer in Westcott's green eyes told Peter that he'd scored a bull's-eye. "Maybe."

"No maybe about it. You would never have left the country now—at this crucial time—if you hadn't."

"I'll have to leave again in about two weeks."

Peter made a mental note to have the men tailing Westcott increase their surveillance during that period. This time Ryan wouldn't give them the slip and get out of the country without one of his men following him. "Let me know *before* you go."

"All right." Westcott turned to study a multicolored toucan that had landed on a nearby perch. "What's happening here?"

"Before you left, I told you that I'd seen the videotape of Lauren Winthrop with Griffith, and I felt she was telling the truth. We had the ocular scanner experts conduct a study."

"Why?"

"You know the ocular scanner is even more accurate than a lie detector. It measures the minutest change in the iris. They did close-up, freeze frames of her eye. Combining those results with the information the voice modulator yielded, we concluded she was telling the truth. She's here to build Ravissant Gallery. Evidently, her painting has a highly personal meaning to her. The stress level in her voice and the response of her iris both indicate she told the truth when she said it was private."

"I told you she was no Mata Hari."

"Lauren Winthrop's penthouse is bugged. Someone is eavesdropping on her. We're not certain who, but we're running it down. What did you say to her the night you had her visit Griffith?"

"No bugs picked up our conversation. I remembered everything you boys taught me. Turned on all the damn water in the bathroom before I *whispered* to her T.J. wanted to see her."

"The bugs in her place are the most sophisticated available. Whoever is listening heard you and knows she's seen Griffith." Peter cast a furtive glance over his shoulder. "It won't matter unless it's Carlos Barzan."

"So find out if it is. Those bugs are transmitting the info to a recorder. Locate it and you'll have the answer."

"We're investigating. But recorders for these new bugs are tiny, the size of your wallet. It might be in Winthrop's building, across the square, or in a mobile unit circling the area. The possibilities are limitless. To make matters worse, Grosvenor Square is honeycombed with buildings inhabited by wealthy people who don't wish to have their privacy invaded." He nudged Ryan, indicating they should move along and appear to be interested in a pair of parrots. "The only thing we know for certain is that the recorder isn't in her penthouse—we've checked."

Ryan studied Peter. "You haven't told her about the bugs, have you?"

"No. If she knew, she might inadvertently do or say something to tip them off."

"Do you have any idea who it is?"

"The CIA notified us that a drug cartel may be trying to involve Ravissant Publishing in producing bogus prints."

"It could be Barzan, trying to hide drug money through the phony prints just the way his son intended to launder money using diamond production as a front." Ryan shook his head in disgust. "With the diamond process, they could have disguised tremendous profits. Same thing with phony prints."

Peter paused by a thicket of bamboo, ignoring the cooing of two mating macaws. "I wish it were that easy. You know I'd like to take down Barzan, but the CIA's evidence points to the Medellin Cartel. I'm afraid what we have here are two separate—but very volatile—situations. Leave the print fraud to Interpol. Concentrate on Barzan coming after Griffith. Report anything, no matter how inconsequential it might seem."

"All right," Ryan agreed. "You checked all the names I gave you, and they're clean?" At Peter's nod, Ryan added, "No more word on the operative Barzan sent here?"

"Nothing. But our mole is still in place and sending back increasingly detailed information. We should have more very soon," Peter added, confident the MI-5 plant would crack Barzan's computer system any day.

"They bought a title at a auction?" Irek shook his head. "They now lord of what?"

"Kitty and Tex Halford are now Lord and Lady Avon Bishop," Vora answered, her eyes on Lauren, who was gazing out the Jaguar's window at the spring twilight as Irek drove her home. Vora guessed she was thinking about Ryan Westcott. He'd been back several days, but he hadn't once come into the gallery or called. Of course, Irek talked to him daily.

Lauren turned to face Vora. "The Texans who leased your house purchased a peerage?"

"Yes. The minute Maggie Thatcher's son, Mark, married that girl from Texas, there has been a stampede of them to London, horning in on all the social events they could. Every year Robert Smith holds a title auction in Painters Hall. That's where Kitty and Tex picked up their title."

"Deke zabeb," muttered Irek as he rounded Berkeley Square.

"Why would anyone sell their title?" Lauren asked from the backseat, sounding only vaguely interested.

"Some people need the money. Other titles aren't in use, like Lord and Lady of Stratford St. Andrew. That manorship was given by Henry VIII to his fourth wife, Anne of Cleves.".

"She did not have—how do you say it?"

"Descendants. No. Anne was beheaded. Remember Henry had all those wives?" She smiled as Irek shrugged. He wasn't interested in going back in history much farther than 1917. "So now Kitty and Tex have a title to go with a mansion in Belgravia. They'll be moving in a week after the exhibition."

"What come with the titles? Land? Castle?"

"Nothing. They may use it socially, of course. And on their stationery or—I don't know—have it monogrammed on their towels," Vora said.

"Monogram?"

"Embroidery done by machine."

"On towels? *Deke zabeb.* Westerners is crazy."

Silence reigned as they drove down Mount and turned right on South Audley. Neither Irek nor Lauren seemed particularly concerned that Vora had leased the only home she'd ever known to the most obnoxious couple on earth. It had taken all the fortitude she could muster to give up Archer Leighton's home. But she had to make her own life now. A flutter of misgiving went through Vora.

She was moving into a red-on-red flat light-years from Harrods. Without staff, she would have to learn how to cook. To top it off, the copy of *Larousse Gastronomique* the clerk at Hatchards had sold her might as well have been written in Greek. But these were minor inconveniences. The real problem was Irek. Would love be enough?

Irek reached his hand across the console and covered hers. She looked into his smiling brown eyes. How could this be a mistake? He must love her, not because of what she was—but in spite of it.

The Jag battled its way up Grosvenor as Lauren asked, "Irek, do you have Ryan's telephone number?"

"Yes. But he tell me not to give it to anyone. I am only to use if emergency."

"I see." Lauren's voice sounded forlorn.

"I don't think Ryan would mind if—" Vora began.

"No. He said it was important to put the number in my head and nowhere else. He tell me several times."

Irek had a stubborn streak that was hard to overcome. The Jag glided to a halt in front of Lauren's building.

"Irek, why don't you go in with Lauren and dial the number for her? She won't look. That way you'll be helping her without breaking your promise."

"Do you think Ryan would care?" Irek asked.

"No," Vora fibbed. She hadn't the foggiest what made Ryan Westcott tick, but Lauren had confided in her that she was interested in him. Vora couldn't imagine why he was giving her friend such a hard time. "I'll wait here with the car."

"Thanks." Lauren winked. "See you tomorrow."

Lauren looked away as Irek dialed Ryan's number. He handed her the telephone and mouthed the words good-bye. Before she had a chance to respond, Irek was out the door.

"Yes?" asked the curt voice of the Sikh.

"May I speak with Ryan . . . Westcott?"

"Who is this?"

The sound of his voice chilled her. "Lauren Winthrop. Is he there?"

"Wait."

The clonk of the receiver being dropped on a table rang in her ear. *Don't let him be angry with me. Make him understand.*

She mentally reviewed what she'd told herself during the ten days Ryan had been gone. Even with all she'd been through, she'd led a sheltered life as far as men were concerned. She didn't know why she was drawn to Ryan Westcott. Wasn't she looking for a different type of man? Yes, but what type? It certainly wasn't Grant Fraser, nor would it be another man like her first husband. Her marriage to Ozzie had been a union of convenience for them both. Next time, she'd marry for love, but right now, she was compelled to see Ryan again.

"How the hell did you get this number?"

The receiver shook in her hand. "I-Irek dialed it—but don't be angry with him. He didn't let me see it."

An exasperated huff. "What do you want?"

"I-I'd like to talk to you."

"You had your chance."

"Ryan, I'm sorry about what I said. I'd like to see you."

Silence.

"Please. Could I buy you a drink? We could meet at Harry's Bar."

"No."

"Please. I must talk to you."

"Meet me downstairs in your lobby."

She could barely control the spasmodic trembling in the pit of her stomach as she raced into her bedroom. She didn't have time to do more than brush her teeth and freshen her lipstick. She went out past the snoring hall porter, Jeeves. If he wasn't such a nice old man, she'd complain to the management. All he ever did was bring in the mail and catnap.

In front of her building, the moon brightened the sky as it hovered over the massive eagle perched along the roofline of the American Embassy. She waited, watching the lights of the cars as they sped around Grosvenor Square, keeping her eye out for the Aston-Martin. *What are you going to say?*

Suddenly, Ryan walked around the corner, hurrying up Grosvenor from Carlos Place. He wore the bomber jacket unzipped with his hands shoved in the pockets. As he came nearer, she noticed the light breeze was ruffling his dark hair across his forehead, emphasizing hostile green eyes. She tentatively walked toward him.

"Thanks for coming," she said, thrilled to hear how normal her voice sounded.

His eyes roved over her, taking in her practical Ferragamo pumps and conservative brown dress beneath her open coat, but he didn't say a single word.

"Shall we go for a drink?" She dredged up an encouraging smile.

"No. Let's take a walk."

He turned and she followed him, heading toward Brook Street with Ryan walking so fast that she had to jog to stay beside him. Head forward, his hair was buffeted by the wind that was now in their faces.

"How have you been?"

He stopped and whirled to face her. "You dragged my ass all the way over here to make small talk?"

"I-I said I was sorry." Her words were a suffocated whisper.

"That's not good enough. I want to know why I remind you of Rupert Armstrong."

"You don't. I-I don't know what made me say that. It slipped out."

"Bullshit."

"Honest. I didn't mean it. Couldn't we start over; pretend I never said those things?"

Her placating words did nothing to diminish his anger. He walked forward, less rapidly this time, but with as much determination in his stride. She tagged along with her head cocked to the side studying his stern profile.

"You're exactly like your mother. Exactly."

"What?" *Where had such an outrageous statement come from?* "How could I be? I haven't seen her in years."

"You're not going to use me, Lauren."

"Wha-what do you mean?"

He gripped her chin with a hand still warm from being buried in his pocket. "I'm not a fucking stud service."

Stud service? Is that what he thought she wanted—to sleep with him? Didn't he know it went much deeper than that? She jerked away from his hand. "Calling you was a mistake. I'm nothing like my mother, and I'm not just looking for sex."

"Could have fooled me. You want to get laid. Admit it. You want it, but you're afraid of it."

She gazed down at the toes of her shoes. He had a point. She had been afraid. No more. But she wasn't merely looking for sex.

He prodded her with his index finger, poking her shoulder. "You're planning on running me through the wringer then dropping me the way your mother did T.J., aren't you?"

"No. I'm—" She stopped herself. She did have in mind a casual affair when she'd called him. What else could there be? Ryan Westcott didn't have long-term potential for any woman. Certainly not her.

"You're a manipulator just like your mother. You still wear your wedding ring. Why? To ward off undesirable men, letting only men you like know you're a widow."

"No, I—"

"You married an old man so you could push him around. Now you've got another old fart, Fraser Grant—"

"Grant Fra—"

"Who the hell cares? Point is, you go for old wimps you can wind around your finger. Ever been out with anyone your own age—before me?"

She nodded, but it was a lie. She wanted to run away from him, but she couldn't let him know he was right. Older men reminded her of her father and made her feel safe.

He moved closer, standing toe to toe with her, assessing her with scornful eyes. "A tight-ass too. Your mother all over again."

She stepped back. "You're wrong"—another step back—"I'm not uptight."

He advanced one step, overtaking her, his face inches from hers. "You wear that tight bun like you're fifty years—"

"It's a chignon. It's fashionable."

"You're afraid to let your hair down. You wear dowdy clothes that keep every inch of you covered. You're a prude."

She turned away. There wasn't any point in letting him insult her. He hated her mother and had transferred that hate to her. She'd misjudged him when she'd thought him sensitive. Obviously, Irek Makarova was a special case, and that was why Ryan had been kind to him.

Ryan grabbed her by her shoulders and spun her around. "I don't know what the hell I see in you. Don't contact me again —unless you're willing to make a commitment."

"Commitment?" The word came out as if she were being strangled.

"For crissake, Lauren. A commitment. You know, what you women have been bitching about for centuries. Women always want men to make a commitment. Now I'm telling you. Don't come near me unless you're willing to commit yourself to me. I'm not having Fraser Grant sniffing around my woman, or that prick, Tibbetts."

He released her arms and walked away, tossing his parting volley over his shoulder. "A commitment or nothing."

22

As Vora rushed to Brown's Hotel, she wondered about Lauren's cryptic message asking Vora to meet her for breakfast. Something important must have happened last night when Lauren had spoken with Ryan Westcott.

"Good morning, Mrs. Leighton." The doorman swept open the massive oak door, and Vora murmured a greeting.

Utterly English, Brown's was more an institution than a mere hotel. With its mellow paneling, stained glass, and slightly old-fashioned decor, it had charmed visitors from Napoleon to Roosevelt to today's cadres of Japanese businessmen. When Archer had been alive, Vora had accompanied him to Brown's twice a week to have tea by the fire in the Albemarle Room.

Entering L'Aperitif, Vora saw Lauren seated at a table in the corner with a waiter attentively standing by. Vora eased herself into a chair and quickly ordered black pudding and coffee. Watching as Lauren ordered, Vora decided something had upset her friend. "What's the matter?" she asked when the waiter left.

"I need a new hairstyle and new clothes."

Vora couldn't believe it. She'd spent days shepherding Lauren around, outfitting her in beastly little dresses suitable for the Queen Mother. Countless times, Vora had pleaded with Lauren to let Basil have a go at her hair. She'd refused.

"I want a different look. Something . . . sexy. I'm certain Ryan will attend the exhibition of the Courtright Collection at the Barbican Centre tonight. I want to surprise him."

"You spoke with him then?" Vora asked and Lauren related the details of her encounter with Ryan. "What does he mean by a commitment?"

"He didn't say . . . exactly."

"Changing for a man isn't a good idea. Believe me, I know. I've tried dieting, lengthening my hair, and dozens of other ploys. What worked was being myself. And even then building a relationship isn't easy. Irek refused to live in my 'museum.' I dislike Thameside living. The road to the Isle of Dogs has gone to the dogs, yet he adores the whole area. But I'm happy because I love him, and I found I like myself just the way I am."

As the waiters arrived with their breakfasts, presenting the food with a flourish intended to remind the customers that Brown's served the best breakfasts in London, Vora continued, "Don't change yourself to please Ryan Westcott."

"I'm not. Ryan made me take a close look at myself and I don't like what I see. He forced me to examine my past. I've never gotten along with my mother. I look exactly like her, so I've always feared I'd become the same self-centered person."

Vora nibbled on the black pudding and thought about the mother she'd never known.

"My mother never should have had children," Lauren said. "She wasn't the least bit interested in me or my brother, Paul. You see, she was a country girl who'd come to London. Because she was strikingly beautiful, she managed to land a job as a cloakroom attendant at the Ritz. Grandmother claimed watching all those wealthy people made Mother want to marry a rich man."

Vora nodded. London had always been a magnet for country girls with the same dream.

"She met my father when he attended an embassy party at the Ritz. Mother thought because he was an American with the foreign service that he must be wealthy. They were married two weeks later and he was posted to Japan."

"She didn't love him?"

"No. They were horribly mismatched. Papa spoke five languages and had an unfailing intellectual curiosity, but he wasn't interested in making money. On the other hand, my mother loved material things, and she constantly socialized. They could have gone out every night, but my father refused. They'd have horrible rows and she'd accuse him of being dull and a failure."

Vora couldn't decide what was worse, fights or her uncle's wall of silence.

"Mother also blamed me for Papa not making more money. He'd been offered a position in Yemen, which would have meant a better position with more pay, when Mother discovered she was pregnant with me. He wouldn't leave Japan and go to a country where the medical facilities were questionable."

Vora had difficulty imagining a mother who'd be so cruel as to tell a young child that she was at fault for marital problems.

"My father was killed when a typhoon hit Japan. His office building collapsed. They didn't find his body for days."

"How awful. Was your mother upset?"

Lauren shook her head, then toyed with the eggs that she'd yet to taste. "I think she was relieved. She whisked us back to England and dumped us in Box-on-Stroud with her mother, then she went to London."

"Did you see her very often?"

"No. I didn't see her for another two years until I was fifteen. She remarried, but we weren't invited to the wedding." Lauren pushed her plate aside, her eyes downcast. "When Nana died, Mother didn't even come to the funeral."

Vora wished that she could comfort her friend, but she had no idea what to say. It was obvious she'd loved her grandmother very much, and her mother's actions had cut deep.

"After Nana died, Mother had no choice but to send for Paul and me. Until I arrived in Marrakesh, I'd never dreamed people actually lived in such big houses—had so many servants. I'd always shared a room with Paul. There I had my own room, but I missed Nana. And, of course, Papa."

The emotion in her voice startled Vora. As Vora listened,

she pictured Lauren arriving in Marrakesh almost twenty years ago.

On the day they arrived, Lauren didn't see her mother until dinner, when a servant escorted her into a banquet hall where Caroline waited, dressed in a blue gown straight from the pages of *Majesty*. Lauren couldn't suppress an admiring sigh. She barely noticed her brother standing on the far side of the large room or the man with him, her new stepfather. Lauren's eyes lovingly focused on her mother. *You should see her, Papa. She's more beautiful than ever.* Lauren's arms ached to hug her, to kiss her. Two years was a lifetime. How she'd missed her mother.

As Lauren reached out to her, Caroline asked, "What happened to your hair? Why isn't it in braids?"

The stern expression on her mother's face and the disapproval in her voice halted Lauren. She dropped her arms to her sides. Caroline cast a sidelong glance at the red-haired man across the room, but she made no move to give Lauren a welcoming kiss or even a hug.

"I'm fifteen now, Mother, too old for braids," Lauren said quietly.

"Nonsense." Caroline's long-lashed blue eyes studied Lauren. "From now on wear braids. They make you look . . . sweet."

"All right," Lauren reluctantly agreed as her mother led her across the room.

"Rupert, darling," Caroline said, her voice filled with warmth. "This is Lauren."

Lauren felt Rupert Armstrong's eyes on her with a look so critical that she forced herself to study the marble floor beneath her feet. She'd never seen anyone like him. His hair was as red as the sun setting over Cornwall, but his face was as pale as the moon. God almost forgot to give him eyebrows, remembering only at the last moment and putting a few red wisps over black eyes that gleamed like coals from the devil's chamber.

Please make Rupert like me, Papa. I know he must be wonderful or Mother wouldn't love him. After her father had died, Lauren had continued to talk to him as she had when he'd been alive. They'd shared a special closeness, a special love. Lauren felt if she kept talking to him that she'd never lose him.

At the table Lauren listened to her mother discussing last night's party with Rupert. He smiled and laughed at Caroline's chatter, seemingly charmed—as men always were—by her mother.

"Rupert, darling, about the children," her mother said in a tone that implied Lauren and Paul were toddlers not teenagers and couldn't possibly be included in the discussion. "I've enrolled them in school in France. They'll leave next week just in time for the fall term."

Rupert didn't look up from his soup. "Lauren's too young to be away from home. Only Paul goes."

Caroline's flawless complexion reddened and she cast a scalding glance in Lauren's direction. "Of course, darling."

"Bad news," Paul said as they went upstairs. Neither of them had dared to talk during dinner.

Lauren was stunned. She and Paul had never been separated. But she felt better when she reminded herself that she'd have her mother. They'd never been close, not the way she and Papa had been. But now things would be different.

"Can you believe the way Mother listens to Rupert?" Paul asked. "The minute he said no, she agreed."

Lauren decided that was odd. Mother had always argued with Papa—about everything. The pickiest things.

Paul draped his arm across her shoulders and hugged her. "Don't worry. I'll write often, I promise. Everything will be all right."

But it wasn't. Because she didn't speak French, one of the two languages spoken in Marrakesh, she was lost at École Française where all classes were conducted in French. Being fluent in Japanese was of no help either, so Lauren never volunteered an answer in class.

In algebra Lauren sat next to Angelique Dubarry, who was the prettiest girl in school. She had thick hair the color of a Hershey bar and eyes a half shade lighter. The first day Lauren had said hello in her best French. With a sweep of her mascara-thickened eyelashes, Angelique had looked through her. Lauren hadn't spoken to her again until the end of the first week, when she'd been unable to understand the assignment. Angelique had written it down for her.

Lauren stayed up until three in the morning finishing the lesson. When she handed it in, she discovered she'd done the wrong pages. The teacher had waved his arms and screamed something in French. Beet-red with shame, Lauren was sent to the headmaster. He said Lauren was failing all her classes and would be moved down one form to be with students who were a year younger.

Her mother burst into Lauren's room, waving the note from the headmaster. "How could you disgrace me like this? What am I going to tell Rupert?"

"I don't understand French. I need a tutor."

"Nonsense. You're just not concentrating." She marched over to Lauren's desk where she had her algebra book open with a French-English dictionary beside it. Caroline seized the paint box Paul had given Lauren for her fifteenth birthday and opened it. "What's this?" With a brittle crack, she snapped the brush in half and tossed it in the wastepaper basket. "Forget painting. Concentrate on your French."

Anguish seared through Lauren, taking her sinking spirits even lower. But she didn't cry. Arguing with her mother was futile. She'd begged her mother not to make her wear braids, which made her look like Heidi, but it hadn't done any good. To make matters worse, without Paul, an acute sense of loneliness stalked Lauren. No one came by her locker to chat. No one waited for her after class. No one saved her a seat in study hall. No one liked her. No one.

Lauren came to school each day with a sense of dread. She kept her eyes downcast, avoiding the other students. One day, Lauren was eating lunch alone when Angelique sashayed up to a nearby table and took the seat her friends had saved for her.

Papa had told Lauren a thousand times never to be fooled by a beautiful face—it would only lead to misery. How right he was, she thought, remembering leaving the algebra class to a chorus of snickers. Through lowered lashes, Lauren watched Angelique flirt with the boy beside her.

Todd Haile. A year older than Lauren, the cocky American spoke fluent French as well as English. He paraded up and down the halls, teasing and laughing—a clown—but everyone adored him. Who could resist those laughing blue eyes and hair like freshly minted gold? Of course, she never looked directly at Angelique's boyfriend. Each day Lauren passed Todd in the hall, but she looked down, embarrassed by her braids and her nonexistent French.

When a burst of laughter came from the adjacent table, Lauren assumed Todd had made another joke. But then she caught her name. She choked down the last bite of her sandwich. Everyone in the room was roaring now—except her.

"Lauren," Todd called. He said something in French but she only understood one word, *cheveux*, hair. Everyone laughed and some of the boys banged the table in glee. Angelique had tears streaming down her happy face.

Heat surged to Lauren's cheeks and she felt her throat closing up. Her braids. They were making fun of her braids. With all the dignity she could muster, Lauren headed for the door, but Todd caught up to her before she could make her escape. He grabbed her arm, saying something in French. Total silence had replaced the raucous laughter. She stared at the books in her arms; she didn't need to look up to know every eye was on her. "English," she whispered. "Say it in English."

In French tinged with an American accent, Todd repeated what she'd said for the benefit—and intense amusement—of his friends. "Since they put you back with the babies, we all thought you were just plain dumb. But you speakie zee English."

She felt the hot sting of tears behind her eyes, but refused to give him the satisfaction of breaking down.

"Everyone is wondering if your hair is really blonde, or do you bleach it?" He held up one of her braids, exaggerating his inspection of it to garner another round of laughs. She jerked her head away. "There's only one way to tell, for sure, and they've elected me."

As he repeated what he'd said in French to a mounting crescendo of hoots, it dawned on Lauren what he meant. Through tear-blurred eyes, she smacked him with an open-handed whack that echoed through the room, silencing the laughter. Then she ran out of the room and down the corridor. She darted into the rest room and locked herself in a stall.

As the girls trooped in and out, Lauren remained hidden in the stall. *Help me, Papa. Tell me what to do.*

When the bell rang, she didn't return to class. She peeked out the door to be sure the halls were clear and saw Todd Haile waiting outside.

He charged in saying, "I knew you were in here."

She bolted into a stall, convinced he intended to rip her panties off and check her hair color. Before she could lock the door, he barged in. Whirling around, she faced away from him, saying, "Touch me and I'll scream. You'll get in trouble."

He didn't respond, but she could hear him breathing, planning his next move. She imagined him taking her panties and showing them to everyone. *Help me, Papa.*

"I'm sorry. I've behaved like a total jerk," he said, his accent sounding like the American westerns Nana watched on the telly.

The slight tremor in his voice did little to soothe her. Instead, it confused her; fresh tears seeped from her closed eyes and rolled down her cheeks. He was merely teasing her. He moved closer and put a warm hand on the back of her neck. Her stomach dropped to her toes as she steeled herself for a fight.

Todd traced slow circles with his thumb across the bare skin where her braids parted. "I'm sorry. It was a mean thing to do." He spun her around to face him and his expression became incredulous. "You're crying. You care what people think?"

"Of course I care."

"I want to be your friend. Please forgive me."

"I-if I forgive you, will you let me out of here? I want to go home."

"Only if you let me walk with you."

Down the block, he stopped and put his hand on Lauren's arm, halting her. "I really am sorry. I thought you were stuck up like your mother. She never speaks to anyone unless they're rich. At least, that's what everyone says. I kept trying to say hello to you, but you always looked away as if I wasn't worth noticing. I wanted to get your attention. It was a stupid thing to do."

Anger replaced the tears still trembling in her eyes. "Don't you dare say anything bad about my mother. She's beautiful. Perfect. I only wish—"

"I'm sorry. I can't say anything right, can I?" His contrite expression underscored his words.

"I'm not stuck up." She felt compelled to defend herself even though he was the one in the wrong. "I didn't think anyone liked me, especially you."

"Why wouldn't I like you? You're the prettiest girl I've ever seen—even if you do wear pigtails like an eight-year-old."

Pretty? Her? Impossible. She walked on, not hazarding a glance at him, but cursing the stupid braids. Why did Mother insist she wear them, anyway? It seemed to Lauren that her mother wanted her to look younger, but act like an adult. She ignored Lauren most of the time, expecting her to take care of herself. The closeness Lauren had anticipated when Paul left hadn't developed. Lauren doubted it ever would.

Todd stopped Lauren at the Jardin du Harin, pausing beneath an umbrella of crepe myrtle. He lowered his head and his lips brushed against hers, then gently covered her mouth. School books clutched to her breast, she burrowed against him, his arms encircling her. A shudder coursed through her, sending a ripple of warmth through her body. Stunned, she had the almost overpowering urge to remain in his arms. But she pulled back, remembering how he'd humiliated her.

"I've got to go," she said, hoping he didn't hear the quiver in her voice. "It'll take me forever to do my homework."

"Don't you speak any French?"

He probably kissed girls everyday, she decided as she shook her head, telling her heart to stop beating so fast.

"Have your parents get a tutor. Madame Murard is good."

"They don't believe in tutors."

He considered her words for a moment, then said, "I have an idea. My dad's with Coca-Cola. We've been in six countries since I started school. Mom always buys tapes to learn the language. You could use her French tapes." He smiled that easygoing smile no one could resist. "What subject is giving you the most trouble?"

She wanted to say everything, but thought she'd really sound dumb. "Algebra."

"I'm a whiz at math. I'll help you."

Over the next weeks, Lauren's grades slowly improved, not only because she had the tapes and Todd coaching her, but because she spent most waking hours studying. She didn't want to disappoint Todd. One day he asked her to go to a Saturday matinee at the Lycee Movie House, but she had get permission from her parents.

Rupert's eyes assessed her carefully. "With Todd Haile? Absolutely not. No dating until you're seventeen."

"Seventeen? Paul dated when he was fifteen."

"Shut your mouth," Mother yelled, then lowered her voice demurely after a quick glance at Rupert. "How dare you question his decision? Go to your room."

No dating until she was seventeen, a year and a half from now. Todd would toss her aside and take up with Angelique again. Goodness knows Angelique was always hovering around, giving Lauren dirty looks. The next morning Todd was waiting for her at the school's gate.

But after she told him, he said, "We'll work it out. You can go to the movies with a friend and I'll meet you there."

By the break for the Christmas holidays, they'd managed to meet twice at the Lycee. But even the hours holding hands and stealing kisses in the darkened movie house couldn't compare with how happy she was every day. Being with Todd, having friends, even if they were his friends first, gave her a new sense of confidence.

The midyear report came while Paul was still at home for the Christmas holiday. Her scores placed her near the top of her form, and her brother insisted she ask the headmaster to put her back with students her own age. After the headmaster agreed, Lauren proudly told her mother, but she didn't seem particularly pleased. Todd was overjoyed. That was enough for Lauren.

Just before summer vacation, the school buzzed with news of a costume ball being held by Comtesse de Breteuil at her Villa Taylor. A select few students, including Todd and Angelique, had been invited to attend along with their parents. Angelique was going as Cleopatra. Lauren easily imagined her in a clinging gown hugging her full breasts. With her dark eyes and hair, she'd be a stunning Cleopatra. Lauren envisioned the play Angelique would make for Todd.

Lauren arrived at home one day just before the ball and found a package from Paris. Her sixteenth birthday. She'd forgotten. Paul had sent a set of oils with brushes of assorted sizes, a wooden palette, and a tube with a roll of canvas in it. She raced up the stairs, anxious to try out the oils.

Inside her room stood a crystal vase with an enormous cluster of pale violet orchids with throats of a deeper hue. Who else knew it was her birthday? She tiptoed up to the vase and removed the small card.

> One more year—it won't be long.
> Love,
> Todd

She touched the delicate blossoms, amazed that anyone as wonderful as Todd Haile could like her. But love? Impossible.

Her mother walked into her room with a white chiffon gown draped over her arm. She spotted the orchids. "Where did these come from?"

Lauren quickly pocketed the card. "It's my birthday. A boy I know from school sent them."

"Do you have any idea how much these cost? You're altogether too young to have anything this expensive." She called to the upstairs maid. "Put these flowers in my room."

Tears welled up in Lauren's eyes, but she fought them back. Her father's words came to her: It's the thought that counts. She slipped her hand into her pocket and clutched the card.

Her mother leveled cold blue eyes on her. "There's a party tomorrow night at Villa Taylor. Rupert says you may come."

Lauren remained silent; Rupert had been out of town, returning only last evening. The party invitations had been out for well over a month. It had been Rupert's decision, not her mother's, that she should attend. Why? Lauren wondered. Then she realized an invitation from the Comtesse was an edict. She owned the most famous landmark in Marrakesh, Villa Taylor. Its tower could be seen from any point in the city.

"I haven't got a costume."

"I have an old Valentino here. I'm never going to wear it again." She handed Lauren the gown and a length of gold braid. "Make a toga. You're going as Cleopatra."

Lauren walked over to the table where the orchids had been. She ran her hand over the wood surface. Wasn't a girl old enough for flowers whenever a boy cared enough to send them? Even her unhappiness over the loss of the flowers couldn't diminish her pleasure over going to her first real party. She could hardly wait. But she wasn't going as Cleopatra.

On the evening of the ball, Lauren rode in the backseat of the limousine with her mother and Rupert, who were dressed as Marie Antoinette and Louis XVI. Lauren adjusted the tiara she'd made herself, fashioning a sun between two horns, then smoothed the skirt of the Cleopatra-style dress. She felt Rupert's eyes on her again with an unwavering stare that made her nervous. From the moment she'd come downstairs, he'd been looking at her hair. No more braids. She'd cut her hair so it skirted the top of her shoulders and had cut deep bangs. Her mother had been furious, but Lauren didn't care. She wasn't wearing braids anymore.

As they stood in the receiving line, a servant explained the adults would be dancing in the ballroom while the teenagers would be having their own party out on the terrace. At midnight, there would be a supper and the costume promenade with prizes for the best costumes. Lauren glanced at her mother, who looked every inch the regal queen. A sure winner.

Lauren started to whisper to her father in heaven that he'd be proud, but stopped. Would he? Now Mother had all the things he never could give her. Would he be happy to see her with Rupert? Lauren glanced over her shoulder at her stepfather. He was looking at her again, an indecipherable expression on his face. *Oh, Papa, I would give anything to have you here with me tonight for my first party.*

After they'd passed through the receiving line, Lauren found the terrace of the Moorish villa and paused in the shadows watching the group of boys and girls dancing to a rock band. Todd was half a head taller than the other boys, so she easily spotted him. Dressed as a Barbary pirate, he was dancing with Angelique. She wore a white dress similar to Lauren's except it was more revealing, making Angelique's bosom even more dramatic.

Lauren stared down at the gentle swell of her breasts. "Come on, you two. Grow," she whispered under her breath.

"Lauren?" someone called when the dance ended. "Is that you?"

Todd turned, Angelique's hand possessively clasping his arm, and Lauren's stomach knotted.

"Wow!" He deserted Angelique and made his way over to Lauren. "You look terrific."

"I didn't know you were invited." Angelique had followed Todd. She eyed Lauren suspiciously as Todd scoured her with admiring eyes. "Who are you supposed to be?"

Lauren touched her headpiece. "I'm Isis, the Egyptian goddess of fertility."

The band began playing a waltz, and Todd swept her into his arms. She snuggled close.

"I'm glad you're here." He studied her face. "I can't get over your hair. You look . . . fantastic."

For a long moment, she looked up at him. "Thanks for the flowers. They're beautiful."

"I saved my money for months. Because you're special—to me."

She stared wordlessly at him, her heart hammering. Special. He really though she was special. Amazing.

"Let's go up to the top of the tower," he suggested. He led her up a steep set of stairs to Villa Taylor's famous watch tower.

Todd pointed to the full moon as it lingered over Djebel Toubkal, the highest peak of the snow-tipped Atlas Mountains. "This is why Churchill had Roosevelt carried up to this tower. Have you ever seen a more spectacular view?"

"Never."

"Churchill painted lots of watercolors of Marrakesh, you know."

"Really?" Papa had bought every one of Churchill's books.

"Yup. After Churchill lost the election, he came here and stayed a long time."

"I can see why he wanted to paint the city," Lauren said, truly appreciating Marrakesh for the first time.

In preparation for Ramadan, the holiest of Moslem holidays, which lasted a month, the numerous mosques were strung with thousands of fairy lights that twinkled like stars blowing kisses. At the heart of the city was the crown jewel of mosques, Koutoubia, with its golden cupola lit by floodlights. The miles of ramparts lining the *medina* had turned to a liquid silver under the opalescent light of the bright moon. And in the distance, the haunting call of a courting tomcat begged for a mate.

When Todd took her in his arms, it seemed the most natural thing in the world. She'd kissed him before, but tonight instinct told her to part her lips. Enthralled with new, strange sensations, she felt his tongue graze her lips and she dropped her jaw a fraction of an inch. His tongue swept into her mouth, seeking hers. A sweet, melting heat radiating through her, she edged her tongue forward to meet his.

Her pulse hammered wildly as he continued to kiss her. Giddily aware of how rapidly her heart was beating, she pressed herself into the firm curve of his body. She felt the rigid bulge and drew back.

"I'm crazy about you," Todd whispered, his blue eyes luminous in the moonlight.

She drew a long, uneven breath. Paul had told her about sex. But not enough. He never said anything about her feeling so . . . so willing.

Tenderly, Todd again lowered his lips to hers. He brushed his lips against hers until she let his insistent tongue caress hers. Todd slipped his hand down the gentle swell of her chest. Circling a breast with his hand, he cradled it, stroking her erect nipple through the filmy fabric. Weak-kneed, she clung to him, kissing him long and lingeringly. A quiver built deep in her stomach and she felt curiously light-headed.

Todd smoothed back her hair, running his fingers slowly through it. "We'd better get out of here."

She didn't want to leave, but was afraid to protest. After all, Paul had warned her about "loose" girls. Losing Todd's respect was unthinkable.

He led her back to the terrace where the band was playing a

waltz. She snuggled against Todd, both arms around his neck as his arms circled her waist. Out of the corner of her eye, she saw Angelique, her eyes on Todd. Lauren looked up to catch his reaction. Instead, she saw Rupert standing on the edge of the terrace watching her.

Just then, a servant appeared tinkling a silver bell directing them inside for the costume promenade. The teenagers gathered around the punch bowl for one last glass of pomegranate punch, grumbling about not wanting to parade around the ballroom with their parents. While worrying about what Rupert might tell her mother, Lauren accepted a cup of punch from Todd. As she turned, Angelique plowed into her, spilling the punch down the front of Lauren's dress.

Lauren raced across the terrace and into the powder room and sponged off her dress.

"There you are." Mother stuck her head inside the door. "Hurry up or we'll miss the promenade."

Lauren turned to face her. "Mother—"

"Why, you clumsy little fool. How could you? Wait for me in the car."

Three miserable hours passed before her mother and Rupert left the party. As they drove home, Caroline financially dissected the party—cost of the flowers, cost of the catering, cost of two bands. On to the people. Cost of their jewelry, cost of the gowns, cost of the various antiques in Villa Taylor.

When they were inside their home, Rupert told Lauren, "Go to your room and wait for me. We'll discuss your behavior."

Caroline looked puzzled. "If it's about the dress—"

"I'll handle this."

"Of course, darling." Caroline left without another word.

Filled with apprehension, Lauren went to her room, removed the soiled gown, and placed it across her bed. Clad in her nightgown and robe, she waited for Rupert, hoping he hadn't seen her come down from the tower with Todd. Rupert had made it clear that she wasn't to date or be with boys until she was seventeen. Would he ground her for the summer? Pilar Colbert's family had invited Lauren to their home in Agadir. Everyone went to the seaside resort in the summer.

Lauren counted on spending every day at the beach with Todd.

The door to her room opened and Rupert walked in, dressed in a brocade robe with satin lapels that resembled a long smoking jacket. It skimmed his knees, leaving the rest of his bony legs bare except for his feet, which were covered by Porthault slippers. Sipping a glass of brandy, he gazed at the dress.

"I-it was an accident. A girl bumped into me."

He quirked the few hairs that passed for an eyebrow, then placed his drink on the nightstand. She watched, her anxiety growing as he came toward her. She stepped back.

"What were you doing with that Haile boy?" His voice had a threatening quality that she'd never heard before.

"Dancing, that's all." Lauren's heart knocked against her ribs as she noticed the strange glint in Rupert's eyes. What if he beat her? No one had ever hit her.

"Did Todd kiss you?"

"No." She took another step back.

He closed in on her. "What were you doing in the tower then?"

"He kissed me once," she confessed, realizing that lying was only making him angrier.

He was standing so close now that she could smell the brandy on his breath and the stale odor of sweat mingled with bay rum after-shave. A malicious smile crossed his face. Danger. She sensed it in the same way an animal knows it's being stalked. She darted to the side, but he stepped in front of her, blocking her escape.

"Try being nice to me." One pale hand, prickled with red hair, reached for her as the other released the sash on his robe, revealing his naked body.

"Help me, Papa!"

A sleepless night brought a gray dawn and the threat of rain as thunderheads rumbled over the Atlas Mountains. Lauren lay in bed, staring at the ceiling. What should she do? Common sense told her to tell her mother about Rupert's visit, but her instincts told her that her mother wouldn't want to know.

She debated for hours, trying in vain to find the words to describe what Rupert had done.

When she finally mustered the courage to go downstairs, Lauren found her mother giving the servants last-minute orders. She and Rupert were leaving that day to spend the summer in the south of France. "Mother, may I speak with you?"

"I'm busy. Our plane leaves in two hours." Caroline's arctic blue eyes swept over Lauren, apparently missing her tear-swollen eyes. "Rupert tells me that you disobeyed him. You're grounded all summer."

"Mother," she lowered her voice, "last night Rupert—"

"Your father spoiled you. Rupert believes in discipline and so do I. Don't ruin this, Lauren"—she waved her hand, indicating the villa—"by disobeying him."

Caroline turned and rushed from the room.

The days ticked by, long and lonely. Lauren wasn't allowed to receive or make telephone calls, nor was she permitted to see her friends. Finally, Paul came home. Lauren threw her arms around him, hugging him with all her might. She couldn't bank the tears she'd held back since her ordeal with Rupert.

"Hey, why are you crying? I'm home now." As she dried her eyes, he led her over to a sofa. "Let me tell you about Paris." Paul rambled on and on about his school, his friends, his girlfriend, and the hours he'd spent on the Left Bank. Each time he came home from Paris he seemed happier. "I wish you could be there, too."

"So do I," she mumbled, utterly ashamed yet searching for a way to tell him about Rupert. But how could she tell Paul something that would shatter the life he so obviously loved? If Lauren told, her mother would leave Rupert. Where would the three of them go? Back to London where they'd be poor again. Mother would despise that and probably blame Lauren for it. Mother would never be able to earn enough to send Paul to a private school in Paris. He might blame Lauren too.

She stared down at Paul's fingers twined through hers and hoped she'd never have to tell him. Perhaps Rupert wouldn't do it again.

At the end of the summer, her mother and stepfather returned. During dinner that evening, Rupert behaved as he had before the party. He never acknowledged Lauren's presence. Her mother chatted incessantly, thrilled with France—the shopping, the restaurants, the parties. Paul joined in, regaling his mother with anecdotes about his life in Paris. Lauren knew she'd made the right decision. The two people she loved most were happy. She'd have ruined their lives by exposing Rupert.

The hall clock struck midnight and Lauren was sitting at her easel painting when she heard a noise in the hall. At first, she thought it was Paul. Ever since she could remember, he'd had trouble sleeping. Perhaps he was going for a walk. Shuffle-clop. Shuffle-clop. Wrong. Those were Porthault slippers shuffling up the marble hall.

The shuffle-clop came closer. Lauren hid in her closet, silent sobs raking her body until Rupert opened the closet door. His hands—spiked with red hair—reached for her. She turned her face away, terrified by the flare of possession in his eyes. Her mind struggled with the decision. Scream and bring Paul from next door. Or submit?

She chose silence.

When Rupert left, Lauren stumbled to her feet and went into her bathroom. She reached for a washcloth and saw her reflection in the mirror. She froze. Her hair was shorter now than it had been the night of the party and blunt cut to her chin. In the dark bathroom, she looked exactly like her mother—the woman Rupert loved.

Lauren raced to the easel and grabbed her canvas scissors. Back in the bathroom, she switched on the light. "Oh, Papa, why couldn't I look like you?"

With determined whacks, she chopped off her hair into a sawtooth cut that might have been done by a five-year-old. Perhaps, if she made herself as ugly as she felt, Rupert wouldn't touch her again.

The next day, the first day of the new school year, Lauren marched into school, ignoring the stares and snickers her hair prompted. They couldn't hurt her. Not anymore.

Lauren hadn't seen Todd for three months, but she didn't look for him. All men were like Rupert—except Paul, of course.

She didn't care about any of her classes until she arrived in art class. Her eyes never once strayed to the opposite side of the room where Todd Haile sat. When the lunch bell rang, she didn't look up from the sketch she was making.

"Hi. How've you been?" Todd asked, coming up to her.

She didn't respond, hoping silence would make him go away.

"Why'd you cut your hair? It was pretty long." He waited, but she didn't answer. "Lauren, please look at me."

Her eyes met his and she unwillingly remembered how thrilled she'd been to be his girl.

"Why didn't you answer my letters?"

Letters? Rupert was reading her mail, she fumed. The urge to kill her stepfather welled up in her once more.

"I told my mother about you. She said we should be honest with each other."

He'd discussed their relationship with his mother? How odd. Lauren couldn't imagine confiding in her mother.

After a moment's hesitation, Todd added, "I love you."

"You're disgusting. I hate you."

His quick intake of breath and rapid exit told her she'd hit the mark. Lauren returned to her sketch, relieved she was rid of Todd forever. What would Papa say? she suddenly wondered. *You've become an evil person like Rupert Armstrong. Don't let him ruin you. All you have to do is live through this. It'll be over one day.*

She ran down and found Todd in the lunchroom. His back was to her, so she tapped him on the shoulder. "It's not you that I'm disgusted with. It's me. I hate myself." She left before he could reply.

Halfway down the hall, Todd caught up with her. He held out his arms and she rushed into them, not realizing until that very moment how much she needed him. The touch of his hands was almost unbearable in its tenderness. So unlike Rupert's hands.

"Are you still my girl?"

"If you understand I can't go all the way with you."

"That doesn't matter." His eyes, intelligent and honest, assessed her. "I meant what I said. I love you."

She didn't respond. It was inconceivable that he loved her

in spite of not being able to have sex with her. What would Todd think if he knew about Rupert? If he found out, she'd lose his respect. His love. She prayed she wouldn't become pregnant. How could she ever explain?

Lauren made it through the next year—Rupert was gone most of the time—because she had Todd. She prayed Rupert would stay away forever. Disappear. Be killed in a plane crash. Die in a fiery automobile accident. Anything.

The following spring just before her seventeenth birthday, Todd told her, "Bad news. Dad's been transferred. We're leaving Monday."

"Why are you leaving so soon? Why not finish school here, then join your father?" she asked, her shaking hand on his arm.

"You don't know my parents. Family, family, family. Togetherness until—" He smiled, and Lauren could tell that no matter what he said, he loved them. "This is a big promotion for my dad. He'll be head of the French division of Coca-Cola."

Regardless of how much she'd mentally prepared herself to be without Todd next year when he went away to college, Lauren wasn't prepared for this.

"I spent all night thinking about us," he said. "You've never really leveled with me. I have to know now. Do your parents beat you? Is that what's wrong?"

Too ashamed to admit the truth, she answered, "Yes. My stepfather beats me."

"Why? You're perfect. Any parent would be glad to have a daughter like you."

"I don't know." She felt the coward for having submitted for so long. What would Todd say if he knew the truth?

"I have a plan. I'll be eighteen this June, so I can do whatever I want. I'll be getting control of a trust my grandmother left me. I want you to come to Paris and marry me."

"Oh, Todd." It was a crazy idea, but the thought he loved her enough to marry her made her want to cry. "I'm underage. I couldn't get out of Morocco."

"Seventeen-year-olds can fly without their parent's permission. I'll send you the money for a ticket as soon as I can."

Lauren considered the situation. This was the answer to her

prayers. She doubted she could exist through another year of Rupert's abuse without Todd. If she married him, there would be nothing Rupert could do to force her to return.

As the end of June and Todd's eighteenth birthday approached, his encouraging letters from France made Lauren really believe she was getting away from Rupert. When she went down to dinner one night after Rupert had returned from a long trip, she looked him in the eye and smiled, confident she'd soon be rid of him forever.

A sinister smirk curled Rupert's lips. "It's really too bad about the Hailes."

"Yes," Lauren agreed, thinking he was referring to their move.

"The Coca-Cola executive?" Her mother asked in a tone that said: Who cares?

"The whole family was killed last week in a traffic accident."

"No! It can't be I just got a letter—" A heaviness centered in her chest, threatening to crush her lungs. She bolted from the table and charged up the stairs. In her room, she flung the paint box open and found Todd's last letter. It had been postmarked ten days ago.

Rereading his last words through tear-filled eyes, it seemed impossible he'd died. She would never again see his happy blue eyes or hear his heart-warming laughter, a deep chuckle that could make her smile no matter what had happened the night before. How could he be gone?

Did it hurt to die? Of course it did. *Please God, tell me he didn't suffer.* She took some comfort knowing Todd was in heaven now with his family. With Nana. With Papa. *Watch over him, Papa. I love him so.*

23

Tears swam in Vora's eyes as she listened to the conclusion of Lauren's story, the utter horror of her friend's unspeakable ordeal engraved forever in her mind. How could she have complained to Lauren about her senile uncle? Compared to Rupert Armstrong, Uncle Nigel had been a blessing.

"After I got away from Marrakesh, I didn't relate very well to men," Lauren said. "I was afraid of them. When I left Ryan last night, I sat up for hours thinking about my past. Now I understand that I've been dressing conservatively so I won't attract men. What I'm really afraid of is not being able to say no—the way I couldn't say no to my stepfather."

"Are you certain Ryan is the right man for you?" Vora thought that Lauren needed a more understanding man than Ryan appeared to be.

"Yes. I've been attracted to him from the first night we met, but I couldn't handle my feelings until I came to terms with my past. Looking back, I appreciate what Todd Haile did for me. Without knowing what was wrong, he unselfishly gave me his love. All these years, I've thanked God for sending him to me. And I've asked myself a thousand times what might have been—had Todd lived."

The waiter removed their uneaten meals and inquired if

the food had been unsatisfactory. Vora choked out a polite reply.

"I feel something is bothering Ryan," Lauren said. "He's deeply troubled, the way I was when I met Todd. Ryan needs someone to love him. What can happen? Nothing I can't handle. I'm strong now. I refuse to walk away without giving it a try. I don't want to ask myself 'what might have been' the way I have with Todd."

"Thanks for taking me on such short notice," Lauren told Basil Blackstoke after she'd spent the afternoon shopping with Vora, then had come to his salon to have her hair styled.

"Think nothing of it, ducks." He led them to his chair.

"Root job. Root job," chanted the scarlet-throated parrot swinging from the perch behind his station.

"Hush now." Basil blew a kiss to the bird and then motioned for Lauren to sit. He pressed a rat-tail comb to his lips and studied her. "Classic bone structure, classic." He plucked the pins from her chignon, releasing her ash-blonde hair. "Fine hair without a hint of natural curl."

Waiting off to the side, Vora watched him part Lauren's hair and comb it straight along her jawline.

"I'll blunt cut it to here. You can wear it in a classic—"

"Couldn't I have one of those tousled styles?"

"Definitely not." Basil stamped his foot, his mock-miffed expression on his face. "Those Ubangi perms are out of style—"

"I didn't mean a tight perm. How about something natural, but not a classic pageboy?" She looked anxiously at Vora. "I don't want to look like my mother."

"All right, ducky." He gave Vora a disgusted look.

Vora checked her Piaget, deciding Irek had finished painting for the day, and she would be able to speak with him. She'd convinced him to get a telephone and an answering machine. That way he could hold his calls while painting, but she could still reach him. Tonight she wouldn't be seeing him. She and Lauren had agreed to keep Irek out of the public eye until the night of the exhibition. Vora planned to attend the Courtright Exhibition with Lauren. "I'm going to call Irek."

Basil smiled; he knew how much she loved Irek. They'd

discussed him often as Basil styled her hair. "Use the private line in my office."

Inside Basil's office, Vora dialed and waited, gazing at the photographs of celebrities lining the wall. Nanette Newman, Theresa Russell, Judy Richardson, Glenda Jackson. Followed by the royal ranks. Lady Jane Churchill, Lady Chichester, Vicountess Weir.

And Vora's own picture taken a good fifteen years ago. She read the caption. 'To my dearest Basil. With love, Vora Leighton.'

Irek was right, she decided as the answering machine, not Irek, came on the line. She had used the word love too easily.

"It's me," she said to the answering machine. "I—"

"Vora." Irek came on the line. "I do not like this machine. Today I have calls from three stock brokers and Lloyds trying to sell insurance. What do you want?"

She didn't let his characteristically gruff tone upset her. "I called to tell you how much I love you."

With a glass of Boodles in his hand, Ryan edged his way through the mob viewing the Courtright Collection. Julian Agnew was discussing a Robert Ryman painting with two men. T.J. had several of the minimalist painter's works, so Ryan moved past the prominent gallery owner with a brief nod. A series of Sean Scully's paintings were next. Ryan examined these closely. Should the Courtright family decide to sell, he'd be interested in the Scullys. He preferred these earlier works to the ones Scully was currently producing.

Ryan wandered across the Barbican's exhibition hall to where the metal sculptures were on display. He stopped to avoid Lady Fiona Farnsworth. The doyen of the aristocratic collectors had been confined to a wheelchair for the last few years.

"Slow down, I say. I can't see a bloody thing." She whipped the ivory-handled cane she always carried through the air.

The toadstool with patent leather hair pushing her wheeled her closer, and Ryan maneuvered himself around the far side of the sculpture. He spotted Vora Leighton across the room talking to a blonde whose bare back was to Ryan. A riot of blonde curls and showgirl legs beneath a slinky black number.

Looked promising. He swilled the remainder of his gin and headed toward Vora with a smile. After last night, he need a diversion. He had to stop thinking about Lauren.

As he approached, the blonde turned and he stalled midstride. Lauren? Sonofabitch! She beamed at him, a starburst of excitement firing her blue eyes as she walked toward him.

For a second his guard dropped, but he quickly recouped. Wary, he noted the black dress that fit her body like a shadow at high noon. It swagged across her slim thighs and flared open as she moved to reveal a tantalizing glimpse of leg. But it was the navel-tickling neckline that surprised him. Christ! If she took a deep breath, she'd be ready to join the topless tootsies on page three of *The Sun*.

Every pair of male eyes deserted the Courtright Collection to follow Lauren. Out of nowhere, red-hot talons of jealousy materialized, clawing at Ryan. He fought the urge to punch the jerk who'd just stopped her to say hello. She laughed, a low throaty sound that carried across the small distance separating them even though her words didn't. He turned away and quickly crossed the hall ready to leave, reminding himself that he didn't give a damn about her.

"Ryan, wait."

He turned and saw Lauren coming toward him. He had to admit she was breathtaking. Great hairdo—rumpled. Looked like she'd just gotten out of bed. The overpowering urge to haul her into his arms and kiss her gripped him. *She's trouble, buddy, remember that.*

"What do you want?"

"You," she said, her voice an intimate whisper.

Sonofabitch! *Had she done all this for him?* With a cool glance, he studied her as she slipped a warm, soft hand into his, deliberately not responding to her opening gambit.

"I'm ready to make that commitment."

Commitment? Hell, she'd called his bluff. He never thought she'd do it. He wanted to settle down. Someday. Not now; not in the middle of this undercover operation. If he softened and lost his edge, who knew what might happen?

She held up her left hand, displaying immaculately manicured coral nails. "I took off the ring. I cut my hair, and I have a whole new wardrobe." She turned slowly, giving him another agonizing look at her sexy body. "What do you think?"

He shrugged dismissively, masking his feelings with indifference. *Don't let her get to you, buddy.*

"I did it for you." Her unsteady voice was a shade shy of a whisper. "Most of the things you said last night were true, though my reasons for choosing older men and continuing to wear my ring are different than you think. I'm ready to make changes in my life."

Didn't she know what she was doing to him? Until last night, she couldn't have had any idea. He'd carefully hidden his true feelings even from himself, telling himself he couldn't possibly be attracted to Caroline Armstrong's daughter. Yet he was. During last night's tirade, he'd lambasted Lauren with every half-baked thought he'd ever had about her, trying to punish her. What the hell had prompted him to add the commitment bit, he couldn't imagine. There was no place in his life for a woman—not right now.

"I'm committed to you."

Those silken syllables spoken so softly echoed his own longing. A longing to sit and talk and laugh—like an ordinary man. Against his better judgment, he wanted her. As he struggled with his conscience, Lady Fiona tapped him with her cane.

"I say there, Mr. Westcott," she said, staring up at him from her wheelchair with rheumy blue eyes. "Do you know if the Courtrights will be selling this collection?"

"Perhaps, Fifi," he said, watching Lauren out of the corner of his eye. If she were his, he would never let her out of the house in that sexy dress. "Word is Sotheby's will auction it next fall."

"Sotheby's." She sniffed and banged her cane on the floor. "I won't deal with them since that despicable Australian affair."

Vora Leighton joined them as Ryan nodded his agreement to the dowager. Since it had been revealed that Sotheby's had loaned the Aussie tycoon, Alan Bond, part of the fifty-four million dollars he'd used to purchase van Gogh's "Irises," many collectors had become skeptical of the house's practice of guaranteeing sale prices. By promising the seller a price and turning around to lend the buyer the funds, many thought the market was being artificially inflated.

"And now Christie's has followed suit," Lady Fiona huffed, glaring at Vora and Lauren. "I'm not buying anything from an auction house."

"Private dealers are a better choice," Vora said.

"What would you know?" With her cane, Lady Fiona prodded the servant waiting behind her wheelchair, signaling her desire to move on. "You're exhibiting that Communist."

"He's a British subject now," Vora said.

Lady Fiona wiggled her cane at Vora as the servant wheeled her away.

"She's just the type of collector who will talk Irek down, giving everyone the impression he's terrible without even seeing his work," Vora said.

"That isn't a wheelchair," Ryan said. "It's a rolling throne. But she'll come to the exhibition. Wait and see."

Ryan noticed the distressed look on Vora's face. He followed her gaze across the room and saw Mootzie McCallister with Clive Holcombe. Mootzie was wearing a purple Spandex dress that came to mid-thigh, hugging her body.

"She looks like ten pounds of crap stuffed into a five-pound sack." His comment didn't get even a suggestion of a smile out of Leighton. She didn't still have the hots for Holcombe, did she?

"I understand," Lauren said quietly, "that Mootzie has set him up as a furrier. He designs high-style furs like the Fendi sisters and sells them at Beyond Mink in Knightsbridge."

"Great, a pelt pusher," Ryan said. "Next she'll have him in the underground stations. I can see it now. Mootzie's Tootzies. Sox Trot. Mink Monger."

"I think I've seen enough," Vora said, walking away.

"I'm going to stay a while," Lauren said. "Ryan will take me home, won't you?"

"Sure," he heard himself say, and she responded with a winsome, little-girl smile.

What was he, crazy? Lauren was a nut like her mother. She'd walked out on him once already. Now she'd done an about-face. Didn't make sense. He needed answers.

"Why don't you see your mother?"

"Is there somewhere we could go and talk in private?"

Downstairs inside Biroum's, they found a table in the corner. Ryan ordered a gin for himself and Malvern Water with a double twist of lime for Lauren. She swizzled the straw through the drink, her eyes on the double twist. "You know, my father's been dead almost twenty-five years, yet I miss him still."

Ryan took a drink, realizing Lauren loved her father deeply. The way he'd loved his mother.

"When my mother remarried, she went for what she'd missed the first time around—money. I was too young to understand. I assumed she'd married a kind man like Papa." A strained note had crept into her voice. "I never knew there were men like Rupert Armstrong."

She frowned, her eyes taking on a faraway look as if she were reliving her story. Almost of their own volition, the words tumbled from her lips. As her terrible story unfolded, Ryan's anger at her vanished, wiped away by astonishment. Even the golden glow of the gin didn't help. He put the near-full glass down and steeled himself for the rest of the details. Long before she came to Todd Haile's death, Ryan wanted to kill Rupert Armstrong.

How well Ryan remembered that bastard putting on his pince-nez glasses. They magnified his elliptical irises—like those of a snake—as he'd examined the phosphorus contracts. With a flourish, he'd signed the documents. Death sentences for thousands of an endangered species. Killing Rupert would be too kind. Ryan had a better idea. He would be in Marrakesh again—soon.

"What did you do after Todd died?" Ryan asked. He watched Lauren carefully as she continued.

When Paul returned home from school in Paris a few days after Lauren had learned of Todd's death, she was too despondent to be happy about the armada of art supplies that he'd brought her. She hardly noticed that Rupert had left for Kenya and she no longer had to dread midnight when he usually came shuffling down the hall, his sinister hands ready to grab her.

For the next week, Paul tried to cheer her up by taking

Lauren to explore the *medina*. Founded centuries before by
camel breeders who were fanatic converts to Islam, the old
section had a mysterious aura that the newer French quarter
with its Parisian-style boulevards lacked.

Lauren observed the piety of the faithful when the *muezzin*
called them to prayers. The men collapsed to the ground,
kneeling on prayer mats, facing east toward Mecca. The Moslem women moved into the shadows, remaining standing obediently while their men prayed. Apparently, Allah only listened to men's prayers. Lauren wondered if God heard her
prayers. If he did, he'd show her a way to get away from
Rupert.

One day, Paul and Lauren found themselves in Jemaa-el-
Fna, the heart of the *medina*. Called "Assembly Place of the
Dead" for all the men executed on this site at the pasha's
whim, the square now attracted every tout, sleight-of-hand
artist, and petty thief imaginable as well as scores of legitimate
vendors. Awed by flocks of cartwheeling acrobats and stilt
walkers, Lauren and Paul were even more fascinated by the
Guinean dancers. Twirling and stomping as they rattled iron
castanets, their white tunics billowed as they spun in endless
circles. The black tassels on their fezes whirled like the rotors
on a helicopter, and their gold teeth sparkled in the summer
sunshine.

"They're exorcising demons," someone nearby explained.

Lauren wondered if they could rid her of Rupert Armstrong. Just then, one of the dancers motioned for Lauren and
Paul to follow him. They ventured deeper into the *medina*
where reed-roofed stalls housed vendors hawking various
wares. The dancer said something in fractured French and
pointed to a woman swathed in indigo fabric. Her skin had a
patina of mottled blue from the dye in her clothing. She belonged to a group of Bedouin nomads that periodically wandered in from the Sahara. Distinguished by the blue fabric
that they hand-dyed, they were well known for their talent as
silversmiths.

As the woman beckoned them inside her stall, Paul said,
"I'm going to buy you something special."

Inside, Lauren squinted at the old crone seated on a foot-
stool, hunched forward, chanting in Arabic as she showed

them a tray of silver bangles. An accordion of fat, her body
had blue sand in its creases. The cloying scent of jasmine
incense intensified by the summer heat in the close stall made
Lauren slightly dizzy. But Paul didn't seem bothered. He
examined the bracelets carefully, selecting one with an inta-
glio pattern. The reverse of embossing, an intricate design
had been stamped into the smooth silver.

Paul paid the old woman and led Lauren outside once
more. He slipped the bracelet on her wrist. "I hope this cheers
you up. I'm sorry about Todd. I know how much he meant to
you."

Lauren wanted to tell him about the plans she and Todd
had made, about her need to get away from Rupert. The
words wouldn't come. "Thank you for the bracelet."

Paul took her to a sidewalk cafe that served cool drinks.
They sat in the shade watching the activity in the square,
sipping their drinks.

"Todd's not the whole problem, is he?" Paul asked, his eyes
questioning her. "Every time I come home, you seem . . .
different."

"I'm growing up," she said quietly. Her words brought a
flash of insight. She was seventeen—grown-up. Almost. If she
could get away from Rupert, she'd have to hide until she was
eighteen and could legally be independent.

Lauren looked up and found Paul studying her with a concerned expression. "You know I love you . . . no matter
what." His gentle hands cradled hers as he ran his thumb over
the silver bracelet. "There's nothing you can't tell me. We've
always talked in the past. But since we moved to Marrakesh,
you've become . . . withdrawn."

She felt guilty for having shut her brother out, so she told
him part of the story. "I was planning to run away and marry
Todd. If he'd lived, I would be in France right now."

"I'm sorry he was killed, but seventeen is entirely too young
to marry." Paul smiled indulgently. "Anyway, how'd you
think that you'd get out of Morocco?"

"Seventeen-year-olds can get exit permits," she replied
tightly, seeing herself, permit in hand, boarding a plane that
would take her away from Rupert Armstrong forever.

Paul lowered his voice and leaned toward her. "This isn't

England. Women don't have the same rights in Moslem countries. And women don't get permits at seventeen without a male family member's approval. Do you think Rupert would give you permission to leave? Come on, be serious."

The ray of hope that she'd glimpsed vanished, taking her ebbing spirits even lower. Enduring another year until she was eighteen seemed impossible. She grasped at one last straw. "Paul, you're a male relative. Couldn't you get me an exit permit *now*?"

"Now? What's your rush? You still have one year of school."

She had to risk telling her brother the truth. No one else could help her. "You said you love me. I want to go away this week before Rupert returns."

Paul's blue eyes, a mirror image of her own, narrowed. "You'd better tell me what's going on." When she hesitated, he took her hands in his, saying, "There's nothing you can't tell me."

She took a deep breath. *Help me, Papa. Make him understand.* "Sometimes . . . at night . . . after midnight, Rupert comes into my room." She braced herself for Paul's reaction, but he merely smiled at her encouraging her to continue.

"And?"

Staring at Paul's gentle hands, but seeing Rupert's, she elaborated, not omitting any detail. When she'd finished, Paul gazed at her blankly as if he didn't believe her.

"My God!" he said after a long pause. "Why didn't you tell me before now?"

"I didn't tell anyone, not even Todd. Where would we go if Mother left Rupert? She couldn't support us. You wouldn't be able to continue school in Paris. I'd ruin your life."

"That doesn't matter. I love you. I'm not letting that bastard touch you again." His voice had an edge to it that she'd never heard before.

Tears came to her eyes. Her world could be upside down, but she could always count on Paul. She studied the empty glasses on the table for a few minutes before the solution came to her. "I have an idea. There may be a way to get me out of Marrakesh *and* keep you in school. Have you heard of anyone in Paris who makes fake identity cards? If I had one, I could pass for a citizen and hide until I'm eighteen and can legally be on my own."

"Easy," Paul answered, then grinned. "My friend Marcel got one for his German girlfriend. All we have to do is get you to Paris. Getting the money for a plane ticket will be the hard part."

"No. It won't," she said with more conviction than she felt.

When she finished explaining her plan, Paul shook his head saying, "This is a crazy story. Mother won't believe—"

"Sure she will—if you say exactly what I told you."

"Shouldn't we tell Mother? Maybe she'll—"

"Since when has Mother ever worried about us?" Lauren asked, remembering throwing a rose from the garden on Nana's pine casket as the damp earth was being shoveled into the grave. Mother had been "too busy" to return home for the funeral. "She didn't even love her own mother. We have to take care of ourselves."

"You're right. All we have is each other."

"When I get to France," Lauren continued, "you tell Mother I ran off with an artist. That way she won't be angry with you. You'll still get money for school. If we're careful we both can live on it and no one will be the wiser."

Paul led her out of the *medina*. "You're not a good liar. Are you up to this?"

She thought of her father and Todd. They'd both been unfailingly honest, but she felt certain they'd approve of this scheme. "I can lie if I have to."

They returned home and found their mother in her suite wearing a quilted white satin robe, reading *Elle*.

"We'd like to talk to you, Mother," Paul began.

She saved her place with an ostrich feather bookmark. "What about?"

"Lauren is—" Paul shook his head, seemingly profoundly distressed. "Lauren is pregnant."

"What?" Mother vaulted to her feet and charged toward Lauren. "You little slut—"

"Now Mother"—Paul stepped between them—"what good is anger at this point? Lauren knows she has made a mistake, but—"

"Who is the father? He can damn well marry you."

Lauren hesitated, remembering her father's warnings about lying. She choked out, "Todd Haile."

Paul eased Mother back onto the chaise. "So you see, we have a problem. What we need to do is handle this without Rupert finding out."

"Yes," Mother agreed, white-faced, "if Rupert found out—"

"He won't," Paul assured her. "All you have to do is give us money. I'll rush her to Paris and get the matter taken care of there. Lauren can be back before Rupert returns. He need never know she went anywhere."

"Rupert didn't follow you to Paris?" Ryan asked.

"He did. But it took him months to find me. My brother arranged for me to hide in Calais. Rupert turned Paris upside down, assuming I was near Paul. His investigators finally tracked me down."

Ryan watched her, mentally applauding Lauren's courage for striking out on her own at seventeen. There was a depth and power to her that he'd never suspected existed.

"I knew Rupert would come," she said, still using that far-away voice. "I worked days in a flower-stand. At night, I lay awake in the garret I rented, listening for his footsteps. When I heard them one night just days before my eighteenth birthday, I was ready. I'd been planning for months. I answered the door with a loaded gun in my hand. Unfortunately, I was shaking and the gun fired prematurely. The bullet clipped his foot."

"What did he do?" Ryan asked, amazed she'd do something like this. Not that the bastard didn't deserve it, but it was difficult to imagine Lauren shooting to kill.

"When he was released from the hospital, it was a few days after my birthday. He couldn't force me to return to Morocco. He promised he'd get me. He told me to never stop looking over my shoulder. I didn't listen to his threats. I assured him next time I'd aim for his heart."

"And your mother?" Ryan asked, curious about how Caroline Armstrong had handled the situation.

"I don't know what Rupert told her. She told Paul that she never wanted to see me again."

Ryan scooted across the leather banquette and put his arm

around Lauren. It had been much worse than she'd admitted. No matter what Buck Westcott had done, Ryan had always had his mother. What would it have been like to go through hell without being able to turn to your mother?

"Once I was over the hurdle of confronting Rupert, I moved to Paris and studied art, earning money by translating for Japanese businessmen. I entered therapy and put my life back together. Then I met Osgood Winthrop. I felt safe with him because he reminded me of my father. When Ozzie died, I moved to New York to be near my brother."

Ashamed of himself, Ryan felt guilty. Since he'd met Lauren, he'd refused to give her a break. Told himself she wasn't entitled to one. He was wrong and he hated himself for it. She deserved someone wonderful, not a jerk like him. But he couldn't tell her that, not now, not after she'd confided in him. What the hell, he thought as he made a decision he hoped he wouldn't later regret.

"I'm not promising anything," he said. "Let's see what happens after we spend some time together. You'll have to understand there are certain things in my life that I can't share with you—right now. You'll need to trust me."

She wound her arm around his neck and brought her soft mouth up to his for a kiss. As her lips met his, she whispered, "I trust you."

He let her kiss him as he ran his fingertips across her bare back. When she eased her hand up his thigh, she was a little clumsy at it. He gave her high marks for trying; she achieved the desired effect.

"Come over to my place for a . . . nightcap," she said.

Ryan smiled, scrambling for an excuse. No way would he make love to her and let the bugs record it. His alternative was taking her to Palace Green. Stirling would be pissed. Tough.

"My place," he said, rising and picking up her sable.

"Ryan, I'm nervous there. I don't—"

"T.J. isn't going to bother you. He can't sleep unless he knows I'm safe inside Palace Green."

"All right," she agreed as he helped her into her fur.

On the way across the city to Palace Green, he told her

about his imprisonment in Zaire and her mother's refusal to help T.J. get him out.

"Poor man, no wonder T.J. doesn't like me. I must remind him of someone he loved who—"

"He doesn't hold it against you, believe me. He has your painting in his room."

"Really?" She hesitated a moment and he angled his head sideways to get a better view of her face. "Could you swing by my place? There's something I want to show you."

"Sure," he said although the last thing he wanted to do was go into her penthouse. During the drive, he asked her a few questions about Ravissant Publishing, hoping to see if he could gather a few clues on the print fraud for Stirling. She didn't know much. Ravissant wasn't running any prints until after Irek's exhibition. The print fraud idea sounded like a wild goose chase to him, but he couldn't think of any other reason anyone would bug her home.

As the lift's brass cage rose to her penthouse, he had an idea. "Bring a change of clothes. Something casual. I need to drive up to Bourton-on-the-Water tomorrow."

"Sounds like fun. Can Iggy come too?"

"Definitely." He waited for her to get out, then followed her into the vestibule where the hall porter greeted them with the news Tabatha had gone out for the evening.

"Follow me." Lauren smiled over her shoulder and led him into the conservatory and flicked on the lights.

Immediately, the painting on the easel caught his eye. Sonofabitch! It was a portrait of him. A damn good likeness. He studied it for a moment, pretending not to be affected by the effort she'd obviously put into it. Did he really look that unapproachable? He glanced at her and was touched by the anxious-to-please expression on her face. How could he ever have thought she was like Caroline Armstrong?

"I don't know what to say. It's wonderful."

"Then you like it?"

He swung her into his arms, locking his hands around her waist. His demanding lips met her eager ones. He had to remind himself the damn place was bugged as he kissed her.

"Get your clothes," he said, reluctantly releasing her.

While she gathered her things, Ryan inspected his portrait.

Strange, she had the primer on too thick. Think she'd know better; she'd been around art for years.

"I'm ready," Lauren called and Ryan left the conservatory.

On the drive to Palace Green, Lauren told him about Tabatha Foley. He decided Lauren was a soft touch. Reminded him of his mother.

They drove into the compound, past the sentinel of cameras and the Rottweilers that went berserk at the delicious prospect of having someone to attack. Inside the garage, he parked the Aston-Martin and helped Lauren out of the car. He cleared the ocular scanner first, then waited for her. Carrying her Vuitton tote with her change of clothes, he passed through the metal detector concealed by an archway.

At the low buzz and flash of lights, Ryan turned to Lauren. "It's your keys. Toss them on the table, and then back up and walk through the archway again."

"I just have one key." She took a keyring out of her purse. "Ravissant's keys are on another ring."

Puzzled, Ryan waited for her to pass through the metal detector again. It took a fair-sized ring of keys to trigger the alarm. But when she tried again, it buzzed. Silent as a shadow, Adi appeared with Iggy.

"What's wrong?" Lauren asked.

"Nothing. Probably a bunch of coins in your purse. Give me it and your coat." He nodded to the Sikh to check them.

Adi gave the pot belly a stay command. Sitting on her plump haunches, she lifted her snout and sniffed repeatedly, wagging her tail.

"Nothing," Adi said, his eyes on Iggy.

"Try it again, Lauren."

The alarm sounded again, and Ryan checked the monitor. Christ! It registered high on the scale. Enough metal for a gun or an equally deadly weapon.

"Did you calibrate this today?" Ryan asked and Adi nodded.

"What's the problem?" Lauren asked. "I don't have any metal."

"I'm not sure." Ryan fought the uneasy feeling creeping over him.

The antiquated girandole in the foyer cast deep shadows on the ancient oak beams that cross-hatched the ceiling. In the dim light, Ryan took in everything about her, from the cluster of untamed curls to her sexy silhouette. Any fool could see she didn't have a gun on her. It would be damn near impossible to conceal anything beneath that dress. Unless she had some weird weapon hidden in her underclothes. He recalled the deadly Tomcat knife that had landed him in prison. Undetectable. The knife snapped down to less than four inches.

"I can't violate Griffith's security. You can't enter until we can clear you. Take off the dress."

24

"Take off my dress? Here?" Lauren couldn't believe he'd ordered her to do this.

"Adi," Ryan said. "I'll handle it."

As the Sikh silently disappeared down the shadowy hallway, Lauren cursed herself when she guessed what might be triggering the alarm. *How could you have been so stupid?* Why hadn't she noticed the metal detector the first time she'd been here?

"Ryan, I can explain."

"I think you'd better," he said, his expression as stern as his words.

"I'm wearing a merry widow."

"What in hell is that?"

"It's a modern version of an old-fashioned corset. It has stays that run"—she gestured indicating the area from below her breasts to the top of her hips—"from here to here." Heat flooded her cheeks; she felt incredibly silly. "I guess the stays must be metal."

Ryan gave her a blank look as if he thought she might be making this up. He put his hands on her waist and squeezed. "Jesus. It's a vise."

The time spent at Janet Reger's selecting something seductive had suddenly become the worst idea she and Vora ever

had. All night, she'd barely been able to breathe because the
merry widow was so confining, and now she'd been robbed of
the surprise.

"There's a sucker born every minute." He grinned, his
green eyes sparkling. "Most of them are women."

"It's supposed to be sexy."

He studied her a moment, then shook his head. Laughing,
he pulled her into his arms. "You're a nut, know that?"

Not giving her a moment to answer, he kissed her, forcing
her lips open with a thrust of his tongue. A rush of passion
spiraled through her, dismaying her with the magnitude of
her own desire. Her instincts were right. He was the man for
her.

As his tongue mated with hers, something cold and wet
touched the back of her calf. She pulled back. "What—" She
looked over her shoulder and saw Iggy sniffing. "Why does
Iggy have her nose up my dress?"

"She's never seen a merry widow."

He again kissed her, his hands squeezing her bottom. The
detector's alarm buzzed and the red warning light flashed—
they must have leaned the wrong way. Ryan switched off the
monitor.

"Let's go upstairs and get you out of that contraption."

Lauren picked up Iggy and held the pot belly up to her
neck so she could take a deep whiff of perfume.

"She's missed you," Ryan said, as he guided Lauren down
the long hall.

"I've missed you both." Lauren saw the flicker of hesitation
in Ryan's eyes. She was right. He needed to know someone
cared. Really cared.

As they climbed the stairs to his rooms, she glanced around.
Despite the walls hung with paintings that would have given
most houses a closed-in feeling, Greyburne Manor seemed
strangely empty. Maybe it was the ominous silence. The only
noise she detected was their footsteps on the plank floor.

They cleared the ocular scanner outside his rooms, and he
led her through the darkened chamber into the bedroom
where he switched on the bedside lamp to reveal an unmade
bed with Iggy's pillow still at the foot. She put Iggy on the bed,
and the pot belly tripped, catching her foot in the tangled

sheets before she nosed under the pillow and pulled out something.

"My bra!" Lauren yanked the satin-and-lace swatch of fabric out of Iggy's mouth. It had once been the palest shade of peach, but now it was tattle-tale gray, probably from being dragged across the floor. "How could you let her ruin this? It was outrageously expensive. Now I'll have nothing to match the panties."

"Panties?" Ryan grinned. "Iggy would love a pair of panties." He slowly moved his hand down Lauren's back to the zipper. "On the other hand, she might prefer a merry widow."

He deftly removed Anouska Hemple's dramatic creation and tossed it across the chair where Iggy had hidden the last time Lauren had been here. As Ryan's eyes roved over her body, a suppressed laugh quirking his mouth, Lauren felt utterly ridiculous.

"Shouldn't we save the chair for Iggy?" she said to fill the awkward silence.

"Nope. Tonight, she's insisting on a ringside seat."

Lauren glanced at Iggy. She sat on her pillow, her head cocked to one side as she watched them with soft brown eyes. A man who slept with a pig. Okay, an exorbitantly expensive miniature Vietnamese pot belly, not some barnyard beast. Still, Ryan was eccentric. She shouldn't feel so foolish in this getup.

A slinky version of an old-time corset, the merry widow was made of black French silk with the troublesome stays concealed by delicate lace. Black satin garters held up sheer black nylons with razor-point seams.

"A merry widow, huh?" He fingered the silk cord that laced up the front, his eyes roving over the wispy demi-bra that barely concealed her nipples. Tugging on the drawstring, he unlaced it. "Can't imagine why any widow wearing this contraption would be merry."

Neither could Lauren. She took her first deep breath of the evening, having felt all night as if she were being strangled at the waist.

"But it's sexy as hell."

He undid the garters, his fingertips leisurely grazing her

thighs, lingering longer than necessary. He eased the one-piece garment off and tossed it over his shoulder. As he lowered his face to her breast, Lauren kissed the top of his head, inhaling sharply as her body instantly reacted to his touch. His tongue curled around each nipple in turn, coaxing them upright. When he lifted his head, she cradled his face in her hands and met his lips eagerly.

With unsteady fingers, she removed his jacket, then fumbled between moist kisses as she unbuttoned his shirt, wishing she were more practiced at the art of seduction. She faltered with his belt buckle but finally managed to get it undone and eased down his zipper. With alarming swiftness, the fullness of his arousal was revealed. She inched her hand across him and squeezed gently. He pushed himself more deeply into her palm, urging her to use more force. When she did, he scooped her into his arms and carried her to the bed.

As he nestled in beside her, Lauren sensed a slight hesitation, a reserve that hadn't been there the first time they'd made love. "You're not holding back because of what I told you about Rupert, are you?"

"I don't want you thinking about what that bastard did. I don't want to be rough with you."

"The first time we made love, you didn't know anything about my past and it was wonderful. Be yourself."

Ryan lifted her hair from the nape of her neck. As he kissed her, he caught a trace of Bluebells clinging to her skin. His pulse accelerated immediately, reminding him just how much he wanted her. She'd gotten to him, Ryan admitted.

While he kissed her with the ardor she remembered, her tongue dancing with his, her hips tilting to meet his, she realized she'd never felt this way. Before, she'd made love tentatively, afraid to give fully. Not wanting to lose control. Now rising passion driven by love urged her to let go. Give herself completely. Forget the past.

"Shit!" Peter Stirling rarely cursed, but this occasion called for it. His agent, Adi, had just alerted him that Ryan Westcott had taken that Winthrop woman into Greyburne Manor. What the hell did Westcott think he was doing? Every time someone went in there, it violated their rigid security.

Why Lauren Winthrop? They hadn't discovered anything amiss with her, yet Peter's sixth sense told him something was wrong. Too many coincidences. Someone—they still hadn't been able to run it down—was bugging her penthouse. Now she was in Greyburne Manor. Again.

He poured himself a brandy and collapsed into his well-worn leather chair; propping his feet up on the matching hassock, he mulled over the situation. Like a man caught in quicksand, he was slowly being sucked down. Every time he turned around the case had a new twist. The complications he could handle, but not the women. Too unpredictable. They led with their hearts, not their heads.

He took a swig of brandy, reluctantly tempering his position as he recalled his most successful case. A woman. A startlingly beautiful woman had been the key. During the Blitz, Peter had been assigned to the British Embassy in Washington, where the diplomats were pressuring Roosevelt to join the war against Hitler. Under the direction of Sir William Stephenson, Peter led the brigade of British undercover agents whose job it was to spy on the Germans hovering around the capital.

He spotted the gorgeous Amy Thorpe at one of the numerous picnics held in Rock Creek Park for the city's embassy personnel. A favorite with all the men, Amy didn't strike him as spy material until she married British attaché Arthur Pack, and he was posted in Poland. There she'd tired of her dull husband and begun a series of flirtations with men in the highest political circles.

Peter believed the Warsaw government possessed plans for one instrument that would help the British win the war. Polish scientists had worked on the Enigma coding machine. Using it, the Germans had a method of communicating that couldn't be broken, even by a legion of expert cryptographers. Her sense of patriotism brought Amy into the fold, and she had a remarkably easy time gathering the plans that allowed the British to have access to every message Hitler sent. Before anyone else. The most spectacular intelligence coup of the war had been achieved by a woman.

Spurred by memories of that highly successful operation, Peter had recruited Julia Hartley for the Barzan case. A wide-

eyed blonde with that overbred manner of English aristocrats
whose trust funds substituted for cranium capacity, she was
the last person anyone would suspect of being a graduate of
the London School of Economics. Computers were her speciality, but even with her impressive background, she hadn't
unraveled Carlos Barzan's skein of financial holdings. Peter
never suggested she use any of her sexual skills to gather
information, but the reports she kept sending indicated it
wasn't her word processor she'd been fondling. A budding
Amy Thorpe.

Julia's latest information had alerted him to still another
visit to London by David Marcus. Last time, his men had
spotted a buxom blonde entering the suite where Barzan's
assistant was staying. For this visit, Julia had booked Marcus a
suite at the Hyde Park Hotel, and Peter's men had arranged
to be in the room next door. The Concorde had landed over
an hour ago, and Marcus should be at the hotel by now. It
might not mean anything, but Peter would never be comfortable until he knew the blonde's identity.

Women. There were just too many of them in this case. His
thoughts again returned to Lauren Winthrop. He'd assigned
extra men to investigate her, and they'd spoken with virtually
every person who'd ever known her. Nothing. They all liked
her and described her as energetic and hardworking. Except
for the Armstrongs. Caroline and Rupert, when interviewed
—supposedly for *Harpers and Queen*—said she'd been an un-
ruly child who'd run away to pursue a career in art.

They were holding back something. He sensed it the moment he'd heard the tape. His instincts told him to assign
someone to check further on the Armstrongs. At this rate,
Peter decided he'd be investigating half of the world before
he closed this case. But he didn't have any choice. Somewhere, there was a common denominator in all this. But
where?

The obvious explanation was that Barzan had contracted
with Lauren Winthrop to parlay herself as Carolyn's daughter
into Griffith's good graces. Since the technicians using the
ocular scanner and the voice modulator had cleared Lauren,
that didn't seem to be the angle. But Peter didn't trust all the

newfangled gadgets. His instincts told him Lauren Winthrop was Barzan's operative.

Tonight, his agents informed him that she'd approached Westcott, wearing a sexy dress. Naturally, Ryan had taken the bait and asked her home. The man's brains were in his jock strap.

Peter reconsidered. No. Westcott would be careful. No matter how much of a playboy he was, getting Barzan was Westcott's top priority.

Weary, David Marcus climbed the half flight of stairs from the Hyde Park Hotel's foyer to the lobby level and turned to the left. At the reception desk, he handed over his confirmation slip, then checked his watch. As soon as he had his room number, he would call Tabatha, who was waiting by a pay phone in the Knightsbridge Underground station.

"Does this room have a view of Hyde Park?" David asked as he was given his key.

"No, sir. You didn't specify—"

"Of course I did. I want a view of the park. Why else would I stay here?" David fumed. Julia had flubbed it. He switched hotels with every visit to London, not just to keep anyone from noticing his young visitor, but to make Tabatha happy. He couldn't risk being seen with anyone so young in public, so he made it a practice to give her a thrill by staying at the top hotels, even if he didn't particularly care for them. The St. James Club—too many rock stars. The Ritz—over gold-leafed and stuffy. Blakes Hotel—too much black.

He'd selected the Hyde Park, which boasted the only close-up view any hotel had of Rotten Row and The Serpentine. In the morning, Tabatha would get a kick out of seeing the boaters on the Serpentine and the soldiers exercising their horses on the row. With luck, Prince Charles would trot along the bridle path as well.

"Mr. Marcus, we could give you a room, but not a suite, facing the park."

"I'll take it. What's the room number?"

When he'd gotten the key, he walked around the corner to the telephone and called Tabatha. She answered immediately. Then he hurried upstairs and ordered a late dinner

from room service. Even before the food came, Tabatha's curt
knock sounded—the Knightsbridge station was less than a
block away.

"Hi," she said as he opened the door.

"Hello," he said as his eyes swept over her body. She wore a
pale yellow shirtwaist that made her look young. So young.
And emphasized her breasts. His prick rose to the occasion.
"Come in. I've ordered dinner."

Tabatha sauntered in and tossed her Harrods shopping bag
on the bed. Turning her back on him, she walked over to the
expansive window and gazed out at the park. He smiled inwardly. Give the kid a thrill. Why not?

He answered the knock at the door and directed the waiter
with a dinner trolley to the small table in the corner. After
he'd tipped the man and hurried him out the door, David
guided Tabatha to the lobster dinner. The thought of eating
one more morsel made him want to unnotch his belt—again.
Flying on the Concorde was a feeding frenzy at supersonic
speed.

He popped the cork on the Cristal bottle and poured them
each a glass. "To your shop."

The glasses clinked and Tabatha smiled, which was rare, but
David knew mentioning her shop would do the trick.

"Have you thought of a name for it yet?"

She paused to swallow a bite of lobster before answering.
"Bangles."

"I like it," he lied. Stupid name. "Here's the present I promised you." He tossed five thousand pounds on the table near
the crème brûlée. "Has Lauren finished the painting yet?"

"No. She's been busy with the exhibition."

"See if you can encourage her." Since the bugs had picked
up her call to Westcott, David now had Griffith's telephone
number. All he needed was the completed painting, and the
trap would be set.

"I'll try, but she's tied up with the exhibition."

Patience, David thought as he watched Tabatha attack a
lobster claw. Things were ahead of schedule. Barzan would be
pleased. When he'd sought a way to penetrate Griffith's security, Barzan had discovered T.J.'s affair with Caroline Armstrong. Rupert had been livid when Barzan had told him of

Caroline's deception. Barzan had offered to make Armstrong even richer by using Armstrong's exporting company to smuggle drugs if Rupert would let Caroline come to London to lure Griffith out of his Palace Green fortress. Rupert refused, but suggested using his stepdaughter, a dead ringer for Caroline, instead. As it turned out, Lauren Winthrop was proving to be a wiser choice.

"I'll be back next week. I'm going to Switzerland, but I'm returning for the Russian's exhibition," David said, mentally planning to cancel the reservation his secretary, Julia, had made at Brown's and book his personal favorite, the Savoy, instead.

"Get undressed," Tabatha ordered, switching to her assertive mode.

David went over to the bed and stripped, tossing his things on a cranberry-colored damask armchair. He lay down and waited for her to come to him. By now, he knew the routine. She'd tease him until he was crazy. Then she'd disappear into the bathroom and take her sweet time undressing.

Tabatha polished off the crème brûlée and looked down at the empty plate as if she was considering licking it clean. Tossing the napkin onto the table, she rose and crossed the room. Hot and hard, David watched her, anticipating her unbuttoning the shirtwaist. She stooped, giving him a tantalizing glimpse of her shapely legs, and picked up the terry cloth slippers with Hyde Park Hotel monogrammed on them in royal blue. She put them inside her Harrods shopping bag.

Casually, she sat down beside him and ran her fingertips up his bare leg to his balls, then up his shaft. "In a bad way, aren't you?"

He nodded, his eyes on her glorious tits. So young.

Tabatha stood up and went into the bathroom, taking her bag with her. All the soap and complimentary toiletries would be gone. He didn't care. Nor did he mind knowing she'd be in there for half an hour or more while he waited. And waited.

Twenty-three minutes later, she emerged, naked, but with her hair brushed down over her breasts concealing them. Oh Lord! She was planning on royally working him over. He could feel it coming. Nobody did it better. Nobody.

"Roll over," she demanded.

He obeyed and lay there anticipating a slap or perhaps a whack with one of the terry slippers. Instead, a cold stream of liquid was poured down his spinal column. Gently, she massaged his back, spreading the lotion across his tense muscles with deft fingers. Good Lord! Where did she learn all this?

Her hands moved lower and lower. Across his buttocks to his upper thighs. They accidentally grazed the back of his balls, and he groaned. She moved her hand away, and he relaxed, expelling an agonizing breath. Back again—a teasing, fleeting touch. He held his breath. Waiting. Wondering what she'd do next.

Suddenly, she straddled him and leaned forward, her hair flowing across his back, tickling him. Two hard nipples raked through the curls brushing his back. Up and down, back and forth. She moved slowly, waltzing the hair across his back. Torturing him with those big nipples.

So young. He loved it.

As Ryan turned the Aston-Martin off the M5 at Cheltenham, Lauren gazed out the window at the thistledown riding the breeze, lofting high toward the spring-blue sky. Everywhere she saw the apple green of freshly sprouted leaves before they would darken into the deep green of maturity. Squads of swaying bluebells and dog's mercury in full bloom painted the gently rolling meadows with spring's vibrant palette of colors. Bright yellow butterflies lazily floated through the air, their wings spread wide to welcome the warm sunshine.

"I never expected the Cotswolds to be this beautiful."

Lauren smiled at Ryan, and he returned her smile with genuine warmth. Despite the fiasco with the merry widow, last night had been an unqualified success.

"You haven't been outside of London much, have you?"

"No. I went by train once to Box-on-Stroud in the West country where I'd lived briefly with my grandmother. I've wanted to travel, but I've been too busy."

"I'll take you to Rye one day soon. It has a very different look than this or the West country."

Lauren nodded, pleased that they were making plans. They'd been up most of the night talking, getting to know each other better. As tough as he seemed, Ryan did have a gentle side to him. He'd arisen early this morning and loaded the Aston-Martin with presents from every exclusive shop in London, from Asprey where he'd bought an antique cameo to Swain, Adeney, Brigg where he'd purchased a handmade umbrella. He must love his Aunt Tillie tremendously to go to all this trouble for her birthday.

"Is your Aunt Tillie your mother's sister or your father's?"

"Neither. She was my mother's best friend."

"Oh," she said softly as Iggy, who was snoozing in her lap, squirmed, opening one sleepy eye before dozing off again. Last night, Ryan had told her about losing his mother. She'd been startled at how keenly he still felt her loss. Why not? After all these years, she missed her father.

"Aunt Tillie is all the family I have. My mother never had a decent present. Anything she wanted, she had to save Green Stamps to get. I do what I can for Aunt Tillie. For years she lived in Stow-on-the-Wold, but she wanted to move to Bourton-on-the-Water, so I bought her a cottage."

Lauren understood him. He indulged his Aunt Tillie because he hadn't been able to buy things for his mother. Paul had spoiled Lauren, bringing her presents from Paris because he knew Mother neglected her. Ryan and Paul were very much alike. They were men she could trust. And love.

Ryan brought the car to a stop at a yellow road sign with a picture of a black frog on it. Thousands of toads the size of a pence were hopping across the road.

"Don't let Aunt Tillie intimidate you," he warned. "When I called her this morning and said I was bringing you, she practically went into orbit with happiness. She's dying for grandchildren. She pictures us married already."

And you? She wondered if he wanted marriage and children, but forced herself not to ask. Let things take their course. After all, they were just getting to know each other. Then why did this feel so . . . right?

After the last toad hopped across the road, Ryan gunned the engine. South of Cheltenham, he turned down a lane marked Leckhampton Hill and stopped the car. "Let's stretch our legs," he said as he helped her out of the car. "You'll like this view."

Lauren put the half-awake Iggy on the ground and the pot belly followed them, ambling along as they walked up an incline. They rounded the bend and a limestone karst came into sight.

"The Devil's Chimney." He pointed to a tall rock column that time and the wind had sculpted into a formation that did look very much like a chimney.

"It's great," Lauren said. "And the view is unbelievable."

Below the cliff lay a green valley dotted with stone farmhouses and sectioned off by hedges rather than fences. Lowing milch cows, recently milked, called to their calves as the cowbells they wore echoed across the verdant countryside. In the center of the valley lay the town of Cheltenham with its clusters of thatched-roofed houses, village green, and church spire.

Ryan put his arm around her and pointed across the valley. "Those are the Malvern Hills. That's where all that Malvern Water you guzzle comes from."

A rustling in the bushes stole their attention from the panoramic view. Stumbling noisily through the thicket after a wood warbler, Iggy disturbed a bevy of speckled wood butterflies and a pair of nesting bobbies.

"Come on, Iggy," Ryan said. "You'll never catch a bird. You're too clumsy."

As the pot belly tripped through the underbrush, sniffing and wagging her tail, Ryan turned to Lauren. "She doesn't get out often enough. This is good for her."

Back on the road, they traveled through the rural area until they came to Bourton-on-the-Water.

"It's called 'the Venice of the Cotswolds,' " Ryan said, then briefly contrasted it to the squalor of Venice, California, where he'd grown up.

There wasn't any comparison. The river Windrush bisected the hamlet, flowing leisurely by stone cottages with slate roofs and Elizabethan houses framed with half-timber. At regular intervals double-arched bridges spanned the narrow waterway and provided choice spots for picnickers while children waded in the water below. The well-cultivated gardens boasted early purple orchids and the lighter-hued bee orchid as well as the more exotic musk orchid.

Ryan parked the Aston-Martin in front of a stone cottage with a blue door. Before he could get out, a plump woman rushed out, wiping her hands on her apron. Ryan bear-hugged her as Lauren got out of the car and put Iggy down on the cobblestone.

"Aunt Tillie," Ryan said. "This is Lauren Winthrop."

She beamed at Lauren and extended her hand. Instantly, Lauren knew her fears about Aunt Tillie not liking her were unfounded. As she chatted, effusively welcoming Lauren, she realized Aunt Tillie would like anyone Ryan liked.

Iggy sniffed everything in the front yard while they brought in all the presents. Decorated with English pine antiques and displays of Coalport china, the cottage had a homeness to it that was uniquely English.

"What did the doctor say?" Ryan asked as he guided Aunt Tillie to a chair and handed her a present.

"I'm getting an ulcer. That's all. Nothing to worry about." She smiled at Lauren as she unwrapped the first gift. "I had a bit of a problem with my tummy and Ryan made me go to the doctor."

The paisley umbrella in the box brought tears to her eyes. So did the cameo, the stationery from Smythsons, the assortment of marmalade and preserves from Fortnum & Mason, the potpourri from Colefax & Fowler, the tablecloth from the General Trading Company, an enamel box from Eximious, and a hat with sun pleats across the brim from Philip Somerville. But the gardenia fragrance from Penhaligon's was the hit of the party. Iggy took one whiff, rolled over, and played dead.

"I think she prefers Penhaligon's Bluebells," Lauren teased. "As long as you were in there, you should have bought her some."

Ryan winked at Aunt Tillie. "No way, Lauren. You promised her."

"All right." Lauren tickled Iggy's soft belly and instantly revived her. "I'll bring you some Bluebells to go with—" She stopped herself before she said merry widow. When they'd awakened this morning, they'd found Iggy snoozing on top of the dratted corset, a black satin garter between her teeth.

"I adore Iggy," Aunt Tillie said. "I'm on a list at a breeder to get a pot belly. When Ryan first brought her here, I thought she'd smell or have fleas, but she's cleaner than a cat."

"Pot belly's don't get fleas?" Lauren asked.

"Nope. There's something in their skin that fleas don't like." Ryan stroked Iggy's soft fur. "They're the perfect pet. Smarter than dogs, and easier to housebreak. More sensitive noses than bloodhounds."

"Ready for a bite to eat?" Aunt Tillie asked.

A bite proved to be a gigantic shepherd's pie in a fluted casserole, spring lamb seasoned with fresh herbs, hot dill bread, and baby vegetables with marjoram.

"Do you like to cook?" Aunt Tillie asked her.

"Very much. I don't have the time right now, but I hope to soon. I'd love your recipe for this shepherd's pie. It's the best I've had."

Ryan grinned as Aunt Tillie said, "Ryan's mother gave it to me years ago. It's the traditional recipe, but add half a cup of sour cream to the mashed-potato topping."

Everything was so delicious that Lauren overate and had no room for the fresh fruit compote or the trifle made with ladyfingers Aunt Tillie had baked fresh that morning. When Ryan suggested they all take a walk along the river, Lauren readily agreed, anxious to enjoy her day out of the city.

The weather held, bright and dazzling in its clarity, which was unusual for spring when showers could replace sunshine in a matter of moments. With Iggy clumsily tagging along behind, they strolled along the path flanking the river. Darting water bugs ruffled the smooth surface of the shallow water. Soon they had a flock of school children around them asking curious questions about Iggy.

After they'd circled the hamlet, Aunt Tillie showed them a shortcut home, and they left the picturesque river to go down a side street. They came to a run-down house with a dovecote in the weed-filled front yard. Hundreds of pigeons were roosting in the wooden hutch and their white droppings littered the ground. Iggy sniffed, then squealed and ran to Lauren and hid behind her skirt.

"What do you think?" Aunt Tillie asked Ryan.

"It's shi— . . . I think it's the biggest pile of manure I've ever seen inside the city limits."

Lauren choked back a laugh as Iggy nuzzled her ankle, contentedly sniffing. She'd bet anything Aunt Tillie never heard "her boy" cuss.

"The town council's trying to take care of it." Aunt Tillie shook her head.

They spent the rest of the afternoon chatting and nibbling on an unending array of goodies Aunt Tillie brought out. Despite her enthusiasm and ready smile—particularly for Ryan —Lauren thought Aunt Tillie looked tired. When dinner was over, Lauren insisted on doing the dishes for her. She finished and returned to the drawing room and found Ryan sitting on the sofa beside Aunt Tillie.

"We need to be getting back," Ryan said when he saw Lauren.

Aunt Tillie jumped up. "Wait. I have something for you." She returned a few minutes later with a Fortnum & Mason hamper. "A few little things I baked for you."

Ryan hugged her, then kissed her on both cheeks. "It was wonderful. I'll ring you later in the week."

"Thanks for having me," Lauren said. "And for giving me your recipes."

"You be good to my boy, you hear?"

Outside, the sun was a golden halo on the horizon as the plum twilight deepened, casting purplish shadows across the land. But the night promised to be warm and clear and filled with the lingering scent of flowers as an early chorus of frogs chirped spring's lullaby. On the wall bordering the cottage, tiny specks glistened against the gray stone like strings of miniature lights.

"Glow worms. They eat snails," Ryan explained. "They're all over this area at this time of year."

Lauren eased herself into the Aston-Martin, hating to leave the beauty and serenity of the Cotswolds. Ryan climbed in and stowed the hamper in the backseat while Iggy hopped into Lauren's lap. Ryan leaned over and kissed Lauren.

"Thanks for being so nice to Aunt Tillie. You made her day."

"*You* made her day. 'Be good to my boy.' I swear, you have her bamboozled. If she heard the way you really talk, she'd—"

"Wouldn't matter. She was in love with my mother's

brother, Garth. I look exactly like him. No matter what, she would love me."

"Why didn't they marry?"

"He was killed in the war. She never got over him."

Lauren closed her eyes for a moment, experiencing Aunt Tillie's anguish and years of loneliness. Some men were destined to be loved forever.

"If anything happened to you, I would never get over it, either." Instead of holding her feelings inside as she once would have, she told him what she'd been longing to say. "I love you."

25

Dead Man's Hole. Reputed to be the coldest spot in England, the frigid point on the Tower Bridge was where bodies from the bloody tower had been heaved into the Thames. Even on this spring day, it was colder here than anywhere else in London.

"What's going on with Lauren Winthrop?" Peter Stirling demanded.

Ryan shrugged, having expected this confrontation. He had no business spending time with Lauren right now. It was imperative he keep his instincts finely honed. Barzan was bound to make a move soon.

"I've buried my share of careless men. Are you going to be one of them? Get rid of her before you jeopardize everything."

"All right," Ryan reluctantly agreed. How could he do it? Tell her what, a total lie? He could ask her to wait, but it might take another three years. That wouldn't be fair. If things worked out, he could go back to her, and she would understand. Or would she?

"Have you found out who is bugging her penthouse?"

"No." Stirling lit his pipe. "We've swept the gallery and Ravissant Publishing as well as Makarova's place. No bugs in any of those locations. You would think anyone planning to fraudulently reproduce the gallery's prints would have bugs at least in the publishing house."

"What about that lawyer she used to date, Grant Fraser?"

"Nothing. He's here with Lloyds preparing the suit against Pan Am over the Lockerbie crash. He'll return to the States soon, where the settlements don't have limits, to try the case." Stirling puffed on his pipe, then added, "We even checked out Lauren's brother, Paul. Nothing."

"Rupert Armstrong," Ryan said instinctively. He went on to tell Stirling about the ivory smuggling.

"We know about it and we've kept our eye on him for years. What would that have to do with Lauren Winthrop, anyway?"

Ryan hesitated. Lauren had shared the personal details of her life under the assumption he'd never tell. Did he have the right to violate her confidence by telling British intelligence? He decided he did. Her life might be in jeopardy.

He outlined the harrowing experience Lauren had described to him, then added, "I think Armstrong is a big enough bastard to want to hurt her."

Stirling puffed rapidly on his pipe, his expression skeptical. "Why now? He's had years."

"Because now she has money. She's on the verge of being really successful. He wants revenge."

"It doesn't sound plausible, but since we're taking a look at the Armstrongs anyway, I'll tell the boys to dig deep." Stirling tapped his pipe on the rail of the bridge, emptying it.

Leaving Stirling, Ryan returned to his car and got in, wondering where to go. Tight rows of clouds with leaden underbellies promised showers soon, or he would jog through Hyde Park to think things out. He didn't want to spend the afternoon in Greyburne Manor without anyone to talk to. The place was like a tomb. Depressing as hell with all those paintings hanging, macabre reminders of the past. He revved the engine and decided to visit Irek Makarova, who lived nearby. As he walked into the building, Finley Tibbetts emerged.

"Hello," Tibbetts said with that affable, clubby manner he always faked.

Ryan nodded and went inside, bypassing the lift for the stairs. He pounded on Irek's door and the Russian immediately answered.

"Ryan." He slapped him on the back. "Good to see you."

"Was Finley Tibbetts just here?" he asked as he came into the flat.

"I give him an interview."

"Really?" This surprised Ryan. He thought the plan had been to keep Irek under wraps until the exhibition.

"Lauren arranged it. I talked exactly the way Dr. Digsby say. Finely and I now are friends."

"I see," he said, but he couldn't imagine "Finely," who was only impressed by pomp and pounds, liking Irek.

"Did you come for a special reason?"

"I wondered if you wanted to go to lunch."

Irek looked out the floor-to-ceiling windows facing the Thames. Rain pelted the pewter-colored water and whitecaps tossed spume skyward, indicating the wind had picked up. A nasty day that matched Ryan's mood.

"I will make us lunch." Irek grinned. "I have food left over from last night's dinner. We make much, much more than we eat."

He followed Irek into the small kitchen as he talked about learning to cook with Vora. Ryan glanced around. Leighton had made a difference. Gone were several of the totally tasteless items that had caught Irek's fancy when Ryan had taken him shopping. But he was wearing yet another watch, a phony Rolex. Makarova still had a mind of his own.

Irek came up with the remains of a jugged-hare pie and a good-sized portion of cassoulet of monkfish as well as half a bottle of Wiltshire Stitchcombe '84. The food was excellent, but Ryan found talking with Irek depressed him. The Russian burbled with happiness as he chatted nonstop about Vora. Learning to cook. Forays to the country. Trekking through the tarns—the small picturesque lakes—of the Lake District. All the things that Ryan would give anything to do with Lauren.

As Ryan checked his watch, he realized Lauren would be at the airport to meet her brother, who was arriving a week before the exhibition to do some sightseeing. He supposed he should go over there this evening. How could he possibly turn down a woman who'd told him her most intimate secrets? A woman who loved him.

The deep-seated ache of loneliness, which had been there so often these last few years, hit him full force. If he could have walked away, trading every material thing he had to make this work with Lauren, he would have. Only one person could make him hurt her.

His father.

Smiling at Lauren, Paul walked down the jet-way with a young boy on his shoulders. Next to her brother walked a short lady carrying a sleeping girl. Lauren kept her smile on hold as she watched the woman. A conflagration of wild curls framed her heart-shaped face and clashed with the orange mumu cloaking her plump body. This couldn't be Geeta Helspeth. Paul's wife, Marcy, had been a statuesque brunette who had once been a runway model for Claude Montana when they'd lived in Paris. Every woman he'd ever dated had been a slim, striking beauty.

When he reached Lauren, Paul swung the boy to the ground and hugged his sister. "God! It's great to see you. I've missed you." He turned to the woman. "Honey, this is Lauren."

"Hi. I'm Geeta." She smiled, a warm affectionate smile. "And this is Demi—short for Demitri." She indicated the young boy. "And Monique."

"I-I love your work. When your glass sculptures were at the Met, I went to see them three times." Lauren knew she was babbling, but she couldn't get over the woman who'd won Paul's heart. Geeta blushed and looked at Paul. Lauren realized she was shy. Didn't she know how famous she was?

Monique tugged on Paul's trouser leg. "I have to go potty."

By the time, they'd gotten the children to the loo, claimed the baggage, and piled into the limo Lauren had rented for their stay, it was dark. The heavy rain had subsided, leaving a gentle spring shower in its wake.

Tabatha greeted them at the penthouse door and directed Jeeves and the chauffeur to take the luggage to the guest rooms. Twin seek-and-destroy missions on two feet, the children raced around the penthouse peeping into every drawer and opening all the closets. In less than ten minutes, every mirror had fingerprints all over it.

"They'll settle down," Paul assured Lauren as Geeta wandered off for a bath and a nap before dinner. "Where's the television?"

"In the study," Lauren said, amazed at how casual Paul seemed with the little monsters.

"Turn it on, put them in there, and hope for the best."

Lauren led them into the study. Flipping the channels with the remote control, Demi argued with his sister about what to watch as Lauren and Paul eased out of the room.

"You look happy," Paul said. "Are you?"

"There's this wonderful man. I—"

"Grant? When he called for your address, I assumed you two would get back together."

"No, not Grant," Lauren said as she guided him down the hall into the conservatory and stopped in front of the portrait. "Ryan Westcott."

Paul studied it for a moment. "He looks a little stern."

"He isn't. He's a softie."

He inspected her work. "You've hit your stride, Lauren. Your technique has really improved. Is this all you've done?"

"Yes. I've been terribly busy. I'll paint more as soon as I get some free time."

Paul checked the canvas. "I don't like to criticize, but you've got the primer on too thick. It's shiny."

Lauren put her finger up to her lips. "Tabatha gave it to me. It's probably from a discount shop. I didn't want to hurt her feelings by not using it."

Paul nodded, looking at the portrait thoughtfully. "You love him, don't you?"

"Very much. He's totally different than the other men that you've seen me with."

"Like Geeta." Paul put his arm around Lauren. "She's nothing like Marcy, and yet I love her very much. She doesn't let anything upset her. Whatever happens, happens."

Lauren hugged him, understanding. As much as he'd loved Marcy, her driving ambition hadn't helped Paul. He'd left his job as a photographer, which he loved, to work in a New York advertising agency as an art director. He'd left Paris to please Marcy, but, like his father, Paul had never been suited to the high-pressure environment.

"Lauren," Tabatha called through the conservatory door. "Mr. Westcott is downstairs."

"Tell him to come up." She hugged Paul. "I'm dying for you to meet him. I told him everything. And I mean everything about us."

"I told him you were home. He said to come down."

"I'll be right back," Lauren said to Paul. "I'll bring Ryan up to meet you."

As she passed the study, Lauren noticed how quiet the room was. She peeked in and saw the children watching one of the satellite channels being transmitted from Paris. The actors were nude. She signaled for Tabatha to get her brother, then raced down the servant's stairs into the lobby. Ryan was waiting, his back to her, looking out at the square.

"Why are you waiting down here? I want you to come up and meet my brother," she said, but when he turned, the smile froze on her lips. Something was dreadfully wrong.

"I want to talk to you in private. Let's go for a walk."

Her mind a tumult of unnamed fears, she walked beside him as he went west toward the American Embassy.

"What's the matter?"

He halted, leveling cold green eyes on her. "Us. We're not right for each other. This isn't working."

"B-but . . ." He couldn't mean this. They'd had a wonderful weekend. Hadn't they?

"Find yourself a nice guy who'll love you. Not me. I need my freedom."

"Give me a chance." She dropped her lashes quickly to hide the hurt. Had she imagined their attraction, their compatibility? Had she become a victim of her own repressed passion? Obviously she had.

For a moment his expression softened, then it became cold and closed again. He turned his back on her and walked into the dark night.

Peter Stirling munched on a piece of overdone chicken from the take-away counter at Drumstix, and reviewed the preliminary reports on Rupert Armstrong. Shady character. The hum from across the room alerted him to the FAX machine spitting out a message. It had to be Julia Hartley; she was the only one with the number. Out cranked the piece of paper with only one word on it: Intrepid.

Peter threw the chicken bone to the floor and clapped his hands. Julia had discovered the password to Barzan's computer system. Now she had access to his financial records. It would just be a matter of time before the American authorities charged him with tax evasion. A cheap shot, but Peter didn't care. It had taken care of Al Capone, hadn't it? With Barzan out of the picture, most of the cocaine coming into England would be stopped.

Peter would prefer to put him on trial here in England for attempted murder, which would carry a stiffer sentence. But it didn't look as if it was going to work out that way now. Too bad. The MI-5 had spent a fortune—not to mention several years—devising an elaborate trap for Barzan.

Peter carefully folded the paper. Intrepid. Code name for the late Sir William Stephenson. A famous flying ace in the First World War, he'd gone on to shape British intelligence, making it superior to that of England's enemies. Good old Intrepid would be proud. The Americans, the French, the West Germans, and even the Israelis had been after Carlos Barzan for years. But the Brits had cracked the case.

Not so fast. Peter reminded himself that too much had gone wrong with this case already. Last time he visited London, David Marcus had changed rooms and Stirling's men hadn't been able to react quickly enough to get an adjacent room. They'd seen a blonde go up. But she never came down, which was preposterous, of course. When Marcus returned next week, they'd have Brown's covered. That blonde wouldn't get by them again.

Peter was tempted to call Westcott and give him the good news, but he didn't. He might still need him as a backup. Years of work in the intelligence field made him wary. This trap had been Westcott's idea. He was positive Barzan would come after T.J. again. Ryan had been patient for three, going on four years. A few days more couldn't make much difference to him.

*   *   *

Lauren lay in bed telling herself to go to sleep. She couldn't. Her mind kept replaying her time with Ryan. He cared for her; she was certain he did. Then why the about-face?

A soft knock interrupted her thoughts. She went to her door and opened it.

Paul walked into her room saying, "You weren't asleep." When she shook her head, he continued, "Do you want to talk about it?"

Again, she shook her head. What was there to say?

"You had a fight with Ryan?"

"Yes," she reluctantly admitted. "Not a fight really. He doesn't want to see me any more."

It felt so right having Paul to talk to again that she found herself pouring out the whole story from the first time she'd met Ryan in the gallery to this evening's finale. "I somehow failed him," she said, ending the story.

"Stop it. You haven't failed anyone. Don't blame yourself. Remember what Dr. Renault said."

It had been years since she'd seen the psychiatrist, but Lauren could still hear his words. *It's not your fault.* Back then, she'd blamed herself for Rupert's behavior. Her self-esteem had been nonexistent. A typical profile of an abused child, the doctor had assured her.

"It's not my fault," Lauren said, and Paul smiled encouragingly. "I did what I could."

"If you ask me, Ryan sounds like a real crazy-maker. You're better off without him, babes."

Lauren doubted that but didn't say so.

"This news will cheer you up." Paul grinned. "I'm opening a gallery early next month."

"Really? Is Geeta lending you the money?"

"No. When she had an exhibition at the Nedra Matteuchi Gallery in Santa Fe, I met a man and we discussed opening a gallery for photographers. He offered to be my partner."

A cold, sinking feeling hit her. "Who?"

"Carlos Barzan."

Vora tiptoed into the bathroom and quietly closed the door. She had to pee every few hours, it seemed. Her queasy stomach flip-flopped. Mercy. Why had she ever thought she wanted to be pregnant? She eased into her silk robe and went into the kitchen. The shutters were open and the mauve light of another resplendent spring dawn brightened the room enough for her to see the tea kettle. She filled it and reached for the tin of Lapsang Souchong.

When Dr. Osgood had told her she was pregnant, it seemed impossible. She and Archer had tried so hard to have a child. Nothing had worked. Now, when she least wanted it, she was pregnant. Irek would marry her, of course. But how would he feel later? Would she hold his interest once he could choose from any woman around? Would he dump her as Clive had?

Riddled with self-doubt, she opened the front door to get *The Times*. The teapot whistled for attention as she scanned the front page and hustled to get it before it woke Irek. She poured the hot water in the Spode teapot she'd brought from home. Then she turned to Finley's column. She read it twice, the second time through tear-blurred eyes, before picking up her personal telephone directory.

Dr. Digsby answered on the first ring.

"Vora Leighton, doctor. Have you seen *The Times*?"

"Naturally. Don't worry. God will take care of Mr. Tibbetts."

Vora slammed the phone down. The man was a bona fide nut. How did he expect Irek to overcome a scathing review that called him 'a slimy Bolshevik with artistic pretensions'?"

"Vora. Come back to bed."

She hid the newspaper beneath the Porsche sales brochures Irek had been collecting.

26

"I'm going to tell the bastard to go to hell."

"Lauren, please don't. It'll only make things worse." Vora looked over her shoulder at Irek, who was across the gallery talking with Tabatha Foley.

"I'm not letting Finley get away with it. He'd given me his word not to publish anything about Irek before the opening." Lauren checked her watch; in twenty minutes the exhibition officially opened. "You keep Irek calm. I'm going to adjust the lighting."

For the fifth time that evening, Lauren rechecked the lights. She moved around the main salon and then into the smaller gallery. He's destined to be a famous artist, Lauren assured herself. Despite Finley Tibbetts.

She paused in the center of the small gallery where Tabatha's figurine was on display. Two overhead spots accentuated the translucence of the porcelain with its delicate lines and the subtly blended colors.

"I really like Mr. Makarova," Tabatha said as she came up behind her.

She smiled to see the happy expression on Tabatha's face. Lauren had taken her to Basil and he'd restyled her hair into layers of loose curls that framed her face and softened the line of her nose. He'd applied a cellophane rinse that had given her russet curls an incandescent glow.

Miss Marple at Harrods had selected a peach chiffon gown for Tabatha to wear to the opening. Instead of trying to disguise her enormous breasts, the strapless sheath pushed them up like twin Uzis. Personally, Lauren thought it was a bit old for her, but she looked pretty nonetheless.

"I've never seen any painting as beautiful as 'Velma Liubov'.' Why won't he sell it?"

"I'm certain Velma is very special to him." From where Lauren stood she could see Irek. His eyes sang arias of love to Vora who stood beside him. She wore an Anthony Price original, a swirl of mossy-green organza and deeper-green seed pearls that complemented her auburn hair and brought out the gold tones in her eyes. Lauren realized even perceptive Tabatha hadn't noticed Velma was Vora. The freckles should have done it, but Irek's style was Impressionistic enough to make positive identification of the subject almost impossible.

"Stand beside 'Perfection' and introduce yourself to the guests. Remember what I told you. Be on the alert for reporters from *Apollo, Connoisseur, Art and Antiques*, and the local papers. I'll nip in as often as possible to check on you."

Lauren left Tabatha and went into the main gallery where the first guests were arriving. Among them was David Marcus. She took the stairs to the lower level to avoid having to talk to Barzan's assistant. After successfully dodging him on the contract matter, she wanted to avoid a confrontation with him tonight.

Downstairs, the caterers were garnishing platters of cheese, carving firm wheels into animals, placing wedges in artful ice sculptures while portable ovens heated *encroûté* selections. Sally Clark deserved a medal. She'd transformed the limiting cheese menu into a work of art. How the Tanqueray Silver would go over, Lauren wasn't so sure. The bar had everything anyone could imagine to go with vodka from a simple olive to guava juice.

Too late to worry about it, she decided as she walked through the offices to the outside stairs leading to the street level. Halfway up, she saw Ryan Westcott going into the gallery. She waited until he'd entered. Her heart thudded and the ache of regret she'd felt too often in the last week returned. *Not tonight. You don't have time.*

But she had noticed Ryan was wearing a sport coat and open-neck shirt. He probably wanted to make Irek feel comfortable. At Dr. Digsby's insistence, Irek had selected his own outfit for this evening. Rather than choosing the traditional dinner jacket most men wore to openings, Irek had dressed in charcoal Italian-style trousers with pleats at the waist and legs that nipped in at the ankles. The cuffs of his silver-gray shirt were rolled back to reveal a Batman watch with a fluorescent dial. The Hermès belt with the gold buckle must have been Vora's contribution. Irek looked handsome, but most important, he was relaxed. Happy.

Please, Lauren prayed, *make tonight a success. Irek's suffered enough already.*

"Shit!" Peter Stirling threw the copy of *Punch* on the sofa. At this rate, he would be talking like Ryan Westcott by morning. What else could go wrong with this case?

Last week, Julia Hartley had been all set to access Marcus's computer. Then Barzan's secretary developed shingles. Since David Marcus was abroad, Barzan had commandeered Julia. He had her trotting all over Manhattan with him. Wasting her time.

Now Peter's man had just called. David Marcus had already stayed in Switzerland longer than his original itinerary had indicated. This evening, his plane had arrived late from Zurich. Did he check in at Brown's as planned? Hell, no. The limo had deposited him at the Savoy. Great. They were madly scrambling to position themselves at the Savoy while Marcus attended the Ravissant opening.

The only promising development in the past week had been with Rupert Armstrong. His exporting business was generating more cash than the products warranted. How many Berber rugs could he sell in England? Customs agents were set to inspect his next shipment.

Ryan finished his vodka on the rocks—he still preferred gin —and looked around the gallery for Lauren. Where the hell was she? The glitterati were arriving by the dozens. Lord and

Lady Brocket, Rocco Forte of Trusthouse Forte, Roger Moore, Kenneth Branagh. A gaggle of Guinnesses. Jane Seymour. Art dealer David Ker with fellow dealer Julian Agnew.

And the American contingent. Ann Getty with Gordon in tow. New York dealer Barbara Guggenheim. Linda de Roulet, the heiress to the Payson fortune. She'd sold Picasso's "Au Lapin Agile" for almost forty-seven million dollars. Should give her enough to pick up a Makarova or two with a few pounds to spare.

People were here. But would they buy?

Despite Finley's bashing, the press were crawling all over the mountains of cheese and guzzling vodka. The art magazines. The foreign papers. London *Times* food critic Jonathan Meades—sampling the Vinnie blue *encroûté*. A guy from *Time Out*, the arbiter of current trends. The tasteless tabloids. All had their photographers dogging their heels. The squads of television reporters had their mini-cams. The stage was set. Now someone buy something.

At the gallery entrance, Ryan saw Lauren escorting Lady Fiona Farnsworth as her attendant pushed her rolling throne into Ravissant. Jesus! He wondered what to call the color of the halter-top dress Lauren wore. The palest shade of lavender imaginable, it clung sensuously to her luscious curves, emphasizing her narrow waist and long legs. She brushed back an errant lock of hair and laughed, the light catching her crystal-blue eyes. For the briefest moment, his gaze met hers. He forced himself to look away.

Vora rushed up to him. "No one has bought anything."

"For crissake, it's only nine fifteen. No one's here yet. Relax. We've all done everything we could do." Damage control had been the order of the day since that prick's story broke. They'd all banded together and followed up the engraved invitations with telephone calls.

"How can Irek take this so lightly? Do you know what he said?" When Ryan shook his head, Vora continued, " 'A *zek* has nothing to lose.' He doesn't care."

Out of the corner of his eye Ryan caught Lauren again, speaking with Jeffrey Archer. Flirting. "What's a *zek*?"

"A prisoner," Vora said as she looked across the room, her love for Irek clearly reflected in her eyes.

"Irek's seen hell. Whatever happens tonight won't throw him."

"But I want so much for him to have the success he deserves," Vora said, waving at a new arrival. "There's Basil."

A short man wearing white cowboy boots with white-suede jeans tucked into them sashayed toward them. His white-foulard cowboy shirt was topped by a bolo tie with a hunk of turquoise the size of a fist anchoring it. Christ! His hair stood on end, making him look as if he'd received an electrical shock. Talked like he'd been permanently short-circuited, too, punctuating every sentence with "ducky."

Ryan nodded, his eyes on Lauren, as Vora introduced him to Basil Blackstoke. Still stationed at the door, Lauren greeted Lady Antonia Fraser and Harold Pinter. Ryan didn't care for Pinter's plays and hadn't read one of her historicals. But what the hell, if they bought a painting.

"There's Lord and Lady Glenconner," Vora said as Colin Tennant and his wife came through the door. "They're in from St. Lucia in the Caribbean. He's built a hotel there, you know."

Ryan didn't. And he didn't give a damn. Vora flew off across the room to greet the peers, and Ryan noticed Lauren now had Andrew Lloyd Webber by her side. Lauren had delivered most of the luminaries of the Groucho Club.

Now if they'd just get off their duffs and buy something. He looked over at Irek. The pain-in-the-ass Lady Fiona had him backed into a corner.

"How do you like my boots?" Basil asked.

Ryan looked down at Basil's feet. He'd forgotten all about him.

"They're white alligator. Very rare, ducky. They're found only on the banks of the Limpopo River."

"They're okay if you get off killing an endangered species." What a cocky little shit. Where did he get his money? Was there that much profit in shampoos and blow-drys? Basil drove a vintage Bugatti and had recently purchased the penthouse at 3a Palace Green, the pricey complex up the street from Greyburne Manor. David Goldstone had cornered the marble market to build it. The penthouses went for four million pounds—over seven million dollars.

A lot of money for a blow-dryer queen. Then Ryan remembered Basil had a line of hair products called Miracles. An image of Lauren wearing that merry widow came to mind. Women paid ridiculous prices for crap they didn't need. Basil's shampoo sales alone probably outranked most galleries.

Vora stalled Lord and Lady Glenconner and waited for Lady Fiona to stop talking to Irek. While they chatted, Vora looked around at the nearly full gallery and saw many of them were Archer's clients. They'd respected her enough to come when she'd called. That surprised her. *Now, please, let some of them buy something.*

"Introduce us to the artist," Colin Tennant demanded, and Vora was forced to join Irek even though Lady Fiona was still there.

"All you're serving is vodka?" Lady Fiona groused before Vora could introduce the Tennants. "I *loathe* vodka. I only drink sherry."

"Try Breeze Sea," Irek said.

Sea Breeze, Vora mentally corrected him, deciding Irek was nervous after all. He hadn't been dropping his articles in weeks, nor had he been reversing his words. But she refused to embarrass him by correcting him.

"A Brie Cie? Never heard of it." Lady Fiona dismissed the drink. If she hadn't heard of it, it didn't exist. But she was smiling at Irek. And fluttering her ancient eyelashes.

"You will like," Irek said with a cute grin.

Vora introduced the Tennants and motioned for a waiter to take their order.

"Two martinis," Colin Tennant said, "stirred, not shaken."

"A Brie Cie for me." Lady Fiona winked at Irek.

"Pardon?" the waiter said.

As Vora drew him aside, Lady Fiona railed about how much better off Russia would have been had Trotsky not been murdered. "She means a Sea Breeze." The waiter still looked puzzled. Lauren and her American drinks. "Grapefruit juice and cranberry juice with two jiggers of vodka."

The Tennants looked bored and many other guests were milling around waiting to be introduced to Irek. Vora was wondering how to get rid of the old biddy when Ryan came to her rescue.

"Fifi, let me show you Irek's work." He nudged the attendant with the greasy hair aside and wheeled the protesting Lady Fiona away.

Vora quickly introduced the other guests, then left. Irek didn't need her to hold his hand. The gallery was filling rapidly, many of them Archer's clients. She roved around greeting them and avoiding Lady Fiona. But she did notice the old woman had consumed the Brie Cie and had ordered a second.

Lauren waited at the door, encouraged by the turnout. Discouraged by the lack of sales. People were viewing the exhibition, quaffing Bloody Marys, Screw Drivers, Vodka Tonics, and Martinis. But they weren't buying. The cheese was going fast, disappearing into hungry mouths on Carrs biscuits, wedges of toast, Fortt's saucer-sized crackers, and vegetables. But no one was buying.

The tight band of tension around her rib cage cinched in still another notch. She glanced over at Irek. He was laughing and joking, oblivious to the nonexistent sales. Women were drawn to him, Lauren decided as she noted the enraptured looks on many of the female faces. He exuded power and low-key animal magnetism that women found appealing.

The valet tapped Lauren's shoulder. She'd told him to alert her to the arrival of Finley's Silver Shadow Rolls-Royce. She recognized Pimerton, Finley's chauffeur, as he stepped out to open the door for the art critic. Lauren dashed the sort distance from the door to the curb.

"Don't bother to get out. You're not welcome in my gallery."

"I don't understand your attitude, Lauren—not a'tall. You can't be upset that I spoke my mind? After all, the press must be free to report without—"

"What you did defies journalistic ethics. And you know it. You didn't honor off-the-record comments. You didn't verify facts. Irek is not a 'common criminal.' He was detained for his political views like Solzhenitsyn or Sakharov." She paused for a deep breath, resisting the urge to slap his smug face. "But above all, you lied. You promised not to release this story until after tonight."

"A misunderstanding. Nothing a'tall to—"

"Take him away."

The chauffeur smiled and winked at Lauren as he drove away. She turned and saw Geeta and Paul walking toward her. As usual, they were late. Geeta Helspeth was never on time. But Lauren couldn't help liking her. She laughed at herself and everything around her. Most of all, she enjoyed life without taking anything too seriously. She was perfect for Paul.

At least he was happy. Since Ryan had told Lauren that he wanted his freedom, she'd been miserable and lonely—despite the constant ruckus the children caused and the demands of the exhibition. She'd never offered herself so completely to a man. She'd never wanted to before now. His rejection had left her questioning her judgment, her feelings.

"Hi," Paul hailed her. "Good turnout?"

"Great. Better than we expected."

Lauren guided them inside and found Vora. "Introduce Geeta around," she whispered. "Be sure she meets the press, but stay with her. She's shy."

Checking her watch, Lauren saw it was almost ten. Where was Tak? He'd promised to come. She'd rung Claridge's earlier; he had a reservation, but hadn't checked in. Twisting her silver bracelet, she made herself take a deep breath. Nothing had sold.

Across the main gallery, she saw David Marcus talking with several men she didn't recognize. Seeing him brought Carlos Barzan to mind. It struck her as extremely odd that he would seek out Paul. It was even stranger that Barzan would swear her to secrecy about his ownership of Ravissant while he didn't mind revealing his deal with Paul. Right after Paul had told her, Lauren had been about to confide in him when Demi had appeared. Monsters were hiding in the mirror on the guest-room wall and he was frightened. Paul had left to comfort him and Lauren hadn't had the opportunity of speaking to her brother alone since then.

She supposed it was coincidence that Barzan had been at Geeta's showing. After all, she was one of the world's foremost sculptors, and Barzan was a prominent collector. Still, Lauren didn't like his deal with Paul. This meant she would continue to have Barzan as her partner even after she finished with Ravissant.

Did it matter? He'd given her free rein at Ravissant and hadn't tried to manipulate the market. But the fact that he must have known about the gallery's outstanding debt disturbed her. When she had a chance, she planned to ask him about it. She saw David Marcus coming her way and mentally sharpened her fangs.

"Where's Makarova's contract?" he asked without preamble.

"We have a verbal agreement." She looked him right in the eye, daring him to question her judgment. Despite their pale color, his eyes had almost a caustic intensity.

"You probably won't need it. Nothing is selling. Next time, I'll see the contract *before* I permit an exhibition."

"If I don't have Mr. Barzan's complete confidence, I'll take the next plane home."

"Now wait a minute." He smiled, his albino-blue eyes even more threatening. "Don't get huffy. You've done very well so far, but good business practices dictate—"

"Excuse me," she said and walked away, waving to Takgama Nakamura.

That bitch. If he didn't need her to get to Griffith, David would have told her to go to hell. Fuming, he finished his Gibson. He gazed around the room hoping to spot another high-profile financier. It gave him a perverse sense of pleasure to talk with them and know he controlled more money than they did. He'd just finished a discussion with Robin Leigh-Pemberton, governor of the Bank of England. When David didn't recognize any other financiers, he strolled into the smaller gallery.

As he scanned the room looking for someone he knew, he noticed an astonishing redhead with the biggest tits he'd ever seen. High and full, they crowned a shapely body. His prick hardened. He couldn't see the woman's face because her head was turned toward the person next to her. Just as he broke into the group, she turned. Tabatha? What in hell was she doing here?

"Hello," she said, extending her hand with all the aplomb of a sophisticated lady. "I'm Tabatha Lynn Foley."

"David Marcus." He shook her hand and watched, stunned,

as she introduced a cabal of reporters from various art magazines.

With her new hairstyle and those clothes, she was all grown up. Almost beautiful—nothing a nose job wouldn't cure. He was achingly hard now, remembering what she'd done to him last time they'd been together. Suddenly, he saw himself with her. Now. Next year. Ten years from now. Tabatha Foley could grow up and he wouldn't dump her. Why would he? Her performances couldn't be topped.

"What direction do you see your career taking?" asked one bespectacled man with a notepad and pencil poised in his hand.

"I'll want to improve my craft, of course. So, I'll be taking classes at St. Martins—"

What the hell was going on here? Did these men think she was an artist? "I thought you made jewelry," David interjected.

"Jewelry?" asked another reporter, making it sound like a four-letter word.

"Mr. Marcus is correct," Tabatha said evenly. "I make jewelry as a sideline. An artist's life isn't easy. I have to support myself."

"Of course," they said sympathetically.

David's blood pounded in his brain, making it hard to hear. He wanted to kill them all. And her. He'd discovered Tabatha, shown her a good time. She wasn't going to walk out on him.

Lauren rushed up. "Tabatha, guess what? 'Perfection' has been purchased by the Metropolitan Museum in New York."

"Is this your first sale?" asked one of the reporters.

"Of course not," Lauren answered for Tabatha. "I sold her first piece in one day. She'll be doing many more."

A tall man elbowed his way into the group. "Geeta Helspeth is in the other room."

The reporters bolted for the main gallery. Lauren followed them, leaving David and Tabatha beside "Perfection." *Please,* Lauren prayed, *let someone buy something of Irek's now.* She spotted Dr. Denton Digsby at the entrance, but decided to join Tak, who was still talking with Irek. She was weaving her way through the crowd when she heard a crash and the chorus of "oh nos" behind her.

"What happened?" Lauren asked Tabatha after she'd raced back into the smaller gallery. The remains of "Perfection" were scattered about the floor.

Her face ashen, Tabatha shook her head, but David Marcus said, "Someone bumped into the pedestal."

"Don't worry," Lauren tried to reassure Tabatha as she signaled for a waiter to sweep up the shards of porcelain. "I'll speak with the gentleman from the Met. I'm sure he'll be glad to have first choice of anything else you make."

Lauren left wondering just how the piece had fallen. True, the gallery was crowded, but the pedestal was heavy with a secure base. What else could go wrong? Nothing of Irek's was selling and the one piece they'd sold had been destroyed.

"The guy standing next to her did it. He was the only one close enough and big enough to rock that pedestal."

Lauren looked into Ryan Westcott's compelling eyes as he moved up beside her. She swallowed hard, assuring herself she had a much stronger guard up than last week.

"You must be mistaken. Why would David Marcus do that?"

For a moment she thought his body tensed, but perhaps it just was the barely controlled power she often sensed when she was around him. Seeing he had no answer, she walked away.

He caught her arm and whispered, "Try not to be angry with me. I didn't mean to hurt you."

He didn't *mean* to hurt her? "Don't come around anymore. After tonight you're not welcome in Ravissant or in my life."

Lauren stalked off as fast as she could. She would always love Ryan, but he didn't need to know it. And she certainly wasn't going to allow him to drive her crazy. She'd spent too many years already putting her life back together.

"Hello, gorgeous." Grant Fraser nabbed her.

"Hi," she said, her eyes skipping across the crowd for Tak. Had he left already without buying anything?

Grant put his arm around her. "Everyone is having a ball. I was just speaking with Terrence Holbrook, a Lord of Appeal."

"Did he buy anything?"

"No," Grant said, obviously impressed by the man whose position was equivalent to that of a Supreme Court Justice.

"He can afford two Makarovas, not just one."

Grant put his arm around her. "You're taking this too seriously. Marry me and you won't have a thing to worry about—ever."

Watching Fraser paw Lauren only made Ryan more irritable. She was angry with him; Ryan didn't blame her. He'd royally muffed it when he'd told her he wanted his freedom. He should have told her something else. Anything else. It had hurt her so much she was now angry. In time, her anger would harden into hate. He couldn't risk it—not when he'd waited this long for a woman like her.

Ryan shouldered his way through the mass of people and past Lady Fiona ordering yet another Brie Cie as he left the gallery. Outside, he saw Takgama Nakamura speaking in Japanese to Yasumichi Morishita. Rumor had it Morishita was planning a takeover of Christie's. Ryan hoped the Monopolies and Mergers Commission wouldn't approve such a bid. Hadn't the Sotheby's takeover been a lesson?

He crossed the street and went into the Coach & Horses where he called Stirling. "Why wasn't I given a photograph of David Marcus? I'm waltzing around him at the Ravissant opening, and I didn't even recognize him."

"I thought you'd met. Didn't you have several meetings with the Barzans?"

"Yes, but I never met Marcus."

Ryan heard Stirling nervously puffing on his pipe. "An oversight. Awfully sorry. But I don't think it will matter. He's Barzan's bean counter—nothing more. And we have a tail on him—"

"The bald guy. I spotted him as soon as I found out who Marcus was," Ryan said and went on to tell Stirling about the incident with the figurine. "I'm positive Marcus deliberately destroyed that piece. If your man was doing his job, he'll be able to verify it."

"Why would Marcus do that?"

"How the hell do I know? Take a closer look at him. Maybe he's counting more than beans."

"We are." There was no mistaking the weary note in Stirling's voice.

"Anything more on Lauren Winthrop?" Ryan asked, not caring if Stirling guessed this was the real reason for his call.

He wasn't worried about Marcus. Barzan would come gunning for T.J. personally. Again.

"No. She seems to have a clean record. But we haven't found out who's bugging her penthouse."

Ryan rang off, thankful Lauren wasn't under suspicion. He'd known all along she wasn't involved, but he'd owed it to T.J. to be positive. Now that Ryan was certain, he wasn't losing her. He had too many lonely nights behind him not to recognize the right woman when he met her.

On the way back to Ravissant, Ryan saw Lauren come up the stairs from Ravissant's office level to the street with David Marcus. They were having an animated discussion but Ryan was too far away to hear what they were saying.

"Nakamura and Morishita offered to buy all Irek Makarova's works and you refused to sell?" David asked.

"Yes." Lauren didn't bother to disguise the animosity she felt for David Marcus. She couldn't imagine why he'd done it, but she suspected Ryan was right. David had deliberately destroyed Tabatha's figurine. Then he'd appeared downstairs —uninvited—just after Lauren had refused Tak's offer.

As soon as she got the chance, she was going to discuss the Barzan situation with Paul. She had no intention of establishing yet another partnership with Barzan that would include his troublesome assistant. She would bankroll Paul's gallery, not Barzan. Then they could maintain their independence.

"Why would you do such a stupid thing?"

"I have no intention of letting anyone—not even my friend Tak—buy more than two of Irek's works. It's the mark of a speculator—future competition. I learned my lesson from the Saatchi affair. Often he bought whole collections. Now he's having financial difficulty and is unloading them. That makes it hard for the artist's own dealers to make any money. To say nothing of the artist who makes a profit only on the original sale. If Tak and his cohort resell Irek's works in Japan, Irek loses and Ravissant loses."

"You're a better businesswoman than I thought."

As David returned to the gallery leaving Lauren outside, she questioned rejecting Tak's offer. She hadn't told David, but Tak had hinted he would spread the word that he found Irek's works inferior. As always Tak played to win—not caring if he dealt from the bottom of the deck, something she remembered from the conversations she'd heard when she'd hostessed for him at the Sake Sistahs.

I can play hard ball, too. Like most Japanese men, Tak undoubtedly found her assertiveness offensive, but she didn't care. No more kowtowing for her. As Irek's representative she had to think of his best interests, not Tak's. If the Japanese were willing to buy the entire collection, Irek would be a winner. Maybe not tonight—but someday. Hopefully within the year so she could make a healthy profit and get rid of Barzan and his henchman, Marcus.

She turned her head as a Turbo Bentley caught her eye. A burst of high-pitched giggles heralded the arrival of Mootzie McCallister escorted by Clive Holcombe. Lauren stifled a groan. What if Mootzie bought something? That might be worse for Irek's reputation than anything Finley Tibbetts had printed or Tak might say.

"Lauren." Ryan Westcott appeared beside her. "I'd like a word with you."

Over her protests, he ushered her down the street and stopped in the doorway of Culpepper The Herbalist. He guided her into the dark alcove at the shop's entrance where no one could see them.

"Make this fast," Lauren said.

Ryan hesitated. How could he explain his strange behavior? "I'm crazy about you. I—"

Lauren barely controlled her gasp of surprise. Paul was right. Ryan Westcott was a crazy-maker nonpareil.

"I blew it the other night. I didn't mean what I said."

"Don't do this to me," Lauren said, utterly astonished at the sincerity in his voice. "Not now, not in the middle of this—"

"Last week I should have told you the truth. I've never cared for a woman the way I do you. I don't want my freedom, but I can't see you right now."

Wordlessly, she stared at him, her heart racing pell-mell. During the past week, he'd spoken to her dozens of times in her dreams, recanting his words that their relationship wasn't working. Yet she couldn't believe he was actually saying it.

"Why didn't you just tell me that in the first place?" *Why did you torment me with the thought I'd lost you forever?*

He cupped her chin with his hand, shattering the hard shell she was trying to maintain. Suddenly, she was all too aware of his firm thigh brushing hers and the seductive warmth emanating from his body. She prayed he had a logical explanation. Right or wrong, every fiber of her being wanted to forgive him.

"I'm involved in something that has gone on for over three years. Who knows how much longer it'll last? I didn't want you to wait not knowing—"

"Isn't that my decision, not yours?"

He gently pressed his lips to hers, a caress more than a kiss. "Will you wait even though I can't discuss my problems with you? Even though we'll have to see each other on the sly—if at all?"

"I'll wait forever if necessary." She stood on tiptoe and kissed him, a heated kiss that left no doubt she meant every word. Reluctantly, she stepped out of his arms. "Let's get back. Irek needs us."

"You go and I'll follow. It's important we not be seen together too often."

He's an unpredictable man, she told herself as she hurried up the street to the gallery. But she loved him. Not since Todd Haile had she felt so much in love. She was prepared to wait. Why not? She'd been waiting for him, needing a man like him without even knowing what she'd been missing.

"There you are," Dr. Digsby greeted her. "Quite the media event, isn't it?"

As she nodded, Digsby noted the look of concern on Lauren's face. It pleased him that she genuinely cared about Irek. He turned and followed her inside saying, "The Princess Royal is here and the Princess of Kent."

"Really? Where?"

Digsby watched her closely. She had the most extraordinary eyes—flawless blue, like the blue salvia that grew near his country home in Sussex. "Over there with Irek. Come on. I'll introduce you."

"Don't bother."

He decided that she'd declined not out of shyness, as many did when confronted with royalty, but because she wasn't impressed by titles. He wished he could share the truth with her. He'd put pressure on them both to appear tonight. Michael, Princess of Kent, was on the hot seat from critics who didn't like her book. Digsby had advised her to go ahead and write another. Who cared what they said about you as long as sales were up?

Princess Anne was a more difficult case. Her impending divorce and the publication of love letters sent to her by an attaché had been the subject of a royal roast in the press. The squawk about using her military attachés for non-military activities had driven the princess to Digsby. He'd advised her to stay the course and keep appearing in public—like tonight— and show she had nothing to hide.

"It's the photo opportunity of the decade." Digsby marveled at the flashbulbs popping like firecrackers. "Where else can the press get a picture of Mootzie McCallister with Lord Widener or the Princess Royal with Eric Clapton?"

"Despite Finley, do you think the press likes Irek?"

"Definitely. His colleagues know Finley is a blowhard."

"Then why hasn't anyone bought a painting?"

"Several have sold."

Lauren dashed over to the reception counter. "Has something sold?"

"Yes. Arianna Stassinopoulos Huffington bought two."

"Really?" This encouraged Lauren. Arianna had been a former president of the Cambridge Union, the elite debating society, the first foreigner to be selected. She'd gone on to write a scathing book about Picasso that claimed his later works reflected his diminishing artistic powers as well as his moral degeneration. Arianna was a woman who knew her mind and wasn't easily fooled.

"Sybille Bedford purchased the landscape of Kiev in winter."

"Great." Sybille had always been Lauren's favorite novelist. Years ago she'd read *A Legacy,* and she had *Jigsaw* on her nightstand right now. Inviting the Groucho Club was paying off.

"Jeffrey Archer is taking two, but he and his wife are trying to make up their minds which two."

Lauren silently vowed to buy all of his books. In hard cover.

"Has anyone marked these sold?" she asked, barely able to contain her joy.

"Mrs. Leighton is handling that."

Lauren threaded her way through the crowd as she searched for Vora, noting that television crews from the Beeb and Thames Television had arrived.

"Can you believe it?" Lauren whispered when she found Vora attaching a gold-foil sold sticker to "Nyet," a landscape as seen through the bars of Christopol Prison. Lady Fiona had purchased it.

"More than half sold." Vora hugged Lauren. "I can hardly wait to tell him."

"He doesn't know?"

"Who can get near him? Anyway, I don't want to go over there right now."

"Because of Clive?" Lauren asked, seeing Clive and Mootzie among the throng surrounding Irek.

"I don't care about Clive anymore. But watch Mootzie."

Mootzie was openly flirting with Irek, giggling loudly at everything he said.

"Irek's too smart to fall for that tramp."

"I'm concerned Clive is jealous of Irek. He's everything Clive isn't, and now Mootzie is making a play for him. He might say something or do something to embarrass Irek."

Lauren watched Clive standing beside Mootzie and scowling at Irek. She skimmed the crowd, searching for Ryan, and found him in the corner handing Lady Fiona yet another Sea Breeze. "Go tell Ryan to help out."

As Vora went for Ryan, the receptionist signaled to Lauren. Five times she flashed four fingers. Twenty pictures sold. Suddenly, the best of all worlds seemed possible—a sellout. Finley Tibbetts could chew a root.

"Lauren, may I have a word with you?" Tak appeared at her elbow speaking Japanese.

"Yes," she replied in English. His earlier threat made her wary. Although fluent in Japanese, she had no intention of letting him manipulate her. This was her turf. English her language.

"I wish to purchase 'Velma Liubov'.'"

"It's not for sale. We're merely displaying it to indicate the

direction Irek's career is taking." As she spoke, she decided
Tak's threat to discredit Irek had merely been a maneuver to
frighten her. He'd realized Irek was destined to be a premiere
artist. Even Tak, with his billions of yen, couldn't stop him.

"A half million pounds."

He couldn't mean almost a million dollars. The most they'd
asked for any piece in the collection was just under a quarter
of a million dollars for "Volga," a wintry scene on the river. It
had yet to sell.

"Don't you think Mr. Makarova has the right to hear my
offer?"

"He won't take it. That portrait means too much to him."

Tak's inscrutable expression became a knowing smile. "Every man has his price."

"I'll tell him, but now isn't a good time," she said. The
camera crews were adjusting their lights, poised for an interview. Out of the corner of her eye she spotted Dr. Digsby.
Grinning. Maybe now was the perfect time.

"Come on." She took Tak's arm and guided him up to the
mob clustered around Irek. The cameras were running, the
interview was getting under way. In the center of the intense
light, Irek stood alone while Mootzie and Clive as well as a
host of other guests waited nearby.

"Irek," Lauren said, interrupting the reporter. "Mr.
Nakamura has offered half a million pounds for 'Velma
Liubov'.'"

"Everything else has sold," Ryan added, walking up beside
her. He was followed by a host of guests, including Princess
Anne.

The crowd gasped. His first exhibition—a sellout. And an
astounding offer from one of the world's wealthiest collectors.
Unprecedented.

"It is not for sale," Irek answered without hesitation.

"Divine. Simply divine," said Dr. Digsby as he came up
behind Lauren.

"One million pounds," Tak upped his offer.

A twitter of surprised whispers filled the room. Lauren's
eyes swept the gallery for Geeta and Paul. Like everyone else,
they had joined the tight circle. Confident no one could see
her, Lauren reached down and squeezed Ryan's hand.

"Not for sale," Irek replied immediately.

"Mr. Makarova, which painting is 'Velma Liubov' '?" the television reporter asked.

Irek stepped aside, revealing the portrait behind him. The crowd erupted in shocked chatter as everyone moved closer and dozens of flashbulbs exploded while the video cameras zoomed in for a closeup.

"One and a half million pounds." Tak's voice cut through the din.

Irek paused for a moment, studying Tak, and Lauren assumed he had weakened. *Remember, every man has his price.*

"This is painting of woman I love. It belong to me. Always. It has no price."

"Two million pounds."

Silence ricocheted through the gallery. All eyes were focused on Irek. Waiting. Wondering.

"The Lord be praised. The Lord be praised."

Lauren didn't turn around when she heard Dr. Digsby's incantation. She just squeezed Ryan's hand, thinking the offer had exceeded the record for an artist's debut.

She looked for Vora and found she'd wiggled her way up to the perimeter of the circle, not too far from Lauren. A tight frown furrowed Vora's brow. Her eyes were on Clive Holcombe. He'd edged closer to the portrait and was studying it carefully. Clive then looked at Irek with a grimace that telegraphed hate.

"Deke zabeb," Irek said, then laughed. "You peoples crazy. No painting worth this much money. Crazy. Listen to Irek. 'Velma Liubov' ' is not for sale."

"You tell him, my boy," came the inebriated voice of Lady Fiona as she clutched her Sea Breeze with one hand and waved her cane with the other. Her rolling throne had nudged its way in beside Mootzie, who was gazing at Irek, mesmerized.

"Hallelujah!" cried Dr. Digsby as pandemonium broke loose.

While the television reporter recapped the events for the live broadcast and the camera panned the crowd, zooming in on the Princess Royal, Lauren ventured a look at Ryan. He was staring at Irek. No. Just beyond Irek to Clive Holcombe, who was standing much too close to the portrait. Suddenly, Lauren wished she'd asked Halford Shead for more insurance.

With a smirk, Clive whispered something to Irek.

"I kill you if you ever say that again," Irek said in a loud voice as he swung both powerful fists at once. The first blow hit Clive in the ribs. The second landed squarely on his jaw, sending him reeling. He collapsed into Mootzie's arms, knocking her to the floor at Lady Fiona's feet.

The reporters went wild, flashes popping faster than machine gun fire. The television cameras focused on the unconscious Clive as Lady Fiona tried to revive him by pouring the remains of her Brie Cie on him.

"A media event. God loves it."

27

As soon as Clive hit the floor, David hustled Tabatha out of the gallery, confident no one would notice them leaving together. He was right. Except for Princess Anne's bodyguards, who hurried her away at the first swing of the Russian's fist, no one else left.

"The Savoy," David told the taxi driver as he climbed into the backseat of the salon-style cab beside Tabatha.

"I thought you were staying at Brown's," she said.

This was the first complete sentence Tabatha had uttered since David had broken her figurine. He'd taken a hard line and had explained to Tabatha that he wasn't giving her money unless he guided her career. That tack hadn't gotten him very far. She'd been sullen ever since.

"I like the Savoy better. You'll enjoy the gardens facing the Thames."

She sat silently staring ahead, her chest lifting ever so slightly with each breath.

"I want you to come to New York," he said, voicing the plan he'd been mulling over in his mind. "I'll set you up in a penthouse like Lauren's, only nicer. You'll have your own maid to wait on you."

She eyed him suspiciously. "Why?"

"Because I like you. I like being with you."

"Is that why all you ever show me is a bed?"

He put his arm across the back of the seat but didn't touch her. "When you're in New York, I'll take you wherever you like."

Her expression brightened.

"Let's start tonight. We're going to have dinner in Savoy's Grill Room."

She rewarded him with a suggestion of a smile. He let his fingers graze the top of her bare shoulders. "Best crème brûlée in London."

That earned him a full-fledged smile. It was worth the risk of being seen with her in public. Tonight she looked twenty-five—old enough to be with him.

"Did you mean what you said about bringing me to New York?"

He dropped his hand to her bare shoulder, caressing her silken skin with his fingertips. "Absolutely. You can go to art school there if you like."

"I forgot to tell you. Lauren finished the portrait of Ryan Westcott."

David smiled. Wait until Barzan got the word. "I'll buy you something special."

"Don't. Just don't make me dress like a little girl any more." She took his free hand and placed it on her breast. "I'm a woman."

Through the sheer fabric, he felt a hot spiraled nipple. "I know, angel. You're exactly the woman I want."

"Show me."

Her voice had that aggressive quality he loved. But tonight was going to be different. He needed to show her who was boss. Beneath his hand, her prominent nipple begged for attention, but he refused to caress it. Instead, he kissed her long and hard, driving his tongue deep into her mouth.

A startled gasp came from Tabatha as he kissed the sensitive spot just below her ear, then circled its coiled ridge with the tip of his tongue. Her breath came in short little pants as he kissed her neck. The throbbing heat of his arousal threatened to snap his composure, but he wouldn't give in. As much as he wanted to, he never touched her breasts.

Casually stroking her knee, his lips again found hers and

their tongues locked. Inching his hand upward, his fingers trailed across the smooth nylon until he reached a garter then bare skin. Hot, delicious bare skin, getting more moist as his hand traveled upward. No panties, of course. Feeling how much she wanted him fired his blood even more.

"Who's in charge?" he asked, easing his hand from between her thighs.

Flushed, with a few stray wisps of hair curled in damp ringlets around her face, Tabatha's eyes were heavy-lidded with passion. "You are."

He yanked the top of her sheath down, baring her breasts.

Ryan waited in the shadows of the outside stairwell for Lauren to come out of the gallery. The last few guests were drunkenly straggling out. He hated to see what the party at Basil Blackstoke's would be like. Ryan had never seen so many people in the bag. It had definitely been an exhibition no one would forget. Not only had Irek sold out and refused Nakamura's offer, but he'd knocked Clive out, then refused to say why. Great copy. Even better on television.

Finally, Lauren emerged and Ryan whistled. She turned, saw him motioning to her, and came down the stairs.

"How would you like to go away with me for a week or so?"

"I'd love to, but what about the gallery?"

"Leighton can handle it. You won't be running Irek's prints for another two weeks. What's there to do except ship off what sold tonight?"

"But my brother's here."

The distress in her voice didn't surprise him. Her brother would be the kicker. Ryan had known it all along. It was a crazy idea, anyway. He would never have thought of it except another week without seeing her depressed the hell out of him.

"Paul will understand," she said, startling him. "Where are we going? What shall I bring?"

He adjusted the high-ruff collar on the taffeta cape she wore and picked up a strand of blonde hair. "I can't tell you yet. But we have to leave within the hour. Just bring summer clothes in a single duffel. Skip all that junk you women usually haul everywhere. Wait for me in front of your building."

She nodded. Just what he liked: a woman who knew when not to ask questions.

"Lauren, two other things. Bring your passport. And don't tell anyone you're going with me."

Vora eased herself out of bed, trying not to awaken Irek. She slipped into the bathroom and closed the door before switching on the light. She examined her body in the mirror. Her waist was an endangered species; her nipples had a purplish hue. She wouldn't be able to hide her pregnancy much longer.

Vora didn't know what to do. She honestly didn't. If Lauren were around, she would help her. But she wasn't. She'd disappeared three days ago, leaving a terse note about being called away on business. Lauren had left a similar message for her brother and Vora had covered for her, telling him that she was in Paris on business. But she knew better. Lauren was with Ryan Westcott.

Vora had ruled out an abortion. She wanted this baby even if Irek no longer planned on marrying her. He hadn't mentioned it once since the exhibition. Now that he was the toast of the town, every woman wanted him.

"Vora?" Irek called.

She pressed the button that locked the door and hastily donned Irek's terry robe.

"*Otkroyte*—open up!" He pounded on the door.

Vora swung the door open and Irek charged in naked as she stood there, the oversized garment hanging on her like an enormous choir robe.

"What is wrong? You in here every night."

"It's the flu, I think. I—"

"When will you tell me about my baby?"

How did he know? she wondered, then decided it didn't matter. What was important was neither of them had been honest with each other. "When will you tell me what Clive said?"

Irek led her back into the dark bedroom and switched on the bedside lamp. He dropped to the bed and patted the seat beside him. Vora slowly lowered herself to the bed, frightened by the earnestness in his eyes.

"Liubov'," he said, shaking his head. "I did not know what it means until I met you. I want you to marry me. I want our baby."

"You do? Honestly?"

He leaned toward her, smoothing back the cluster of curls that grazed her cheek. "I love you, Vora."

She refused to let the past ruin her future. "What did Clive say?"

"Dushinka, you do not want to know."

"Yes, I do. Love has no secrets."

"He wanted to know if . . . you still insisted on being on top."

Vora closed her eyes and asked herself what in heaven's name had she ever seen in Clive Holcombe. Clive had never loved her. Unlike Irek, he'd gladly taken what she'd offered: clothes, a car, trips.

"I can't explain," she whispered. "I was a different person before you. I—"

"If you love me, no thing matter, *dushinka.* No thing. Say you will marry me."

"Yes, of course," she whispered, fighting back tears.

He eased off the robe and pulled her under the covers. He kissed her, a slow, loving kiss, and she decided she liked the red-on-red flat that was miles from Harrods. As long as she had Irek, she was happy.

His kisses trailed down her neck and across her breast, lingering on each nipple. He eased himself lower, planting moist kisses on her ribs, her tummy. The rasp of hair on his chest seared a sensuous path as he moved down her body.

"Irek, what are you doing?"

"Let baby sleep." He moved his head between her thighs.

Afterward, she lay against the solid wall of his chest as he fell asleep. The opalescent light of early dawn sent slanted beams of light through the plantation shutters. Vora couldn't sleep, so she rose and went into the kitchen to make some tea.

She told herself the halycon days she and Irek had enjoyed before the exhibition were gone forever. Not only was there the baby to consider, but she would need to help Irek or he would never paint again. Overnight he'd become a national hero. Jaguar had given him an XJS convertible. Carrs had named their new biscuits "Liubovs." Pomodoro was touting pepperoni pizza loaded with anchovies—The Makarova Special.

Wilber McCallister had sent a lifetime supply of cashmere socks as a reward for opening Mootzie's eyes before she married Clive. Irek had been invited to dine with everyone from Princess Diana, who was miffed at missing the bash, to the Cocteau Twins, who'd asked him to a vegetarian buffet in their Soho loft. Lady Fiona went on a prime-time chat show and told the world via satellite how to make Irek's favorite drink, the Brie Cie. The next day the Ritz, Connaught, and Claridge's began serving the concoction and many private clubs followed suit.

Naturally, Tanqueray was eternally grateful and had sent seventeen cases of Tanqueray Silver. They'd asked him to do a series of commercials. They were hounding him to prepare a book of his favorite vodka recipes.

Irek laughed most of this off with *deke zabeb,* but the media pressure was hard to ignore. *The Times* had printed a full-page editorial lauding Irek's principles and describing the unanticipated departure of their art critic, Finley Tibbetts, as "regrettable." *The Sun* and the *Daily Star,* which catered to those who preferred not to read, ran a series of photographs. Of course, the knockout punch was on page one. Both tabloids praised Irek's gallantry for decking Clive because he'd made an off-color remark about Princess Anne. Her popularity rating went up immediately, and Dr. Digsby charged her double.

The international furor hadn't been any less tumultuous. A man without a price. The world marveled. Irek insisted he had his price. If Nakamura had threatened to send him back to Russia or harm those he loved, he would have given him the painting. No one listened—except Vora. Dr. Digsby explained the media created their own message. Once a story was in print, God had spoken.

As Vora poured the tea, the luminous dial on the telephone-answering machine caught her eye. She punched the message button and expected to hear Lauren. Instead, Egon Laurent's voice asked her to call him immediately. She erased the message, thinking the print wholesaler based in Paris wanted to order prints of Irek's work. But why had he called here and not the gallery? She checked the clock, then dialed Paris.

"Egon?" she said when he answered. "Vora Leighton returning your call."

"Did you know someone is going around offering to discount Irek Makarova's prints?"

"Ravissant Publishing has exclusive rights. We haven't printed anything yet. No one can possibly know which ones we plan on running."

"Artists International is offering 'Velma Liubov,' 'Volga,' 'Nyet,' 'Zeki,' and 'Kiev,' " Egon said, his voice filled with concern. "They're available immediately."

Too shocked to respond, Vora couldn't imagine how anyone knew exactly which prints they would be running. Anyone could have guessed "Velma Liubov' " because of all the publicity. No one except Vora and Lauren knew which others would be printed, not even Ryan. Except for Irek, of course. Someone had leaked the information weeks ago in order for prints to be ready now just days after the showing.

"These are unauthorized prints," Vora said, her voice shaky. "Let me contact the—"

"I was positive that they were. As successful as Makarova's exhibition was, the prices wouldn't be discounted. You realize some wholesalers will take advantage of this opportunity—without asking questions."

"Yes," Vora agreed. Most galleries purchased their prints from wholesalers. Years ago, there were but a handful of wholesalers in each country and galleries like Ravissant representing a special artist knew them personally. But with the advances in printing techniques and the public's appetite for poster art, hundreds of wholesalers had appeared overnight. "Thanks for letting me know."

Vora hung up and stared into space, puzzled about who had told the counterfeiters. This could set Irek's career back. Any prints that circulated from a discounter would be low-quality reproductions fraudulently signed and numbered. But people would see them and judge the caliber of Irek's work accordingly.

As Vora considered the possible suspects, she kept coming back to Lauren. Who else could it be? Irek would have no reason to sabotage his own career. That left Lauren. But why had she done it after working tirelessly on the exhibition? When Finley's article came out, it had been Lauren who'd relentlessly pursued the members of the Groucho Club. And they had come through, purchasing the majority of Irek's works. It just didn't make sense that Lauren was behind this.

Vora pondered the situation and reviewed the various ways anyone else might have known which prints Irek had authorized. With a sinking heart, she picked up the telephone and dialed Interpol.

"See why they call it the Red City?" Ryan asked as the twin-engine plane swooped low over Marrakesh.

"Everything looks red—the plains, the miles of walls, the houses," she said mechanically. If she'd known Marrakesh was their destination, she never would have come. When she'd left with Paul, she'd vowed never to return.

Yet here she was—for the love of a man. She glanced at Ryan, wondering if she'd done the right thing. Was he involved in some illegal activity? Three days ago, they'd left London, hidden aboard a fishing trawler bound for Spain. They'd landed there in the middle of the night and made their way to Gibraltar. Circumventing passport checkpoints, they'd again left in the dead of the night aboard a garbage scow destined for Sebta.

Only when they'd boarded the private plane on the final leg of their journey did Ryan reveal he was taking her to Marrakesh. As the plane landed, Lauren closed her eyes. *Don't be silly,* she told herself as the plane skidded to a halt. *Rupert Armstrong can't hurt you now.*

The dry warm air greeted her as she stepped from the plane. The cloudless sky was sapphire blue, a perfect backdrop for the brush strokes of snow still left on the august peaks of the Atlas Mountains.

"I'd forgotten how beautiful it was." Lauren glanced around at the myriad date palms, their fronds whispering in the gentle breeze blowing down from the mountains.

Ryan guided her to a dilapidated Rover and tossed their two bags in the rear. He cleared the layer of red dust off the windshield with the wipers and they were off, riding the bumpy road into the city.

"Ochre," Lauren said as she looked out at the city. "That's the color of Marrakesh. Not red. Not pink. But ochre. I'll have to blend that color when I paint."

Ryan paused at the gate of a walled compound and tooted twice. Where the hell were the guards? Someone was supposed to be on duty around the clock. A sleepy-eyed guard stumbled out of the villa followed by the pack of Rhodesian ridgebacks. He smiled reassuringly at Lauren as the fortress-style gate swung open.

Poor kid. She'd been amazingly understanding. He knew she was worried about him. Probably thought he was a criminal.

"Will we be in Marrakesh long?"

Not long, he wanted to say, but didn't. He needed to know she trusted him. "We'll be here a while. Why?"

She didn't answer immediately. On the way in from the airport, she'd been quiet, preoccupied.

"I have to see my mother. But I don't want to go anywhere near Rupert Armstrong."

"Are you sure?" Ryan asked. He didn't want Lauren around that black widow.

"Yes." Lauren turned to him, her blue eyes fired by determination. "There's something I have to tell her."

What? Ryan wondered but he didn't press her. "You could meet her this afternoon at La Mamounia or a cafe or—"

"Somewhere private. Mother isn't herself when others are around. She's always on display."

"I've got it. In the *mellah*."

"The Jewish section of the *medina*? No. Mother would never go there."

"She would if she thought T.J. wanted to meet her. I know the old house where they used to go." Ryan brought the Rover to a halt in the garage at the rear of the compound. "I'll send one of the servants with a note that says *Amour ne se change*." "She'll come."

"You're sure? Maybe after all this time—"

"Caroline will come. She sent T.J. dozens of letters. He

returned them unopened." Ryan reached inside the backseat for their bags. "I can't go with you, but I'm sending Hassan."

"I don't want anyone with me. This is something I have to do myself."

"I understand, but I insist Hassan accompany you. The *medina* isn't a safe place for a woman alone."

28

The *medina* hadn't changed since the days Lauren and Paul wandered the maze of streets. But then, it had been the same for centuries. Woven reed mats were strung between buildings, providing shade for the narrow corridors that served as streets. In the corners men squatted, eastern style, and sat on the backs of their calves. The women scurried about, their eyes downcast, their faces hidden by veils.

At Ryan's insistence, Lauren wore a burnoose and a veil. Beneath the summer-weight cape, she was hot. And nervous. She forced herself to concentrate on the sights and sounds around her, not on the impending confrontation.

As they traversed Jemaa-el-Fna, Lauren looked for the Rijel Zuraq, the legendary "blue men" of the desert, hoping to spot the old woman who'd made her bracelet. She wasn't there, of course. They'd only seen her that one time. She'd been ancient then.

Even if the silversmith wasn't around, the usual dog and pony show was in full swing. It was still too early in the afternoon for the Guinean dancers, but the snake charmers were busy demonstrating their skills to clusters of tourists from polyester America. As usual, the camera-happy visitors were snapping shots of the snake charmer with a deadly looking snake hanging from his nose. He twirled in circles as the reptile's fangs clamped onto the tip of his nose. For his efforts, he earned a few coins.

Nearby, a water bearer posed beside a man with garlands of cameras while his wife took a picture. The scarlet costume of the water bearer featured a wide-brimmed hat with hundreds of tassels hanging from the rim. Across his chest were dozens of highly polished silver cups, and on his back was a leather jug of water. Supposedly, the water was "safe" for tourists. Lauren knew better. One sip of the water and "Allah's Revenge" was sure to follow.

Beyond the crowded square Hassan led her up narrower and narrower streets. This was the business section of the *medina*, where artisans, not con artists, toiled. She stopped outside one building, recognizing the weavers immediately. Berbers. While Arabs had an eastern heritage, Berbers were related to Europeans. They looked very much like the French. She admired the Berber culture because women were allowed to have a say in their own lives. Unlike Moslem women, they were even allowed to own land.

True artists, she thought, as she watched them handle the hand-dyed yarn spun from mountain goat fleece. Two weavers stood on each side of a gigantic loom while young girls, five or six years old, scuttled back and forth, tying off the knots. In another year or so, their fingers would be too large to assist the master weaver directing the operation, and they would be replaced by younger children. Moving with the grace of ballet dancers, the weavers worked the treadles, snapping the shuttle back and forth and banging the woof with a powerful stroke.

"We must go." Hassan tugged on her arm.

She followed him as she pondered the similarity between the weavings of American Indians and the Berber designs, which made similar use of chevrons and lozenges. In recent years the light tufting the Berbers favored had become fashionable. Westerners pressed the small Berber population for more and more rugs. Even Paul wanted one.

"Here." Hassan indicated a door at the end of a darkened corridor so narrow they couldn't walk side by side.

Lauren lifted the ancient lever and the blue door opened with a tortured creak. Inside a single oil lamp burned, barely illuminating the room. Unlike the rest of the *medina*, the *mellah* had never had electricity.

It was hot inside the room, and Lauren removed her burnoose and veil as she inspected the shadowy area. In a dark corner was a bed with a reed mattress. It was hard to imagine her mother making love to T.J. on it. But who knew? She'd never understood her mother.

The floor of the room was beaten earth and the walls were mud-brick. A photograph of a man on a camel circa 1880 had been nailed to the wall. Curious. Back then, Jews hadn't been allowed to own camels. Nor could they have horses or donkeys. Anywhere they'd gone, they'd had to go on their own two feet.

She wandered over to take a closer look at the camel. Like most this beast had a haughty air. Legend had it, only the camel knew every one of Allah's names.

As usual her mother was late. Caroline always made an entrance. Always. Lauren paced the small room until she finally heard the lever lift. She withdrew into the shadows beside the bed.

Her mother swept into the room, her eyes widening to combat the sudden darkness. Lauren saw herself in twenty years. Flawless skin almost unlined and stretched over high cheekbones. Hair that was now silver not blonde, yet becoming because it softened the faint lines around the eyes and mouth.

Her mother paused, dramatically undoing the burnoose she wore to reveal a stunning white dress that tastefully hugged her body, emphasizing her youthful figure. "T.J.?"

Lauren stepped forward. "No. He isn't coming."

Her mother gasped. "W-what are you doing here? Where is T.J.?"

For a speech rehearsed so many times, Lauren was dismayed when the words refused to come.

"I demand to know what's going on."

"Aren't you glad to see me . . . Mother?"

She nervously patted her perfect hair. "Well, I was expecting . . ."

"T.J. Griffith doesn't want to see you. I just used his message to get you here. I have something to tell you."

Caroline's expression hardened into a well-remembered display of irritation. "What?"

"Do you know the real reason I ran away?"

Her glacial-blue eyes swept around the room as if seeking an avenue of escape. "That was a long time ago. It doesn't matter."

"It does to me." Like Rupert's hand clamped around her neck, a suffocating sensation tightened Lauren's throat. "I ran away because Rupert kept forcing himself on me."

"I don't know what you're talking about. Without Rupert's money—"

"You know exactly what I mean. He forced me to have sex with him," she said, suppressed anger firing every word. "You knew all along what he was doing. But you didn't do anything to help me. Did you?"

As the flaming Moroccan sun set in the west, its rays becoming a soft coral, Ryan paced the veranda. The *muezzin* shrieked, his tremolo separating the faithful from the infidels with his call to evening prayers. Where the hell was Lauren?

In the garden below, the guards were reverently kneeling on their prayer rugs, their heads pressed to the ground facing Mecca. Hassan better not have left Lauren alone while he prayed in some damn mosque. Anything could happen in the *medina*.

He heard the telephone ringing and went to answer it, knowing that during prayers no one else would.

"Mese el khair."

"Ryan Westcott," Stirling said.

"Yes," Ryan said. He'd hoped this call would be from Lauren.

"He's coming to London. How soon can you get back?"

Barzan. Making his move at last. "At noon on Friday I'm leaving from Tindouf."

"No. Don't go over the border into Algeria. The Polisario has attacked several border installations. Use the airstrip at Zagora." Stirling rang off without another word.

An overwhelming sense of anticipation filled Ryan. The waiting was over. With luck, by this time next week, he would be a free man. And Carlos Barzan would be where he belonged—behind bars.

Ryan walked across the tile floor as he reminded himself that he would have to be at his best if he was going to trap Barzan. It was difficult to fight an enemy when you had no idea of where or how he would strike. Perhaps Stirling knew more than he was saying. A cautious man, he rarely said much on the telephone.

Of course, this meant Ryan couldn't see Lauren again once they reached London. Where was she? Just then he heard a car pull into the drive. He ran to the door and expelled a relieved sigh when he saw Lauren's blonde head.

"Sorry we're late. After I talked to Mother, I had Hassan take me to see some Berber rugs. Paul—"

"Shopping? You went shopping?" He'd been worried pissless and she'd gone shopping.

Lauren wound her arm through his and kissed him on the cheek. "Uh-huh. But I didn't find what I wanted."

"Jesus! Can't take a woman anywhere but she shops."

Lauren snuggled against him. "Typical female trait. You'd better get used to it. If I can stand your swearing, you can put up with an occasional shopping spree."

It was hard to be angry with her when she looked at him with those blue eyes. He guided her into the study and poured himself a gin and a Moroccan-grown *boulaouane* for her. She accepted the glass of white wine and sat on the ottoman-style sofa. He wanted to know how it had gone with her mother, but he refused to ask. She respected his privacy; he had to respect hers.

"I'm sorry you were worried," she said as he sat beside her. "Paul wants a Berber rug for his entry hall." She put her glass on the leather drum table. "He was on my mind the entire time I spoke with my mother, so afterward I went to find him a rug."

"How was your mother?"

Lauren didn't know how to express the intense sense of relief she felt at confronting her mother after all these years. "Mother denied everything, but I pressed her until she finally confessed she'd known all along Rupert was molesting me."

Her words froze in his brain. And an image of his own

mother surfaced, her loving smile vividly clear. Across his childhood memories—some pleasant, others not—he felt the power of her love.

"Thank God you had your brother."

She didn't respond. Instead, Lauren looked across the room at the woven tapestry on the wall. "At first, I was upset you'd brought me here. Now I'm grateful. I feel so much better now that I've talked to her."

"Why didn't you tell me the truth?"

"For years, I've kept the door shut on those horrid memories. You forced me to reevaluate myself and the past. Recently, I decided the therapist who counseled me in Paris was right. He claimed the ultimate betrayal comes from the parent who allows the situation to continue. He said in many cases the mother either consciously or subconsciously knows."

Again, Ryan thought of his mother. She'd allowed Buck to beat him—until Ryan could protect himself. Why hadn't she gotten out? "Sometimes women are afraid to be on their own and stay with men they should leave. My mother did."

Lauren couldn't imagine a father who wouldn't be proud of Ryan. He'd told her about his youth and all his athletic and academic awards. Why hadn't his father loved him?

"Mother wasn't afraid. She was selfish and greedy. She confessed she never loved my father or Rupert. She married for money and position. Sacrificing me never bothered her. Even now, realizing I know doesn't upset her. She was more concerned T.J. hadn't met her."

"I hope you told the bitch to rot in hell."

"No. As I walked out the door, I told her I forgave her."

"You're kidding," he said even though the sincere expression on her face indicated she meant every word.

"Something Irek said put it all into focus for me. He forgave Russia instead of dwelling on what he can't change. I'm not hating my mother and letting it eat away at me. I've closed the door on the past."

"Does this mean you forgive Rupert?"

"I feel sorry for him. He's a sick man."

"He's sick, all right." Ryan's voice teetered between anger and disbelief. Proved what he always thought—women were too damn soft. "Armstrong's in bed suffering from vigilante

justice. Moslems make the punishment fit the crime. Cut off a
hand for stealing or an ear for eavesdropping. That sort of
thing. They have an interesting garrote they use on the family
jewels."

"You're joking." It sounded so barbaric, Lauren could
hardly comprehend what Ryan had said.

"You didn't think I'd let that bastard get away with it, did
you? I told Hassan to look into it. I'd rather have taken care of
Rupert myself, but the local boys got to him first." Ryan noted
the shocked expression on her face. She was courageous when
she had to be. Still, she was a soft touch. "While you were with
your mother, I stopped by to see Rupert. I wanted to make
certain he knew who was behind it. I told him you sent him
your love."

Hundreds of horseback riders in flowing white robes
charged at them, their Arabians galloping full speed. Her
heart in her throat, Lauren sat on the ground beside Ryan as
the Berbers thundered toward them, waving rifles. Suddenly,
the riders stopped dead in their tracks. They pointed their
rifles at them and fired. The shots pierced the air of the high
Atlas Mountains and echoed up and down the steep gorges to
the nearby summit, Tizi N' Tichka. The Arabians pivoted,
their riders shouting war whoops, and retreated.

"Scared?" Ryan asked.

"A little," Lauren admitted. "I knew it was a *fantasia*, but
when they came so close to us, I was worried."

"They've trained since childhood to ride with that preci-
sion. The plains have always belonged to the Arabs, the mountains to the Berbers. They're prepared to defend them. This
show demonstrates their skill, their readiness to go to battle to
defend their land."

"But Ryan," Lauren said as she looked around at the gathering of Berbers at the festival, "what could they defend with
those rifles?"

Ryan rose and helped Lauren to her feet. "Remember Af-
ghanistan. The Berbers are cast in the same mold—independent mountain men. They've lived the same way for centuries. They'll defend their land if they have to, but I doubt they

have anything to worry about. King Hassan leaves them alone."

"You'd think he would explore the Atlas for minerals or something rather than battle the Polisario for the Sahara."

"Maybe he will one day. Who knows?" He smiled at her. "Do you want to stay and watch the *guedra* or would you rather look for a rug? We can't do both. I have to be in Ouarzazate by dark."

"Let's find Paul a rug. I've seen the *guedra* before," she said, recalling the Berber girls doing a dance of the seven veils while seated. It was quite a show, but she wanted to surprise Paul with a Berber rug.

They wandered around the remote village and inspected the rugs hung on looms built from the poles supporting the huts. The weavers had abandoned their stations to attend the festival, leaving half-finished rugs. Beside each loom was a stack of completed rugs to be sold to wholesalers and sent to Europe or America.

Lauren selected a rug for Paul, and they went to find the weaver. The man was supervising the *mechoui*. A sheep's carcass was roasting on a hand-cranked spit over a bed of charcoal. When Ryan explained what they wanted, the man smiled and nodded to his wife, indicating she should handle the negotiations. Like most Berber women, she sought good fortune by wearing heavy silver jewelry studded with odd-shaped stones.

"For you?" the woman asked in Arabic as they walked to her hut.

"For my brother," Lauren explained.

The woman smiled, creasing the tattoo on her cheek that identified her tribe. They haggled for ten minutes and finally settled on a price.

"Hey, just what every woman loves," Ryan teased as he tossed the rug in the back of the Rover. "A deal. Factory direct and below wholesale."

"It's my Christmas present for Paul." Lauren climbed into the Rover.

"Should I be jealous?" Ryan asked as he fired the engine. "You love him very much, don't you? He was there when you needed him."

"I love you both—in different ways."

He drove away from Telouet, heading toward Ouarzazate. He kept his eyes on the treacherous road, but his thoughts were on Lauren. She was a woman of strength and purpose. Through sheer determination, she'd saved Irek's exhibition by mustering the members of the Groucho Club. Calling on a bunch of intellectuals had been a stroke of genius. They'd led the way, buying Irek's work without caring what the critics thought.

Ryan supposed he was glad she didn't hate her mother or that piss-poor excuse for a man, Rupert. Bitterness would change her. He loved her just the way she was. Forged from a hellish past, she'd become a strong woman.

As they rode down the mountain, Lauren gazed out the window. She'd never been on this side of the Atlas Mountains. Unlike its verdant west face, the African sun had blistered the east side, leaving a barren terrain. But when they reached the Draa Valley, small villages were strung along terraced fields of maize and barley.

Finally, she saw Ouarzazate on the horizon. Concrete bunkers instead of Arabic buildings. Undoubtedly, the same architect responsible for the American Embassy in London had designed this outpost on the threshold of the desert. She was relieved when they drove past the eyesore to a *Kasbah*.

They stopped at a mud-brick building with a weed-filled flower bed staked out by rows of broken beer bottles turned upside down. After Ryan left her inside the hut and went off to do some business, Lauren lit an oil lamp as the *muezzin* wailed, calling the faithful to evening prayers. She wandered into an adjacent room and found a single bed with a reed mattress like the one she'd seen in the *mellah*.

It still surprised her that her mother had met T.J. there. She must have loved him. But not enough to help him when he needed it. Would her mother have come all this way not knowing what was going on? On faith. For love. Of course not. She was a shallow woman. Perfect for Rupert.

But what about T.J. Griffith? Every time Ryan spoke of him, she heard the reverence in his voice. He must be a wonderful man. Ryan didn't respect many people. But why hadn't T.J. seen through her mother? Don't condemn him. She reminded herself of her own father. Now that she was older, she recalled many of his comments. He'd found out about her mother when it was too late. He might well have left her had it not been for Paul and Lauren.

Griffith had been wrong about her mother. Lauren hoped he wasn't wrong about "Midnight in Marrakesh." When she returned to London, she intended to devote more time to painting. Now she was older, stronger. She wouldn't let the critics discourage her.

She lay down on the reed mattress, planning how to rid herself and Paul of Barzan and trying not to wonder about Ryan. Things would work out was her last thought as she fell asleep. Haunted by the past, uncertain about the future, her dreams quickly became tortured nightmares. Disembodied hands relentlessly pursued her, roving over her body.

With a start, she awoke in total darkness. A hand clamped over her mouth; another was in her hair. Rupert. Terror surged through her. After what they'd done to him, he would kill her. She clawed at him as she kicked and bit his hand.

"Lauren, stop it." Ryan pinned her with his large body.

"Ryan?"

"Do you know anyone else in Ouarzazate?"

"I was having a bad dream. I didn't hear you come in."

"I was trying to be romantic."

"You know I have this thing about hands in my hair."

"I was just smoothing it out of your face." He rolled off her. "You screamed and I put my hand over your mouth before you roused the entire *Kasbah*."

"Did you finish your business?" she asked as she touched his bare chest, caressing the warm skin.

"Uh-huh." He kissed her slowly, then rolled onto his back. "C'mere."

She jumped to her feet and hastily shed her clothes before she moved on top of him, noticing the healthy hard-on beneath her thighs. Churning her hips, she nestled against it. His hands grasped her buttocks and squeezed. As they kissed, their tongues mimicked the movement of their hips, and she clutched at his shoulders, leaving half-moon prints on his skin.

"Once I thought making love to you would get you out of my system, but I was wrong."

He took one nipple between his lips and sculpted it with his tongue until it was erect. Moist heat fired her body as she guided him into place. They gasped at the same time.

Ryan held her hips still. "Do you have any idea how much I love you?"

29

Even though it was June a wintry fog obscured the English countryside as their plane descended at a remote airstrip. It glided down, then bumped along the rough tarmac as the Israeli they'd picked up in Ouarzazate muttered something in Hebrew. An ache of regret replaced Lauren's happiness. When would she see Ryan again? Suddenly, she wanted to return to the dusty route of ancient caravans, the road from Ouarzazate to Zagora. Sharing the old desert lifeline between oases with caparisoned camels and donkeys, Lauren had been content just to be with Ryan. She no longer worried about his mysterious activities. She trusted him.

"I'll have Adi bring Paul's rug over to your place," Ryan said as the plane taxied up to a hangar. "Someone is waiting for me. This will have to be good-bye."

Gathering her into his arms, he pressed his open lips to hers. She clutched him, quivering at the sweet tenderness of his kiss. Too soon, he broke away and rose. Ryan guided her down the metal stairs to where an old man smoking a pipe waited. He scowled at Lauren.

"What the fuck do you think you're doing with her?" Peter shouted when they were alone.

"You said she wasn't a suspect," Westcott answered with his usual insolent tone.

"That was last week. I had no idea she was with you." Peter silently cursed his men for losing Westcott on the night of the opening. Too many cars, too many drunk people, too many excuses. Too late now. He lit his pipe and took a long draw, marshalling his thoughts. "She's the one."

"What do you mean?" Ryan's brows met in a tight frown.

"She's Carlos Barzan's operative. She'll try to make the hit soon."

"Unfuckingbelievable! Lauren couldn't possibly—"

"What kind of proof would you like to see?" Peter was amazed that a tough nut like Westcott had been hoodwinked by Lauren Winthrop. Working with amateurs was torture. Time to retire. "Our mole untangled Barzan's computer records. Lauren Winthrop purchased Ravissant with funds from Carlos Barzan. He's currently financing her brother as well."

"He's tricked her. She can't possibly—"

"I'm afraid not. Lauren's been inordinately clever. She's had Tabatha Foley relaying messages to Barzan via Marcus."

Ryan turned away from Stirling's accusing gaze. Lauren couldn't possibly be involved in this. But Peter Stirling was a careful, methodical man who wouldn't make accusations he couldn't prove. A flash of pain more intense than anything Ryan had ever experienced shot through him. Had he been conned by Caroline Armstrong's daughter? "What about the bugs in her apartment?"

"They wanted the telephone number at Greyburne Manor. Apparently, Barzan intends to call T.J."

Peter let Ryan absorb that while he thought of just how big a coup this was. Thanks to Julia Hartley, the Americans had Carlos Barzan thirteen ways to hell on tax evasion and fraud. Since Vora Leighton had foiled Barzan's efforts to flood the market with bogus prints to cover his illicit drug profits, the Brits had him nailed on the print fraud scheme. Peter had persuaded the Americans to hold off on arresting Carlos Barzan, believing the MI-5 could get him on attempted murder and stick him with a much longer prison term. But now Winthrop might put an end to the MI-5's plan.

"What did you tell her?" Peter asked.

"Nothing." She didn't suspect the truth, did she?

Peter resisted the urge to chastise Ryan any further. The anguish in his voice painted a vivid picture. Ryan had fallen in love with a beautiful woman. It wasn't the first time. After all, once Peter had been head over heels in love with Amy Thorpe.

"You know, women are a great deal more skilled at deception than men. In my experience female amateurs have always made the best spies. Now take Amy Thorpe," Peter said, trying to ease Westcott's guilt. "She gave us the plans for the German's super-secret coding machine. They never knew it but we had access to all the Nazi's intelligence communiques. Then we arranged for Amy to return to Washington. There, she finagled the Italian navy's code books from their former head of intelligence. She even managed to get the Vichy French navy's code books from them as well."

Ryan tuned out Stirling's comparison of Lauren to Mata Hari and Aline, Countess of Romanones, who'd spied for the OSS during the Second World War. At last, Ryan understood his father's fatal attraction to Caroline Armstrong. Bewitching bitches. Like T.J., he should have known better.

Why was it he learned his lessons too late? After 'Nam, Ryan had told himself he'd seen his last killing. The experience in Zaire had etched the consequences of unnecessary death in his mind. But nothing topped his experience with Robert Barzan. Nothing.

The crazy kid had gotten wind of the diamond experiments they were conducting. Robert had insisted T.J. and Ryan discuss the financing with his father, Carlos Barzan. Thinking Barzan might provide capital to help finance the expensive experiments which could take years, Ryan and T.J. had met with Carlos several times. They'd decided to risk their own money and not take in a partner, gambling they could develop the process before they ran out of funds—or before someone else filed a patent.

They never imagined that Robert Barzan would pull an idiot stunt like appearing at the lab intent on stealing their test results and prototype machine. When he'd drawn the gun, Ryan and T.J. had assumed Robert was bluffing. He wasn't. As T.J. struggled with him, the gun went off, mortally wounding Robert. While they were futilely attempting to revive him, the MI-5 arrived. They'd been tailing Robert as part of an ongoing drug investigation. The MI-5 convinced T.J. and Ryan to cooperate with them in their efforts to trap Carlos Barzan and shut down his drug operation. According to the MI-5, Barzan's one weakness was his son.

To satisfy the press, British intelligence concocted a story about an underworld figure killing Robert in a diamond scam, but they made certain Barzan found out the truth. Then they waited for Carlos Barzan to make his move. Barzan had built his empire on his own and had a reputation for always taking care of troublesome people himself. He would come after T.J. personally. Then they could nail Barzan with an attempted murder charge.

Ryan had tried to get T.J. not to become involved, but T.J. wouldn't listen. His country needed him; he wanted to help. Ryan suspected he relished the challenge. When months passed and Barzan didn't react, Ryan and T.J. had become careless and overlooked a car bomb. A horrible mistake. Another lesson learned too late.

"How will Lauren try to do it?" Ryan asked.

"We don't know," Stirling ruefully admitted. "As I told you before, our information is that Barzan wants to be personally involved. If not, I would close this case now and let the Americans handle it. But Carlos Barzan is scheduled to fly in this evening. It appears he'll strike—using Lauren as a decoy—within the next three days. On Saturday, he's set to appear as the honoree at a charity function at the Kennedy Center. He won't miss that." Stirling sympathized with Ryan. How much could one man take? "Don't worry, we're onto Winthrop now. Her hall porter, Jeeves, is one of our men. He has a contingent of extra agents to help him. We're monitoring our own bugs in her apartment. We'll know exactly how she plans to do it—in advance."

It was afternoon when Lauren arrived at Paddington Station. During her long wait for the train and the ride into London, she'd worried about Ryan. Was he in trouble? Should she telephone the police? No. He was expecting that old man who'd met him at the plane. Ryan could handle his problems.

Lauren took a taxi to her penthouse and rushed upstairs. She greeted the hall porter, then asked, "Is Tabatha in?"

"Miss Foley didn't return last night," Jeeves said.

Lauren wasn't surprised. Whenever Tabatha's boyfriend was in town, she spent the night with him. Lauren didn't approve, but she didn't have the right to reprimand the girl.

Once inside, she tried Paul's number in Santa Fe. She owed him an explanation for her sudden disappearance. He didn't answer. She dialed Geeta's number but no one was home.

Lauren quickly showered and changed clothes. If she hurried, she could get to the gallery and spend several hours working before time to close. As she left the flat, she paused in the kitchen and wrote Tabatha a note, thinking she would return sometime this afternoon and could run an errand. Lauren put money on the counter so Tabatha could buy a bottle of Bluebells at Penhaligon's. When Adi delivered the Berber rug that Lauren had bought for Paul, she would send the cologne to Iggy. She wanted to wait and deliver Ryan's portrait personally.

As Lauren walked into Ravissant, she met Vora. "Sorry I ducked out on you. I—"

"You'll never believe what happened." Vora motioned for Lauren to come into her office. "Phony prints of Irek's work turned up everywhere last week. Luckily, a wholesaler in Paris alerted me before too many hit the market."

"How?" Lauren asked, taken off-guard.

"Awfully sorry, it was my fault. I opened my big mouth and the criminals knew exactly which prints we intended to run." Vora's sherry-brown eyes clouded with regret. "I handled it, though. I called Interpol, and they intercepted most of the prints."

"Why would you say anything to anyone? We agreed—"

"Don't make me feel any worse." Vora sank into her chair. "How do you think I've felt having to face Irek?"

Lauren sat on the edge of Vora's desk. "What happened?"

"You know how close Basil and I are—were. When he styled my hair, he asked me which prints I liked best. I told him and he decided those would be the ones we would print. He repro-

duced them from the shots in the catalogue. You can imagine
how cheap and shoddy they were."

"Why would Basil do such a thing?"

"Money. He's been living beyond his means for some time.
His hair products aren't selling as well as he led people to
believe." Vora's voice became unsteady. "I told the authorities I suspect he was involved in Archer's death."

"No!"

"I believe Archer called Miracles on the afternoon he died.
Basil must have taken the call in his private office. He never
gave me the message."

"Fraud is one thing, but murder?"

"The day Archer was killed"—Vora's voice rose another
octave—"I came into Miracles and confided in Basil that
Archer was worried and considering going to the police for
protection. At the time, I never dreamed Basil was involved,
so I didn't tell the authorities he knew any of my business."

"What made you suspicious of Basil? You two have been
close, and he insisted on throwing the reception for Irek."

"When I received the call from the wholesaler, I racked my
brains wondering who did it. At first, I thought you were
involved."

"Me? I would never—"

"I know, but you'd disappeared. I didn't know what to
think. You were with Ryan, weren't you?"

Vora didn't notice Lauren hadn't answered as she rushed
on with the story. "When Basil was cutting your hair, I used
the telephone in his private office. I saw my picture on the
wall and realized how long we'd known each other and how
much of my business I'd confided in Basil. Like many lonely
women, I told my hairdresser too much. He could easily have
guessed which prints we would run."

"What did Irek say about all this?"

"He understood. You know Irek, he doesn't let much upset
him." Vora blushed, deepening the color of the freckles she
no longer bothered to hide. "There was so much bad news I
forgot to tell you the best news ever. I'm going to have Irek's
baby." Vora beamed. "You know, this print crisis brought us
closer together. I'm secure now. I know he truly loves me. At
last, I've managed to banish Archer's ghost. He overwhelmed

me. I'm not making that mistake with Irek. We had a long discussion and I told him how much I hate living on the Thames. We've compromised. Since we both like the country, we're moving to Pildowne Crossing."

"Baby?" Lauren muttered, disbelieving. "You're getting married?" So much had happened in the short time she'd been away.

"I'm due in early December, but we'll be married and settled in our country home long before then. There's a stable we'll convert into a studio. Irek can work in peace. Believe me, we've had nothing but a barrage of reporters and other people since the exhibition. This move will make us both happy."

"Sounds great. I can imagine the pressure you've endured. Every paper I read carried the story. I would say Ravissant is the best-known gallery in the world right now. And we did it. Two women."

"I want to thank you, Lauren. You gave me the courage—"

"We did it together." Lauren wanted to ask what Clive had whispered to Irek, but didn't. Vora would tell her if she wanted her to know. "What needs to be done here?"

"Nothing. Irek reached a decision about his work." Vora's tone was hesitant. "He refuses to allow us to produce any of his prints, now or in the future."

"But that's cutting off a very lucrative market. I'm certain he'll change his mind as soon as this fraud ring is arrested."

"He won't, and I agree with him. Two days ago I sent out notices to all the wholesalers and the major dealers, saying Irek Makarova's works wouldn't be available as prints. Any prints that do surface are counterfeit."

"That's a pretty drastic reaction," Lauren said, torn between secretly applauding Irek's stance and her own desire to profit from the prints. She'd already met the terms of her deal with Barzan when the exhibition had been a success. Anything she earned from now on would be her profit, not his.

"He has an even more revolutionary idea. For every painting he sells, Irek plans to give another to a museum with the condition it not be resold. Irek thinks the escalating price of art hurts museums. They don't have the funds to compete with the private investor. Since Irek's prints won't be available for the public to see, he intends to make sure major museums have an original."

Lauren nodded. Irek's altruistic actions made her ashamed of her greediness. "I see his point. Except for the Getty, few museums in the United States can compete because of the skyrocketing prices of art. And the changes in the tax laws have made it financially unattractive for individuals to donate their collections to museums."

"The common man will never see great art if it's all in private collectors' hands. Irek doesn't want that. At heart, he identifies with the average man." Vora smiled sheepishly. "I guess I'm a commoner, too. I don't have much money left. When the bogus prints flooded the market, I sold everything to buy back those prints that had gone out before Interpol stopped the distribution. I could have just issued a statement repudiating the prints' authenticity, but I didn't want anyone to see any of those shoddy prints."

"Irek let you?"

"I didn't tell him. When he found out, we reassessed our priorities. That's when we decided to buy a country home together with the funds from the sale of my uncle's estate and use Irek's money for the improvements and redecorating. Now we're really partners, but we don't have much cash."

"What did you two buy at Pildowne Crossing, a country home or the entire town? What about the money from Belgrave Square and all the Impressionist paintings Archer left you? What about the proceeds from Irek's exhibition?"

"Archer didn't leave his art collection to me. I have the use of it, but it's part of one of those perpetual trusts intended to sustain the Leighton dynasty into the next century. After Irek bought a Porsche 959, he gave the remainder of his money to a group that helps Soviet artists resettle in the West." Vora checked the simple tank watch she'd bought when she'd sold her Piaget. "I have to leave straightaway. Irek makes me tea every day—decaffinated, of course. Irek worries constantly about the baby . . . about me."

Lauren kissed Vora's cheek. "Tell him I said thanks for making you so happy."

Vora left and Lauren went into her own office. She called Paul again. Neither number answered. As she hung up the receiver, her hand still on it, the telephone jingled twice. "Hello?"

"Lauren Winthrop? This is Carlos Barzan."

"Yes?" Lauren expected him to congratulate her for Irek's successful opening.

"It's urgent that I talk to you. I'm arriving this evening. Can you meet me at Harry's Bar tonight at ten?"

As the mantel clock struck eight P.M., David Marcus paced the luxurious hotel suite. Where did Tabatha come up with Eleven Cadogan Gardens? One of those little, exclusive in spots off Sloane Square, it had no hotel sign, yet it prided itself on superb service. David had to admit he'd never been in a hotel more keenly attuned to its guests. Tabatha knew what he liked. And how to please him.

It wouldn't be long now before he could move her to New York. When Lauren had disappeared, she'd given them a start and they thought it might be necessary to find another way of delivering the painting. But Lauren had arrived home this morning. Barzan had landed two hours ago. With luck, David would replace Barzan in a day or two. As soon as T.J. Griffith was dead.

A twinge of guilt crept into the remotest corner of David's brain, but he suppressed it. Nice guys didn't make it to the top. He'd worked too long and too hard to turn back now.

A knock on the door announced Tabatha Foley. He hadn't even suspected how much he wanted her until the night of the exhibition when he thought he might lose her, but he'd turned the tables and had her eating out of his hand again. Dinner at the Savoy with their legions of minions parted Tabatha's thighs quicker than money. She craved luxury. He would give her whatever she wanted. As long as she gave him what he needed.

"Come in, angel," he said as he opened the door.

Tabatha wore a black wig and enormous sunglasses despite the late hour. He liked the way she followed his directions. Now that the end was in sight, he didn't want a single slipup.

"Better hurry," he said. "I made dinner reservations at nine at Overtons."

Tabatha sidled up to David, a mischievous look in her eye.

His prick froze as she unbuttoned the row of buttons below his tie and traced her long fingernails through the gray hair on his chest. She pulled up her lightweight cotton sweater, then took his hands and centered his palms on her bare nipples. They instantly jumped up to greet him. His heart stopped. What would she do next? He never knew.

The knock on his door surprised him. The maid had already turned down the bed. Puzzled, David looked at Tabatha. He went to the door and put his eye to the peephole. Jesus H. Christ. Carlos Barzan. How did he get the room number from a hotel whose hallmark was discretion and whose clientele entered manor houses and castles in the visitors' book rather than mere street addresses? Why hadn't Barzan used the house telephone as he normally did?

"Tabatha, wait in the bathroom until I call for you," David whispered as he buttoned up his shirt. He blessed her for unquestioningly obeying him.

"Carlos," David said as he swung the door wide. "I thought you were staying at the Ritz." A creature of habit, Carlos Barzan always took the same room at the Ritz overlooking Queen's Walk in Green Park.

"I am," Barzan said as he entered the suite.

David nervously glanced around. Nothing of Tabatha's was anywhere in sight. Despite his drug dealing, Carlos Barzan was a straitlaced man. He would never approve of David dating a girl young enough to be his daughter. It would ruin the respectable image Barzan so carefully cultivated.

"Is everything set?" Barzan asked.

"The painting's ready. You have Griffith's telephone number. The bugs in Winthrop's flat confirm she returned today."

"Where has she been?"

"Who knows? Does it matter? She can't possibly suspect anything." David couldn't forestall a smug smile. "It's up to you now to get Lauren Winthrop into Greyburne Manor. Unless you want me to do it."

"No. I want revenge. I've never let anyone do my dirty work. That's how I've stayed on top. Show your enemies no mercy."

Barzan walked across the suite to the windows which overlooked the garden. David followed, still puzzled about why Barzan had come.

Barzan leveled his black eyes on David. Instinctively, David stepped back. "When T.J. Griffith dies, I want him to know I killed him. I planted the car bomb, you know. I'm glad it didn't kill Griffith. He's had three years to live looking over his shoulder, wondering when I'd strike again. This time I'm going to tell him just before I kill him."

"Why didn't you tell me the truth?" David wondered out loud. Barzan had never admitted he'd personally planted the car bomb that had all but killed Griffith. What else didn't David know?

"Why haven't you told me how much money you've stolen from me over the years?"

"Well—I-I," David sputtered as Barzan turned his back on him. Jesus H. Christ. How had he found out?

"You didn't think I would let you get away with it, did you?"

"Look, I can explain—"

Barzan whirled, aiming a thirty-eight with a shiny chrome silencer at him.

Lauren checked her watch—ten twenty. Carlos Barzan must have been delayed. She was debating whether to order another Malvern Water with a double twist of lime or not, when he walked into Harry's Bar. Barzan saw her, came over, and sat beside her.

"I've come about your brother," he said, his black eyes studying her intently. "He must have told you that he asked me to finance a gallery he was putting together. I did it to accommodate you. Your initiative with the Cassatt prints, and now your success with this Russian, tells me I've found the best adviser available. That's why I've come to you rather than·going to the authorities."

"What are you talking about?" she asked, a pulsing knot forming in the pit of her stomach.

"He's part of a print fraud ring operating worldwide."

"Impossible. Paul would never do anything like that." There were few things she would stake her life on. Paul's honesty was one of them.

"I have proof."

Barzan reached into his inside breast pocket and withdrew an envelope. As he handed it to her, Lauren noticed the speck of blood on his collar where he must have cut himself shaving. She read the document, a cold metallic finger of panic tracing its way across the back of her neck. It was Paul's signature—unquestionably—accepting payment for prints by Irek Makarova.

"There's some mistake. Let me talk to Paul. I've been trying to reach him all day, but he's been out."

Her brain struggled to make sense of this. The magnitude of the problem boggled her mind as she remembered what Vora had told her. There was an ongoing international investigation. If Paul were involved—by some mistake—he might be arrested. Jailed. In a psychological twilight zone again.

"I can't have my name ruined. I'm being honored Friday night at the Kennedy Center, you know, by the Society of Distinguished Americans."

She managed half a smile, her anxious thoughts on Paul.

"I'm calling off our deal," Barzan said, his voice taking on an ominous note. "As far as money is concerned, I have a check right here for the half million I owe you. We're even; you've earned it. Ravissant has become the world's premier gallery. I won't have your brother's criminal activities ruining what I've strived so hard to build."

"You?" Lauren was tempted to throw her Malvern Water in his tanned face and tell him to go to hell. But a quick tally through her mind's archives reminded her of all Paul had done for her. She had to help him.

"I'm giving you a chance to leave gracefully. I'll have this little matter taken care of"—he waved the document she'd read—"if you fly home with me tomorrow at noon. I can make certain Paul's name never is implicated in the scandal, and you will still have a pristine reputation as an adviser."

"Tomorrow?" she asked, deciding to stall for time. She was positive Paul hadn't done anything illegal. If she had enough time, she could prove to Barzan this was a mistake. "I can't leave so soon. I have to—"

"Tomorrow," he interrupted, an unmistakable note of menace in his voice. "Or I go to the authorities."

Grim reality gnawed at her. If she didn't do as he said, Paul would be arrested. How had he gotten himself into such a mess? She supposed she should be grateful to Carlos Barzan for giving her the opportunity to protect Paul—and her own reputation.

"Pack only what you need and have your maid send the rest. My solicitor's office can handle the details on your penthouse and the gallery."

She nodded, her thoughts on her friends. On Ryan. How could she explain her sudden departure? She guessed she could straighten things out in America and then return to explain.

"Is there anything you have to do for Ravissant before you leave?" Barzan inquired, his tone now cordial.

"No. Vora Leighton is perfectly capable—"

"What about Finley Tibbetts?"

"What about him? He lost his job at *The Times*."

Barzan smiled knowingly. "I understand he'll be joining the *Apollo* staff. Shouldn't you send him a little gift and a note of apology?"

"How did you know we had words?"

"It was in Ross Benson's column. Personally, I commend you for not allowing Tibbetts to set foot in the gallery. But I have the long-term interests of Ravissant to consider. Apologize to him."

She nodded because she had no choice, but she resented his dictatorial attitude. Once she had this straightened out, she would avoid Carlos Barzan. "I'll have Smythson send him a leather address book with a note from me enclosed."

"Great. That should do it." He signaled for the waiter. "Now, what about Ryan Westcott?"

Disconcerted, she looked away. How could Carlos Barzan know about Ryan?

"Remember, his boss, T.J. Griffith, is one of the major forces in the art world. We wouldn't want to rile him, would we?" He smiled at her as the waiter arrived. After ordering a cognac, Barzan continued. "Haven't you done a portrait of Westcott? Shouldn't you give it to him before you leave?"

"How did you know about the portrait?" Her sense of anxiety heightened. Something wasn't right here.

"Tabatha Foley told my assistant, David Marcus. She

bragged how talented you were. Perhaps, one day I can arrange for you to exhibit your work at Ravissant."

Lauren ignored the exhibition carrot he dangled under her nose, remembering Tabatha speaking with David Marcus at Irek's opening. Strange, how small things could come back to haunt you. Lauren wanted to wait to give Ryan the painting. Right now, he had business to attend to. He'd made it clear he didn't want her around. "The painting isn't quite ready yet."

"Finish it tonight." Barzan's tone verged on anger. "I want Griffith to patronize Ravissant. Leave London with everyone singing your praises. That way your career won't suffer . . . or your brother. Deliver that portrait."

"All right," she reluctantly agreed.

"I'll send a car for you tomorrow. He'll take you by Smythsons for Finley's gift, then on to Griffith's. I'll meet you at the airport."

Vora snuggled against Irek's burly chest and munched on a Walkers petticoat tail topped with lemon curd.

"Shortbread with lemon curd." Irek shook his head in mock disgust.

"Pregnant women have strange cravings." She licked the lemon curd off one unmanicured finger. "Do you know where I would like to spread a little lemon curd and lick it off?"

"*Deke zabeb.* Keep the lemon curd away from me."

"It's all right to make love," Vora assured him. "I crave it as much as petticoat tails with lemon curd." She offered him her lips and edged her hand between his thighs as the telephone rang.

"Do not answer," Irek said, caressing her enlarged breast.

Vora had already lifted the receiver. "Hello."

"I'm sorry to call so late," Lauren said, her voice distressed. "My brother isn't well. I'm flying to Santa Fe tomorrow. I don't know when I'll be back."

"Oh no. What's wrong with him?"

"I-I'm not certain. Hopefully it's minor. But he needs me. You'll have to handle the gallery on your own."

"Don't worry," Vora said firmly. The exhibition had taught her that even without Archer, she could manage things.

"I'll call you soon," Lauren said, her voice sounding unusually hesitant. "I need to talk to Irek."

"It's Lauren," Vora told Irek. "She wants to speak to you."

"Lauren," Irek said, a smile in his voice. "I did not have the chance to thank you for my exhibition. Thank—"

"Irek, could you do me a huge favor? I don't have Ryan's number. Could you call him for me and tell him I need to come by tomorrow at ten?"

"Sure. I call him. Glad to."

The merry widow sizzled in the flames and with it the bra. Iggy stood on the hearth squealing her protests.

"Sorry," Ryan said as he patted the pot belly's head. He couldn't stand the sight of anything that reminded him of Lauren. Since he'd returned to Greyburne Manor, he'd spent the entire day securing Griffith's priceless art collection in the hermetically sealed vault in the basement. Knowing the strike was imminent, Ryan had protected the art by putting it in the lead-lined chamber. That accomplished, he'd left Adi to double-check the security devices Ryan had already checked. He flopped down on the sofa and closed his eyes. Iggy hopped up beside him and settled herself into the crook of his arm.

"We made a big mistake, sweet cheeks. Lauren fooled both of us, didn't she?"

Iggy oinked her agreement just as the telephone rang.

"Westcott?" Stirling asked when Ryan picked up the receiver.

"Yes." He sat up, Iggy on his lap.

"We intercepted a shipment of Berber rugs from Rupert Armstrong. Rolled inside each were bags of cocaine."

"Great," Ryan said, but it was a hollow victory. "Has he been arrested?"

"Not yet. We're waiting to coordinate this entire operation. We don't want to tip our hand by arresting anyone who'll sound the alarm. Barzan is our top priority. Anyway, it may take a while to convince King Hassan to extradite such a prominent man."

"I see." Ryan's voice echoed his disappointment.

"You'll be happy to hear that we know the method Lauren

will be using. She's ordered a huge bottle of Bluebells by Penhaligon's. I don't know why but—"

"I do." Ryan cursed his stupidity as he told Stirling about Iggy and the cologne.

"You can be sure the cologne inside the Penhaligon's bottle will be replaced with an explosive liquid. I'm sending the bomb experts over to secure as much of Greyburne Manor as possible. All we need to know is when."

Ryan hung up. Never in his entire life had he felt more like a failure—except when he'd been unable to disarm Robert Barzan. The gun never should have gone off. If Ryan had reacted in time, T.J. would never have accidentally killed Robert. If . . . like "what might have been," signified regret. But it didn't change a damn thing.

The telephone rang again and Ryan answered immediately. It was Irek.

"Lauren wants to visit you tomorrow at ten," Irek said. "Her brother is ill. She wants to say good-bye."

DAWN

That was a time when only the dead could smile.
from "Prologue" by Anna Akhmatova

30

Clear and warm, the morning was filled with the chirping of robins flitting through the branches of the trees shielding Greyburne Manor. Brilliant sunshine penetrated the spaces between the leafy branches, stippling the ground with uneven patches of golden light and muted shadows. The dew still clung to the grass as Peter Stirling mounted the front steps and stopped at the entrance. Although the ocular scanner had been temporarily disengaged to allow the bomb squad to enter last night, Peter paused in front of the carved oak door. He glanced over his shoulder half expecting the Rottweilers to pounce, even though he knew they'd been locked in the dog run in the back.

The Sikh, the MI-5 agent Peter had assigned to this case because of his patience, answered his knock. Peter walked in, passing through the metal detector. It fired, emitting a buzz.

"My keys," Peter said and tossed them to Adi before trying again. "Where's Westcott?"

The Sikh nodded, indicating for Peter to go down the hall to the specially equipped room with padded walls. Like the basement, this room had been reinforced with lead, the best protection against a bomb. But it might not be enough. While the bomb squad worked all night, Peter conferred with experts concerning what type of explosive might be in the Penhaligon's bottle.

Peter assured himself things were well in hand. For once, his men hadn't lost sight of anyone. Last evening, Barzan had visited Tabatha Foley and David Marcus at Cadogan Gardens. Then he'd met Winthrop for drinks. What they'd discussed remained a mystery. Last-minute details, most likely. At any rate, it appeared that Winthrop and Barzan were going to do this alone. Late last night Tabatha Foley had visited Boots Pharmacy, then returned to the hotel. She and David Marcus were still in his hotel suite—not even calling room service for morning coffee—showing no signs of leaving the love nest.

Peter walked into the padded room and saw the concealing panels along the walls were open, revealing the security cameras' monitors scanning the grounds. Ryan sat at the table beside the telephone. His face was drawn and his eyes had lost their usual look of defiance. Poor devil. Peter handed him the latest evidence—in case he had any last-minute reservations.

Ryan stared at the check. A half-million dollars drawn on Carlos Barzan's personal account made out to Lauren Winthrop and dated yesterday.

"Jeeves discovered it this morning. It was right on top of her desk." Peter took it back. "I'll keep it for evidence."

The telephone rang and Ryan answered it but it was for Stirling. He listened and hung up with a smile.

"She's on her way. Barzan is following her at a discreet distance."

"Then why the hell did he want the phone number?" Ryan asked.

"Undoubtedly, he'll call T.J. from his limousine. It'll stoke his ego to let T.J. know he's responsible."

Ryan figured Stirling's assessment was correct. Three years was a long time to devote to revenge. Only two things commanded that kind of devotion. A twisted mind. Or love.

"When Lauren comes through the door," Peter continued, "she'll pass through the metal detector. After the corset caper, she knows exactly how much metal it takes to trigger the system, that's why I had you set it lower yet."

"If it fires, you want me to make a joke of it."

"Yes. But quickly hand the Penhaligon's bottle to Adi. He'll rush it to the bomb squad. We want Barzan to think the trap is set. We want him to make that call. That'll give us the evidence we need to convict him."

Stirling took a deep breath. "There's one chance in a million that the bomb isn't in the cologne bottle. She's bringing your portrait and whatever is in her Vuitton handbag. This morning as she left, Lauren showed the painting to Jeeves. As he admired it, he gave it the once-over. Nothing. It's just canvas on wooden stretcher bars, but give it a look yourself."

"I've seen it."

"Take another look. Then give her a passionate kiss and check for hidden weapons like a plastic gun. If you don't find anything, knock her handbag to the floor and get it open as you retrieve it and take a peek."

At the thought of kissing Lauren, Ryan's frustration flared into dangerous hatred. He longed to touch her, all right. Put his hands on her neck and wring it.

Peter left the room and went down the hall to make certain the bomb squad was in place and Adi was standing by. They were ready. His last mission. Peter muttered a silent prayer. In less than an hour it would be over. One way or the other.

"Her limousine just passed the Israeli Embassy," one of his agents told him.

"Somebody get rid of the pig," Stirling said as the pot belly followed him. Sniffing.

"She's already ferreted out four chocolate bars," his man answered.

"A big help, I'm sure."

Peter sought refuge in the padded room along with several of his men, protected by the lead lining the walls and the reinforced ceiling. Ryan waited, a study in casualness. A man about to put his life on the line. He didn't look nervous. Or frightened. Suddenly, Peter regretted not having married, not having a son. Okay, Ryan was stubborn and headstrong, but intelligent. Gutsy. A leader.

All eyes riveted on the entry gate's camera as a sleek Rolls limousine pulled up to the curb. The chauffeur opened the door and Lauren Winthrop's shapely legs swung to the pavement.

Ryan tried to steady his erratic pulse. Despite what he'd

told himself, he wasn't ready for the mindless flash of hatred overwhelming him as he saw Lauren's face on the screen. Her hair fluttered in the light breeze concealing and then exposing her beautiful profile. Over one arm she had a small shopping bag from Penhaligon's. The chauffeur retrieved the painting from the trunk and handed it to her.

"She's leaving her handbag behind." Stirling stated the obvious as they watched her hand the Vuitton to the driver, then ring the bell at the front gate.

Lauren waited, dreading the inevitable security check. She was dying to talk to Ryan. She wished she could tell him the whole story—she hated lying. But now wasn't the time. He had his own problems. *Please, let Ryan settle his affairs as soon as possible, and let me straighten out this mess with Paul.*

All night, she'd been up packing, finishing what business she could. And calling Paul every ten minutes. He never came home, nor was there an answer at Geeta's. Lauren hoped she could reach him and clear up this problem soon.

The gate swung open and she carefully maneuvered the portrait through without damaging it. Her heels clicked on the cobblestones as she walked up the front steps, looking around for the attack dogs. She'd never used this entrance before, but she knew to stand in front of the ocular scanner's fish-eye while the camera above the door checked her as well. Finally, the door swung open and she stepped into Greyburne Manor.

Beyond the arch concealing the metal detector, she saw Ryan waiting with Adi at his side. She walked through the detector, confident it wouldn't go off.

"I left my purse in the car," she said, trying to make light of the situation. Any dope could tell he wasn't happy to see her. "I'm not taking any chances." She extended her hand with the shopping bag. "This is for Iggy."

Without a word, Ryan handed it to Adi, and the Sikh disappeared down the gloomy hall.

"A drop behind each ear," Lauren teased, a bit unnerved by the abrupt reception. "Where is she?" Lauren asked, glancing around for the pot belly as she leaned the portrait against the wall.

"Taking a nap." Ryan's voice was flat, cold.

"I'm sorry I had to come," Lauren said, acutely aware of how much he resented her being there. "I know you're in the midst of something important. But I'm leaving for Santa Fe this afternoon, and I don't know when I'll be back."

He held out his arms to her, but there wasn't any welcoming light in his eyes. She hugged him, wanting desperately to tell him everything. But any fool could see he had the weight of the world on his shoulders. Why should he carry her burden, too? Being in his arms gave her some comfort, so she ignored the punishing force of his mouth against hers. His hands slid down her body, squeezing harder than necessary.

No concealed weapon. No purse. The Penhaligon's bottle was the answer, Ryan decided, and he pushed her away.

"What's wrong with your brother?"

Lauren couldn't lie to Ryan and expect him to respect her later when he learned the truth. She elected to tell him as much as possible without involving him. "One of Paul's business deals has gone sour. He needs me."

"Really?" Ryan's tone was scathing. "I thought he was ill. That's what you told Irek."

Her face became grim, but she looked him directly in the eye as she answered, "It was too personal for me to discuss with Irek."

"Oh? I thought Vora was your best friend."

"She is but . . ." Suddenly, she knew she shouldn't have come. There was a side to Ryan Westcott that she would never understand. He could be sensitive one moment and unfeeling the next. It was something they would have to straighten out before their relationship went any further. He had to learn to communicate. It wasn't a one-way street.

A liar, Ryan thought, but not an accomplished one. Any jerk-off could see this brother bit was a ruse.

"My brother needs me. I wanted to let you know where I was in case you want to find me. I finished your portrait. I'd like you to have it." She handed it to him.

He inspected the back first. Wooden stretcher bars with a wire strung between the sides to hang the damn thing.

"You're supposed to look at the front." Lauren couldn't keep the injured tone from her voice. Was this the man who loved her?

"It's nice." He dredged up a smile as he put the portrait down, leaning it face toward the wall. "T.J. will like it."

"Do you think so? Really?"

The sincerity of her expression caught him off-balance. "Lauren, is there anything—anything at all—you'd like to tell me?" The words were out before he'd realized what he was going to say. Damn her.

She hesitated a moment, wondering if she should tell him about Paul's predicament. What could Ryan do? He would surely tell her to get the facts from Paul before doing anything, which was exactly what she planned to do. What was important right now was letting Ryan know how she felt about him. "I never knew what it meant to love until I met you. Never forget I love you with all my heart."

Her parting words robbed Ryan of his sense of victory. He almost believed her. An Academy Award performance. Shit.

As the door closed behind Lauren, half a dozen of Stirling's men hustled about and Iggy sniffed the air. "Who let you out?" Ryan asked as he headed back to the padded room to confer with Stirling.

The telephone rang and Ryan dashed into the room as Stirling said, "Ten to one, it's Barzan calling to gloat."

Stirling snapped on the recorder and nodded for Ryan to answer.

"Yes?" Ryan said casually, as though he hadn't been waiting three years for this very moment.

"T.J. Griffith?" Barzan's voice had a smile of victory in it. Ryan let him dangle. "Who's calling?" he finally asked.

"Carlos Barzan." The voice was positively triumphant now.

"Just a minute." Ryan partially covered the receiver and yelled, "Adi, get T.J. Tell him Barzan's on the phone."

"Is that you, Westcott?"

"Yes."

"I was having a little chat with a mutual friend of ours the other day."

Stirling mopped his forehead with a linen handkerchief. An eerie feeling crept over him, intensified by the noises in the hall. What in hell were his men doing with the damn pig?

"What friend?" Ryan asked, distracted by the commotion outside the room. Clumsy Iggy was caught somewhere. Again.

"Rupert Armstrong."

"Understand Armstrong's a piss-poor excuse for a man now." Ryan ignored Stirling's silent double take. He hadn't mentioned the garrote incident. Should have used it on Lauren's neck.

A low, cynical chuckle came over the line. "Rupert tells me you're in love with his stepdaughter."

"He has a wild imagination. Must come with no balls." Ryan put his hand over the receiver and whispered to Stirling, "Someone grab Iggy or shut the door. I can't concentrate."

"What's taking Griffith so long?" Barzan asked.

"He's coming. Thanks to you, he doesn't walk so fast anymore."

"How do you like your portrait?"

"Great," Ryan responded, maintaining a false level of casualness, sensing he'd been thrown back in time to the jungles of 'Nam. The enemy had the drop on him.

"Has Griffith seen it?"

"He's looking right at it," Ryan lied. The picture was down the hall by the front door where he'd said good-bye to the bitch. He put his finger over his uncovered ear as Stirling crossed the room and closed the door behind the agents who'd been out in the hall. Iggy was stuck somewhere and bleating for help.

Barzan laughed. "Great. I—"

Like a bullet between the eyes, the truth hit Ryan. He dropped the telephone, bolted past the MI-5 men, charged toward Stirling, screaming, "Iggy! Iggy!"

Stirling blocked him, throwing his body against the door. "No, Ryan. You can't—"

Ryan shoved him aside, knowing he had only seconds before Barzan realized he was no longer on the line and hit the remote control that would detonate the bomb. Ryan jerked open the heavy lead door.

Semtex-H. Plastic explosive—the terrorists' favorite weapon. Iggy had been trying to warn them. The paint. It had to be plastic explosive carefully applied by Lauren.

Don't think of that bitch now. Save Iggy.

As he charged through the doorway—or perhaps a fraction of a second before—an ear-shattering boom rocked the build-

ing. Instinct sent him diving to the floor while chunks of stone
and shards of glass hurtled through the air like deadly spears.
Ryan heard a tortured moan. Pain pulverizing him, he shimmied across the floor on his belly—as he had going up Devil's
Hill in 'Nam—until he reached Iggy.

"It's okay, sweetheart," he whispered to the hank of blood-
ied fur and splintered bone.

But it wasn't all right. For Iggy, it never would be. Her front
legs had been blown off as well as the left side of her face.
Blood was gushing from her snout so fast that she couldn't
possibly live more than a few minutes.

"Thanks for keeping me company," he said, remembering
the long, lonely nights. "I'll never forget you."

With a tortured whimper, Iggy's body went limp.

"Thank God." Ryan didn't want her suffering another second.

A crack ricocheted through the building as the centuries-
old timbers supporting the cathedral ceiling collapsed. The
last thing Ryan saw was Iggy's trusting eyes staring lifelessly at
him.

As the limousine drove up the street, Lauren wondered if
she would ever understand Ryan. A deafening boom thundered. The limousine slammed to a stop, banging Lauren's
head against the door. She turned and saw the gaping wound
that had once been the entrance to Greyburne Manor. She
threw open the door, jumped out, losing a high heel, stumbled
over the curb, and ran around a chestnut tree to the sidewalk.
She kicked off the other shoe, sending it hurling over a low
hedge. Head down, arms pumping, legs flying, she blindly
raced back toward the house, panic and adrenaline guiding
her. Gasping for air, heart hammering, she skidded to stop on
the glass-strewn walk. Miraculously, the wall enclosing
Greyburne Manor was still standing.

"Ryan!" The piercing scream vibrated her entire body as
she banged on the wrought-iron gate's remote-controlled
latch. The video camera dangled from a frayed wire, spitting
sparks at her. With a whoosh, a scorching, suffocating wall of
flame recoiled from the building. The searing smoke clogged

her lungs and she sank to her knees. She screamed again, and again, and again. But no sound came from her tortured throat.

Flash-frozen by fear, she was dimly aware of the people running toward her and the shrieks of sirens as they raced up the street. The churning smoke burned her eyes, making it difficult to see, but she kept her gaze on the spot where the front door had once been. *What on earth happened? Please, Lord, let Ryan be all right. Please hurry, before that building becomes a crematorium.*

A pair of hands slammed down on her shoulders. Instinctively, she tried to jerk away as she was hauled to her feet, not noticing her foot had been cut and was bleeding.

"You're under arrest."

Her hand trembling, Vora put down the telephone as she wondered how to break the news to Irek. She walked slowly into the kitchen where he was brewing herbal tea and arranging tea cakes on a platter.

"What did Dr. Osgood say? Is the baby fine?"

Vora took a deep breath. "The *babies* are fine."

Irek dropped a Bath bun on the counter. "Babies?"

"Twins. Healthy twins."

"Sit, *matiushka*— little mother," Irek ordered, and she sank into a chair. "Up feet."

"I feel fine, honest. You don't have to wait on me."

"Eat," he commanded, beaming as he put the platter of tea cakes on the table beside her. "Eat for three."

"Oooh," she moaned. She would be as big as a cruise ship before long, she thought, as the telephone rang.

They let it ring. Screening their calls with their message machine had become standard practice. Too many reporters, too many fans, too many invitations.

"Mr. Makarova, this is Lawrence Martin with *The Times*," the voice squawked at them from the recorder. "I'm wondering if you have any comment about Lauren Winthrop's arrest?"

Irek bounded across the kitchen and grabbed the telephone. "Arrested? Arrested? What do you say?"

"She was arrested shortly before noon. Winthrop hasn't

been formally charged yet, but my sources tell me she's accused of planting a bomb at the residence of T.J. Griffith."

"Impossible," Irek said unequivocally.

Vora put her hand beneath her breast to still the pounding. The babies were kicking was her first thought, then she realized it was her heart knocking against her ribs. Lauren? A bomb? Never.

"Do you know where Lauren Winthrop obtained Semtex-H?"

"What is Sam Tex H?"

"Plastic explosive. You know, the same substance that brought down that Pan Am jet over Lockerbie. I understand she'd applied it to canvas so it appeared to be a base coat of paint. Do you have any idea where she got it or how she knew it could be disguised as paint?"

"No. And I tell you this. She is not guilty. I know peoples. Lauren Winthrop is the best. She not do this thing. Never."

"Scotland Yard has a lot of evidence against her," the reporter said, his voice still blaring through the answering machine. "Do you have a comment?"

"Fock Scotland Yard!"

"May I quote you?"

Irek slammed the receiver down. "What do we do?"

"A lawyer," Vora said without hesitation. "She'll need a first-rate barrister. Peregrine Tutwiler. He's the best."

Peregrine Tutwiler usually salivated at the prospect of lucrative litigation. "I'll defend you to your last pound" had always been his motto. But after Vora mentioned Lauren's name, he refused to take the case, explaining he accepted only those cases he had a prayer of winning.

Irek was tuned into BBC 1 when Vora came in with the news of the refusal.

"Was anyone killed?" she asked, the full magnitude of the situation hitting her as she saw the television shot of the bombed-out shell that had once been Greyburne Manor.

"They do not know anymore then *The Times* reporter."

"Do you suppose Ryan was inside?"

Irek shook his head, concern etching his face. "What did the lawyer say?"

"He refused to take the case. I'm going to call Dr. Digsby. I know he works closely with Peregrine Tutwiler. Lots of defendants wage media campaigns to strengthen their cases."

"Heavens, no," Dr. Digsby said when Vora asked. "The Lord has spoken."

Clutching the receiver, Vora dropped into a chair, meeting Irek's questioning eyes with a shake of her head. How could she get through to the pudding-head evangelist who equated media images with God's will? She opted for a divine dose of flattery. "I'm certain, Dr. Digsby, that the Lord reveres your good work. If you spoke to Mr. Tutwiler, I'm positive the Lord would give the barrister the proper guidance, and he would take the case with God's blessing."

"Wel-l-l," the doctor waffled. "I believe that is true. But once an event of this importance has been reported so extensively, it is God's will. Impossible to change."

You nut. "The Lord wants you to help. I feel it."

"If he did, it would take an inordinate amount of money. Mr. Tutwiler is expensive. My staff would have to be augmented by an army of private investigators to get to the bottom of this. We're probably looking at close to half a million pounds to change the Lord's mind. He would need it in cash— immediately."

Almost a million dollars. Vora sucked in her breath. They didn't have anywhere near that kind of money—not after the print fraud and purchasing an estate in the country as well as a Porsche. They might be able to raise it, but it would take time. Why was she bothering with this crazy man? Because he alone could deliver Peregrine Tutwiler and a media blitz it would take to keep Lauren's case from being tried in the press.

"What is the problem?" Irek asked.

How in hell had Carlos Barzan gotten away? Peter Stirling asked himself that evening. In the frantic moments after the bomb exploded, Barzan had jumped from his limousine and disappeared into the crowd before the agents tailing him could arrest him. At least they had Lauren Winthrop in custody. Peter stared out of New Scotland Yard's window at the twilight's deepening shadows embracing London. His temple throbbed and he gingerly touched the bandage. Time to retire. When a pig was smarter than him and his men, it was definitely time to get out.

"Who would have thought Semtex-H could be applied like paint?" asked one of the men from Interpol.

"No one even suspected," Stirling admitted. In the past, it had been disguised as candy, as wafers, as kids' toys, even folded like paper. But who dreamed it could simulate paint? No one. None of the bomb experts even mentioned it. The miniature detonator and the filament wire had been a real stinker, too. None of them saw it, and it had been too small for the metal detector to pick up.

That Winthrop woman was a real actress. Despite the tears and her pleas to know about Westcott's and Griffith's safety, Peter wasn't deceived. She was as guilty as Barzan. Now it was up to Her Majesty's government to put the case together. Having so many agencies involved, national and international, made this a jurisdictional nightmare. Never mind, let someone else sort it out. For convenience, they were all using New Scotland Yard's facilities.

"Call the hospital," Peter told one of his men.

"I called five minutes ago."

"Call again." He prayed Ryan would live. Peter supposed he should count his blessings. The rest of his men had all survived with minor fractures and burns. Luckily, the bomb squad had been on site, with their fire trucks and ambulances hovering nearby on Wright's Lane. If they hadn't been, Ryan would have died on the spot.

No such luck for Iggy. She'd tried to warn them with the three oinks that signaled the faint odor of nitrogen that plastic explosives always emitted. But unlike the guard dogs everyone feared, Iggy had become too much of a pet. She'd trumpeted the warning—as she'd been trained—but no one listened. Until it was too late.

Once again, Peter cursed plastic explosives. He should have guessed. Barzan knew Greyburne Manor had the latest in security devices right down to an ocular scanner. But none of them could detect the deadly explosive. The only clue to its presence was an odor of nitrogen so light only the most highly sensitive noses could detect it. Peter had wanted to get a thermal neutron analysis bomb detector that had been designed for airlines to screen baggage for Semtex-H, but the cost had been prohibitive. Even the airlines were dragging their feet about installing them. The only one in England was at Gatwick Airport.

The telephone rang and one of his men answered it. When he put it down immediately, Peter's heart turned to lead, assuming the hospital had called saying Westcott had died. Poor devil. In a way, these last three years—though trying— had been fun. Ryan had been a protégé and a surrogate son. Peter felt like personally killing the woman and Barzan. They'd destroyed one of the most brilliant men he'd ever encountered. Life wasn't fair.

"That was our operatives who've had David Marcus under surveillance," said the agent who'd answered the telephone. "They've been trying to reach us. Tabatha Foley has murdered David Marcus. The maid went into his room this afternoon and was accosted by a young woman fitting Tabatha's description. She tied the maid up and stole her clothes. She slipped out past our men, wearing the maid's uniform."

Peter sighed, thankful Ryan was still alive. "Why would Foley kill Marcus?" He considered the situation. The MI-5 agent tailing Marcus on the night of Makarova's opening had confirmed Ryan's suspicion. Marcus had destroyed Tabatha Foley's figurine. But afterward they'd made up. Had Marcus done something else to the girl? Something so bad that she'd murder him? His sixth sense kicked in. Something wasn't right here.

Women. Peter would go to his grave not understanding them. He decided to go down and see how Winthrop's interrogation was going.

It wasn't. She was still sitting in a holding cell, a vacant look in her eyes. Her foot had been bandaged, but the blood had seeped through the gauze, staining it.

"Is Ryan all right? And Mr. Griffith? Are they alive?"

The plaintive note in her voice wrung Peter's heart, but he shook it off. Strange, she'd yet to ask for a lawyer.

"Please tell me," she pleaded as Peter walked out of the room.

* * *

Lauren stared blankly as Peregrine Tutwiler informed her of the charges he expected Her Majesty's government to file. "Ryan and Mr. Griffith, are they all right?"

Peregrine's blue eyes studied her as if she'd arrived from another planet. "I'll see if I can find out."

"I have no money," she said weakly. Like a ship on an uncharted sea, she'd lost her bearings. She didn't know where she was going. Or where she'd been.

"Irek Makarova has already paid me. He and Vora Leighton insist you've been framed."

It was all Lauren could do not to burst into tears. Her friends had faith in her. Knowing they believed in her gave her courage and the will to fight. Barzan had to be the culprit. He'd planted a bomb in the picture frame or the Penhaligon's bottle. Somewhere. And she'd capitalized on her relationship with Ryan, taking the deadly bomb into Greyburne Manor. That's why Barzan had hired her, paying more than the job warranted. She should have been more suspicious of his motives. She refused to let him get away with this. If Ryan or T.J. had died, she owed it to them to get Barzan.

"Let me assure you of one thing. I'm innocent. I would never harm Ryan Westcott or T.J. Griffith. What I want more than anything is to punish Carlos Barzan."

"Shit!" Peter Stirling threw *The Times* across the floor on the morning following the bombing. The media blitz was on. That daffy Dr. Digsby was behind it. Everyone was criticizing Peter's handling of the operation. The Israelis and Russians led the furor on Embassy Row backed by their royal neighbors in Kensington Palace. How had plastic explosives gone undetected? They all had dogs to sniff for the telltale nitrogen. What was the MI-5 doing with a pig—for God's sakes?

Nobody bothered to check that a pot belly's nose was much more sensitive than a dog's. No one thought to find out how expensive Iggy had been to purchase and train. She had been far superior to a dog—but the media wasn't carrying that angle. Miniature pot bellys were too exotic. Few people had ever heard of them or seen them. Those who had described them as "designer pets," not working animals like guard dogs.

In the days that followed, the media smoke screen intensified. The association of hotels complained Stirling's men had managed to stake out a murder scene yet let the murderess, Tabatha Foley, slip away. The Royal Society for Prevention of Cruelty to Animals demanded an explanation of the methods employed in training Iggy. Museums worldwide criticized Peter for not removing Griffith's art collection to a safe site even though it hadn't been damaged. King Hassan coughed up Armstrong with a scathing protest to the Queen that he should have been informed of Armstrong's activities earlier.

The MI-5 had concealed some facts from the media. No one knew about Ryan Westcott or Julia Hartley's involvement. No link had been established between the print fraud involving Basil Blackstoke and Barzan. And most important, no one knew the authorities were searching for Barzan. Peter believed that they would have a much better chance of catching him if Barzan didn't know he was being hunted.

By the end of the week, Stirling had received stacks of telegrams. It seemed as if everyone who'd ever known Lauren had sent a message urging the investigators to believe her story. He'd seen her several times. Her only question was about Griffith's and Westcott's conditions.

Stirling had to admit Lauren's story was plausible. Not likely but plausible. Stranger things had happened. He wondered if perhaps he wasn't keeping an open mind. Had his love affair with Amy Thorpe colored his perception? Amy had said she loved him, but what she really loved was the intrigue, the adventure, the excitement of spying. He'd been a master spy and she'd been his protégée. He never should have fallen for her, nursing a grudge all these years when she married another. Not every woman was like that. Maybe Lauren was what she claimed—an innocent pawn.

Tabatha Foley had to be the key. No one else could corroborate Lauren's story. But where was Tabatha? Her Majesty's forces were looking for her as well as a slew of sleuths employed by Tutwiler and every reporter in London. Nothing. Where would he go if he were young and on the lam?

"Sir." One of his agents poked his head around the door. "Hospital just called. Westcott is out of critical condition."

Although he wasn't given to prayer, Peter took a moment to give thanks. Then he took the lift to the lower level and made his way to where they were holding Lauren. She looked up expectantly.

"Ryan is going to live."

"Thank God. Thank God." Tears limned her eyes, but didn't fall. "Bless you for telling me. You have no idea how much he means to me," she said, her voice trembling. "I can face anything that happens to me now. Anything."

Shaken, Peter walked out of the room convinced Lauren actually loved Ryan. No one could feign that kind of emotion. Now he was determined to find Tabatha Foley. He reviewed Tabatha's file, noting Lauren's assessment that she was an underage runaway. Home. She could go home if the village was isolated enough. London's multitude of newspapers reached even the remotest backwater. But if Tabatha disguised herself and stayed out of sight, she could hide until this blew over.

Keen observers of class distinctions, like Vora Leighton, said Tabatha had a slight accent. Untainted by the soft burr of the north, her voice had a certain lilt to it that indicated she'd grown up in the south. Peter assigned extra men to canvass all drivers from companies that had sent lorries south in the days following the murder. Had she hitched a ride?

A lorry driver for Rhodda's Dairy reported dropping off a girl in Weymouth earlier in the week. Although she had short blonde hair not brown, the driver had remembered her big breasts.

Peter personally interviewed the driver. "Did the girl say where she was going after you let her off?"

The driver shook his head. "She didn't say much. She slept like—like she hadn't slept for days."

"We need to find her. Is there anything else you can tell us? Anything at all?"

"She dropped a piece of paper with a phone number on it. I pitched it out, but I think the number was a Portland exchange."

Peter sucked on his pipe, not believing his good luck. The Isle of Portland was small. If Tabatha had gone there, he'd have no trouble tracking her. Peter started to leave, thanking the driver.

"You're helping her father, right?" the driver asked as Peter was halfway out the door.

"Her father?" A charge of excitement shot through him. "What did he look like?"

"Older. Black hair." The driver shrugged. "Expensive clothes. He was here yesterday."

Barzan. With pulse-pounding certainty Peter knew Carlos Barzan must be after Tabatha. Why? Shouldn't his first priority be to get out of England? Until now, his trail had been stone cold. Peter assumed Barzan had slipped out of the country. What was he doing chasing a murderess around? Wait a minute. Maybe they'd been too hasty in assuming Tabatha had murdered David Marcus. Just because she'd attacked the maid didn't mean she'd killed her lover. She might have seen the murder, Peter concluded. Forensic experts placed the time of death between seven and midnight the evening before his body was found.

Peter couldn't figure out why she'd waited until the following day to flee. Then he remembered the details in the crime report. She'd purchased peroxide and scissors at Boots. There had been hair and traces of bleach in the sink. What kind of girl could spend the night in the same suite as her dead lover, cutting and bleaching her hair? The same type of girl who could be paid to betray a woman who'd befriended her.

If Barzan read the papers, he wouldn't see his name and wouldn't realize the MI-5 was onto him. But he must have spotted the articles about Tabatha and concluded she'd been hiding in the suite when he shot David Marcus. Undoubtedly, Barzan feared she'd expose him.

"When did this 'father' come to see you?"

"Early yesterday morning."

Barzan had a head start of almost a full day. Unless Peter found Tabatha first, she was as good as dead.

And Lauren Winthrop would most certainly be convicted.

31

Immediately, Peter took the agency's jet helicopter to Easton, the only village on the Isle of Portland large enough to merit a police station. Constable Whitworth met them, and Peter showed him the only picture they had of Tabatha, which had been taken on the night of Irek Makarova's exhibition.

Constable Whitworth shook his head. "Don't know her."

"You're positive?" Peter asked. He knew Whitworth had lived his entire life on the tiny island. If Tabatha had lived here, Whitworth would know her. "Take another look."

Squinting, Whitworth cocked his head to one side and took a second look. "We-l-l-l . . . it could be our Sally Hemstreet all dressed up like his nibs."

"Does her family live nearby? We need to find her," Peter said, dead certain Tabatha Foley and Sally Hemstreet were the same person.

"I'll take you to her straight away," Constable Whitworth said, his expression grim. "Sally's body is in the morgue."

"Christ! Barzan killed her," Peter said.

"No one killed her," Constable Whitworth disagreed. "She died of natural causes. At least that's what Dr. Robinson says."

"Didn't anyone know the authorities were looking for her?"

Whitworth pointed to the picture. "Our Sally never looked like that. Her family used to have a farm east of Southwell, but they couldn't make a go of it. They moved to Australia two years ago when Sally was"—he consulted the cloudless sky—"about fourteen. Several days ago, Sally called the estate agent handling the farm where she once lived. When she heard it was still available, she said she'd take it. She arrived Tuesday morning and paid cash to lease the farm for six months. She spent yesterday gathering supplies like she planned to stay out there forever. She stopped for tea at Tuttle's Tearoom, collapsed, and died of a heart attack. Imagine, so young."

Peter cursed his bad luck. Barzan was always one step ahead of him. "Was there a stranger, an older man in the tearoom?"

"Yes. How'd you know?"

Peter turned to the two agents he'd brought with him. "Fly the body to Fort Halstead immediately. Tell the boys to check for brucine."

"Like the Leighton case?" one agent asked.

"Maybe." They'd yet to prove who had given Archer Leighton the lethal dose. All Basil Blackstoke knew was a contact's name. Perhaps Archer Leighton wasn't important enough to Barzan's organization for Barzan to have done it personally. But Peter couldn't be sure. Barzan took diabolical pleasure in killing those who got in his way.

As Peter's men hustled to carry out his orders, he stood on a rise and let the spring breeze off the English Channel buffet his raincoat, corkscrewing it around his legs as he reviewed the facts. Evidently, Tabatha had heard the killer, but hadn't seen his face or she would have recognized Barzan. How lucky could Barzan get? Now where would he go? The most likely escape would be to pay a fisherman to sail him across the channel to France. But Barzan never did the expected, Peter reminded himself. What was the least likely course of action? To stay here.

Peter, his two agents, and Constable Whitworth went to check out the abandoned farm where Tabatha had lived. Peter surmised that Barzan planned to lay low until one of his cronies could come across the channel and pick him up. Using his own men would avoid raising suspicion by asking a local fisherman to sail him to France.

The farm was down a country lane that wasn't much more than a cow path, choked by spring weeds. In the distance, they saw a weathered gray farmhouse. It appeared to be deserted, but Peter ordered the men to leave the car behind a copse of trees and approach on foot. They circled behind a dilapidated barn that smelled from moldy hay. Inside was a new Ford Escort with a car rental sticker on it. The insurance card in the glove box indicated it had been rented in London to George Marshall.

Peter turned to Constable Whitworth. "Do you know of any George Marshall on the island?"

Constable Whitworth shook his head.

Taking no chances, Peter posted men at the sides and rear of the house, then he went to the front door and eased it open. Inside he found a small parlor, its few pieces of furniture covered by dust-laden sheets. Wild bramble vines had edged through the crack between the window and the sill. In a corner a rat was chewing on a red berry, its stealthy eyes on Peter. The scrims of sunlight that filtered through the drawn curtains revealed footprints on the dusty floor. Peter quietly ventured down the hall to the only bedroom.

Carlos Barzan lay across the bed, sleeping beneath a sheet that served as a makeshift blanket. Peter surveyed the room and spotted a tiny vial on the dusty nightstand beside the car keys. He silently placed the vial inside an evidence bag and pocketed it, betting it was brucine, one of the most highly controlled poisons in the world. With this evidence, Barzan couldn't weasel out of the murder charge.

Peter had planned to sit on the sidelines and enjoy the legal gymnastics that Barzan and his phalanx of attorneys were certain to employ in what promised to be a lengthy trial. Like a fly in a spider's web, Peter had envisioned Barzan futilely trying to extricate himself from the case the MI-5 had painstakingly built against him. But now Peter wanted a quick confession from Barzan. Peter couldn't chance a legion of lawyers advising Barzan to stonewall it while Lauren Winthrop rotted in jail. Who knew? Barzan might—for some twisted reason—never clear her.

"You're under arrest," Peter told the sleeping Barzan in a loud voice.

Barzan didn't move. In the dim light of the room, Peter wasn't sure Barzan was even breathing. Had he taken a fatal dose of brucine? Peter touched Barzan's shoulder and shook him. When he still didn't move, Peter bent over him, praying he wasn't dead. If he were, it would be virtually impossible to prove Lauren's innocence.

In a single explosive movement, Barzan vaulted to his feet, leveling a thirty-eight with a silencer on it at Peter, knocking him backward against the wall. He stared down the barrel of the weapon that must have killed David Marcus.

"I'm Peter Stirling with the MI-5. We have the house surrounded," Peter said with a calm he definitely didn't feel. His two agents and Constable Whitworth might not be able to capture Barzan.

Barzan silently stared at Peter with the most merciless eyes that Peter had ever seen in over fifty years with British intelligence.

"There's no point to killing anyone else. We have the brucine to link you to Tabatha Foley. And we have a tape of you talking with Ryan Westcott just before you detonated the plastic explosive. You said: 'You're dead, Griffith. You killed my son. Now you die.' We have enough evidence to put you behind bars for murder."

Barzan didn't respond. Peter guessed the drug lord must be counting on his money and connections, so he played his ace. "Julia Hartley is one of our agents. She cracked David Marcus's computer system. We know where all your funds are hidden."

The slight narrowing of Barzan's eyes indicated he now felt threatened, but he still didn't say anything as he kept the revolver aimed at Peter's heart.

"We've frozen all your assets," Peter lied, knowing these things took time, but the Swiss had become more cooperative in recent years, especially with drug funds. "You won't even be able to pay for an attorney, so don't think you're getting off." Peter yelled over his shoulder, "Come on in, boys."

As soon as Peter heard his agents coming through the door, he rolled the dice again. "Give me the gun," he said, putting his hand on the barrel extended in length by the silencer. Barzan surrendered the gun without uttering a word.

It wasn't until he was cuffed and in the car on his way to the station that Barzan finally spoke. "The papers didn't mention who died in the bombing. Did I get Griffith?"

"The MI-5 has been on to you for years." Peter couldn't suppress the note of triumph in his voice. "We covered up your son's death and persuaded Westcott and Griffith to work for us. We knew we'd get you sooner or later."

Barzan appeared startled. Evidently, he believed this was a personal feud that didn't involve British intelligence. "You killed Griffith with that car bomb three years ago. We've had Westcott impersonating him since then. We knew you'd try again. This time we were ready for you."

The following morning, ten days after her arrest, Lauren was released. Vora and Irek as well as Geeta and Paul were waiting for her. When Lauren saw them, she swallowed with difficulty, fighting the hot sting of tears building in her eyes.

"How can I ever thank you?" she asked Vora as they hugged.

"We did no thing," Irek said.

"They're being modest," Paul said. "Irek offered to sell Takgama Nakamura 'Velma Liubov'' to raise money to help you."

"You didn't." As agonizing as the past days had been, Lauren's spirits had been buoyed by her friends' faith in her. But she never dreamed Irek would sell the painting that he loved.

"Mr. Nakamura wouldn't take it," Geeta said, "but he gave Irek the money to hire Tutwiler. Tak thinks you're special."

Lauren was so amazed that she didn't know what to say. The numerous people who'd offered to help her still surprised her.

"I'm sorry I let Barzan trick me," Paul said. "When he sent me complimentary tickets to Disney's Epcot Center, Geeta and I thought it was the perfect opportunity to take the kids."

"You couldn't have known how sinister Barzan was," Vora said. "No one knew."

"But if Lauren had been able to reach Paul," Geeta said, "she wouldn't have been duped into believing he'd signed that phony piece of paper Barzan showed her. She wouldn't have agreed to leave London on such short notice."

"It does not matter," Irek said. "Barzan would have found another way. He admitted he'd tried to kill Paul with an overdose of Halcion. Barzan would stop at no thing. "

"Irek's right," Vora agreed. "If Tabatha Foley hadn't been spying on Lauren, he would have found someone else."

Lauren shook her head. "She had so much talent—wasted."

"Don't pity her," Paul said, putting his arm around Lauren. "Come on, let's go home. There's a flight to Santa Fe this afternoon."

Home? Lauren wondered just where that was. *Where the heart is.* Hers was right here in London. "I must see Ryan."

"He does not wish to see you . . . again," Irek said gently. "I explain it was not your fault. Ryan knows all about Barzan's confession. But Ryan says you are like your mother. If you loved him, you would have told him everything."

"I must see him even if it's for the last time."

When they arrived at Portland Hospital, Lauren went in alone. For the thousandth time she cursed herself for not being more suspicious of Barzan's job offer. Because of her naïveté, she'd almost killed the man she loved.

Lauren urged herself through the door to his private room and found him sleeping. She'd told herself to be prepared for how he might look. It didn't help. At the sight of his head, encased in white gauze like a turban, she stifled an anguished cry. *What have I done?*

On tiptoes, she moved closer to the bed. His hands were at his sides as white and lifeless as his face. An I.V. shunt pierced one hand with fluid dripping from a bottle hanging overhead. The leopard ring was missing, she noticed.

She waited beside his bed, willing him to find it in his heart to forgive her. He stirred, opening first one eye and then the other. Without saying anything, he looked at her with that semifocused look of someone heavily sedated.

"How do you feel?" she asked softly.

He squinted, as if making sure she wasn't an apparition. "What do you want?" His voice was hoarse, strained.

She touched his hand with her fingertips, but he jerked it away. "I want you to know I'm sorry. I never meant to hurt you or Iggy. As long as I live, I'll never forgive myself."

He turned his head away. There might have been tears in his eyes, but she wasn't sure.

"I know you're upset about Iggy," she said.

"No. I'm not. She was specifically trained to detect plastic explosives. She was just doing her job. That's all."

Lauren knew he didn't mean what he was saying. Peter Stirling had told her exactly what had happened, but she didn't argue. "I'm sorry about Iggy." Lauren struggled to keep her voice even. "She was wonderful."

"Thanks to you, there wasn't enough left of her to sweep up with a broom."

Lauren took a deep breath, fearing her eggshell composure would shatter. She had expected his vehemence—she deserved it. And more. A happy, loving creature had been destroyed because she was too stupid to be suspicious. Mercifully, no other lives had been lost. "I would do anything in my power to change what happened. Anything. Please, believe me."

"Forget it. No one can change the past." Obviously in pain, he added, "You had your chance. If you'd even once mentioned Barzan was financing—"

"You never told me about T.J. or—"

"That was different. I was involved in a top-secret government operation."

"You're right," she conceded. "I would have told you about Barzan if I'd had any idea how important it was."

"I even gave you a last chance when I asked if you had anything to tell me. You could have told me the truth."

"I didn't want to burden you with my problems. Paul—"

"Paul. Always Paul. He got you away from Armstrong, so you've dedicated your life to him."

"That's not true. I help him when he needs me."

"So go to him now. Get out. I don't need you."

Hours later, Ryan awoke slowly, fighting his way through cushioning layers of sleep, and found Paul sitting beside his bed. They'd been introduced at Irek's exhibition, but hadn't exchanged more than a few words. Ryan felt like smashing Paul's face in. *Stop it. He's not responsible. He can't help it if he's a carbon copy of his sister.*

"If you feel up to it, I'd like to talk to you," Paul said.

"What about?"

"About Rupert Armstrong."

"Who cares?" Ryan snapped. Armstrong was behind bars where he belonged. So what? It still wouldn't bring back T.J.

"When my mother married him I was young, impressionable," Paul launched into his story, ignoring the censure in Ryan's green eyes. "She cherished being rich, so I thought that money was everything."

Ryan shifted uncomfortably; the drug had worn off and the throbbing pain had returned.

"After a few years in France and an unhappy love affair, I achieved a sense of values. I realized money couldn't buy happiness."

"Get to the point," Ryan said, wondering why he had to hear Paul's life story. Promised to be a real yawner.

"Early on, I had my mother figured out. I knew she didn't love anyone but herself. Lauren couldn't see that. She's too innately good."

"For crissake, I don't want to hear about Lauren." Thinking about her only reminded him that he couldn't trust her.

"Lauren married Ozzie, taking on an old man with a third-rate gallery. She made it into the best watercolor gallery in Paris. In New York, she brought me through a crisis when my first wife died."

"What's the point? What about Armstrong?"

"The point is Lauren has never had a chance in life. Rupert Armstrong, a sick old man for a husband, a third-rate gallery, a weak brother . . . then Carlos Barzan."

"Don't try to convince me to give her another chance—"

"Barzan lured her to Ravissant. You made it easy for him by falling in love with her. He—"

"I'm not in love with her."

"Good." Paul eyed Ryan with obvious distaste. "Because I don't want her to have anything to do with you."

That took Ryan by surprise. He tried to figure Paul's angle.

"My sister is too good for you. Like Irek Makarova, she has inner strength. She gives everything to those she loves. She hated working in the Sake Sistahs, kissing up to Japanese businessmen like some geisha girl. But she did it to help me." He studied the I.V. bag dangling above Ryan's head. "I'm the last person in the world to deserve that kind of devotion."

Alerted by the raw emotion in Paul's voice, Ryan watched him carefully.

"I've always had trouble sleeping. Often I prowled around the villa late at night. I saw things, heard things. Like Mother, I knew what Rupert was doing to Lauren. But I was young—confused. Afraid of Rupert." Now staring out the window at the June twilight, Paul hesitated, then slowly continued. "For over a year, I put off doing anything. Finally, I couldn't stand it. Instead of confronting the bastard, I took the coward's way out. I hustled Lauren out of Marrakesh while Rupert was away."

A pulsing knot tightened in Ryan's stomach, and he had to remind himself he didn't give a shit about Lauren. Or he would have rearranged her brother's face.

"She forgave me," Paul said. "As soon as we were out of Marrakesh, I told her the truth, and she forgave me. That's what kind of a person she is."

"She forgave you? J-e-e-esus! She's dumber than I thought."

Snowflakes as large as thistledown drifted through the air, adding to the knee-deep snow that had already fallen. The soft hiss of the rising wind through the pines promised the storm would continue through the night into Christmas day. The sounds muffled by the deep snow, Lauren locked the door of her gallery in Santa Fe.

Beyond the Rainbow, the gallery she and Paul had opened six months ago after she'd left London, was at the end of a pedestrian street called Pirate's Alley. Before the Spanish had come to New Mexico early in the seventeenth century, Canyon Road had been nothing more than a dusty trail leading to the Pecos Pueblo. It still wasn't much more than a country lane except that now world-famous galleries lined the street. Beyond the Rainbow was located on a less prestigious offshoot of the famous street, but Lauren was proud of her gallery nonetheless.

She was proud of herself, too. She had traced a few of her early works that she'd sold to the New York decorator and repurchased them. Displaying them in Beyond the Rainbow,

Lauren ignored wisecracks like "If I buy this will it blow up?" No longer fearing rejection, she continued painting, adding to her collection. Her paintings were selling—slowly, but steadily—to noted collectors.

She drove home and parked near a tall aspen, its spindly branches bowed with fresh-fallen snow. As she trudged through the knee-deep drifts to the door of the adobe that she no longer shared with Paul since he'd married Geeta, Lauren heard the telephone ringing and hurried to answer it. "Merry Christmas, Vora."

"How did you know it was me?" Vora asked.

"Lucky guess," Lauren said with a laugh. "You were up nursing the twins and couldn't get back to sleep, right?" Since Larisa and Anatoly had been born, Vora was in the habit of calling after their late-night feeding. As a *volki*, a godparent, Lauren was thrilled to be kept posted on the twins' progress.

"Right," Vora admitted. "I called to wish you Merry Christmas and to tell you some interesting news. Your mother married that Frenchman she's been living with since Rupert was jailed."

"Mother always lands on her feet," Lauren said without enthusiasm. Years ago, she'd given up trying to understand her mother. Their meeting in Marrakesh closed the door forever.

"I just thought you'd want to know," Vora said. "I guess Caroline won't be coming to Rupert's trial next month."

"Bet on it," Lauren said, wondering if Vora and Irek had heard from Ryan. Asking would only reopen the wound. Since his patent had been registered, Griffith International was now one of the premier companies in the world.

"How are you doing?" Vora asked. "Christmas can be a hard time to be alone."

"Stop worrying." Lauren kept her tone upbeat. "I'm not alone. Paul and Geeta and the monsters are just across the street. I'm making Christmas Eve dinner for them."

In truth, Lauren had never felt more lonely. She warned herself not to think about Ryan, but couldn't help it. She still could see the hate firing his green eyes. *Don't dwell on what you can't change. Life is too short.*

Striving to keep her spirits up, she rang off and lugged in

piñon wood, then started a fire. A knock on the front door reminded her that Demi was coming over early to light the *luminarias* lining her porch. She took a handful of long fireplace matches to light the votives. Weighted with sand, the small bags with candles had long been a Southwestern holiday tradition.

She swung open the heavy oak door and found Ryan. He wore T.J.'s bomber jacket with the collar upturned, snow dusting his shoulders and dark hair. Her heart beat erratically.

"It's cold out here." He tossed his head, flinging the snow off.

She stepped back and let him walk past her, praying he'd forgiven her, but she wasn't going to beg him. Besides visiting him in the hospital, she'd written him countless letters. He knew how sorry she felt.

He reached for her and pulled her into his arms. Her pulse thudded as her heart refused to believe what her mind told her. He really was here. She'd thought that she'd never see him again. The touch of his lips on hers erased her remaining doubts and fears. Between kisses, he said, "I'm sorry I've been such a bastard."

"I'm sorry I—" She began only to have the words cut off by another tender kiss.

"Let's start over, here and now. No more saying 'I'm sorry.'"

"What made you change your mind?"

"Your friends wore me down, then your brother talked to me. Even Peter Stirling was on your side."

Lauren knew exactly what Paul had told him. "I love my brother too much to let that one mistake stand between us. Besides, I could have told a teacher"—she shrugged—"or someone. But I was embarrassed, afraid. Paul and I have had years of happiness together since then."

"Part of what happened was my fault," Ryan admitted. "I couldn't tell you the truth. We were caught up in something that was bigger than both of us." His green eyes were serious as he studied her. "I realize I wanted to punish you because, like your mother, you couldn't be trusted. I thought you would have told me the whole truth—if you loved me."

"Despite my promise to Barzan, I would have told you if I'd

known it was important. I never suspected." She sighed. "My father always said to beware of things too good to be true. I should have known."

With the tip of his finger, he traced the line of her jaw. No woman on earth was more loving than Lauren. In denying he loved her, he'd only become more bitter. It was impossible to punish her without hurting himself. "How about trying for some happiness of our own for a change? Marry me?"

Tears brightened her eyes as he slipped the leopard ring on her finger. "Yes," she whispered.

"I would have come sooner, but Aunt Tillie died last week. She'd had cancer for some time but she'd kept it from me. I found out just after I got out of the hospital. I've been staying with her since."

"I feel terrible," Lauren said. "She was a wonderful lady."

Ryan's pain was evident in his eyes. "She, too, helped me put things in perspective. Aunt Tillie told me she would have forgiven Uncle Garth anything had he lived, but once he was gone it was too late. I thought of my father. You know, I never told T.J. that I loved him. My pride wouldn't let me."

"I love you," she said, her voice a notch above a whisper. "I always would have, even if you hadn't come back to me."

"I love you, Lauren. Never doubt it." In a soft, moist kiss, his tongue sought hers, taking her breath away. Suddenly, he pulled back. "Hold it. I almost forgot. I have a surprise for you in the car. Come on."

He guided her out to a new Range Rover and Lauren saw the Berber rug she'd picked out for Paul rolled up in the back. Ryan opened the door and pointed, not to the rug but to the front seat.

At first she couldn't tell what was in the small basket. It appeared to be a short-haired puppy. Then the creature cocked its head and yawned, curling its pink tongue. Iggy. A sharp ache gripped Lauren as she remembered what she'd done.

"Pick her up," Ryan urged. "Go on."

Lauren hesitated, and the pot belly let out a whimper. Gingerly, she petted it and the piglet licked her hand. Just like Iggy. "What's her name?"

"I was waiting for you to name her, but I had an idea."

"What?" Lauren asked as she picked up the pot belly and nestled her against her breast. Was this what Iggy had been like as a baby?

"How about Mootzie?"

Lauren couldn't keep from laughing. "Mootzie. Perfect."

Ryan put his arm around her as she gave the tiny pot belly a finger to suck. "She needs you, Lauren." He put his coat around them both, sheltering them from the wind-driven snow. "I need you."

AUTHOR'S NOTE

I never gave much thought to artistic freedom until China first opened its doors to the West, and I traveled through the country with my husband. Along the Li River, we came to a small village where local artists were selling their paintings. A young artist clearly had remarkable talent and we purchased one of his traditional Chinese landscapes. Our interpreter told us the artist had many paintings he considered better, but since the subject matter wasn't approved by the state, he wasn't allowed to sell them. My husband and I were anxious to see his other work, yet to do so would have placed all of us in jeopardy. Today, that painting hangs in my living room. Often I pass it and wonder what happened to the artist. The Cultural Ministry still dictates what Chinese artists paint, subjecting their talent to the whims of the state.

Until recently, artists in the Soviet Union suffered similar repression. In writing this book, I marveled at the tremendous dedication Russian artists have shown. Eli Beliutin and his students of the Abramsevo School spent over two decades painting what they wanted without ever knowing if it would be exhibited. Finally, *glasnost* came and many of them are now receiving long-overdue recognition. Others died—waiting.

One man who died needlessly was Russian author Anatoly Marchenko. Unlike Sakharov or Solzhenitsyn, Anatoly Marchenko wasn't part of the Soviet *intelligentsia*. He was an ordinary man who wanted to write, but the state didn't approve of his subjects. That didn't stop Anatoly, and he continued to smuggle his manuscripts to the West where his three books were published. He died in Christopol Prison, under mysterious circumstances, having been incarcerated for most of his adult life.

In writing *Midnight in Marrakesh,* I was often inspired by Beliutin's devotion to his craft and Marchenko's tenacity.

With them in mind, I created the fictional character Irek Makarova. Some of his experiences are based on similar events related by Marchenko in *To Live Like Everyone*. And Ryan's prison scenes were inspired by horrors Marchenko described.

While thousands of artists, writers, and dancers were censured by the state, I think the plight of the great Russian poetess Anna Akhmatova epitomizes what they endured. An acclaimed poetess before the Second World War, she survived the Siege of Leningrad, becoming the voice of hope for the blockaded people, only to find herself denounced after the war. Her works could no longer be published, her husband, poet Nikolai Gumilyov, was executed and her only son sent to prison. But she never lost her faith, continuing to write and refusing to emigrate.

Akhmatova believed that coming to terms with the situation without compromising her artistic integrity required her to remain in Russia. Turning her back on her past, on her people was unthinkable.

"Requiem"

No foreign sky protected me,
no stranger's wing shielded my face.
I stand as witness to the common lot,
survivor of that time, that place.

I remembered Anna Akhmatova's strength and courage as I did background research for my character Lauren Winthrop. Experts tell us one out of three women in America were sexually abused as children. Their recovery and future happiness depend heavily on their ability to come to terms with the past—not deny it or bury it. And that takes courage—a special fortitude not unlike that of Beliutin or Marchenko or Akhmatova—because every fight, whether it ultimately benefits an individual or a nation, begins with a personal commitment.